HIDE AWAY

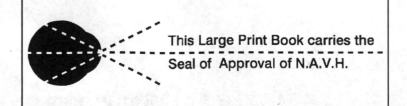

This Large Print Book carries the
Seal of Approval of N.A.V.H.

HIDE AWAY

IRIS JOHANSEN

LARGE PRINT PRESS

A part of Gale, Cengage Learning

GALE
CENGAGE Learning·

Farmington Hills, Mich • San Francisco • New York • Waterville, Maine
Meriden, Conn • Mason, Ohio • Chicago

LIBRARY OF CONGRESS CATALOGING-IN-PUBLICATION DATA

Names: Johansen, Iris, author.
Title: Hide away / Iris Johansen.
Description: Large print edition. | Waterville, Maine : Thorndike Press Large Print, 2016. | © 2016 | Series: Thorndike Press large print basic
Identifiers: LCCN 2016009100 | ISBN 9781410485281 (hardback) | ISBN 1410485285 (hardcover)
Subjects: LCSH: Duncan, Eve (Fictitious character)—Fiction. | Facial reconstruction (Anthropology)—Fiction. | Women sculptors—Fiction. | Large type books. | BISAC: FICTION / Thrillers. | GSAFD: Mystery fiction. | Suspense fiction.
Classification: LCC PS3560.O275 H53 2016b | DDC 813/.54—dc23
LC record available at https://lccn.loc.gov/2016009100

ISBN 13: 978-1-59413-947-5 (pbk.)
ISBN 10: 1-59413-947-4 (pbk.)
Published in 2016 by arrangement with St. Martin's Press, LLC

Printed in the United States of America
1 2 3 4 5 6 7 20 19 18 17 16

HIDE AWAY

CHAPTER 1

Community Hospital of the Monterey
Carmel, California
She was alone.

She mustn't panic. After all, she was eleven years old and had been taught to take care of herself. She had always been told that someday she might have to face this.

Cara Delaney leaned back against the door after leaving Eve Duncan's hospital room and tried to smother the fear that was surging through her. Her heart was beating hard and her throat was tight. They were going to send her away. It was all very well to tell herself she had known that it might happen someday, but it still came as a shock. She wasn't ready to face it yet.

But she'd better get ready. She'd been on the run most of her life and should have been prepared for the day that there would be no one here to help her. Her sister, Jenny, had been killed; Elena, who had cared for

Cara since she was born, had been killed. Now Cara was the only one left, and if Eve had decided she didn't want her, she'd have to find a way to face the loneliness and protect herself.

What was she thinking? Cara thought in sudden disgust. She had been feeling so sorry for herself that she had forgotten that it was Eve that she was supposed to be worrying about. It was Eve who had to be taken care of as Cara had promised. Jenny had died so that Cara could live and so had Elena. Now it was Cara's turn to give back.

She drew a deep breath and opened her hands, which had been clenched into fists. She could work through this, she just couldn't give up. There had to be a way . . .

"Cara?"

Margaret Douglas was walking down the corridor toward her, a concerned look on her face. Margaret was Eve's friend, and she had taken over Cara's supervision to keep her out of the hands of Child Services. She had been kind to Cara since Eve had been in the hospital, and Cara liked her. But Cara didn't want kindness now.

She wanted to go back into that room from which Joe Quinn had sent her and start the battle to keep her place at Eve's side.

■ ■ ■ ■

What on earth had happened to Cara, Margaret thought. Her gaze was fixed worriedly on the child's face as she came down the hall toward her. Cara's lips were tight, and there was a tension about the muscles of her shoulders. Maybe it was just the accumulated trauma of the last days that had finally hit home. What wouldn't be wrong with an eleven-year-old child who had gone through what Cara had suffered in the last few days, much less her short life, Margaret thought bitterly. She and her sister, Jenny, were the daughters of Juan Castino, the kingpin of a drug cartel in Mexico City, and they had been kidnapped as an act of vengeance by Salazar, the leader of a rival drug cartel. Jenny had been killed, and Cara had been taken on the run by her nurse, Elena, for eight long years. Just a few days ago, Elena had been murdered by a hit man, James Walsh, hired by Salazar to find them. Cara had later been cornered by Walsh, who had come close to killing her. Only Eve's intervention had prevented it, but it had landed her in this hospital with a concussion. Yes, Cara had every reason to look tense.

"Hey, what's the problem?" Margaret stopped in front of Cara and smiled gently. "Anything I can do to help?"

Cara shook her head. "I don't think so. I think it has to be me. Something has gone wrong. I could tell when Joe Quinn came into Eve's room and sent me out here. It's probably about me. He said it wasn't and that I didn't do anything wrong. But what else could it be?" Her hazel eyes were glittering with moisture. "Eve said they were going to take me home with them for a while. But Joe probably thinks that the reason Eve was hurt was because of me. He's right, you know."

Margaret reached out and gently touched the child's dark hair. "You don't know that he's upset with you, Cara. Joe is very fair. He knows that Eve does what she thinks is right, and nothing stops her. Yes, she was hurt trying to save your life. But Joe was there almost immediately afterward, and he was concerned for you as well as Eve." She cupped Cara's thin shoulders in her hands. "We were all concerned. It was a nightmare finding you and trying to keep you safe from that horrible man. There was no way Eve was going to stop."

"I know," Cara whispered. "Jenny said to trust Eve, that she would never stop until I was safe."

Margaret stiffened. "Jenny? Cara, your sister, Jenny is —" She hesitated. There was no other way to put it. "Jenny isn't with us. She died eight years ago."

Cara nodded. "I know that, but she . . . I dream about her." She looked at Margaret defiantly. "And she doesn't seem . . . Do you think I'm crazy?"

"Who, me?" She brushed the hair back from Cara's face. So much intensity in that small face, those wide-set hazel eyes that were more green than brown. The winged brows and pointed chin. In the few days since she'd come to know the child, she'd become aware of how much emotion and intensity lay behind that usually reserved expression. Intensity and strength. Strange to think of a child as being strong, but Cara's life had been different from that of other children. She'd had to be strong and enduring to bear the constant change and terror of being on the run. Even now when Walsh, the man who'd been hunting her had been killed, she knew she wasn't safe, that there might be another killer on the horizon. That life had made Cara mature beyond her years, and Margaret was constantly finding out new and different facets to her character. "I'm the last one to think anyone is crazy because of a few dreams. A lot of people think I'm a little weird because I don't march to their drummers."

"You don't seem weird," Cara said. "You seem . . . nice."

"One doesn't exclude the other. You seem nice, too." She stepped back. "And a dream can just be a memory."

"Yeah," Cara nodded. "But it seems like more." She paused. "I think Eve dreams about Jenny, too."

"It wouldn't surprise me. Eve has a kind of sensitivity to people like us. That's why I get along so well with her." She added gently, "I know this is all strange to you, Cara. *We're* strange to you. It's only been a couple days since you met all of us. We blew into your life at a time when everything was terrible and scary. You even lost your best friend, Elena, to that monster who was hunting you. You probably don't know whom to trust or how to react to all of us. You don't know where you're going next."

"You're wrong. I know where I'm going." Cara looked over her shoulder at the door of Eve's room. "I'm going with her. I have to take care of her. She needs me."

Margaret's brows rose. "Really? Everyone needs affection. But other than that, Eve's pretty strong, Cara."

"I have to take care of her," she repeated. "I promised Jenny."

"In that dream you had?"

She didn't answer directly. "I promised her." She went on in a rush, "And, like I said, Eve was going to let me stay with her and Joe for a while. She said so." She was frowning. "But when Joe came into the room a few minutes ago, I could tell that he was upset. Maybe he changed his mind."

"I doubt it." She tilted her head curiously. "What would you do if he did?"

"I'd go with her anyway. I'd find a way." Her gaze was still fixed on the door. "I have to take care of her."

Determination, intensity, and total commitment. Margaret shook her head with amazement. All of them had been so focused on finding and saving Cara during these last weeks that they had been thinking of her as helpless. She might have been in danger, but there was nothing helpless about this child. "Well, soon she'll be out of the hospital and on her way home. She won't need taking care of." She smiled. "Though I'm sure that she'll still want your company, Cara. You're jumping to conclusions. Come on, let's go to the waiting room and I'll buy you a soda."

She thought Cara was going to refuse, but

then the girl turned away from Eve's door. "Okay. I can't do anything right now anyway."

"Very sensible," Margaret said, as they strolled down the hall. "There's probably not going to be anything to do anyway. Maybe it's your imagination."

"No," Cara said soberly. "It's not imagination." She glanced back over her shoulder at Eve's door. "Joe was . . . tense. Something *is* wrong . . ."

Mexico City, Mexico
Something was wrong, Alfredo Salazar thought impatiently. In his last report, Walsh had told him that he had located Castino's kid and that bitch, Elena Pasquez, who had hidden her all these years, and that they'd be dead within days.

Why the hell hadn't he heard from him? It was making him damn uneasy. He'd been losing faith in James Walsh lately, but there was no doubt he was an expert once he set his sights on a victim. What could have gotten in his way?

Or who?

He reached in his desk drawer and pulled out the dossiers he'd compiled from the reports Walsh had given him.

Eve Duncan. Joe Quinn. Cara Delaney.

There were other dossiers but none as important as those three.

Eve Duncan, forensic sculptor who had restored the skull of Jenny Castino after her bones had been recently unearthed. He glanced at her photo. Not to his taste. Slim, red-brown hair with hazel eyes. An attractive, interesting face, but he preferred exotic and voluptuous. Evidently she was brilliant because she was considered one of the world's most gifted forensic sculptors.

Also very determined and stubborn. He'd warned Walsh that he should get rid of her before she got in his way. But she was an artist, a sculptor, and not equipped to go up against an enforcer of Walsh's capabilities.

He glanced at the Joe Quinn dossier. Brown hair, brown eyes, strong jaw. Detective with the ATLPD, ex-FBI, ex-SEAL. He had lived with Eve Duncan for a number of years and was said to be extremely loyal to her. He was undoubtedly deadly and capable of interfering with Walsh.

He glanced at the photo of the child. Cara had only been three when Walsh had taken her from the Castino home. Her sister Jenny had been nine, but they'd had the same high cheekbones and winged brows. That damn Eve Duncan had reproduced Jenny's features almost exactly when she'd been sent that skull of the skeleton buried in northern California and found by the Sheriff's Department. Now Walsh was sure that she was trying to locate Jenny's sister, Cara.

Which could mean disaster for Salazar.

And he wasn't about to sit here and wait any longer for word from Walsh. If he hadn't completed the kill, it was time he was taken out himself.

He reached for his phone.

It rang before he could dial.

Ramon Franco.

Which did not bode well. When Salazar had begun to have his doubts about Walsh's efficiency, Franco was the young man Salazar had sent to shadow him and make certain he was performing effectively.

"Walsh is dead," Ramon Franco said harshly as soon as Salazar picked up the call. "Killed. I just found out last night, and I've been scrambling to get information. I told you that you should have sent me to take care of that kid. He bungled the kill, and now there are police all over the place. We'll be lucky if they don't trace anything back to you."

Son of a bitch!

Salazar's hand tightened on the phone as the fury tore through him. "That can't happen. I've spent eight years covering Walsh's incompetence. I won't let that bastard's death toss me into Castino's jaws for him to chew up. Who killed him?"

"Eve Duncan."

So he had been wrong. Evidently the artist had a few more lethal skills than her credentials suggested. He had warned Walsh that she was a possible problem when the woman had gone on the hunt for him after he had stolen her reconstruction of Castino's daughter's skull. Now she was no longer a problem; she was a major pain in the ass. "For God's sake, Duncan is only a forensic sculptor, and she managed to put down Walsh? How many people has Walsh killed over the years? He should have been able to squash her like a bug. How did it happen?"

"It could have been an accident. Her statement to the police claimed they were fighting on the high ledge of a cave, and he backed off and fell to his death." He added, "Or she might have outsmarted him. Castino's other daughter, Cara, was in the cave, and you told me she was the target."

"The last target," Salazar said bitterly. "And Walsh couldn't even manage to find and kill an eleven-year-old kid."

"He found her in that cave, but he

17

couldn't finish the job. Eve Duncan got in the way. He managed to kill her nursemaid, Elena Pasquez, but no one else. I would never have let that happen."

"And when the police start digging into who that kid really is, they'll toss her back to her father, Castino, and he'll go after me. He's just waiting for a chance to break the coalition agreement."

"Then we have to make sure he doesn't have a reason to do it until we're strong enough to bury him and all the rest of the men in his damn cartel. Give me the word and I'll erase Walsh's death and that little girl as if they'd never existed." His voice was suddenly impassioned. "You haven't been fair to me. Haven't I always been loyal to you? From the time I was twelve, I did everything you told me to do. No kill was too hard. Yet you sent me here to Carmel to watch that bumbler, Walsh, just to make sure he was going to be able to finish the kill on the Castino kid. It was a job for a beginner. I may be young, but I'm no beginner."

"No, I know you're not." He tried to make his tone soothing. Franco's tone bordered on insolence, and he was tempted to cut him down to size, but he might need him. He was the man on the spot, with all

18

contacts in place. Better to handle Ramon Franco with kid gloves. The young recruits always lacked discipline, but they were also the ones most eager to prove themselves in blood. He was only nineteen, but his kill record with the cartel was impressive. He was quick, lethal, and totally vicious. "That's why I trusted you to watch Walsh. I never knew when I would have to have someone good enough to take over. Walsh had the experience, but he was going downhill, and I couldn't trust him." He paused. "Not like you, Franco. I see myself in you."

"You do?" Franco was silent, then said haltingly, "I'm honored, sir. It's just that I don't understand. You told me so little about what was going on with Walsh. I felt . . . like an errand boy."

Which was exactly how Salazar saw him. But circumstances dictated the errand boy be promoted until Salazar could take charge himself. "I don't want any of my other men to be jealous of you. Particularly not now. I'd rather you concentrate on getting me out of the mess Walsh made up there in Carmel. You're going to have to dance a fine dance to save the situation. But you're a smart boy, and I know that you can do it for me."

"I'm a man, not a boy."

"Of course you are. But it's not a bad thing that others believe you to be a boy, so they won't suspect how very deadly you can be. I've seen you use that ploy before."

"Sometimes."

"Often. Do you think I haven't been watching you? Use your brains and that smile the ladies like so much."

"Then tell me what I need to know. Tell me what Walsh knew, what I should have known from the beginning."

A definite touch of arrogance, Salazar noticed. "You know the beginning. You grew up with it. The drugs, the vice, that son of a bitch, Juan Castino, constantly moving into my territory. He acted as if his cartel was the only one in Mexico, and every time anyone came close to taking him down, he managed to come out on top. I had the brains and the plans but Castino had the contacts and was always just ahead of me. If I hadn't managed to form a mutual coalition of all the cartels in Mexico, he would have eaten me alive. I can rein him in as long as he knows I have the backing of the coalition behind me."

"Until we find a way to kill him. That's the best way. Don't worry. I'll do it for you."

So simple, so incredibly naïve. "I know you will. But it has to be staged very carefully. I can't let any of the other cartels know that I'm getting ready to jump Castino." He paused. "Or that I yielded to temptation eight years ago to twist the knife and make him hurt. They might turn against me."

"Because you arranged with James Walsh to kidnap Castino's two little girls and their nanny and kill them? They all probably wish they'd had the balls to do it."

"They'd chop me up and serve me to Castino. And then move into my territory and split it up." His voice was laden with frustration. "It was going to be so simple. Walsh would kill them, and there would be no bodies or anything to connect me to it. I'd be able to sit back and watch Castino suffer, then, when the time was right, I'd make sure he joined his little girls in the graveyard. But Walsh screwed it up. He left me hanging and vulnerable if Castino finds out I paid Walsh to kill them. We have to fix it, Franco."

"I can do it if I work fast. I don't think that Castino knows anything yet. The kid's name on the police report is Cara Delaney, and Walsh is only suspected of being a serial killer. Nothing about Castino."

Hope and relief shot through Salazar. "You're certain?"

"I paid a good deal of your money to bribe

21

a look at those reports. No mention of Castino . . . or you."

"Yet."

"As you say. But there may be a way to keep you safe if we work fast. Eve Duncan hasn't made a statement yet. She's in a local hospital being checked out for concussion, and her lover, Joe Quinn, isn't letting her be interviewed."

"Where's the kid?"

"She's being taken care of by a friend of Duncan's, Margaret Douglas."

"Not at Child Services? They're big on Welfare shit in the U.S."

"No, I'm sure. I knew you'd want to know where you could put your hands on her."

"Oh, yes." His hands around her throat to end this nightmare. "Then it appears you may have a multitude of targets in the near future. You need to find out how much Duncan knows about Cara Castino . . . and me. I have to know I'm safe from Duncan before I move forward again."

"You'll be safe. It's only a question which target I hit first." His voice was suddenly eager. "You tell me and it will be done. Duncan? Quinn? The kid?"

"You're moving too fast. I want you to go to that hospital and report back to me. Do you understand?"

"If I took out Duncan, it would stop the —"

"Report back to me," Salazar repeated. "Is that clear?"

"Yes, sir." He was silent. "I didn't mean to argue. You're the *Pez Gordo,* the big boss. I'm just concerned."

He was concerned because if Salazar and his cartel fell, he could be part of the collateral damage, Salazar thought cynically. It was obvious Franco was very ambitious. "Then it's time to use that concern in the way I told you."

"I'll leave for the hospital right away. I won't disappoint you." He hung up.

Franco was moving fast and was eager to please but Salazar still wasn't sure that he would obey instructions if an opportunity presented itself.

Oh well, Franco was a superb assassin, and Salazar was just angry enough with the way Eve Duncan had spoiled his plans that he was willing to take a chance that Franco wouldn't pay her a fatal visit in her hospital room without taking appropriate precautions. Salazar rather liked the idea of Duncan's lying helplessly in that bed in her room while Franco moved around that hospital like a lethal buzz saw.

But if Franco decided to do it, he'd damn

23

well better do it right.

Community Hospital of the Monterey

"Cara has good instincts," Eve Duncan said as she turned back to Joe after watching the child walk out of her hospital room. "You're not easy to read, Joe. I'm glad that whatever you're upset about wasn't about her. Though I'm not sure she believed you. It would have been difficult explaining a sudden change of heart. Do you know, I'm starting to look forward to having Cara staying with us for a while?" She shook her head. "Remember, we were talking on the day Jane left for London about how my life may be changing? Then all of this happened. Do you suppose Cara is the change?"

"Not necessarily."

Eve went still. She couldn't miss that jerky roughness in his tone. "What are you talking about? What *is* wrong?"

"Not wrong. Strange. Bizarre." He shook his head. "I don't know what else."

"Stop playing around with words. Talk to me."

"I don't know how to say it."

"Just tell me."

"The hospital has the results from all the tests they've been running on you. The doctor stopped me in the hall to go over them."

24

"The results? Joe, I know you've been ramrodding everything connected to my treatment since you brought me to this hospital, but that's going a little too far. Why go over them with you and not with me?" She tried to smile. "Some terrible disease popped up that he thought you should break to me?"

"God, I'm not doing this right. No terrible disease. You're very healthy and ready to go home. He just didn't want you to leave the hospital without knowing."

"Joe, what are you trying to tell me?"

"In my completely clumsy and inadequate fashion." He reached out and took her hand. "I'm trying to tell you that you're going to have a child, Eve."

"You're joking," Eve said dazedly. "It's some kind of mistake?"

"No." Joe's hand tightened around her own. "And no. To both questions. I wouldn't have dared come in here if I hadn't made sure the doctor had checked and double-checked. You're pregnant." His teeth bit his lower lip. "And that goes to show how upset I am. *We're* pregnant. I can't quite take it in either. I went into shock when the doctor told me."

"Tell me about it," she said weakly as she

sat up in the bed. "It wasn't supposed to happen. I thought it couldn't happen. It wasn't as if we weren't careful."

"I didn't think so either," Joe said. "We did everything right. Or maybe we didn't. But I don't know how we could have done anything different." He shook his head. "I'm a little confused on that point at the moment."

"Me, too." She met his gaze. "I . . . feel lost. I can't quite grasp it." She reached up and ran a hand through her hair. "How . . . long?"

"Barely. A few weeks. You must have conceived before we left the Lake Cottage to come out here to California."

"I remember when I was pregnant with Bonnie, I didn't know for months."

"Things have changed since you were sixteen. They can tell within five or six days now."

She nodded. "The whole world has changed. My whole life has changed. I'm not the same person."

"Yes, you are. You've just been tempered by experience." He lifted her palm to his lips. "And this particular experience may do some more very intricate tempering. Just don't let it throw you. We'll think about it, then make decisions."

26

"Decisions." No, she couldn't make decisions right now. Her head was whirling, and all she could think about was the fact that in nine months she would bear a child. It was impossible. No, it was going to happen. "How do you feel about it?"

"As dazed as you." He grinned. "Kind of . . . primitive. I've never fathered a child of my own. I suppose that's a natural reaction. I . . . like it." His smile faded. "I never suggested it to you. After all you've gone through, I thought that it had to come from you. I know what you went through when you lost your Bonnie; when she was killed. After we adopted Jane, I believed that might be the way we should go."

"So did I." She moistened her lips. "And now I'm wondering why we never talked about having a child of our own. Did I just bury my head in the sand? My God, Joe, I must have sensed you'd feel like this. Was I so afraid that I avoided facing it?"

He didn't answer.

Because he knew it was true, she realized. She was his center, and he wouldn't allow her to be hurt even if it meant being cheated himself. "You should have spoken to me about it."

He shook his head. "I have you. That's enough, more than enough." He leaned forward and kissed her. "Now stop fretting about me, you have thinking to do."

"Thinking," she repeated. "You said decision. You know I won't have an abortion. I couldn't do that."

"That's not what I meant. You told me once that you'd intended to adopt Bonnie out to a good home before she was born. Then, when you saw her, you changed your mind."

Eve stared at him in shock. "You'd consent to me doing that?"

"I have no idea. I doubt it. Every instinct is shouting no, but I just had to bring it up because you'd once considered it. You were a teenager then, poor, virtually alone, and Bonnie was illegitimate. Now you're older, but you have a career that obsesses you, and family would get in the way." He met her gaze. "Whatever your decision, it has to be made with your whole heart. After that, we'll work out what we need to do individually to meet both our own goals. We'll find a way to blend them together."

"Joe . . ."

"Hush." He squeezed her hand before releasing it. "I'm going to go and see about your release papers. You rest awhile, then I'll send Margaret in to help you dress." He paused. "Do you want me to tell her?"

She shook her head. "It's not real to me yet. How can I make it real to anyone else?"

"What about Cara? Do you still want to take her into our home for a while?"

"Of course I do. What are we supposed to do? Let her go back to Mexico and be torn apart in all those cartel wars? She's just a child, and she's already lost her sister and Elena, her best friend. You know that Salazar won't stop hunting her because Walsh is dead. We've got to keep her safe until we can find a way to get rid of Salazar."

"And Juan Castino, her loving father," Joe said grimly. "You're right, she's a pawn. She wouldn't stand a chance if immigration sends her back to Mexico." He turned toward the door. "I just thought that you might want me to handle it myself. You may be a little busy for a while."

"I believe the word is occupied," Eve said dryly.

"Whatever." He glanced back at her. "I wasn't sure that you'd be prepared for the hassle. We're going to have to whisk Cara away from here, keep her real identity from the authorities, and get her to Atlanta. Then I'll get to work on bringing down Salazar's cartel. That should keep him too busy to pay attention to Cara in the near future."

"I agree. But most of those arrangements

are in your court."

"It will overflow."

She nodded. "Then I'll face it then." She smiled. "And a challenge will be good for me. It will keep me from . . . It will distract me."

"I doubt it."

The next moment, he was gone.

He was probably right, she thought. Nothing was going to distract her from this news that had shaken her world. But she had always found that hard work and putting her own problems at the end of the agenda could be a salvation.

But did she need salvation? Why had the word even occurred to her?

All she needed was to adjust to a situation that happened to millions of women every year.

So adjust.

She closed her eyes and leaned her head back on the pillow. Sort out what she really felt and examine it.

Shock.

A natural reaction.

Disbelief.

Also natural.

Fear.

A pregnancy was never easy when you were older.

Of course, there was an element of —

No, don't hide behind that easy answer. There was something else behind it.

Bonnie. Her little girl who had been her entire life during those seven short years before her death. Bonnie. The pain and agony that had almost killed Eve after she'd been taken.

The fear that agony could come back if she allowed herself to love another baby as she had Bonnie. She dearly loved her adopted daughter, Jane, but that was another relationship entirely. Jane had been ten when they'd found each other, and with a maturity that had made them more best friends than mother and daughter. So different from Bonnie. She had been responsible for her from the instant of her birth, and she had lost her. Could she bear the constant worry that another child would be taken from her?

Coward. She was a coward. Mothers faced that threat every single day.

Did you know what a coward I am, Joe? Is that why you never asked?

Well, there was no asking now. It was a fact. Stunning. Life-changing. Inevitable.

Magical.

The word had come out of nowhere.

Because that was the final emotion she

had felt when Joe had told her she was going to have a child.

Magic. Joyous, rich, heady, magic.

She slowly looked down at her abdomen. Flat. No sign that someone was growing, taking on more life with every second. She reached out tentatively and touched the skin of her stomach.

What's happening? It's a crazy world out here, are you sure you want to trust me to take you through it?

Was she expecting an answer from this baby, who had just barely been conceived? Of course not, the question was really for herself. She had lost Bonnie. She would have to do better to prove herself to this child.

Her hand dropped away from her abdomen.

Later. We'll have to work on this. We're just starting out. We have a long way to go.

She sat up in bed and swung her legs to the floor. Time to start living life and not trying to avoid it. She went to the closet and started to take down her clothes.

"Hey, I'm supposed to do all that." Margaret had come into the room. "Joe said I should give you a little while to rest, and here you are ready to jump into your clothes."

Eve smiled affectionately at her. Margaret had been a tower of strength during the last days when they had been hunting for Cara, then Eve's time in the hospital. But then Margaret had shown remarkable strength from the moment Eve had met her. She was young and full of life and possessed instincts and a knowledge of animals that was as unusual as her ability to deal with people.

"I want to get out of here." Eve headed for the bathroom. "And I've done nothing but rest since I got here. I had a mild concussion, and Joe insisted on having those doctors run every test under the sun to make sure I was okay."

"Typical Joe Quinn," Margaret said. "He was a trifle . . . brief when he was talking to me. Is everything okay?"

"Everything's fine."

"Then you might tell Cara. She's not too sure."

Eve stopped at the bathroom door. "She thinks I'm abandoning her?"

"No, it's not gotten that far yet. But who could blame her? She doesn't really know any of us. She's known since she was three years old and her sister, Jenny, was killed almost in front of her eyes, that she had to run and keep on running just to stay alive. Her nurse, Elena, taught her she mustn't trust anyone." She added grimly, "And with good reason. Elena died trying to protect her. Now Cara is alone, and she's trying to come to terms with taking care of herself." She shrugged. "Though she seems more concerned with taking care of you. Do you know she dreams about Jenny?"

"Yes."

"And she told me she thinks you dream about her, too. Do you?"

"Not exactly."

Margaret gazed at her, waiting. When Eve didn't go on, she said, "Okay, you don't want to talk about it. I understand. Well, I don't really, but I would if you'd trust me. I thought that those reports from 'confidential sources' you told our Sheriff Nalchek you received were a trifle suspect when we were hunting down Walsh." She suddenly chuckled. "Though he'd think what I'm guessing now is far more weird than suspect." She took Eve's suitcase out of the closet. "Go on, get dressed. Call if you need me. I'll pack you up, and we'll be set to go as soon as you're ready."

"Thanks, Margaret," Eve said quietly. "Thanks for everything. We would never have found Cara if you hadn't helped. You've been there for me since the beginning of this nightmare."

"Not quite." She tilted her head. "And that sounds remarkably like good-bye. Is it?"

"I prefer *au revoir*." She hesitated. "What Joe and I are doing isn't exactly legal in taking Cara back to Atlanta with us. It's morally right, but you could still get in trouble. You and the Immigration Department aren't on the best of terms."

"We're fine with each other as long as I'm smart enough to avoid them."

And Eve knew Margaret had made a science of avoiding them and keeping under the radar. Eve had never been told why Margaret felt that was necessary and could only be grateful that she occasionally dropped into their lives. "And you might be caught in the cross fire if they find out that we're keeping Cara from her legal father."

"Who is a murderer, drug lord, and general scumbag."

"Joe and I will be working on clearing up her situation, but it will take time. In the meantime, Salazar will be a danger."

"Then I should be there to —"

"No, Margaret," Eve said firmly. "You have too much to lose. I won't have you stuck in a jail while they decide whether or not to deport you." She made a face. "Though I don't even know where they'd send you. You haven't been very forthcoming on that score."

"It's my life, my problems." Margaret shook her head. "I can't convince you, can I?" She shrugged. "Then I won't try. If you need me, get in touch." She started packing Eve's bag. "Do you need to know where to get phony documents for Cara? I know a few good places and some people who will —"

"No," Eve said. "You're out of this. Joe has managed to block any investigation on Cara's background, but there are still problems. It will be a very tentative fix, but as long as they think Cara is an orphan after the death of her supposed Aunt Elena, we may get away with it. We're hoping that Sheriff Nalchek will smooth things over with Child Services and persuade them to let us have temporary custody. He's well thought of in this area."

"He'll do it. He's like you. He won't want a child in danger."

"I believe you're right. We'll have to see. Everything is a little bewildering right now."

"Eve." Margaret was studying her face. "You're sure everything is okay? You look a little . . . unusual."

"Do I?" Trust Margaret to sense a truth that had only just been revealed to Eve.

Unusual? The world was shaking. Everything was changing. She didn't know how she was going to cope. But she would do it. She had to do it.

She smiled at Margaret. "I'm sure it's *going* to be okay. But you're right, I feel a little unusual. Nothing physical. Just a new challenge on the horizon."

"Cara?"

"She's definitely a part of it." She was closing the bathroom door. "I'll be right out, Margaret."

Margaret shook her head as she gazed at the closed door. Eve was going to prove obstinate, but that's what she had expected. She had tried to push her away earlier when she had been afraid to involve her beyond what she considered safe. She would have to find a way to —

Her cell phone rang, and she glanced down at the ID. Kendra Michaels.

It wasn't the first time she had phoned in the past week. Margaret had been too busy to take her calls and had put her off. She was tempted to do that now.

No, Kendra was her friend, and she was the one who had called to ask Margaret to get in touch with Eve when she'd been unable to reach her. She deserved to know what had happened.

"Hello, Kendra. I don't have much time. I have to help get Eve sprung out of this hospital."

"Hospital? And why is Eve in a hospital? And what the hell is going on?"

"I'm going to tell you. I just have to keep it brief, okay?"

"It's not okay, but I clearly have to put up with it. Eve told me practically nothing when she came out here to California except that she needed someone who was woods savvy and wanted you. Since I'm definitely not woods savvy, I had to find you."

"You sound distinctly grumpy."

"I couldn't see why I couldn't help," she said impatiently. "I still don't. Tell me."

"Eve came out here because Sheriff Nalchek had discovered the grave of a nine-year-old little girl at Sonderville, California. He sent Eve the skull to reconstruct. She did a great job and FedExed the reconstruction back to him. But the FedEx truck was hijacked, the driver killed, and the reconstruction stolen. Eve's computer and notes were also stolen that same day. Someone had no intention of letting that little girl's identity be discovered."

"And that pissed Eve off."

"Big-time. She had become very involved emotionally with that little girl, who she called Jenny, while she was reconstructing her skull. She and Joe Quinn came out here to try to find a clue to who that little girl was." She added, "And to catch her killer. That's why she wanted me to go to that grave in the forest and see what I could find."

"And what did you find?"

"Not as much as I would have liked, but I was helpful. Joe and Eve discovered that the name of her killer was James Walsh and started to try to track him. It became very convoluted because Walsh was on the hunt himself. He was an enforcer for a Mexican drug cartel, very nasty character, and had been hired by the head of a rival cartel to kidnap and kill Juan Castino's two daughters. They were supposed to just disappear, but something happened. The older girl was killed, but the younger child, Cara, and Elena, the nurse who cared for the girls, escaped. Walsh searched for them for years."

"Bastard."

"Oh, yes. It was a very bloody hunt. But we managed to find Cara almost at the same time as Walsh."

"Tell me he's dead."

"Yes, a very painful demise. Eve has only

a minor concussion."

"And the child?"

"Cara is alive, but there are still problems. Eve is sure she can work them out."

"And are you sure?"

"Reasonably. As long as she's willing to accept help from her friends."

Kendra laughed. "You?"

"Well, I do like to see things through to the very end."

"I've noticed. An iron will occasionally peeks out from behind all that sunny sweetness."

"Sweetness? How cloying. I feel ill. And in dire need of an apology."

"You'll not get it." She was suddenly serious. "You're okay, Margaret?"

"Sure, I was just drifting along with the current."

"Never."

"Well, sometimes. Now the current is persistently reminding me I have to get Eve out of this hospital."

"Okay, okay. I'll talk to you later. But that explanation was very sketchy. I'll want details." She hung up.

And Kendra would keep at Margaret until she got all those details, Margaret thought ruefully. She was not only brilliant, she had boundless curiosity and fantastic instincts.

And she hadn't liked being passed over for Margaret when Eve needed help. She always liked being in control.

But then, so did Margaret.

So finish packing Eve up, then try to think of a way to get Eve to let her trail along and help put a period to this nightmare that was haunting both her and Cara.

CHAPTER 2

"Will you be all right here?" Joe asked Cara. He gestured to the long bench outside the administration office. "I shouldn't be long. Just signing papers and giving them a credit card. Five minutes, no more."

She nodded as she opened her computer. "Unless you want me to go help Eve."

He shook his head. "Margaret will take care of her." He smiled. "And Eve usually prefers to take care of herself. You'll find that out if you choose to stay with us for a while."

"I'll stay with you." She gazed gravely at him. "And I think that you take care of Eve whether she wants it or not. Let me help."

He studied her face. "It should work the other way around, you know. You're just a kid. You have a right to have people look after you."

"You did look after me. Eve saved my life. You saved my life. Elena always said that I had to look after myself." She moistened her lips. "And now she's gone, and I can't expect any more help from anyone. I have to earn it."

"And you think you should earn your way by helping Eve?"

She nodded. "If she'll let me. If you'll let me. Will you?"

"I believe that can be arranged." He touched her cheek with his forefinger. "I think you'd be a good person to have on her side. She may need it soon."

"I know. I won't disappoint you."

"Just what do you know?" he asked curiously.

She shook her head. "I won't disappoint you," she repeated.

His hand dropped away from her face. "Stop worrying about responsibility and concentrate on healing. You've had a bad couple days." His lips twisted. "No, you've had a bad several years."

"Not so bad. Not all the time." Her eyes stung with tears. "Elena made them good because we were together."

"I'm sure you made them good for her, too," he said gently. He turned away and pushed open the door. "Five minutes. You can even see me through this glass door. If you need me, come and get me."

Her eyes were swimming with tears as she looked down at her computer.

Elena.

Don't cry. Tears never did any good. Elena had always told her that you just had to forget and go on.

But how was she going to forget Elena?

She wouldn't forget. She would lose her if she forgot all the years they'd —

"Would you like a tissue?"

She looked up to see an older boy in jeans and a white shirt who had dropped down on the bench next to her. She could barely see through the tears, but she was aware of dark hair, dark eyes. Her friend, Heather, would have said he was cute, and his hair was cut like one of the members in Heather's favorite rock band.

He handed her the tissue. "You look like you could use it." He took another tissue out of the same pack and dabbed at his own eyes. "Me, too. Life can be crap, can't it?"

"Yeah." She wiped her eyes. "Thanks."

He nodded. "Welcome." He leaned his dark head back against the wall. "I hate this. My dad is in there paying the bill and for what? They couldn't get her well. My mom died anyway."

"I'm sorry." She took a deep, shaky breath. "It seems to be a good hospital. They're doing everything they can for Eve."

"Your sister?"

"No. Not my sister." She wiped her eyes again. "My sister died a long time ago. Do you have a sister?"

"Yes, Nella. She's in the chapel, praying for my mother's soul." His eyes filled again. "That's where I was when my dad called me and said he needed me. I didn't want to come. There didn't seem much I could do, and I felt helpless. I never liked to go to church, but my mother taught me that prayers help. I felt like maybe I was doing something in that chapel, that maybe she could hear me. Stupid, huh?"

She shook her head. "I don't think so. Elena always told me that when you couldn't trust anyone else that you should pray."

"Elena? You said Eve."

"No, my friend, Elena. She . . . died."

"Seems like everyone is dying," he said thickly. "Did it help you to go to church, like it did me?"

"I haven't been able to do that yet."

"You ought to try it. It can't hurt."

"Maybe later."

"That's what I thought when my mom died. All the things I was going to do and say. Sometimes I wasn't even nice to her.

It's bad to put off things." He suddenly jumped to his feet. "Come on, let's go to the chapel. Neither of us is doing any good sitting on this bench. Who knows how long it's going to take for them to pay those bloodsuckers?"

"What?" Cara's eyes widened in surprise. "I can't leave now."

"Sure you can." He pulled her to her feet. "The chapel's only three floors up. You can call down to say where you're going when we get there."

"What about your father?"

"He didn't really need me, or he wouldn't have parked me on this bench and left me to twiddle my thumbs." He was gazing down at her, his dark eyes glittering, his voice soft, persuasive. "Come on. Nella will like you to be there. I'm just a guy, and she's missing Mom so bad."

"I don't know if I —"

"Cara."

Joe was standing in the doorway. "And who is this?" His soft voice had a definite edge.

The boy smiled politely. "Kevin Roper, sir." He dropped Cara's hand and turned away. "I guess you won't want to go to the chapel now." He was heading toward the elevator. "It was nice to meet you, Cara."

"Good-bye, Kevin. Tell your sister I'm so sorry."

"I'll do that." He got on the elevator. "She would have liked to meet you." He nodded at Joe and Cara as the door started to slide shut. "Hope all goes well for Eve."

Joe was still staring at the door as the elevator started down. "It sounds as if you two had a cozy chat."

"His mom just died."

"And you were going to the chapel with him?"

"No. Yes. I don't know. I thought it might not —" She made a face. "I was confused."

"And this Kevin Roper is very persuasive. I caught that from the body language the minute I walked out of the office."

"He'd been in the chapel today with his sister, Nella, praying for his mother's soul. He said his sister needed someone to —"

"And you were in pain and could sympathize." He was taking out his phone as he spoke. "You say he was in the chapel today?"

"Yes."

He dialed quickly, then was speaking into the phone. "Connect me to the chapel." He waited and then spoke again, "I need to talk to Nella Roper. Is she there? Yes, I'll wait." He covered the phone and spoke to Cara. "It's a social-service volunteer. Everyone has to sign in when they arrive. She's checking." He went back to his conversation. "No? What about her brother, Kevin? They were supposed to both be there earlier today. Not at all? Thank you, sorry to bother you." He hung up. "And I would bet that Roper had no mother who died in this hospital. At least, not recently."

"Lies," she whispered.

"Very beautifully executed lies. A handsome young boy who had lost his mother, sits down beside a grieving young girl who needs someone near her own age who might understand what she's going through. Very clever."

"Why would he want me to go to the chapel? I don't —" She stopped. "He took the elevator down, not up. He told me the chapel was three flights up. He wasn't going to the chapel, was he?"

Joe shook his head. "I don't think you'd have made it out of the elevator alive. I imagine he has a few more skills other than being an expert liar."

"Salazar. Salazar sent him?"

"That would be my guess. I can't prove it yet. There's a possibility he might be a child molester or some other kind of creep who planted himself in a hospital where a victim is most vulnerable."

"If he was sent by Salazar, he was going to kill me?"

Joe was silent. "Do you think I like to tell you that? But I have to lay it on the line. If I'd come out of that office a few minutes later, I might have missed you. I'd like to say trust everyone, and you don't have to worry any longer. I'm not going to do that. I don't know how long you'll have to be careful, but you're not safe now. Do you understand?"

"He . . . was nice."

"He was probably deadly."

She nodded jerkily. "I was used to the idea of a monster, I wasn't expecting someone who looked like one of the guys I'd see around school." She drew a deep breath. "But I'll know better next time." She headed for the elevator. "We have to get back to Eve. I mentioned her name. He might try to —"

Joe was already ahead of her, his finger pressing the button. "I doubt if he could bounce back that fast, but we won't take a chance. We have to get out of here."

"I shouldn't have mentioned her. He just seemed — Hurry!"

Two minutes later they were at the door of Eve's hospital room.

No Eve.

Cara stopped short, her gaze on the rumpled bed. "No," she whispered.

"I didn't expect you this soon. All done with the paperwork?"

Cara turned to see Eve standing in the doorway of the bathroom. She felt limp with relief. "Hi. I thought —" She swallowed. "I was scared. I did something stupid."

Eve's gaze narrowed on her face. "I can see you're scared." She looked at Joe. "What happened?"

"She ran into a wolf in sheep's clothing," Joe said. "I left her for a minute in the hall outside the administration office, and he pounced."

"Salazar?"

Joe nodded. "He recruited a young kid who was very good. Smooth as silk and very believable."

"A kid?" Margaret came out of the bathroom carrying three plastic bags filled with Eve's personal items. "That doesn't sound like a recruit to replace Walsh."

"He was good," Joe repeated. "And clever. Salazar might be trying something new. Walsh had to have been a miserable failure in his eyes."

"He was a miserable failure in anyone's eyes." Eve shivered. "But I didn't think that Salazar would have found out that Walsh

50

was dead yet. Much less send a killer to replace him."

"He probably had someone watching Walsh and reporting back to him. I doubt if he would have trusted him after he'd failed him all these years."

"Do you know his name?"

"Kevin Roper. At least, that's what he told us. I'll check with Manez, my contact in Mexico who deals with the cartels, to see if I can verify." Joe glanced quickly around the room. "Have you got everything? We need to get out of here."

"These were the last items." Margaret went to Eve's bag, which she'd set on the floor on the other side of the bed. "She's ready to go." She looked back at him. "Where are you going to take her?"

"We're going home," Eve said. "I told you, Margaret."

"I thought there might be a change of plan." She fastened the suitcase. "Since I'm sure Salazar knows where you live."

"So am I," Joe said. "But it's my home territory. Easier to defend. We can't hide out here with Cara like she did with Elena. I know the police there, and I have friends."

"You won't be hiding at all," Margaret said soberly. "I know something about hiding. It seems like I've done it all my life. You

51

should disappear until you're ready to make your move against Salazar." She glanced at Cara. "You know all about disappearing, don't you? They don't want to make you feel unsafe, they want to put you in a nice, cozy place. But sometimes those cozy places can be traps, and you have to leave them. There's no choice. Your Elena knew that, didn't she?"

Cara nodded. "She knew. She was trying to take me away again when Walsh . . . killed her."

"We'll take care of her, Margaret," Eve said quietly. "I know you mean well, but she's our responsibility."

"And I should butt out?" Margaret shrugged. "I take it that you haven't changed your mind about letting me come with you?" She didn't wait for an answer but turned back to Cara. "You'll get through this and come out on top. Eve and Joe are good people, and they're very smart." She grinned. "So smart that I know they'll call me to help as soon as they realize what a mistake they're making not to let me run this operation."

"We'll keep that in mind," Joe said dryly. He crossed the room and shook Margaret's hand. "And you may be right about cozy traps. I'll have to think about it. But there are elements in play of which you have no knowledge. All I want to do right now is to get Eve home. She may need that cozy trap for a little while."

"Really?" Margaret's tone was speculative. "Interesting." She turned to Eve. "I'd like to go into this, but we should get you and Cara away from here. Come on, I'll walk you down to your car." She linked her arm through Cara's and headed for the door. "Don't worry, we'll find a way around this."

"What way?" Eve asked warily as she followed Margaret from the room. "It's not like you to give up so easily."

"Maybe I'm getting resigned to being pushed to the side." She winked. "Or maybe I'm trying to keep you off guard while I figure out a way to get my own way."

There are elements in play you don't know about.

Margaret stood watching as Joe drove out of the hospital parking lot.

What elements, Joe?

She turned and walked slowly back toward the hospital, thinking. She'd been aware of something odd in Eve's behavior earlier. Joe's words just confirmed it.

Eve may need that cozy trap for a little while.

She went over the events of the last day

53

and tried to put together a reasonable answer.

Nothing.

Forget reasonable. Try reaching out beyond reason.

A few possibilities, some actually interesting.

One or two that were fascinating.

She stopped short in the parking lot.

Yes, incredibly fascinating . . .

But if there was even a chance of its being true, there was no way she could let Eve go off without her help.

Help she'd refused already with great firmness. How to get around it?

She couldn't act herself, so pull the strings. Find someone Eve wouldn't be able to refuse. Not that easy. Eve was a workaholic, and that dictated a fairly solitary life. She had Joe Quinn, her half sister, Beth Avery, a few close friends, Catherine Ling, Kendra Michaels.

And her adoptive daughter, Jane MacGuire.

Margaret would have chosen Jane first except for the fact that she had been suffering from the tragic loss of her fiancé and was only now recovering.

Jane . . .

Margaret and Jane had grown very close

during the past year. She knew Jane would not think twice about jumping into the situation no matter how risky to help Eve.

She also knew that Eve would not want Jane to know about that danger.

She thought about it.

. . . elements in play you don't know about.

What the hell? Why was she being so hesitant? She always ended up going by instinct anyway.

She reached for her phone and dialed quickly. It rang four times before it was picked up. "Jane? It's Margaret, do you have a few minutes? No, that's not right, maybe longer than that. I'm in Carmel, California. I need to fill you in on something that's been going on out here and then ask you to —"

"I almost had her," Ramon Franco's voice was tense with excitement. "A minute more, and I'd have had her in the elevator, then one needle, and she'd —"

"I told you not to make a move yet."

"I wasn't going to do it, but you wanted her dead. Wasn't that the primary goal? There she was, and Quinn had ducked into the administration office. I could tell by the way she looked that she'd be easy if I took her right then. I was right. I was that close to —"

"You didn't do what I said, Franco."

"You said you wanted her dead." He tried to keep the impatience out of his voice. Salazar had once been a man to respect, but he was getting old, and he'd forgotten you had to take advantage of the opportunities when you were on the hunt. "It would have been over almost before it began if I'd taken her out today."

"And it would have roused an inquiry that might have led to Castino. It has to be done quietly. All I wanted was information. Did you get it?"

"Didn't I say I would?" He could tell by the silence on the other end that he'd gone too far. "If I made a mistake, I'm sorry. I only thought to please you." He went on hurriedly, "Eve Duncan was admitted to the ER with a concussion. Not serious. She was released today. The kid is still going by the name of Cara Delaney and has been at the hospital visiting Duncan. After I left the hospital today, I called my contact at the police department, and there's been no interest in Cara. They're leaving her in the hands of Child Services." He paused. "And Child Services has been requested to leave her in the hands of Eve Duncan and Joe

Quinn by a Sheriff John Nalchek, who was one of the lead investigators."

"And no doubt the request was granted." Salazar was silent. "We may be lucky, Franco. It appears that Duncan has no desire for the child to be returned to the loving arms of her father. It may buy us time." He amended. "Buy you time. Find out where they're taking the girl and follow them. But don't touch her until you're sure you can take Duncan down at the same time. And I want a clean kill, with no bodies."

"The kill would have been clean if I'd put the kid down at the hospital. I had it all planned the minute I saw her on that bench. It was just —"

"You were in the middle of a hospital with people all around you. You were taking a chance."

"I would have pulled it off."

"Forget it. You made a mistake. Admit it."

It hadn't been a mistake, Franco thought furiously. It had been bad luck, but he had been superb. He had almost gotten away with it, and this old fool couldn't see it. He had played that kid perfectly. He drew a deep breath and forced his voice to be contrite. "Of course, I made a mistake. I guess I was just too eager to please. I'll handle it the way you want me to handle it. I'll call you as soon as I know what's happening with them."

"Be sure you do that. I wouldn't want to have to replace you. As I said, you have great promise."

"Thank you, that means a great deal to me, sir." He hung up.

He sat there for a moment, fighting the hatred and the anger. How dare that fool humiliate him like this.

Keep calm.

His time would come.

But first he would have to disarm Salazar by giving him what he wanted. Duncan, the kid, and he might throw in Joe Quinn.

San Francisco International Airport
It took Joe five minutes to get in touch with Manez at Mexican Federal Police after he, Eve, and Cara arrived at the boarding gate and were waiting for the flight to be called. He quickly gave Manez the information about Kevin Roper and a complete description. "Nice-looking kid and no accent. I need the verification that he's one of Salazar's men. Will you get it for me?"

"I will do all I can. We need to talk, Quinn."

"I'll be glad to do it later. Right now I

have a limited time before I'm boarding a flight to Atlanta. I need you to go over everything you know about Salazar and Castino and any details about those kids Walsh kidnapped."

"I already briefed you on my take on the matter."

"It was all piecemeal. That was okay as long as I was only concerned with finding Walsh and keeping him from killing Cara. Now I need to know everything so that I can find a way to take Salazar and Castino down, so they can't tear Cara into pieces."

"May I remind you I've been trying to do that for years?" Manez asked dryly. "Where do you want me to start?"

"Tell me about Salazar."

"Grew up in the gangs on the streets. Worked his way up through murder and killing off everyone in his way. Finally killed off the head of the Mulez Cartel and took power. Since then he's been fighting off other cartels and threats from within. Castino has been a constant headache to him. He hates his guts. Castino was starting to take over his territories, and Salazar scrambled to organize a coalition of other cartels in the area. Castino was forced to join or face a gang war that would have been very expensive. Salazar could never show publicly how he felt about Castino." He paused. "But he was my first suspect when Castino's daughters disappeared."

"Salazar's personal life?"

"He has a wife, Manuela, he married when he was seventeen. He has three sons and a daughter. He appears to be a devoted family man. His father was a small-time drug runner and was killed and decapitated when Salazar was starting to run drugs himself. His mother died two years ago."

"Any weakness?"

"Ambition. Other than that, you'll have to tell me."

"What about Castino?"

"He inherited the cartel from his father, Jorge Castino, but he learned well from the bastard. He's more vicious than his father ever dreamed of being. He grew up believing he should own the world, and he's been trying to take it over since his father was killed. He's got a gigantic ego that makes it impossible for him to admit he's not perfect in every way. He hated the idea of the coalition, but he was smart enough not to try to fight it. The moment anyone tried to break it, the others would pounce like ravening wolves."

"Personal?"

"Quintessential macho. Something of a

womanizer in his early years. He married Natalie Kaskov several years ago. She's the daughter of Sergai Kaskov, one of the heads of the Russian Mafia. It might have been a marriage to meld the two Mafias or it might not. She's a beautiful woman, and I can see Castino going a little crazy about her. They seem to be very compatible, and she appears to like the good life as much as he does. She gave birth to the two girls, and the word was that Castino was disappointed not to have a boy. Not that he would admit it, that would have been a failure. So he went to the other extreme and made much of them whenever they appeared in public with him or Natalie."

"And made them targets to all the people who hated him. Send me photos of everyone we've talked about. I want to be able to know them when I see them."

"Hold on a minute." He was gone from the phone and when he came back, he said, "The photos are on their way. I'm curious to know just when you intend to formally make Salazar's and Castino's acquaintance."

"I have no idea yet. I'm just looking for a hook. I want to see what Salazar saw that would lead him to take a chance that could get him gutted. He must have hated Castino big-time to kill his kids."

"Salazar didn't look too closely at the situation, or he would have noticed that neither Castino nor Natalie paid the girls any attention when they weren't on display. Of course, after the girls were kidnapped, they were both supposedly heartbroken. Natalie in constant tears and Castino threatening vengeance if his girls were not returned to him."

"Just the effect Salazar wanted."

"He didn't let it show," Manez said. "Salazar's been very understated for the last few years. No one suspected him."

"He was walking a tightrope with his hired killer, Walsh. I imagine every minute they were afraid of being butchered by Castino if he found out Salazar had paid for the kidnapping."

"No one could prove it."

"The situation is changed now. We have Cara." Joe looked across the jetway at Cara and Eve standing in front of the huge windows. "And as long as Cara is alive, she's more of a threat than she's ever been to Salazar. Find out who this Kevin Roper really is, so I can identify that particular threat."

"I'll work on it. But I'm not going to be your clerk, Quinn. You and Eve Duncan are the smallest pieces in my puzzle of how to control these cartels. But I'll ask around."

He hung up.

A moment later, Joe's phone pinged, and the e-mail photos arrived.

Just two photos but Manez must have thought they were enough.

The Salazar photo showed a tall, handsome, heavyset man in his forties with a thick head of black hair and dark eyes beneath a beach umbrella beside a swimming pool. He was wearing slacks, his white shirt open to the sun. He was sitting next to an attractive plump blond woman in a bikini with her hair tied back in a ponytail. They were both smiling at a young boy sunning himself on the tiles beside the water. Salazar and his wife, Manuela; presumably the boy was his son. A warm family picture. No one would dream that the man was a murderer who would kill a child without compunction.

He scrolled down to the next photo. It was taken on the street outside an outdoor restaurant. Castino was a dark-haired, slim, athletic-looking man who wore an elegant white suit that made his obviously good body appear excellent. He had fine features and a long nose that managed to look almost Roman. He was walking beside a tall, curvaceous, young woman with gleaming dark hair worn in a chignon. Natalie was dressed even more elegantly than Castino and was smiling and clearly talking vivaciously to him. Joe could see a faint resemblance to Cara in that face. Beautiful. Joe agreed with Manez that a man might go a little crazy over her. They were a perfect couple, assured, powerful, striding through life and paying no attention to anything in their path.

Joe could see why Salazar might have wanted to destroy that arrogance with one swift blow.

Yes, Manez had given him a capsule of the two men and their motivations with these two pictures. Joe needed more, but he couldn't push any more right now. Manez and his men were strained to the breaking point with trying to keep order and sanity in this madness of vice and drugs he was facing. He'd help Joe if it wasn't too taxing on his resources. And informants could be expensive and difficult to handle.

He could only hope that Manez would be able to hit it lucky.

"You look absolutely fascinated." Eve's gaze was on Cara's face as the girl stood at the tall windows overlooking the runways.

"That's our plane at the gate. We should be boarding soon."

"I know. I heard them announce it." Cara's gaze never left the plane that was taking off on the far runway. "Look at them. Aren't they beautiful? I've seen lots of planes on TV, but I've never been as close to them as this. Elena and I never had enough money to travel by plane. We always took her car or a bus. But jets have so much power . . . They seem to sing as they lift off, a deep roar and then the higher notes that follow . . ."

"Only you would hear music in that sound," Eve said. "I'm certain that the neighborhoods surrounding the airport aren't appreciating them as you are." Yet it was entirely natural Cara would be able to hear music where others did not. Eve had been told by Cara's teacher that she was an extraordinary violinist though Eve had never heard her play. "And I don't hear anything as delicate as a string instrument in that roar."

"I do. It's a secondary theme, but it's there." She glanced at Eve. "Though it's more for a piano. Jenny would be able to hear it. She always liked the thunder. She'd play for me sometimes . . ."

Before Jenny had been killed when she

was nine years old, before Cara and her nurse, Elena, had been forced to start the long run that had dominated Cara's young life. "You had to be only about three at that time. I'm surprised you remember."

"I remember. I remember everything about her. I didn't start playing the violin until I started school, but then I understood . . ."

"You loved it?"

"It was . . . everything," she said simply.

"I'll get you another violin as soon as we get to Atlanta."

"Thank you." A brilliant smile lit her face. "It will be . . . I won't feel as . . . alone."

"You're not alone, Cara." She reached out and gently touched her shoulder. "I know you probably feel that way right now, but you have Joe and me. Soon you'll have friends your own age. We just have to get through this patch."

She nodded. "And there always seems to be another patch just ahead. But that's the way it is. Elena always told me that we had to ignore the bad times and just enjoy the good times."

"She sounds like a very wise woman."

"She was great." Her voice was unsteady. "I miss her."

"I know you do."

"It shouldn't have happened. Sometimes I thought she was being too careful, but I was wrong." She moistened her lips. "I used to ask her why we couldn't just go to the police and tell everyone that Walsh had killed Jenny. But she said that it was too complicated. That my father was almost as bad as Walsh, and I mustn't get near either one."

"She was right. It wouldn't be safe. And you'd be in the middle of an international incident that could end very badly for you."

"I don't remember my father or mother. Elena said they hardly ever wanted to see Jenny or me. I didn't understand it. You see all those TV shows where the father and mother act all sloppy about their kids." She frowned. "And my father must have kind of liked us if that other guy, Salazar, thought he'd be sad if he killed us."

"I don't know what he felt. I've heard he's a very bad man. I do know that environment would be totally wrong for you. That's why we want you to stay with us until we can sort this mess out."

Cara nodded. "I promised Elena I wouldn't try to go back to see him or my mother. It's just hard to understand. I know Walsh was a terrible man. I know Salazar, who hired him, is bad. But it's not easy to think of your father as being just as bad and maybe hurting you." She spoke haltingly, trying to work it out. "But there are so many bad people out there. How can you tell who you'd be safe with?"

"You can't. Be careful and watch your back," Eve said. "I'd love to tell you that you have to have faith, and everything will work out fine. But I can't tell you that, Cara. It's not the world you live in right now."

"I know. That's kind of what Joe said."

"But you still came close to real danger when you trusted that boy at the hospital. I would have thought that you'd be more cautious."

"He wasn't like . . . I thought he'd lost someone like me. I wanted to help him."

"And he caught you off guard."

She nodded. "It won't happen again. I'll know better next time."

"Let's hope there won't be a next time," Eve said grimly. "Maybe Joe scared that slimeball away."

Cara gravely shook her head. "I don't think so." She turned back to the window again. "He didn't act scared. I believe I'll see him again."

Eve's brows rose. "You don't appear frightened."

"I know him now. I'm scared, but I know who I'm facing." She added, "It's all part of this business of not understanding. Nothing is what it seems. All the time that Walsh was hunting us, he was just a faceless monster. It was almost a relief when I actually saw him. Now he's dead, and there's someone else. I have to learn what I'm facing. I guess I was expecting someone who was like Walsh."

"And he wasn't."

"No, I think he might be even worse. He made me . . . care. But now I know the face of this monster," she said quietly. "And I'll never forget it."

Lake Cottage
Atlanta, Georgia

"It's beautiful here," Cara said softly as she climbed the steps to the front porch. "I love the lake. Elena took me to a motel in the hills that had a lake for a weekend last year. But it wasn't like this. I'll like being here until you send mc away."

"Who said we were going to send you away?" Eve asked as they watched Joe unlock the front door. "I told you that this was a time of exploration while you decided what was best for you. You might like the lake, but you might not like the life Joe and I lead. We're pretty boring most of the time."

"I'm used to boring," Cara said. "Unless

69

Elena wasn't working, I had to stay by myself in the apartment and not invite any of the kids over to visit."

"Pretty lonely?"

"I didn't mind. I had the music." She wrinkled her nose. "Well, sometimes I did mind, but I knew she was only doing what she thought best. She wanted to keep me safe."

"And she did," Eve said. "She gave up her life to do it."

Cara nodded. "One minute she was there, and then she was gone. I still feel as if she's out there somewhere, waiting for me."

Eve could see how that was possible. Cara had only been told that her friend Elena was dead, and it would have been difficult for her to accept the reality. Eve had avoided going into any details, hoping to spare the child. Now she could see that it had not been a kindness. "You know Elena was murdered. The police had to do an autopsy, and they haven't released the body for burial. After that happens, we'll arrange a suitable service for her." She hesitated. "But we may wait for the service until we're certain you're safe. I'm sure you understand why."

"You think they'll use her as a trap," Cara said flatly.

Eve nodded.

"Anywhere can be a trap." Cara looked around the lake and woods. "Even this beautiful place."

And it was incredibly sad that Cara had found that out, Eve thought. "I won't deny that's true. Our friend Margaret was trying to persuade us that Elena was right to run and hide and not settle in any one place. We may decide that they're both on the right track." She started up the steps. "But while we're here, Joe will make sure we're safe. That's why he insisted on going into the house first to check it out. Stop frowning, you don't have to worry."

"That wasn't what I was thinking about," Cara said as she followed her. "I was think-ing-that he was right."

"He?"

"That guy at the hospital. Kevin Roper."

Eve's gaze flew to her face. "That kid?"

"That monster." She added soberly, "He told me so many lies but there was truth in some of them. He said that I should go to church and pray for Elena's soul. He only meant to lure me away from Joe, and I would have gone. Because it seemed right. I tried to pray for her, but I — It wasn't what — I want to go to a church. Could I do that?"

71

"Of course. After we get you settled, I'll arrange for it. You choose the church, and I'll see that you get there tomorrow."

"Thank you." She looked out at the lake. "Though this is so peaceful, it's kind of like a church, isn't it? I just think that Elena would like me to go to church to pray for her. No matter where we settled, she made sure that she took me to confession and Mass."

"Whatever you like," Eve said gently. "A prayer is a prayer. It's the thought and the love behind it that matters." She opened the front door. "Now come in and let's get you settled. Joe is going to want to take you around and show you the property."

CHAPTER 3

Eve smiled as she watched Joe and Cara stroll down the path that led around the lake. It reminded her of the many times she had watched Joe and Jane over the years. Cara wasn't speaking, and her attitude was reticent, but that was how Jane had been in the beginning, defensive, wary. It had taken months for her to accept Joe after they had taken her off the streets. She and Eve had an instant rapport, but Joe was different. Jane had been in so many foster homes that she didn't trust anyone. But Joe had changed that, Joe always managed to change everything.

She turned away and went back into the house. It was good to be home, but she had things to do. She had to check her messages and see if there was anything pressing. She had put her other assignments on hold to do the reconstruction of Cara's sister, Jenny. There were probably several impatient messages asking when she was going to complete their projects.

She got a cup of coffee and picked up her phone to start going through them.

She'd just begun to scroll down when her phone rang.

Jane.

She hadn't heard from her since before she left for California, when Jane had arrived back in London.

A little odd that she was calling her the minute Eve returned?

"Hi, Jane. What's been happening? Have you been settling into —"

"Why didn't you tell me you were in the hospital?"

Apparently not odd at all. "It wasn't important. A little knock on the head. I'd have been in and out of the ER except Joe overreacted."

"Joe tends to do that with you. That doesn't mean you shouldn't have called me."

"I was hoping you would never know about it. For heaven's sake, you're in London. Why worry you about nothing?" She added grimly, "However, someone evidently saw fit to do that. Should I guess?"

"Margaret."

"That was my first guess."

74

"She thought I should know. She said that you'd sent her on her way, and she didn't think that you and Joe should be left without reinforcements. Good God, what have you gotten yourself into?"

"I'm certain Margaret told you in detail."

"Of course she did. I wouldn't have it any other way." She paused. "What about this little girl? How is she doing?"

"As well as can be expected. Cara's very strong, she reminds me a little of you."

"I haven't been very strong lately. No wonder you didn't trust me. I practically fell apart on you before I left Atlanta."

"You had a right. Trevor was shot and killed before your eyes. And you knew it was because he was trying to save you. It takes a long time to get over a trauma like that. I don't believe you ever really get over it. You just learn to live with it."

"Yes, and it's a tough lesson. But I didn't have to worry you as I did." She changed the subject. "But that's my problem. We're talking about yours. How do you want to handle this? Do you want me to come back there? Or do you want to come here?"

"Neither."

"It's one or the other. I'm not leaving you to face this without me."

"Back off, Jane. We'll handle it."

"Like you always back off when I'm in trouble? We're family, and you know I can't do that. Choose."

"Jane."

"I'll go along with whatever you say, but I really think you'd be better off coming across the pond. I agree with Margaret that you should be running and hiding rather than staked out for Salazar in a cave where he can corner you."

"It's a very nice cave, and you spent a number of years holed up here."

"I loved it. If I didn't think I'd cling too much to you and Joe, I'd be back there right now." She went on brusquely, "But as I said, you'd be safer here. Well, not here in London, but I'm planning on meeting MacDuff and Jock in Edinburgh in a few days, then we'll go directly to the Highlands."

"Oh, yes, the great treasure hunt. Your friend, Lord MacDuff has been trying to talk you into looking for Cira's gold for years." Cira was the ancestress who had come to Scotland from Herculaneum centuries ago and had founded the MacDuff dynasty. There had been legends that she had brought with her a chest of gold coins that would have astronomical value today, but it had never been found. MacDuff and his best friend, Jock Gavin, had been searching for it for years, and MacDuff had reasons to believe that Jane might be able to help them. But Jane had only agreed in the past weeks because she needed the distraction to cope with the depression, Eve knew. "And I believe it's a great idea. Is Seth Caleb going along?"

"No, I haven't seen him since I got back to London from Atlanta." She added flatly, "And I certainly didn't invite him."

Jane's tone was distinctly cool, Eve noticed. But that didn't surprise her. Caleb and Jane's relationship had been volatile since the moment they had met years ago. Caleb was an enigma, and Eve never knew which way he was going to turn. She did know that he probably felt something for Jane that he didn't feel for anyone else on earth. "Since when did Caleb require an invitation?"

"I'm trying to change the status quo in that regard. Look, that's not important. This whole idiotic treasure hunt isn't important. I'll put it off if you want me to come back. Otherwise, you come here, and we'll get lost in the Highlands while Joe is trying to set up a way to make Cara permanently safe from Salazar."

"And I'm supposed to involve you in this mess? No way."

"I'm already involved. The minute Margaret told me what was going on, I was involved. Accept it."

"I won't accept it."

"Yes, you will, maybe not this minute, but it will happen. I'll hang up, and you'll think about it. And you'll realize that we're family, and what happens to one happens to all of us. That's what you taught me when I was growing up, and nothing has changed."

"A lot has changed. You're grown-up, you have a career, you have a life outside —"

"We're family. Make a choice. Call me tomorrow. Or I'll be on the next plane back to Atlanta." She hung up.

She sounded totally determined, Eve thought in frustration. Once Jane made up her mind, there was no changing it. She listened, she looked at the problem from all sides, then she came to a conclusion and forged ahead. This time she had not indulged in the usual analyzing but jumped in with both feet when she'd heard Eve might be in danger.

Which was exactly what Eve would have done.

Family. Because family was everything.

Eve wanted to strangle Margaret. She had probably known exactly what effect recounting what had happened would have on Jane.

Eve had known that, too, which was the reason she hadn't been in contact with her since she had left here for California.

And now she had to find a way to deal with Jane as well as everything else that was going on in her life.

Her hand instinctively went to her abdomen.

See, I told you it was crazy out here. And sometimes the craziness comes from the people you love the most. And if Jane knew about you, she'd be more difficult than ever.

But she didn't know, and Eve wasn't about to tell her. She had a better chance of dealing with the situation the fewer disturbing elements that were present. The presence of this child in her life was definitely disturbing.

Disturbing and yet comforting in a strange way. It was a sign that there were wonderful things in a world where darkness always seemed to be present.

But she still had to fight that darkness, so stop standing here and brooding about what Jane might or might not do. She had until tomorrow to make a decision, and she'd have to talk to Joe anyway.

She sat down on the couch and started to go through her messages.

"You two were gone a long time." Eve looked up from the Hamburger Helper she was stirring on the burner when Joe and Cara came into the cottage. "I hope you worked up an appetite."

"She had a lot of questions," Joe said. "And yes, I'm hungry. What about you, Cara?"

She smiled and nodded. "What are you fixing?"

"Just Hamburger Helper." She made a face. "I'm not much of a cook. Joe and I are working most of the time. We do a lot of takeout." She smiled at Joe. "But Joe is great on the barbecue grill. He'll have to demonstrate soon."

"My pleasure," Joe said. "But we may be a little too busy in the near future." He looked at the simmering skillet. "How soon will that be done?"

"Thirty minutes or so. As usual, I tossed everything in it to make it more palatable. I'm letting it simmer."

"It usually turns out pretty good." Joe turned toward the door. "I have an errand to run. I should be back by then."

"Where are you going?"

"I have something to pick up." He opened the door. "Lock up behind me and don't go out on the porch. Okay?"

Her gaze flew to his face. "Was everything all right out there?"

He nodded. "No signs. But it doesn't hurt to be careful." The door closed behind him.

"You're afraid someone would be here waiting for us?" Cara asked.

"No." She shrugged. "But Joe is right, it doesn't hurt to be careful." She moved toward the door and locked it. "Are you tired from that long walk?"

"You're trying to distract me." She was smiling. "I'm used to locked doors. It was a rule at the apartment." She moved over to the stove. "I sometimes put cheese in the Hamburger Helper. Did you try that?"

"Not this time." She looked curiously at her. "You cook?"

"I did most of the cleaning and cooking at the apartment. We divided up the jobs. It was only fair. Elena was working most of the time just to pay the bills." She looked in the refrigerator and got out some Brie cheese. "Okay, if I put some of this in it?"

"Be my guest." Eve watched her as she carefully cut up some cheese, then blended it in the mixture. "What else did you cook?"

"Oh, hamburgers, lasagna, stew, spaghetti,

mostly easy stuff." She put down the ladle. "But I learn fast. If you want anything else, I'll make it for you."

She chuckled. "We didn't bring you here because we wanted a chef."

"I don't expect you to keep me unless I make myself useful. Why would you? You don't owe me anything." She said soberly, "And I have to stay with you. You might need me."

"Because you had a dream, and Jenny told you that you had to do it? I know you told me that." Eve shook her head. "We want you to stay with us but not because you think you have to do it. Jenny isn't with us any longer. She died a long time ago."

"But I still love her," she whispered. "I'll always love her." Her gaze was clinging desperately to Eve's. "And I think she loves you, too, Eve. I told Margaret I thought you dream about Jenny, too. Do you?"

"No." What could she tell her? Certainly not that she actually had experienced the spiritual presence of her sister, that she'd seen her, talked to her. It would be too much for her to handle. She was only eleven years old. "But I became very close to Jenny while I was working on her reconstruction. I felt as if I knew her very well." She paused. "I still do."

"The reconstruction," Cara repeated. "Margaret told me about what you do. It sounds . . . strange."

"I thought so, too, before I started to learn about it. Then I realized it wasn't strange at all. It was a way that I could bring the lost ones home to the ones who loved them. I just had to be taught that everything was there waiting to be brought out and how to do it." She met Cara's eyes. "And that's what I did with Jenny. In the end, I brought her home to you, Cara."

"Yes, you did." She smiled. "And Margaret told me how wonderfully it turned out. May I see it?"

"I don't have it. It's still being held by the Sheriff's Department in California." And actually seeing the skull from which she'd sculpted the reconstruction might still possibly have a negative effect. She thought that Cara understood but she preferred to introduce her slowly to her work and not on such a personal level. She shook her head. "And I don't think you should see it anyway. Memory is always better."

"You worked on it here?"

Eve nodded at the worktable across the room. "Over there."

Cara walked over to the worktable and touched it with her fingertips. "I think

83

you're right. I don't need to see that reconstruction. She'll always be with me." She looked across the room at Eve. "She saved me, you know. Elena had managed to get Jenny and me away from Walsh, but he almost found us in that forest. We heard him coming. Jenny told me to be quiet, and everything would be okay. Then she ran away from Elena and me toward Walsh. I didn't know what was happening. But Elena did and grabbed my hand and made me run and run and run. She was crying . . ." She swallowed. "Did you know that?"

"Yes," Eve said gently. "But I didn't know that you did."

"Sometimes I did. Sometimes I didn't. I didn't want it to be true. So I tried not to remember." She moistened her lips. "But then the nightmares came, and it would all be there again."

"Do you still have the nightmares?"

She shook her head. "No. For the past few weeks, I've just seen Jenny in my dreams and not that night in the forest. She talks to me and smiles, and I'm not afraid anymore."

"That's wonderful. She wouldn't want you to be afraid. She was very brave herself."

"It seems as if I've been afraid all my life. But I have to get over it. Being afraid didn't keep Elena from being killed. It won't keep

Salazar from trying to kill me. I have to be like Jenny."

"No, fear never helps, but it's hard to fight. We'll work on it together." She paused. "You remember that night when Jenny died. Do you remember anything else? Did Elena tell you anything about who kidnapped you? Or why you couldn't go to the police?"

"Elena didn't know what happened that night. She thought maybe we'd been given something in the food we had for supper, and when she woke up, we were in a truck with a group of workers . . . and Walsh."

"Did she recognize Walsh?"

Cara shook her head. "Elena worked and lived in our house. She didn't know anything about any of the men who belonged to the Castino or any other cartels. But she could tell Walsh was in charge and that he was . . . bad." She moistened her lips. "Her only thought was to find a way for us to escape. But her family had raised her to know that going to the police was an automatic death sentence. She wouldn't risk it. Any more than she'd risk taking me back to Mexico. She said that if my father's enemies had been able to reach me once, they could do it again."

"And how do you feel about your mother and father?"

"I don't remember them. Sometimes I have a vague memory of a woman with dark hair and a lovely smile. But she smiled more at Jenny, than at me." She added simply, "And Elena was my family. I didn't need anyone else."

"You were lucky to have her." She added gently, "I hope you can be as happy with us."

Cara nodded. "If you'll let me stay with you." She turned and moved back across the room toward the kitchen. She stopped as she saw a painting on the wall of the living room. "That's a painting of you." She gazed at the portrait of Eve in her blue work shirt. "I like it. It looks . . . warm."

"It was done by my daughter, Jane. She's an artist and very, very good. She gave the portrait to Joe as a gift."

"Is she very famous?"

"No, she's young and just starting out, but people are beginning to know her name." She started to stir the hamburger again. "She lives in London because that's where her agent and gallery are located."

She went closer to the portrait and peered down at the scrawled signature. "It's signed, but it's not —"

"Not mine or Joe's last name? Jane MacGuire. She's adopted. She was ten

86

when she came to us."

"You must have loved her very much to have chosen her."

"Yes. But we kind of chose each other." She tasted the hamburger and put the lid on it. "The cheese definitely helped. Good job, Cara."

She smiled. "We did it together." She came toward her. "What else can I do?"

"Get some rolls out of the freezer and put them in the oven. I'll get down the plates." She shook her head. "I should have put those rolls in before. This Hamburger Helper is almost done."

"I kept you too busy," Cara said as she opened the freezer. "I asked a lot of questions."

"Yes, you did. And I asked you a few, too." She added, "It's a process called getting to know each other. How do you think we did?"

"Pretty good."

"Me, too. Dinner can wait a little while. Joe isn't —"

Even as she spoke she heard the key in the lock, and Joe came into the house.

"Hi. Just in time," she said. "Cara and I did a joint experiment, and it's very close to —" She stopped as she saw what Joe was carrying. "Is that what I think it is?"

"I called the music store from the airport and asked them to choose the best one they had in stock and have it ready for me." Joe came toward Cara and handed her the black-leather case. "I hope it will do. I don't know anything about musical instruments. I had to trust them."

"I don't care. It will be wonderful." Cara's eyes were glittering with excitement as she took the case and ran to the couch to open it. She carefully took out the violin and ran her fingers caressingly down the glossy surface. "It's beautiful." She began to tune it. "Beautiful . . ."

"I think we've lost her," Eve said to Joe. "I believe I'll even wait to put in those rolls." She took a step closer to him. "You constantly surprise me."

"I just thought it was better she had it sooner than later. She's had a lonely life. Her music was probably a closer friend to her than anyone but her Elena." He smiled as his gaze lingered on Cara's absorbed face. "Until she regards us as good friends, the violin will have to do for now." He glanced back at Cara. "I think we'll give her an hour to become acquainted with it. I'm going to take a look around outside."

Eve walked him to the door. "Have you heard anything from Mexico City?"

"Not yet."

"Kevin Roper might not be connected to Salazar. You said there was a chance."

"A chance." He shrugged. "I have a hunch he is. He was too cool, too bold."

"I hope you're wrong. We need time."

"We may not get it." He paused. "And how are you feeling?"

"Fine. Why shouldn't I be? Joe, I'm barely a few weeks —" She shook her head. "I'm fine."

"Mentally as well as physically?"

She glanced back at Cara, then gave him a quick kiss. "Later." She pushed him out the door. "Be careful."

She drew a deep breath and moved back toward Cara. She'd wanted her discussion with Joe to be private but they could probably have had an in-depth conversation and Cara would not have heard a word. She was totally absorbed, and she might have been on another planet. Eve didn't want to take that chance. What she had learned this morning about having a child was only between the two of them and not to be touched by all the other madness that was going on in her life.

Only this morning. It seemed incredible that such a short time had passed since that moment when her entire life had been turned upside down.

But that time had been filled with worry and adjustment and Cara. And that adjustment was still going on.

I had the music, she had told Eve. She'd had loneliness and fear and death, but she'd also been given the gift that had made all that tolerable. Now she had it again, and it was all there in her face and the loving delicacy of her fingers on the strings.

Joe was a very wise man.

She took her coffee and dropped down on the easy chair across from the couch where Cara sat. She was silent, watching her.

She'd get up soon and put away the food. Supper could wait. Cara needed this nourishment more than any food.

No sign of any intruders, Joe thought as he knelt to examine the grass beside the trail. It was still early in the game. They had moved fast and left the hospital only earlier today. Salazar or his man would have had to move equally quickly to track them down and position themselves for any assault. But Joe had no doubt that assault would come, and he would have to be ready for it.

He wanted it over.

He had anticipated that this nightmare that had tormented them would extend past the killing of Walsh. He had fully expected it. Walsh had only been a hired killer, and Salazar was still hovering on the horizon. Joe had been planning on parking Eve and Cara somewhere safe and going after Salazar himself. But that had been put on hold by the news that Eve was with child. He had been caught off guard, and he had to think and look at all the options.

Just as he had told her she had to look at her options. He knew her, and he knew how she would —

His phone rang. Detective Juan Manez, Mexico City.

"It's about time," he said when he picked up. "I thought you'd contact me sooner. What did you find out?"

"That you should be more respectful of both our friendship and the fact that my sources are not limitless. It should have taken me days, not hours. You're fortunate that I have a forgiving nature."

"And that you want to bring Salazar down with a solid crash."

"I'd prefer Castino, but Salazar will do. If you can't arrange a double event."

"Right now, I need you to focus on Salazar's group. Did you find a Kevin Roper."

"No." He paused. "But I found a Ramon Franco. You would find him interesting."

"One and the same?"

"You tell me. I'm sending you a photo."

"So tell me about him."

"A very nasty predator who pretends to be a follower, but I'd bet we'll have to contend with him in the upper echelons of the cartel in a very short time. The word out is he's very ambitious and willing to take out anyone who gets in his way."

"He's just a kid."

"Nineteen, almost twenty. Did that make you less lethal when you were his age?"

"Good point. Give me his history."

"Grew up on the streets of San Diego, father a drug runner, mother a prostitute. Ramon was acting as her pimp by the time he was ten. But he had a temper, and he caught his mother stashing some of the money for herself. He pushed her down a flight of stairs and broke her neck."

"Charming," Joe said dryly.

"He lost a meal ticket, but he learned from it. No more whores and no more losing his temper. Instead, he ran across the border and started trailing after the drug runners from Salazar's cartel, doing errands, making himself generally useful. By the time he was twelve, he'd graduated to collecting debts for Salazar. He became a sort of protégé of the mob. From then on it was straight up the chain. He dedicated himself to learning everything a good assassin should know, from explosives to poison, to his favorite, the machete. At last report, he'd killed at least fourteen, and that was business. He's smart and not shy of showing muscle to anyone in the cartel who causes him trouble or might get in the way of his rise to the top."

"Faults?"

"Temper, he likes to torture his victims if it doesn't get in the way of completing the job, and vanity, he believes he can talk anyone into doing what he wants."

"He may be right about that. Very smooth." He heard a ping and accessed the photo. Ramon Franco was gazing up at him, smiling recklessly. "You hit it," he told Manez. "It seems Salazar turned loose his pet tarantula on Cara."

"God help her."

"He has so far. Eve and I are attempting to offer a little assistance in that direction."

"She'll need it." He paused. "You've verified through that reconstruction that the child found in that grave was Jenny Castino?"

"If I said yes, you'd be obligated to tell your superiors and they'd be obligated to take action about returning her sister, Cara, to her native country."

"True. But it might also cause Castino to take down Salazar. Or Salazar to take down Castino. Either would be beneficial for us."

"I'm not prepared to sacrifice Cara to do that. We've already lost Jenny."

"I sympathize." He was silent a moment. "But we have a war down here. I don't know how long I'll be able to keep silent."

"You're warning me."

"I'm telling you that unless you can figure out a way to give me the result I want without bringing back Cara, I'll have to reconsider going to California and officially verifying Jenny's identity myself."

"How much time are you going to give me?"

"A week should give ample time to someone of your capabilities."

"Hardly ample."

"All I can afford. The only reason I'm giving you that much is because I remember how Castino and his wife treated those two children before Salazar kidnapped them. They were cared for by nurses, and I had reports they rarely saw them. Castino's wife, Natalie, would trot out the older girl, Jenny, to play the piano at her parties. But other than that, they scarcely had anything to do with them. Natalie was only interested in her parties and shopping. Castino never wanted to admit that anything he owned wasn't the best even though he wanted a son."

"You know a lot about them."

"I know a lot about all of the cartel bosses down here. That's why I'm on the hit list of practically every one of them. It's not only that I wish to break their power, it's sheer self-preservation. Get a plan together. One week." He hung up.

Succinct and to the point, Joe thought as he shoved his phone into his pocket. Manez would do exactly as he said he'd do. He was a good cop, and he'd do the best job he could to protect his people. He had no problem with that, he'd do the same under like circumstances. But it left him less time than he'd hoped to keep Immigration away from Cara.

Get a plan together.

And he would. He just had to line up the enemy and see how to take them down.

In one week.

Not impossible, just difficult. And he had to make sure there was no threat to Eve or Cara.

And no smiling tarantula hovering around them to take his bite.

Well, he was almost sure the tarantula

wasn't on the move here and now. There was no way of being certain, but that was what instinct was all about. Joe had checked the cars, boats, exterior of the house. If Franco was on the property, he was keeping a safe distance and only observing. There was no telling about tomorrow but tonight was —

Music.

He stopped on the trail, his gaze on the lights of the cottage just ahead.

Exquisite, diamond-sharp, velvet-soft. Intricate and complex and yet simple enough to stop the heart. The music wasn't being played, it was being newly created with every note.

"My God," he murmured.

He stood there and let the music flow over him. The composition was familiar, but he wasn't sure what it was. He didn't care. It was enough that it existed. It was enough that the little girl who was playing it existed.

Oh, Cara, what the hell have Eve and I brought into our lives?

Eve was in bed but not asleep when Joe came into their bedroom. Cara was still playing in the living room but they could hear it only faintly back here in the bedroom. "I was beginning to worry."

"I stayed outside for a while listening. I didn't want to disturb — No, that's not true. I just wanted it to go on." He started to take off his shirt. "Is she as brilliant as I think she is?"

"Yes, I don't know about brilliant, but if that's the ability to tear the heartstrings, I think that's Cara. I finally came back here to the bedroom because I thought she might want to be alone with it. She's intensely personal with her music."

"Isn't that the way it is with any artist?"

"I don't know. But I've been lying here thinking about her sister, Jenny. She loved her music, too. I wish I could have heard her play the piano."

"I was talking to Manez, and he was saying that Jenny's mother always made her perform to entertain her guests. Jenny must have been a prodigy as talented as Cara." He'd finished undressing and got into bed and pulled her close. "And I'm sure Cara would be designated the same role if she was sent back to Castino."

"No!"

"Just a comment. It's something we have to face."

"No, we don't. Not if she doesn't go back."

"I thought that was the way you were

heading."

"There's no other way to go. We both agreed that it would be both dangerous and cruel to submit Cara to what she'd go through if she had to be shipped back there. We'll keep her with us until we can work something out."

"That's short-term; if it goes long-term, we'd have to deal with a girl who is quite possibly going to turn out a prodigy. That could be a headache for people as busy as we are. Are you prepared for that?"

"No, I'm not prepared for anything. How could I be? We don't even know if she'd want to stay with us. All she knows is that she had a dream about Jenny, and she wanted her to stay with me."

"A dream? She didn't actually see Jenny as you've been doing?"

She shook her head. "If she did, she prefers to think of it as a dream. Kids these days are bombarded by television shows about ghosts and supernatural stuff. I'm sure that Cara thinks that Jenny's coming to her is like one of those stories, only more real."

"Maybe. Did you tell her that Jenny actually appeared to you?"

"No. The last thing I want is to encourage the fantasy. She needs to face the real world and get on with her life. She's gone through enough tragedy." She paused. "The violin was a master stroke, Joe."

"We promised it to her."

"And you fulfilled the promise." She moved closer to him. "We have another problem. Jane called me while you were gone."

"Why is that a problem?"

"Because Margaret got in touch with her and filled her in on what was going on."

"Yes, that makes it a problem. Reaction?"

"What do you think? She was upset. She pulled the family card."

"Uh-oh. And that means?"

"Ultimatum. One way or another, she's going to be with us. She'll either come here, or we'll go there."

"London?"

"No, Edinburgh. And then the Highlands. She's going on that treasure hunt for Cira's gold that MacDuff has been nagging her about. Remember? I told you she might when she left here."

"The Highlands . . . wild country. Who's going with her? MacDuff and who else?"

"Jock Gavin. You know how close he and MacDuff are. Jock grew up in MacDuff's castle, and they're like brothers. She said that Seth Caleb was not coming, but I imagine he'll show up whether she likes it or not. I don't know who else."

"Quite an entourage . . ."

"Why are you so interested?"

"She offered us an ultimatum. I'm exploring the possibilities."

"We need to get her to stay out of this."

"Yes. What do you think the odds are?"

Eve sighed. "She gave us until tomorrow."

"Then we'll have to think about it." He paused. "I heard from Manez. He identified the kid who accosted Cara at the hospital. Ramon Franco, nineteen, a very ugly customer who very likely killed his own parents and certainly murdered fourteen other people. He works for Salazar."

"You thought that he did," she said. "That means that they're moving very close to Cara."

"And to you. Salazar regards you as a problem he has to remove, or he wouldn't have given Walsh the order to kill you when you were hunting for Cara."

"But it's Cara who is the important one."

"The hell it is." Joe's voice was suddenly rough. "*You're* the important one." He was on one elbow looking down at her. "I'll do my damnedest to save Cara, but *you* have to live. So stop talking bullshit. I'm barely holding on by a thread right now."

She could see that as she looked up at him. His jaw was tight, and a muscle was jerking in his cheek. "Okay. I only meant a child is always more vulnerable."

"Yes." He reached down and touched her belly. "A child is very vulnerable and you should pay attention to your own words. There's a dual reason why you should be working hard to take care of yourself." He rolled away from her and put his arm beneath his head. He added jerkily, "Though we haven't had a chance to even discuss that minor event, have we?"

"It's not minor," Eve said.

"No? It appears to be far down on the agenda."

"It's not minor," she repeated.

"Then what is it?"

"A miracle."

He was still. Then he rolled over to face her. "Is that your conclusion?"

She nodded. "I don't know how it happened or why, but it can't be anything else. I'm confused and scared, but I was lying there in the hospital thinking, and it came to me that you can't argue or reject a miracle. You just have to accept it." She said hesitantly, "At least, I do. You have to make your own decision."

"Oh, do I?" He chuckled, his hand caressing her cheek. "I believe I made my decision the instant I gave you that seed. In case you haven't noticed, I have a thing about responsibility."

"It has to be more than that, Joe. When Bonnie was born, I would have given anything to have someone beside me sharing responsibility. But now I can handle it." Her lips were trembling. "I have to handle it, or I won't deserve to have this child. But you'll have to learn to love — you have to feel the miracle — it has to be more."

"It will be more." He drew her close and cradled her in the hollow of his shoulder. "Just give me some time. I'm going to have a few problems refocusing some of the emotion I give you somewhere else. Okay?"

"Okay," she said huskily. She could feel the tears sting as she nestled her cheek against him. He felt warm and strong, and the musk and spice scent of him surrounded her. "I don't know any woman who would object to a request like that. We'll make it through this, Joe."

"I don't have any doubt. We just have a few obstacles in our path."

"Like murder and drug dealers and keeping that little girl alive," she said. "I'll probably be worried tomorrow but I'm not right now."

Right now, she was close to Joe, with his love surrounding her, the knowledge of the miracle to come, and the faint sound of the music of Cara's violin drifting to them.

It was enough. Tomorrow could wait.

It was after eight when Eve woke.

No Joe.

No sound of the violin.

She jumped up, slipped on her robe and left the bedroom.

"Good morning." Cara was in the kitchen and looked up as Eve came into the room. "I was just going to call you." She gestured to the bacon simmering in the pan. "This is about done. How do you like your eggs?"

"Scrambled." She shook her head. "But you didn't have to do this. I thought we had a discussion about —"

"We did." She made a face as she put bread in the toaster. "But maybe I was feeling guilty about playing my violin so late last night. I didn't even ask permission." Her brilliant smile lit her face. "Thank you, Eve."

"Thank Joe. He's the one who ran out of here to get it for you."

"I've already thanked him. Before he left to check out the woods again." Her smile faded. "He told me that boy at the hospital

103

was one of Salazar's men. Ramon Franco. He said he was very bad." She turned back to beat eggs in a small bowl. "He wanted to make sure I wouldn't trust him again. But that wouldn't happen."

"No, I don't think it would." She sat down at the breakfast bar. "But Joe never takes chances."

She nodded. "I like that. It makes me feel safe about you."

"About us."

She smiled as she transferred the eggs to the frying pan. "But he doesn't really know me. I can tell how he feels about you."

"Feeling takes time to build." Joe had said something like that last night. "But you can trust him."

She nodded. "And he doesn't mind me playing my violin."

"Which evidently means more to you than all his protective instincts."

"Yes. I have to learn to take care of myself now, but if I couldn't play my violin . . ."

"I don't imagine you have any problem with anyone's objecting to your playing."

"You'd be surprised. Not everyone likes the violin. Not everyone likes music."

"Then I pity them."

"So do I." She scooped the eggs on a plate and added bacon and toast. "I think they must be empty inside." She put the plate in front of Eve. "But that's just me. And I have to be polite if I run across someone like that. Elena said it's rude to intrude on someone's space. Do you want some orange juice?"

"I can get —"

"I'm right here." Cara headed for the refrigerator. "Anything else?"

Eve's lips turned up at the corners. "No, you've met all my desires."

"I hope so." That brilliant smile was back. "Because you've met mine." She poured the orange juice. "And I cheated you out of dinner last night after Joe came in with my violin. Joe and I were starved this morning, so we ate before he went out hunting for any bad guys wandering around."

"I'm a little hungry myself." She started to eat. "Good heavens, these eggs are delicious. What did you do to them?"

"Mushrooms and a dash of chili powder. And I crumbled up a little bacon, too."

"They're absolutely wonderful." She supposed she should start thinking more about diet. "And healthy, too. Lots of protein. Thank you."

"You're welcome. I'll just wash up these dishes and . . ."

"Just toss them in the dishwasher," Eve

said. "But you might go and clean up. When I went back to the bedroom last night, I looked up the nearest church. It's St. Michael's, and they have an eleven o'clock Mass. Do you think you can make it?"

"I can make it." She was putting dishes into the dishwasher with the speed of light. "I have to go take a shower. And I don't have a dress I can wear. I guess I'll just have to wear my jeans. Elena always liked me to dress up a little when we went to church. She said that it showed respect to God, and it was a kind of celebration."

"We'll go shopping and make sure you have one next time," Eve said. "And I think both Elena and God will forgive you for a lack of respect this time."

"I do, too." Cara was flying down the hall. "I'll be out in thirty minutes, okay?"

"Very much okay." She watched the door slam behind Cara.

Slamming doors, excitement, and the wonder of the young. So much better than the intensity, the sadness, the wariness that she had seen in Cara before. A foreshadowing of the Cara who could be. It warmed the heart.

But that sadness was still with Cara, and going to pray for her Elena would help. Thirty minutes, Cara had said, and Eve wasn't dressed either. She hurriedly finished her breakfast and started back toward her bedroom.

Joe still wasn't back when Eve and Cara got into the Toyota forty minutes later. She called him as she was backing out of the driveway. "Everything all right?"

"Yes. Just being thorough. The clock is ticking. They've had over a day to start moving. I should be back at the cottage in ten minutes."

"We're not there. I just got on the road. I'm taking Cara to St. Michael's for Mass."

"St. Michael's," he repeated sharply. "I don't like that."

"Special request. She wanted to pray for Elena."

"I still don't like it. Do you have your gun?"

"In the glove box." She felt a ripple of shocked distaste at the thought of having to take a gun to church in order to protect a child. "I'll take it in with me. But I doubt if even Salazar's pet killer would risk a public attempt in a church. Too many people around."

"Franco tried to lure Cara into that elevator at the hospital. We don't know what he'd risk. He's an unknown quantity."

Yes, that was true. The entire situation was unknown and fraught with risk. "You think I should turn around and go back?"

Joe was silent. "No sign of any surveillance. It may be safe. The alternative is keeping Cara locked up like a prisoner. Hell, and it may end up that way. But if this means that much to her, we'll try to give it to her. Go straight to the church. I'll follow you and wait outside." He hung up.

"He didn't like us going?" Cara asked quietly, her gaze fixed on Eve's face. "Is something wrong?"

"Not as far as we know. Joe is just careful."

She nodded. "But I don't want to be a bother to either one of you. If he doesn't want us to —"

"It's okay . . . this time." She reached out and took Cara's hand. "It may change."

"Whatever you say." Her hand tightened around Eve's. "I have to keep you safe."

"Because Jenny said you had to do it? I'm sure that she'd be equally concerned about you, Cara. We'll just concentrate on keeping each other safe." She squeezed her hand and released it. "Now stop worrying and just do what you told me you wanted to do. Think about your Elena and pray for her soul. We should be at the church in ten minutes."

CHAPTER 4

Cara was very quiet as they left the church and walked toward the parking lot after the service.

"Okay?" Eve asked gently.

"No." Cara's eyes were glittering with tears. "She shouldn't have died."

The eternal protest, Eve thought. There was nothing to say, so she just gave her arm a comforting squeeze. "I'm sorry, Cara. She was a good woman."

She nodded jerkily. "And God would be smart if he gave her some kind of special place or job to do. I told him so when I was praying for Elena."

"And I'm sure he'll pay attention."

"I don't know. He took Jenny *and* Elena. If he was paying attention, he'd know that was too much." She shook her head. "Elena would say that's not respectful. But . . . I loved them, Eve."

"I know. But their memory will be with

you forever. You'll never lose that."

"No, I'll never lose that." She moistened her lips. "I was kneeling there and trying just to think of Elena and pray for her. But I kept thinking of Walsh and what he did to Elena and Jenny, and that Franco, who smiled at me and wanted to kill me. Elena believed in Satan as well as God. They had to be sent by Satan. There's so much evil in the world, and maybe God can't keep up with it. Maybe we should help him."

"Joe's a detective, he goes after the bad guys every day. We all have to try in our own way." She added gently, "But you have a few years before you have to find your way, Cara." She had stopped beside her Toyota. "Give it time."

"Things happen. Sometimes there is no time." She got into the car. "So I'll hope and I'll pray, but, just in case, I'll fight, not run. I won't let anyone else be taken from me."

"Do me a favor? Run to Joe or me before you decide to take on the devil?" She was negotiating her way toward the exit. "A little help doesn't hurt."

Cara suddenly smiled. "No, it doesn't. Did I sound silly?"

"No, you sounded like someone who has been hurt and didn't want to be hurt again.

And we have to concentrate on doing that."
They had reached the exit and she waved at
Joe, who was parked in a spot near the
street. "And there's Joe waiting to make sure
that doesn't happen. Now let's go home and
talk about how we're going to go forward . . ."
"Wait!" Cara's hand suddenly gripped
Eve's arm. "I think . . . Near the steps to
the sanctuary . . ." Her gaze was on someone
striding down the street. "No, he's gone."
Eve tensed, her eyes flying to the steps.
"Who?"
"I think . . ." She was breathing hard. "I
only had a glimpse, but I think it was the
man you told me was Ramon Franco. No, I
know it was." Her voice was fierce. "I told
you I'd know him if I saw him again. It
wasn't only his face. He had a way of moving, of cocking his head to the side."
"All of that in a few seconds? No mistake?
You were talking about him and Walsh only
a minute before. You're sure that it wasn't
—"
"It was *him.*" Her gaze was frantically
searching the street. "He was in a hurry. He
went down that side street. Believe me,
Eve."
She did believe her, and a chill was running through her. "I was just making cer-

tain." She reached for her phone and dialed Joe. "Cara is sure that she caught sight of Ramon Franco a few minutes ago. What should I do?"

"Where was he?" Joe fired.

"He was coming from the church or maybe the parking lot. He went down a side street on the other side of the church."

Joe cursed. "He'll be gone by the time I get back there and chase him down. It might be what he wants me to do anyway. I'm not leaving you alone. Turn left and park on the street. I'll be right behind you."

Eve hung up and turned left on Danforth Avenue, and a block later, she found a place to park. A moment later, Joe parked and jumped out of the jeep.

He was beside the Toyota in seconds. "Get out. Go get in my Jeep. Keep off the street."

Eve settled Cara in the Jeep, then ran back to him. "What are you going to do?"

"I'm checking the car. Franco was on foot when Cara saw him. He didn't attack. He wasn't positioned for a shot. He had business to do. And after he completed the business, he took off." He carefully lifted the hood. "Nothing here. I didn't think there would be. It wouldn't be easy to rig anything in the engine without someone's seeing him. I would have noticed him myself. I was watching everything going on while you were in the church. I just had to be sure." He closed the hood. "But I didn't see Franco, and there had to be a reason."

"Rig?" Eve repeated. "Are you talking about a bomb?"

"It would make sense. It's a pretty common method of disposal among the gangs in Mexico City. Manez mentioned Franco was good at all kinds of methods for putting down Salazar's enemies. And a bomb would blow both of you to Kingdom Come with no trace evidence. Salazar would have been pleased with Franco."

"Shit."

"I didn't see him." He started for the rear of the car. "He would have had to stay low and out of my line of vision. Back of the car . . ." He knelt on his hands and knees and looked at the undercarriage beneath the car. "Nothing here." He crawled to the side. "I don't see — There it is!"

"What?" She knelt beside him. "I don't see —" Then she saw it. Near the left rear wheel, small, fastened with duct tape, with a blinking light. She gasped. "We should call the bomb squad."

"Maybe." He was wriggling beneath the car. "Give me a minute."

"Joe." Her throat was so tight, she could

barely speak. She knew he'd been trained to both set and deactivate bombs when he was in the SEALs, but that didn't mean he wouldn't blow himself up. "Get out of there. You are *not* going to disarm that bomb yourself."

"I'm only looking at it. Very powerful but basic design. No remote-control switch. Just a timer." His hands were on the bomb, doing something to it.

"Joe, you'll set the damn thing off."

"No, I told you, it's basic. No problem. If I'd been worried, I would have made you go back in the Jeep with Cara when I first caught sight of it."

"Well, *I'm* worried. Get out of there."

He crawled from beneath the car. There was a streak of oil on his cheek and on the collar of his shirt. "It was set to go off in thirty minutes, about the time you'd get back to the house."

"You turned it off?"

"No, I reset it to allow for the time I spent here examining it."

"What?"

"We're going to let the bomb go off," Joe said. He handed her the keys to the Jeep. "You drive the Jeep. I'll meet you when you get off the freeway. I'll need you and Cara to be seen driving the Toyota as far as the

114

property. Don't worry, the bomb's set for fifteen minutes leeway."

"What are you up to?"

"I'll explain later. No time now." He got into the driver's seat of the Toyota. "Trust me."

Trust him to drive home with a ticking bomb on the undercarriage of that car?

Trust his word that she and Cara would be safe for that last stretch in the Toyota?

No question.

But she was going to kill him later for scaring her like this.

She turned and jumped into the Jeep beside Cara.

"Don't ask. I don't know all the answers yet."

The Toyota was parked in a layby off Quinn Road a mile from the freeway when Eve exited and stopped beside it.

Joe rolled out from beneath it. "Get in. Quick. We lost five minutes."

"What were you doing?" Eve asked as she gestured for Cara to get into the Toyota. "Something wrong?"

What was she asking? The whole situation of a ticking bomb was wrong.

"No, I just wanted to check the undercarriage for any other explosive I might have missed before I let you drive it." He ran to the Jeep and jumped into the driver's seat. "Get out of the Toyota the minute you're on our property and the road is surrounded by trees. Jump out, and you and Cara hit the closest ditch. Don't wait until you get to the house."

"Why?"

"The house and driveway are open and can be viewed easily by a telescope. That's where the bomb was set to go off, and Franco will want to see it. The road in the woods when you first enter the property can't be clearly viewed or accessed. When the bomb blows, he'll think he just miscalculated by a few minutes."

"A *few* minutes?"

"Three, tops. Move!"

She moved. Her foot stomped on the accelerator, and the Toyota jumped forward.

She could see Joe in the Jeep in the rearview mirror. She was passing cars and houses as she drove through the neighborhoods bordering the lake property.

Three minutes.

"Eve?" Cara said softly.

"It's okay." She didn't take her eyes from the road. "We're handling it. Just move when I say move."

Cara nodded and fell silent.

Trees.

In a minute, they'd be on the lake property.

It was a long, long minute.

Trees. Shadows. Lake in the distance.

She braked, hard. A screech of metal. The Toyota turned sideways as it halted.

"Out, Cara!" She threw open the door. "Run for that ditch on the other side of the road."

Cara didn't question. She was already running. She was at the deep ditch before Eve, sliding down the muddy side.

Eve followed her.

One more minute.

"Crawl." Joe was in the ditch beside them. "Get as far away from the car as possible."

Eve nudged Cara ahead of her. "Hurry!"

Thirty seconds.

Eve was panting as she moved through the mud and rocks of the ditch. She could feel Joe behind her.

"Head down!" Joe shouted.

Kaboom!

Deafening noise. Glare of fire. Flying metal hurled into the air.

She was vaguely aware of heavy weight. Joe had sprung forward and covered Cara and Eve with his body.

She struggled to move, to sit up.

"Be still. Not yet. There's still flying metal."

A minute later, Joe moved off her. "Okay?"

She nodded as she sat up and looked at Cara. The girl appeared unscratched but her eyes were wide with disbelief as she stared at the fiery inferno just yards from them. Eve glanced at Joe. "You?"

Joe didn't answer as he reached for his phone. "Get in the woods and hike toward the far end of the lake. Wipe out your footprints as you go. *Now.* Franco may turn up any minute. I'm calling the police and fire department and bringing them on the scene so he won't be eager to do any in-depth search."

Eve grabbed Cara's hand and pulled her into the woods. She called over her shoulder. "You're not coming?"

"I'm going to stay here and appear properly devastated by the tragedy. I'll find you after midnight tonight. Get going."

She was already running. She grabbed a branch from beneath a tree, then another for Cara. "You heard him. Erase the footprints."

Cara didn't question but set about brushing the leaves over the faint indentations on the earth.

The air smelled of oil and smoke and

burning rubber. It was hard to breathe.

Joe was alone. Would Franco get there before the fire trucks and police? No, she could hear the sirens now.

And Cara was now by her side, her expression intent, and Eve could almost feel the aura of protectiveness she was emitting. It's not supposed to be like that, she wanted to tell her. It should work the other way around. But she still felt the warmth and companionship of that protectiveness, and she would take that gift. She was feeling bewildered and had no idea why Joe had staged this explosion. All she could do was be patient and take one thing at a time.

Protect Cara from all dangers.

Get to the far end of the lake.

Erase all signs of their passing.

And wait for Joe to tell her what the hell was happening.

"It's kind of cold, isn't it?" Cara huddled closer to Eve beneath the shelter of a boulder beside the lake. "I think the fire from the Toyota has finally gone out. I don't see the glare any longer."

Eve nodded. "It's been hours since the explosion." She drew the girl closer to the warmth of her body and leaned back against the boulder. "It shouldn't be long until Joe gets here. You've been very patient, Cara. Not one question."

"I didn't think you'd be able to answer them." She wrinkled her nose. "You seemed very frustrated with Joe. And there wasn't much time for explanations."

"You're right there," she said ruefully. "On both counts."

"But you're not angry with him?"

"I'll let you know that when the explanations start coming in."

Cara looked up at Eve thoughtfully. "But I don't think you'll be angry with him then either. You wouldn't have done what he wanted if you thought he was wrong."

"Right and wrong is often a question of opinion. Joe and I aren't always on the same page."

"But most of the time?"

She nodded. "Most of the time."

"And you trusted him to do what was right for us."

"Yes, and I always will. It just may not be the way I would do it. Joe has great instincts, and he's sometimes way ahead of the curve." She paused. "And you can trust him, too. If the time comes when he wants you to do something crazy like blow up a Toyota, you go ahead and do it. He'll have a reason."

She chuckled. "But you still thought it was

crazy to blow up the car?"

She sighed. "I loved that Toyota. It was like an old friend."

"But you know he'll be able to convince you it was the right thing to do."

"We'll see when he —" She broke off, her head lifting. "Shh, I heard something . . ."

Cara stiffened. "Maybe I should —"

"It's Joe."

Joe had moved out of the shadows behind them. He pulled her to her feet, and his arms went around her. "Everything okay?"

"You tell me." She gave him a quick kiss. "We didn't run into any trouble, did we, Cara?"

"No." Cara scrambled to her feet. "Hello, Joe."

"Hello, Cara." He took off the backpack he was wearing. "I want you to know getting your violin into this backpack posed major difficulties. Everything else had to go around it." He set it on the ground. "But I figured I might not be able to get you to budge unless it went with you."

"Went with her where?" Eve asked.

"Edinburgh."

"What?"

"I called Jane and told her you'd made your decision, and you'd be flying out to-night."

"Wait a minute. *My* decision?"

"Well, I let her believe that you were in agreement. And when she heard what was going on, she was in agreement, too. All you have to do is say no, but it would spoil all my plans."

"Which involved blowing up the Toyota," she said grimly. "And causing me to almost have a heart attack while you were driving all the way back here with that bomb underneath it. Not to mention sending Cara and me into the woods while you did your fancy staging for Franco."

"Guilty of all of the above."

"Then tell me why."

"I decided that Margaret was right, hiding in plain sight was too dangerous. I could do all the scouting and take all the safety precautions, and there still might be a slip. You and Cara would be squarely in the bull's-eye. I checked those cars for possible explosives when they were sitting in front of the cottage. When Franco couldn't safely get near them, he waited until you left the property and went to a place where he could access them." His lips tightened. "That can't happen again. You won't be safe, and I won't be able to concentrate on getting Salazar or Franco because I'll have to be standing guard."

"So you staged that bonfire to make Franco think he'd managed to kill Cara and me." Eve shook her head. "But they'll find out that there were no bodies in that car."

"Not for a while. That bomb was very powerful and meant to make it very difficult to obtain either dental records or DNA. In short, there would be a possibility of vaporization, or at least huge difficulty finding body parts. You can be safely in the Highlands before anyone realizes you're alive and gone."

"And where will you be?"

"Wherever Salazar is. He controls Franco. I need one to get the other."

"Mexico City."

"Maybe."

"Dammit, we're going to be at opposite ends of the world from each other."

"Not quite. And only if Franco and Salazar stay on my side. The minute one of them steps toward you, I'll be there."

"I don't like it."

"Neither do I. But it's how it has to be right now." He said roughly, "Do you think I like the thought of sending you over there without me? It's the safest thing for you and Cara. Why do you think that I was asking who was on that hunt? MacDuff was in the 45 Commando of the Royal Marines and won a hell of a lot of medals. He's something of a folk hero in Scotland. Jock Gavin is young, but he might be the deadliest man I've ever met. Caleb is bound to show up, and you know what he is."

Yes, she knew. She had seen Seth Caleb in action and still had nightmares about it. "You've been thinking about this since last night."

"I was searching for a way out for you. This is it. It's the best I can do. It will be like having a Special Forces unit to protect you."

"And who is going to protect you?"

He didn't answer directly. "Manez and the Federales want that coalition of cartels broken up. He wants Salazar and Castino dead. He'll help all he can."

"If you ask him. Not if you think he's going to get in your way."

"I've already started to use him."

"For the time being. But you want Salazar and Castino put down regardless if you get the Mexican police to go along with you."

He glanced at Cara. "So do you, Eve."

"I don't want you dead."

"Neither do I." He smiled. "I'll see that doesn't happen. I have something very special to live for at the moment."

She wasn't going to be able to talk him

out of it, she realized in despair. "I didn't want Jane involved in this, Joe. She's just beginning to be able to cope with her life again."

"We have no choice. *She* gave us no choice. I told her all the dangers. I'm calling MacDuff and Jock before I put you on that plane and make sure they're on board with this."

She made a face. "You really meant it when you said that you're forming a Special Forces unit."

"It's already in place. You have to be safe. Don't give me a hard time, Eve."

"Why not? As usual, it seems like it's all for me and nothing for you."

"Look, you have to protect Cara. I have to deal with Salazar. We both have our jobs to do. We can't do them together."

She knew he was right, she just didn't want him to be right. She drew a shaky breath. "You call me. You keep me informed. I want to know what's happening to you. Do you hear me?"

"I hear you loud and clear." He kissed her. "Under the circumstances, I'm not likely to let you run around those hills without my knowing what's happening." He turned to Cara. "You take care of her."

"I will," she said gravely. "Don't worry, I

know that's what I have to do."

He reached out and gripped her shoulder. "And you might take care of yourself, too. Make it a package deal." He turned back to Eve. "I rented a jet, and you'll board it out of the Gainesville Airport." He checked his watch. "It should be ready for takeoff in an hour. I've arranged a rental car to meet us about a mile from here, and I'll drive there and see you on board."

"That's not necessary. I can get there myself."

"It's necessary. I waited until most of the hubbub about the explosion was over before slipping out of the house and coming here. I don't believe that Franco is still hanging around but I have to be sure you're safely away." He grabbed the backpack he'd set down earlier. "And I'll call MacDuff and ask him to set up the arrival in an airport where you can be under the radar."

"Illegal," Eve translated dryly. "Margaret would approve."

"There are times when Margaret and I agree on the basics of self-preservation. I don't want Salazar to tap his contacts and find that an Eve Duncan arrived anywhere in the United Kingdom. We'd have to do a cover for Cara anyway. She has no documents." He took Eve's elbow. "Come on,

Cara. We need to go."

Eve hesitated, then started with them down the trail. It wasn't a foolproof plan, and some aspects scared the hell out of her. But it was the only game in town, and Joe had made it as safe as he could under the circumstances.

Except for himself.

She knew how he operated. He was clever and he could function in conditions that were intricate and complex . . . and dangerous as hell. He'd done it as a SEAL, and he thrived on it. Some of it was planned, other parts were pure instinct. All of it caused Eve to be afraid every minute that she knew what was happening.

But she wouldn't know, unless he told her.

And that scared her more than anything else.

"Relax. It's not going to be easy, but this is the way to handle it," Joe murmured, sensing that disturbance. "It's only the start of the game. Franco moved forward, and we checked him. That means we're ahead."

She nodded. "Just let me know what you're doing," she repeated unsteadily. "I don't want you to be alone."

"I'm not alone. That ended a long time ago. You're always with me . . ."

The pilot, Jeff Brandel, smiled down at Eve and Cara as Joe turned and walked away from the steps of the jet and headed back toward the rental car. "It should be a smooth flight. Is the little girl a nervous flyer?"

Eve shook her head. "She hasn't done much flying, but she'll handle it well. Right, Cara?"

"It's very interesting. And all the statistics say it's safe." She looked back down at her laptop. "And Joe wouldn't have chosen you if you weren't a good pilot, sir."

"Smart," Brandel said. "Yep, I'm pretty good at my job." He turned toward the cockpit. "And you're right, Quinn is tough. No excuses." He grinned. "A little like my wife. I just got married, and she's making me toe the line." He glanced over his shoulder at Cara. "But having a sweet kid like that one might be worth it." He closed the cockpit door.

Eve watched from the window as Joe got into the car. He sat there, and she knew he wouldn't drive away until the plane was in the air. Joe was nothing if not thorough.

She didn't want to go, dammit.

But the plane was already taxiing down the runway, then lifting off. She could see Joe start the car and drive away.

Cara's hand was suddenly covering her own. "If you don't want to go, tell the pilot to turn around and take us back. You're both doing this for me, aren't you? I don't want you to be unhappy. It hurts me. Go back."

"It's partly for you." Eve squeezed her hand. "But Salazar would go after me anyway. I know too much. The minute I finished that reconstruction of Jenny and started to try to find her killer, I was on his hit list."

"But it's mostly for me."

"Or Jenny. She gave her life for you, Cara. She wouldn't want it to be in vain." Her lips tightened. "I won't let it be in vain. You're going to live and be happy. And we're going to punish all the people who are trying to take that away from you as they did Jenny."

"But you're scared about Joe. I *feel* it."

Eve gazed at her curiously. "Do you?"

She nodded. "Jenny said that I'd feel what you feel just as she did. It's happening." She paused. "Why, Eve? I don't understand it."

"I don't understand it, either." She had

been trying to avoid confronting this subject with Cara. But she would not lie to her. "I can only guess."

"She's . . . not a dream?"

"Not for me. I don't know about you," she said. "I never felt a connection like that before with one of my reconstructions. I knew Jenny, I saw her. We had a . . . bond. I don't know why. We both thought it might be because she was sent to me because she needed help to save you." She added quietly, "But I grew to love her as you do. I was sad when she said she was leaving me."

Cara was silent. "It sounds kind of — Do things like that really happen?"

"You'll have to decide for yourself. It took me a long time to admit to myself that I wasn't having hallucinations when my daughter, Bonnie, came to me several years ago. She had been killed when she was only seven, and it almost destroyed me as well." She smiled gently. "And does it really matter as long as the love is there? Dreams or spirits or hallucinations. Whatever brings you peace and love. I like to think that Jenny and I are better for the time we spent together."

Cara nodded slowly. "She loved you, too."

"In your dream?"

She didn't answer directly. "She loves you.

That's why I have to keep you safe." She leaned back in the seat. "But I'll go anywhere with you, do anything. We don't have to go to this Edinburgh."

"I'm afraid we do." She made a face. "Joe has set it up and he's probably right that it's the safest way to handle it. If there is a safe way. I just wish we didn't have to bring Jane into it."

"The daughter you adopted. She's the one who painted the picture of you. Will she be angry that I'm causing you trouble?"

"No, she'd never blame the innocent. You'll like Jane."

"But will she like me?"

"Count on it. I'm only worried because Jane has had such a rough life lately. She was engaged to be married, and Trevor, her fiancé, was killed. It was . . . difficult." Understatement for the heartbreak that had almost destroyed Jane. "But Jane is coming back to us now. I was glad when she decided to go on this treasure hunt."

"Treasure hunt," Cara repeated with a smile. "It sounds like pirates and that *National Treasure* movie. Sort of fun."

Eve nodded. "It does, doesn't it? But it's been on the horizon for Jane since she was seventeen. She's just been putting it off."

"Why?"

"I almost hate to tell you." Eve's eyes were twinkling. "Dreams again."

Cara's eyes widened. "What?"

"When Jane was seventeen, she was having dreams about a young actress, Cira, who lived in Herculaneum in ancient Italy at the time of the eruption of Vesuvius. I won't go into detail, but the dreams were so real that Jane became obsessed. She thought she must have seen something on the Internet or read something somewhere that might have triggered those dreams. She started to do research and found there actually was a Cira who had survived the eruption and fled to Britain, taking with her a chest of gold coins that in today's market would be astronomical in value. Cira settled there in the Highlands of Achavid, what they used to call Scotland, and founded a new dynasty. But after she arrived there, there were no tales, nothing written, about what happened to the treasure chest. It was as if it vanished once Cira reached Scotland."

"But Jane won't admit it?"

"Jane couldn't care less about the treasure. All she wanted was to have the dreams stop and find out the end of Cira's story."

Cara's eyes were fixed in fascination on Eve's face. "And the dreams about her did stop?"

Eve nodded. "But she wasn't happy about the end of the story."

"Why not?"

"It turned out the dynasty that Cira founded was the MacDuff family. And the current Lord of MacDuff has wanted to find that treasure for many years. He's tried to persuade Jane to go treasure hunting with him."

"Because of the dreams she had?"

"Partly. But also because a statue of Cira was found in the ruins of the theater in Herculaneum, and she resembled Jane. Also, there was a portrait of an ancestress, Fiona, in his family art gallery who looked identical to Jane. MacDuff tried to convince Jane she was a member of his family who had emigrated to the U.S. He even wanted to investigate and try to prove it." She shook her head. "Jane didn't want any part of it. She told him she was happy with who she was, and she didn't want to be a MacDuff, thank you."

Cara laughed. "Because she was your daughter. I can see why she'd feel like that."

"Well, anyway, MacDuff has been trying to get her to go on that treasure hunt for Cira's gold ever since. Maybe he thought because of her connection with Cira it would bring him luck. Jane finally gave in."

"Cira . . . I wonder what she was like."

"According to what Jane found out about her when she was researching, Cira was unique. Born a slave and fought her way from the gutters to fame and fortune. Loyal to her friends, tough to her enemies, honest when she could be."

"It's like a wonderful story," Cara said softly.

Eve could see how she might think so without knowing the harsher details. "Not really. Jane met her Trevor while going through it, and they fell in love. But it wasn't a happy ending. Trevor was killed recently trying to protect Jane."

Cara was silent. "Dreams or nightmare . . ."

Eve nodded. "Perhaps a little of both. If you accept them, you have to accept the risk."

"As you did with your Bonnie?"

"It wasn't risk with Bonnie, it was my salvation."

Cara was silent. "Dreams . . . You and me and now Jane. It's strange, isn't it?"

"Only because we're talking about it. I imagine everyone has their secret dreams. We just have to be sure we don't let them get in the way of living our lives. Mother Teresa once said, 'Life is a dream . . . realize it.' " She reached out and touched the silky hair at Cara's temple. "And that's enough talk, period, for the time being. It's going to be a long flight, why don't you try to sleep?"

"Okay. Will you be able to sleep? You're not going to worry about Joe?"

She probably would, but there was no use troubling Cara. "It's early days. If Joe managed to fool Franco, he'll give it a little time before he starts after him and Salazar." She hoped she was telling the truth. "We may be in a holding pattern."

"You didn't answer me. You'll sleep?"

"Little nag." Eve closed her eyes. "I'll sleep."

CHAPTER 5

"It's done," Franco said. "I told you I'd be able to take care of it, Salazar. A bomb on the undercarriage of Duncan's car. It took out Duncan and the kid in one explosion." He laughed. "And you should have seen Quinn standing there on the road staring at the fire while the fire trucks tried to put it out. He looked sick. I showed him he can't get the best of me. I've been waiting for that since he stopped me from taking the girl at the hospital."

"But he did get the best of you there. Are you sure that he didn't do the same thing this time?"

"The cops questioned the neighbors and two separate women saw Duncan and the kid drive by their houses only a few minutes before the car blew."

"You didn't see it yourself?"

He was silent. "I was waiting for them to get to the house. The car blew a couple miles down the road. But I was there within two minutes, and the bomb did its work. I put enough C-4 to practically vaporize the car and anyone in it. I did a quick check in the woods before the police got there, and there were no bodies or footprints. They were definitely in that Toyota."

"Proof?"

"I'll have it in a few days. It will take that long to scrape together what's left of them and attempt an ID. Which they'll have real trouble getting, especially in the kid's case. But they may be able to tell if it's a woman and a child. I'll let you know as soon as the report comes in." He paused, waiting for the praise he knew wouldn't come. "You said you wanted both of them dead, bodies destroyed, no way to connect you with the kid. I did everything right. Everything that Walsh screwed up on. Admit it."

"I'll admit it when you show me proof," Salazar said. He was silent a moment. "But you may have done a sufficient job. A little showy. Officials in the U.S. don't take kindly to car bombs. It makes them feel threatened. All that terrorist stuff. And Quinn is a detective, and he particularly wouldn't appreciate having his lover blown up in that manner."

"It was perfect. The lack of identification

was just what you wanted."

"And you think Quinn is going to take it without acting like a raging bull? I don't believe that's true."

"Then let me take him out."

"I was just going to suggest that, but wait until you have the ID on Duncan and the kid. And don't do anything as attention catching as that explosion. Something quiet, perhaps even appearing accidental? Or maybe suicide. Give him a day or two after he finds out about Duncan, then take care of it." He laughed. "If he doesn't take care of you first."

Franco felt rage sear through him. "He's no threat to me. Naturally, I'll do what you want me to do. I'll tell you when it's done." He hung up.

Salazar had been taunting him. He probably realized that he was on his way up and might become a threat to him. He wanted the job done, but he didn't want him to feel that he was superior in any way.

He almost wished that he hadn't killed that kid. It might have been a way for him to insinuate himself into the power struggle of the coalition that was going to come when he got back to Mexico. Now Salazar was feeling safer, and he might move against him if he decided he knew too much.

But there were other ways to rise to power.

And it was best to do what Salazar wished for the time being and keep an eye on him for the possibility of betrayal. It was almost sure to come. His life had been a series of betrayals, and he knew how to deal with them.

Just as he knew how to deal with Joe Quinn. He had already taken his woman from him. He had shown him the cost of interfering with him. In a couple days, he would kill the son of a bitch in the discreet way Salazar had decreed.

In the meantime, he would wait and dwell pleasurably on the memory of Quinn standing before that blazing car while Eve Duncan turned to ashes before his eyes.

"They're on their way," Joe said when Jane picked up the phone. "You'll meet them at the airport?"

"I told you I would, Joe. I'm in my car now heading for Scotland." Her hand tightened on the phone. "No chance of your coming now, too?"

"Not now. Take care of them, Jane."

"I will. You take care of yourself."

"No doubt about that. I've never had more reason. I'll be in touch." He hung up.

Take care of them.

Damn right she'd do it, Jane thought. Eve had always been there for her since the moment she'd taken her in after a life on the streets and in foster homes. As she'd told Eve, family was everything, and Eve and Joe had created that family for her. There was no question she'd not let it be destroyed by the scum who had planted that bomb.

She could almost see that blast in her mind's eye. When Joe had told her what had happened earlier today, it had shaken her to the core.

So close to a fiery death.

If that child had not seen and recognized the killer.

If Joe had not suspected what was going on.

Too many ifs. Even one would have been fatal, and she couldn't lose Eve.

Not after she had lost Trevor.

Pain.

But not the terrible agony that had attacked her previously. She was beginning to be able to embrace the good memories and let the memory of the horrible night of his death start to fade. It wasn't a question of forgetting him, that would never happen. But she was alive, and she had to face the responsibilities of being alive.

And the biggest responsibilities were to

the people she loved.

Her cell phone rang, and she glanced at the ID.

Seth Caleb.

Shit.

Not now.

Face it.

She pressed the access button. "What do you want, Caleb?"

"I have a long list, and all of them mutually entertaining," he said mockingly. "Where do you want me to start?"

"I can't talk very long. What do you want?"

"At the moment, I want to know where I should meet you after you pick up Eve and that little girl."

She stiffened. "How do you know about my picking up Eve?"

"Not from you, obviously. I received a call from Joe Quinn, and he filled me in on what was going on. He appears to value my services far more than you do. And he must be very upset if he deliberately set out to bring me back into your life. He prefers I stay as far away from you as possible."

It was true. Caleb had saved Joe's life at one time, but the manner in which he'd done it had instilled a permanent guardedness in Joe. Eve had shared that distrust,

141

but she had overcome it when Caleb had been there for Jane on a number of occasions.

"I didn't ask for you to come. I'm not asking now. We don't need you."

"It sounded to me as if you did," he said. "And I called MacDuff, and he wouldn't admit that he needed me. But he didn't object to my presence on your little sojourn into the wilderness. He thought I might add amusement."

"I don't agree."

"But you and MacDuff are looking at it from two different points of view. You've always been afraid of me."

"I have *not.*"

"Let's say, that you've had moments of apprehension."

"Let's say, anyone with any self-preservation instincts would have moments of apprehension being with a man who has a talent for controlling the blood flow of anyone close to him," she said sarcastically. "That doesn't mean I'm afraid of dealing with you."

"Then deal with me," he said softly. "You're going to do it sometime. Why not now?"

"Because I don't choose to do it. You don't run my life, Caleb."

"But I could do such a magnificent job. You'd have such a good time." He suddenly laughed. "I can almost feel the sparks flying. I'll back away and let you go back in your shell for a while. Are you going to tell me where I should meet you?"

"No."

"Then I'll handle it myself. I'll see you soon." He hung up.

She drew a deep breath. She had no doubt she would see Caleb soon. He moved in and out of her life like a constant shadow outlined in fire, disturbing and bewildering her.

"Then deal with me."

He had meant on the most basic and sexual level. What else could it mean? The sexual chemistry between them had always been there though she'd tried to banish it. Caleb was nothing that she wanted. He was highly sexual, unpredictable, primitive, with questionable morals, and she would never know what he would do next. The ultimate fascinating bad boy.

And Trevor had been everything that she wanted. He had been the opposite of Caleb, honorable, trustworthy, humorous, gentle, loving, understanding. He had even tried to understand Caleb on those last days before he had been killed.

Why was she even comparing the two men? Caleb was a law unto himself, and Trevor was gone now.

Because Caleb was not gone, and she had to remind herself that she mustn't be drawn into that emotional vortex that he knew how to weave. It would be so easy to be swept away, and that could not happen. She had come back to London to devote herself to her work. It had been simpler when Caleb had seemed to vanish from her life after she had returned. She had started painting again, and met with her agent, and become totally engrossed in life as she meant to live it.

Until she had been torn away from it by the phone call from Margaret.

And then Caleb had stepped in as he usually did when she would be most vulnerable.

Not fair. Caleb liked Eve, and Jane knew he would help when she was in trouble whether or not Jane was involved. He would just take advantage of any weakness along the way.

And if Caleb could help Eve, then Jane had to accept it and let him do it. It was Eve who was important, not her relationship with Caleb. She would use him just as he tended to manipulate everyone else he encountered.

She would just have to be careful not to let her guard down while she was doing it.

Jane was standing underneath the harsh pole lights by the hangar when the jet rolled up.

"There she is," Eve said to Cara as she unbuckled her seat belt and stood up. "That's my Jane."

Cara peered eagerly out the window. "She looks a little like you. I didn't expect it since she's adopted."

"She has the same coloring, red-brown hair, hazel eyes." She chuckled as she got the backpack down from the overhead compartment. "Big differences, though. I'm just interesting looking, she's positively beautiful."

"Yes." Cara was studying her. "Is that why you chose her?"

"Heavens, no. I told you, we chose each other." She was still smiling as she nudged Cara before her toward the door. "And your next question is probably did I choose her because she might have looked like Bonnie? Yes, Bonnie had the same coloring, too. But that had nothing to do with it either. We

145

just bonded."

"Do you think I'm nosy? Elena said that it's rude to ask personal questions."

"I think you're curious, but most kids are curious. However, you have to realize it's not considered polite in most circles. But you're entering into a new life, and it's natural for you to be curious about the new people surrounding you. So we'll give you a little slack where manners are concerned." She was starting down the stairs. "But don't expect a permanent exception. Privacy is very important. Now come and meet Jane."

She'd gone only a few yards across the tarmac when Jane ran forward and enveloped her in a hug. "Hi, are you okay? You look fine."

"I told you I was fine. It was just a mild concussion." She gave her another hug and released her. "Joe just wanted to take advantage of a temporary weakness to have them give me a physical. He's always nagging, and I'm always forgetting."

"I remember." She linked hands with her and gazed searchingly at her face. "But that bastard's blowing up the car must have been a shock. It must have shaken you."

"I was too busy obeying Joe's orders to feel much of anything." She wrinkled her nose. "Which was probably one of Joe's

146

strategies." She dropped Jane's hands and pushed Cara forward. "And Cara was so cool that I had to hold myself together to compete. Cara Delaney, Jane MacGuire."

"How do you do," Cara said politely. "Thank you for helping me, Ms. MacGuire. I'm sorry to trouble you."

"Jane." Jane held out her hand and solemnly shook Cara's. "And you're very welcome, Cara. Any friend of Eve's is a friend of mine."

Cara's lips turned up in the hint of a smile. "That's the way I feel, too."

"I suspected you might from what Margaret told me about you." She turned back to Eve. "Do you have any other luggage? We should get going."

"No, we're definitely traveling light." She chuckled. "Cara's violin took up most of the space."

Cara looked stricken. "I'm sorry."

"I'm not," Eve said. "I imagine Jane can fit us out with something for this grand treasure hunt. But we may have you work for it."

"Anything."

"You'll play for your supper," she said with a mock scowl. "And no complaints."

Cara smiled. "I promise. No complaints."

"Where are we meeting MacDuff and

Jock?" Eve asked Jane, as they moved toward the car.

"We were supposed to meet in Edinburgh, but after Joe called MacDuff, he decided it would be smarter to avoid being seen together there if possible. We're going to Hazlet Castle, about a hundred miles north of here."

"Castles," Cara repeated. "And Eve said MacDuff is an earl? It's strange . . . and kind of neat. Should I be extra polite to him or something?"

"No way," Jane said. "He's arrogant enough as it is without pandering to his vanity. Be courteous because he's your host, but don't take any guff from him."

"I never found him arrogant," Eve said.

"You never tried to keep him from getting something he wanted," Jane said dryly. "I've been fighting him over this blasted treasure hunt for years. He'll probably drive us like Simon Legree while we're on the hunt."

"Why does he want it so badly?"

"One, it's horribly expensive to keep up a family property like MacDuff's Run. Most of the great homes have been forced to be turned over to the government because of taxes and maintenance. The money would be a godsend. Two, he's heard about Cira, the matriarch of the family, ever since he was born. He's curious about her."

"And you aren't?"

"Of course I am." She started the car. "But not enough to devote this much time to the relics of the past. I want to move forward."

"Even if it's your past, too? Is MacDuff still insisting you're some kind of distant cousin or something?"

"No, I was firm enough so that he won't make that mistake again. He knew that if he tried to gather me into all that nobility folderol, he'd lose any chance of getting me to search for Cira's gold."

"But why does he think you could find it?" Cara asked curiously.

"He's just playing a hunch." She glanced at Eve. "Did you tell her about those crazy dreams I had about Cira?"

Eve nodded. "Not crazy, just strange. You put together a story with those dreams that had a lot of factual content. I can see why MacDuff might think you'll find a way to provide a very satisfying ending."

She shook her head. "I stopped having dreams about Cira years ago. If there was a purpose, it must have been fulfilled. My chances of helping to find that treasure aren't any greater than yours or Cara's."

"And, if you don't find it, then you'll know

you tried. I hate might-have-beens, don't you?"

"Yes." Jane's lips were suddenly tight. "I do. There's nothing worse."

She was thinking of Trevor, Eve realized. She quickly changed the subject. "Who owns this Hazlet Castle?"

"It's one of MacDuff's properties. More of a glorified hunting lodge than a castle, I hear. We won't be staying there long. I think he said we'd be leaving on the search tomorrow."

"That's good." She added slyly, "Off into the wilds of the Highlands. I wouldn't want to trade one cave for another, even one that looks like a glorified hunting lodge. Someone told me that's not a smart thing to do."

"Ouch," Jane grinned. "But that someone was right, as proved by current events."

"Perhaps. Joe certainly thought so." She pulled out her phone. "And I promised to call him when we arrived in Scotland. I'd better do it now."

Joe picked up the phone at two rings. "You're there?"

"Safe and sound. We're on our way to Hazlet Castle to meet with MacDuff. I'll text you when we reach there. Are you still at the lake?"

"Yes, I'm doing more research on Castino

and Salazar and buying time for you." He paused. "How was the trip? How do you feel?"

"Fine. For heaven's sake, how else should I feel, Joe? It's not as if —" She broke off as she glanced at Jane, who was looking at her with raised brows. The last thing she wanted to do was to start worrying Jane unnecessarily. "No problem. What kind of research?"

"A fishing expedition. I'm trying to find a hook to spear Castino or Salazar or both. I turned Manez loose on going in-depth about everything connected with either one . . . and the kidnapping of the girls."

"We know about the kidnapping. Salazar wanted to cause Castino as much agony as possible without endangering himself or his status in the cartel coalition."

"And that may be the sole reason. When Manez finishes his investigation, we'll be sure."

"No sign of Franco?"

"Not yet." He added, "But I'm sure I'm being watched to see if I'm writhing in pain. I'll go out on the porch occasionally and let him see what he wants to see while I'm waiting on the release of the forensic reports. He's probably got a bribe in place and will find out there was no one in that car about the same time as I do."

"Then what?"

"He'll come after me and try to force me to tell him where you and Cara are."

"And you're looking forward to it."

"It will signal the opening of the game. And give me a chance to pay him back for trying to kill you. Then I move on to the next piece on the table."

Salazar. Eve's hand tightened on the phone. "You're so damn casual. Franco is dangerous. You said so yourself."

"I'm not casual. I'll be very careful. You do the same." He said, "Call me when you're on the trail. I'll keep in touch." He hung up.

"Not wonderfully reassuring?" Jane asked Eve.

"As good as can be expected when it's Joe." She slipped her phone back in her pocket. "He's being very patient, but I can never tell when he'll take off like a rocket."

"He won't do it if he believes it will hurt you or Cara."

"Unless he gets an idea he thinks will move the play along." She shrugged. "But maybe that won't happen. We may have at least until Franco finds out that Cara and I aren't dead." She looked in the backseat. "How are you doing?"

Cara nodded. "I'm okay. Sorry you're so

worried about Joe."

"Hey, it's not your fault. Joe's certainly not worried." She smiled back at her. "I'll make a deal with you. You concentrate on having a good time chasing after Cira's gold and doing kid-type things, and I'll try to do the same thing."

Cara studied her, then she slowly smiled. "I think that would be fun. I've never searched for treasure or anything like that before. Elena didn't like me to play with other kids."

"Well, this time you'll be playing with the big boys," Jane said dryly. "MacDuff and Jock will be quite an experience for you."

It sounded to Eve as if any play or association of any sort would have been an experience for Cara. Always in danger, always having to be careful, always having to accept adult responsibilities while she was still a child. She smiled gently but her voice was determined. "And we'll make it a good experience."

He was out there somewhere.

Joe could feel it.

He moved across the porch to stare out at the lake. It wasn't like that first night when he'd been uncertain that Franco was in the vicinity. Franco was not only out there, he

153

was probably getting ready for a move. It was logical that Joe be eliminated to make the cleanup complete.

But that move wouldn't come until Franco was sure that his initial kill was a success. Joe wasn't sure that Franco would make that decision, but Salazar was seasoned and wouldn't be hasty.

But this waiting was making Joe edgy. He almost wished Franco would get overeager and make his try.

No, give Eve her chance to become lost in those barren Highlands. He could wait. As long as he knew he was accomplishing —

His phone rang. Manez.

"That was fairly quick," he said when he picked up. "You've got something for me?"

"You could say that. I don't have details, but I heard a rumor from a prisoner, one of Salazar's men we picked up on a murder charge. It was secondhand from another prisoner in the same cellblock. He's trying to make a deal."

"Rumor? What the hell good will a rumor do us?"

"I'll leave that up to you to decide," Manez said. "Do you want to hear it or not?"

"I want to hear it. Spit it out."

154

Manez did just that, in one single sentence.

Joe inhaled sharply. "Holy shit!"

Hazlet Castle

Hazlet Castle was a small, two-story, stone structure built around a courtyard and set in rolling hills and surrounded by deep forests.

"It's pretty," Cara said as she got out of the car in the stone courtyard. "But not what I'd expect of a castle. Not like the history books, or fairy tales, or Disneyland."

"As I said, there are castles, and then there are castles," Jane said. "MacDuff's primary residence, MacDuff's Run, on the coast, is more what you'd imagine." She got out of the car. "But you still might like to explore it. I don't believe MacDuff would object."

"Object to what?" A tall, muscular man in black trousers and a herringbone jacket was coming toward them across the courtyard. He looked to be in his late thirties, with dark hair pulled back from his face, olive skin, a lean, interesting face, and eyes that sparkled with intelligence and vitality. He moved with swift, springy strength and he was smiling as he took Jane's hand. "A favor, is it?" The words were spoken with a definite Scottish accent. "I always like the

155

idea of your owing me, Jane."

"I think it's a question of your owing me, MacDuff." She smiled back at him. "Why else am I here?"

"According to Joe Quinn, that's questionable." He turned to Eve. "Hello, Eve, I'm glad to see you. I understand you may make our project more interesting than I anticipated."

"And you're still glad to see me?"

"Quinn was very persuasive. He appealed to my sense of noble purpose." His face creased in a smile. "However, as Jane will tell you, my family earned our title as bands of renegades and cutthroats. But that's not a bad thing as far as you're concerned. I'm much more likely to find your situation interesting." He turned to Cara. "And you're Cara? I'm delighted to meet you."

Jane stepped forward. "Cara, this is the Earl of Cannaught, Lord of MacDuff's Run and sundry other properties here in Scotland and Wales. Known by all his subjects as the Laird." She smiled. "He's John Angus Brodie Niall Colin —"

"Stop." MacDuff held up his hand. "I'm sure that you don't intend this girl to remember any of that so you must be doing it to annoy me."

"Just giving you your due measure of

respect, MacDuff."

"It's about time." He turned back to Cara. "Are you going to follow her example?"

"How do you do, sir," she said gravely. "You have a very pretty place here."

"But you find it small and unlike a Disney castle."

"I didn't know you heard me. Was I rude?"

"Honest. But I don't take offense. I completely agree with you. It's small and gradually crumbling into the earth. That's one of the reasons we're going to find Cira's gold and invest in a multitude of renovations on this and my other properties."

"You're certain you can find it?"

"Life is never certain, but I believe with Jane I have an excellent chance." He glanced at Jane. "Now all I have to do is convince her." He turned and gestured to the huge oak door. "Please, come in, and I'll ask Jock to show you your rooms while I finish making the soup I put on when we arrived a few hours ago. Nothing fancy. There aren't any servants here, a circumstance of which I'm sure that Quinn would approve. So you'll have to tolerate dust and the most basic of food."

He threw open the door. "Jock," he called. "Come and see Jane and Eve and meet our young guest."

A fair-haired young man with light eyes and a brilliant smile came across the paneled foyer toward them. "At last. Saved from boredom and kitchen duties."

Cara stopped, gazing at him, dazzled. She had never seen a more beautiful person or a warmer smile. Beautiful, yes that was the word. She would no more call him handsome than she would call a concerto handsome. His shock of blond hair framed a face with perfect features and gray eyes that seemed to glow against the tan of his skin. And that smile seemed to hold all the warmth and understanding in the world. He was now embracing Jane, and Cara couldn't stop looking at him.

"Hello, Jane. It's been a long time. I heard about Trevor." His voice was gentle. "Is there anything I can do . . ."

"No." She hugged him, then turned away. "Nothing. Thank you."

"You're staring, Cara," Eve whispered with amusement.

Cara couldn't take her eyes from Jock's face. "He's wonderful," she whispered back. "It's not only that he's so — there's something else . . . inside."

Eve nodded. "You're right. I'll tell you about him later."

MacDuff suddenly chuckled, his gaze on

Cara's face. "Jock, I believe that you've managed to redeem my humble estate in her eyes. This is Cara Delaney. Jock Gavin. Tell me, Cara, is he Disneyland enough for you?"

"MacDuff," Jane said with a frown.

Jock's gaze swung to Cara. With one swift look he saw, analyzed, and stepped in to heal any hurt. "Don't pay any attention to him." His tone was light, teasing. "MacDuff is just jealous that I fill his shoes better than he does. You're perfectly right, I should have been the earl and he the housekeeper's son. Now tell the lass you're sorry, MacDuff."

"He doesn't have to do that." Cara looked MacDuff in the eye. "Yes, I do think he's like a prince from a Disney fairy tale. But life isn't a fairy tale, and people aren't always what they seem. I'm sure you do have some qualities that people admire."

"Ah, no backing down yet no overt rudeness that might be detrimental to Eve or Jane. Extraordinary." MacDuff tilted his head. "And I appreciate your trying to spare my feelings when I was so impolite as to poke fun at you." He bowed. "Shall we start again, Cara?"

She smiled. "You do seem more like an earl now. Though I've never met one."

"And you'll never meet another one like

159

him." Jock laughed. "He passes muster every so often." He turned and headed for the staircase. "I've been ordered by MacDuff to find you rooms. Would you like to come with me?"

"By all means." MacDuff turned and went down the hall. "I'll be in the kitchen. We'll have a bite to eat in an hour or so. Then we'll go over the maps I have of Cira's castle, Gaelkar. I believe that's the place we have to start . . ."

There were several bedrooms on the second floor, and the three that Jock showed them were furnished comfortably. But all the rooms were dusty, and Jane gazed ruefully around the last bedroom. "I feel like getting a broom and starting in to work." She turned to Jock. "But it would take too long. I'll just open the windows and freshen it up. I hope there's decent plumbing?"

"Sufficient." He shrugged. "And MacDuff did the best he could when he realized that it might be up to us to offer protection to Eve and Cara. He decided it would be best to disappear and not leave any trace, so he whisked everyone out here."

"And I appreciate it," Eve said quietly as she crossed to the window and gazed out at the hills. "Though I hope we won't need that protection."

"It will be what it is." He turned to Cara. "You couldn't ask for a finer man or a better defender than MacDuff. He can be impatient, and he's not always gentle, but he's been my friend since I was a boy, and I could not ask for anyone more loyal."

"Were you really the son of his housekeeper?" she asked curiously.

"Aye. From the time I was a toddler, I was in and out of his castle, MacDuff's Run."

"You were his friend?"

"As much as a wild lad could be a friend to anyone. He was the Laird, and sometimes I fought it. He was a better friend to me than I was to him. I tried to make that up to him later." He changed the subject. "Do you have many friends?"

She shook her head. "I had a friend, Heather, but she wasn't . . ." She stopped. "I couldn't spend much time with her. So I don't really know if she was my friend at all. I guess my only real friend was Elena." She moistened her lips. "But she was enough. I didn't need anyone else."

Time to step in, Eve thought. She could see Cara was on the edge, and she didn't need the trauma of explaining the loss of the woman who had cared for her all these

161

years. Cara was in a strange new world and surrounded by people who meant her well but were also alien to everything she knew. "I think it's time to wash up and go down to have supper with MacDuff, Cara." She made a shooing motion with her hands. "Use that first bathroom down the hall. It looked fairly clean. Jane and I will try to freshen up these bedrooms."

"I can do it," Cara said.

"Yes, you can, but I prefer to do it myself. We'll take turns in the bathroom." She was opening the windows. "Jock, is it safe in the courtyard?"

His brows rose. "Yes, I went over the entire castle and made sure it was all safe when we first got here. I didn't expect anything else. MacDuff alerted the guards that watch over this property to go through it when he knew we were coming. They're some of his old Marine buddies and very sharp. And there was no way anyone not authorized could get close to it after that without our knowing it. They'd report everything to MacDuff. Why?"

"There's no use making Cara stay around when we're going over MacDuff's plans. It will only bore her. After supper, we'll let her go outside in the courtyard and amuse herself." She turned back to Cara. "Be sure

162

to take your violin when we go down to supper."

"My violin?" Her face suddenly lit. "I won't bother anyone? Is it okay?"

"More than okay. I doubt if anyone will even hear you through these thick walls. If they do, they'll receive a gift. Now get going."

Cara whirled toward the door. "I'll hurry, then I'll come back and help you." She suddenly looked back at Jock. "I do have another friend. I have Eve." Then she was gone.

Jane gave a low whistle. "Now that's a responsibility. She reminds me a little of myself at that age."

Eve shook her head. "No, you were much tougher. She had her Elena to remind her that the entire world wasn't garbage."

"She seems pretty tough to me," Jane said. "Most kids would have fallen apart after what she's gone through."

"You're probably right. It's just that she seems to quietly endure while you were such a fighter. Though I believe that leaf may be turning. I'm seeing signs that there's a change in the offing."

Jane was smiling. "And, however like or unlike we are, we have one thing in common. We managed to seek out one Eve Duncan and chose her as our friend." She came across the room to where Eve was standing. "And we thank God that she took us into her life."

"This may be only temporary as far as Cara is concerned. We may not be able to give her the life she needs."

Jane leaned forward and kissed her cheek. "Let's take one day at a time. I have a hunch that new things are going to happen in your world."

"Do you?" Eve smiled curiously. "You may be right. We'll have to see." She turned to Jock, who was staring at them with a quizzical expression. "What do you think, Jock? Are there new things on the horizon for all of us?"

"That would be interesting." He turned toward the door. "And now I'd better go down and help MacDuff prepare us supper. He's fairly competent, but you can't trust these upper-crust types with the basics." He glanced back and smiled. "I'm glad to see you both again. It's been too long." He had a sudden thought. "And, Jane, Seth Caleb phoned and asked me to tell you that he'd see you tonight."

"I can hardly wait," she said without expression.

"Did I detect a hint of sarcasm?" He

paused. "Do you wish me to get rid of Caleb for you? MacDuff thought he might prove helpful in an emergency, but if you want him gone, just say the word."

"I didn't say that," Jane said. "I doubt if we'll need him, but I won't cheat Eve and Cara of his help if you think he's valuable."

"Whew," Jock said with mock relief. "I really didn't want to have to make the attempt of disposing of Caleb. I can handle most skills but that blood thing freaks me out a bit." He lifted his hand. "Remember, supper in an hour."

He closed the door behind him.

"You didn't tell me Caleb was coming," Eve said. "Though I suspected he would."

"If Joe hadn't called him, he would have known nothing about it. He announced he was coming along when he phoned me when I was driving up from London."

"I'd bet that he would have known about it regardless," Eve said. "He keeps an eagle eye on you."

"And that used to make you uneasy."

"It still does, but I've learned to accept the fact that I have to let you handle Caleb. If I find that you're wibble-wobbling, I'll step into the picture."

"Wibble-wobble. I wouldn't do that. Caleb would run right over me."

165

"Probably. But I've occasionally noticed that he allows you to escape punishment when I thought he'd pounce. He definitely has a weakness where you're concerned."

"Not that I noticed."

"You didn't watch him in that hospital in Atlanta when you were in a coma. He was driven." She paused. "And I was grateful to him. He saved your life. Jock may make fun of that 'blood thing,' but you wouldn't have lived if Caleb hadn't gone in and strengthened those arteries."

"I told him I was grateful, too."

"But he disturbs you, so you want to push him away. I understand, and it might be best for you. But you'd better learn how to cope with him or he might . . . Just learn how to cope." She turned away. "Now let's see if we can make a dent in this dust in the next half hour. We might smother if we have to inhale this stuff during the night."

CHAPTER 6

After a meal of beef soup, cheese crackers, and fruit, that turned out to be surprisingly good, MacDuff took them immediately to his study. A fire crackled in the huge fireplace, and the room smelled of pine and the leather of the oversized furniture.

"I'll get the plans." MacDuff went to the shelf in the bookcase behind his desk and drew out a large rolled paper. "I had a new schematic of the castle drawn eighteen months ago, so this should be fairly current. The one before was done in 1994. Still not too old when you remember that the castle is ancient. It was difficult to get anything but a basic map of the ruins." He unrolled the paper on his desk and anchored it on all four corners. "Here it is. As you can see, there's nothing much left. A dungeon, one wall, a staircase, and a few bedchambers, the courtyard. The first floor is a maze of rooms, some blocked by fallen walls."

Jane reached out and one finger traced the curving staircase. "I'm surprised that there's that much left."

"I'm not," MacDuff said. "Cira came from a culture that knew how to build to last. Look at the Coliseum." He pointed to the wall encircling the castle. "And she would have made sure that no invaders would get in and destroy what was hers." He met Jane's gaze. "You're the authority. Isn't that right?"

"How do I know? I'm not an expert on Cira."

"Close as it comes," MacDuff said. "Those dreams you had about her panned out historically." He paused. "And since you're almost certainly her descendant, there's something to say for ancestral and racial memory."

"You're the only one who believes that."

"Because you're too stubborn to let me prove it." He shrugged. "But maybe it will prove itself." He tapped the wall again. "Would you 'guess' that Cira would build those walls strong enough to repel an army?"

"It's logical considering what we've discovered about her character. She was intelligent, strong, and superdetermined or she would never have survived. I was always amazed that she was able to remain a decent human being along with it."

Eve laughed. "You're being so cautious, Jane. Play his game, it won't hurt. I know from what you went through during that time that you felt you knew Cira. Just go with the flow."

"Thank you." MacDuff inclined his head toward Eve. "I realize your opinion carries more weight than mine."

"I don't want anyone to assume that what I went through with those dreams of Cira had any basis in truth," Jane said. "Imagination, maybe. Perhaps something freaky that has nothing to do with your precious ancestral memory."

"Why are you objecting so strongly?" Jock asked curiously.

"Because I'm a realist," Jane said. "What happened to me when I was seventeen has all kinds of explanations, and I may never know which one is true. I had a weird experience, then it was over as if it had never begun. I forgot it, and I'm only revisiting it because MacDuff asked me to do it."

"And I'm very grateful," MacDuff said. He looked down at the schematic again. "Do you suppose this wall was Cira's idea? She wed her Antonio, and he was very strong-willed, too."

"It was Cira," Jane said. "She was an ex-slave and she was nearly fanatical about being free. She wanted her family to be safe at all costs." She smiled. "At least that's my opinion."

"It's on a hill," Eve said. "And it's rough country. Will we be spending all our time at Gaelkar?"

"Presumably. Unless the search leads somewhere else," MacDuff answered. "Why?"

"I have a different agenda than you. I have to protect Cara. I'll have to check out the surrounding countryside. I need to know what kind of problems I might have if Franco shows up."

"I'll help you," Jock said quietly. "We'll do it together. You'll find me very competent."

She didn't doubt it. More than competent. Superb in hunting, absolutely unstoppable when he went in for the kill. When Jock was in his wild teen years, he had run away from home to see the world. Tragically, that journey had led him to be kidnapped by a man who was conducting experiments on a group of chemically brainwashed boys and training them as assassins. It was incredible that Jock had managed to survive and become the person he was today. "I don't want to take you away from the search."

"I can do both." He grinned. "I'm a man of many talents, aren't I, MacDuff?"

"And some of them X-rated," MacDuff said dryly. "And often very annoying. He'll do exactly what he wishes to do and leave Jane and me to do the actual work."

"I do what's important." He dropped into a chair and stretched out his legs. "But I don't have to pay attention at the moment. Continue while I sit here and enjoy the fire . . ."

"You will tell us if we disturb you?" MacDuff asked. "We wouldn't want to let our planning get in the way of your relaxation." He bent over the schematic. "I was thinking about looking into the dungeons first. They're at the lowest point, and there might be passages that lead beneath the —"

The meeting lasted more than a full hour longer before MacDuff tied up the last details and dismissed them to go to their beds.

"At last," Jock said as he opened the library door for Eve and Jane. "Very boring, MacDuff," he said over his shoulder. "You could have made it more entertaining."

"I'll try to do better next time."

"I didn't find it boring," Jane said, as they moved down the hall. "He was very thor-

171

ough. He's obviously spent a lot of time and work on it. He's made an in-depth investigation into that castle."

"I didn't find it boring either." His eyes were twinkling. "But you have to keep MacDuff in line. He's far too used to everyone kowtowing to him." He looked at Eve as she went past the staircase toward the front door. "You're going out to the courtyard to gather your chick and bring her in from the cold?"

Eve nodded. "Cara would probably stay out there all night if I didn't go get her. She has a tendency to become obsessed." She smiled. "And I dare you to refer to her in such a flip manner after you hear what that chick is creating out there."

"Really." He looked intrigued. "Then by all means let's go and see. I'm always ready to take a dare."

Jane was already opening the door. "I'll go with you. I've been curious about —" She stopped as the strains of Cara's violin flowed over them in a wild, passionate, flood of sound. "Dear God." She turned and gazed at Cara sitting on the edge of the fountain, the violin tucked beneath her chin. "That's coming from her?"

"The chick." Eve went down the steps toward the courtyard.

Jock was right behind her, his gaze on Cara. "Does she know how good she is?" he asked quietly.

"Maybe. But she doesn't care, it's all about the music."

He was silent, listening. "And do these bastards who want to kill her realize what they're taking away? To kill any child is a sin beyond belief, but they also want to rob all of us."

"They don't care. She's only a chess piece."

"Is she?" His face was hard in the moonlight. "Then I believe I should enter the game. I don't like being cheated of anything. Not her life, and certainly not that talent."

"Not a chick?" Eve asked.

"It was said in the most affectionate way." He smiled. "And I still might use it if she suddenly discovers how extraordinary she is, and I have to take her down a peg."

"Like MacDuff? I don't believe we have to worry. As I said, it's all about the music." She was only a few yards away from Cara, and she deliberately moved into her field of vision and stopped.

It still took Cara a few minutes to notice she was there. And a moment more to reluctantly lift the bow and stop the music. "Is it time to go in?"

"I'm afraid it is," Eve said. "It's been a long day. Time to get to bed."

She nodded and got to her feet. "I like it here, Eve. The music is stronger here than I've ever felt it. Even when I'm not playing, I can hear it."

"I know what you mean." Jane came closer to her and sat down on the edge of the fountain. "I'm no musician, and I can almost hear it. Some places seem to make their own music. The Highlands are like that. I think you'll like Gaelkar."

Jock nodded. "Aye, wild and wonderful things have happened there, haven't they, Jane?"

She met his eyes. "And how would I know? I've never been there. But it's deep in the Highlands."

"Well, we should be there by tomorrow night and she can judge for herself." He took Cara's hand. "May I escort you inside, mademoiselle?"

"Much better than chick," Eve murmured.

She watched as Jock and Cara walked back to the front door. The beautiful, strong young man and the small, fragile young girl. There was something very touching and old-world about the protectiveness that Jock was showing the child. She glanced at Jane as she started after them. "Coming?"

174

"In a moment." Jane dipped her hand into the water of the fountain and let the drops slowly fall back into the water. "I'll be in soon."

Eve stopped. "Okay?"

"I should be asking you that," Jane said. "I just want some quiet time."

Eve nodded and started up the steps. "I'll see you upstairs."

"Eve."

She looked back at her.

"I'm glad you came to me. I'm glad you trusted me to help." She smiled. "We'll get that little girl through this."

"Yes, we will. We can get through anything together." She blew her a kiss. "Family."

Jane watched Eve disappear into the castle and close the front door.

She stayed there, her eyes on the door.

Waiting.

One minute passed.

Two minutes passed.

"Dammit, what are you doing, Caleb?" she said impatiently as she turned to glare at the shadows of the stable across the courtyard. "What game are you playing?"

"No game." Seth Caleb strolled out of the shadows toward her. He was wearing a black turtleneck sweater and khakis, and the moonlight glimmered on the white thread in his dark hair and lit his high cheekbones, deep-set dark eyes, and full lips. "I was just admiring you in the moonlight. I don't often get a chance to observe you without your getting nervous. How long ago did you realize I was here?"

"I don't know. Not right away. Maybe I saw a movement."

"Then why didn't you sound the alarm?"

"Because I knew it was you."

"How?"

"You sent me a message you'd be coming tonight."

"Yes, I did." He stopped before her. "So it was entirely reasonable that you'd come to that conclusion." He smiled. "But reason had nothing to do with it, did it? You *felt* me here."

"Think what you like, Caleb."

"Oh, I will. I just want you to admit it to yourself, if not to me. We have a connection. It's been there from the beginning. Electricity?" He tilted his head. "Yes, along with something, deeper, less civilized. I sense you all the time when you're anywhere around me."

"I don't want to talk about this."

"Then be honest, Jane."

"It . . . might be possible. You gave me

blood when I was hurt and you have that . . . thing with blood."

His brows rose. "Thing?"

"Hell, what else can I call it? What are we supposed to call it? I'm sure it doesn't have any technical name. I don't know anyone else who's able to manipulate the blood flow of anyone he's close to. It's too weird." And dangerous, she thought. It wasn't only healing that he could control if he chose to use that talent as a weapon. She had seen him do it, and that power frightened her. "And you have to admit it's hard to describe."

He nodded. "Unique, as far as I can determine, outside my family. A small gift, but my own."

"Well, it evidently worked for me at the time. And, since I don't have any idea how it works, I might still be subject to some kind of residual — but it doesn't mean anything." She stared him in the eye. "Can we talk about something else? Like what you were doing lurking in the shadows while Cara was playing?"

"I wasn't lurking. Is it too much to believe that I didn't want her to stop when I arrived here tonight? I heard her playing while I was still driving down the road, and I parked outside the gate and walked up to the courtyard. I thought I'd take a few minutes for myself before I went in and became what you thought me to be." His lips twisted. "Haven't you heard that music soothes the savage beast."

"I believe the quote refers to 'savage breast'."

"I've always thought that my way was more appropriate. And you probably do, too. We've been together during many occasions when my true nature came to the forefront. Isn't that what you see when you look at me, Jane?"

It was true. They had known each other for a few years, and Caleb had seemed to appear whenever she was involved in a situation that was threatening. She had a sudden memory of a time when they had been together in the Alps and Caleb's throwing a body down before her like a savage giving a gift to his mate. The man he had killed had been attacking them, but all she had been able to remember was the savagery and pleasure in Caleb's face.

He laughed. "You're having to think about it. Are you afraid you're going to hurt my feelings? You're not usually so diplomatic."

"You're not a beast. You do have your primitive side. I don't know what you are, Caleb. I don't believe you want me to know. I do know you're intelligent, complex, and can be amusing. I know I owe you my life when you came to me in the hospital."

"And you may never forgive me for that." His smile was gone, his tone fierce. "You wanted me to let you die so that you could join your lover in the great beyond? I wasn't about to let that happen. I won't let you go, Jane."

"You gave me an invaluable gift. It doesn't matter whether I wanted it or not. I still have to be grateful for what you did." She smiled faintly. "And I'm sure that you're arrogant enough to believe that you have control of my life, but forget that. I'll run my own life. I have no intention of dying. I was wrong. There are people who need me. And two of them are in that castle." She got to her feet. "I didn't want you to come because you're always disturbing. But you're here, so make yourself useful. The only thing I want from you is for you to keep Eve and Cara safe." She added deliberately, "And not to get in my way while I'm trying to do it. Do you understand?"

"Of course. You're always very clear with me. Much more clear than you are with anyone else. It's as if you think I'll step outside bounds if given the excuse." He was smiling again. "I'll be very careful not to do that. I'll let you ignore me as much as you're capable. I'll be wonderfully helpful and make certain that all goes well with your world."

"And what are you going to get out of all this, Caleb?"

"Opportunity." He headed for the front door. "It's all I need . . ."

Eve had thought she would be tired enough to sleep, but she realized after an hour of tossing and turning that wasn't going to happen. Not surprising. She was still charged from the flight from Atlanta, and it seemed that every moment since then had been full of renewing relationships, making sure that Jane was okay with what was happening, and Cara was comfortable in this new environment. It was like a new and different life from the one she had left behind her in Atlanta.

And she should be grateful that life appeared to be so different. Talk of ancient ruins and treasures instead of bombs and threats of death at every turn. She *was* grateful. She just wanted to be back with Joe and working to have this nightmare over. It might be safer for her, but what about Joe?

Don't think about it. Do her job as Joe was doing his.

Cara.

She got out of the huge bed and padded across the room to the adjoining room, where Cara was sleeping. She quietly opened the door and peeked at the girl in the bed across the room.

She was fast asleep. It was clear Cara had not had the same problem as Eve. But then children usually slept well. She remembered Jane had no problems until she was in her teens, and Bonnie had been able to curl up anywhere and drop off. Eve had found her so many times in the hammock in the yard with her hand tucked beneath her cheek and her red curls mussed from play.

Bonnie . . .

Eve quietly closed the door and went over to the casement window that she had left thrown wide when she went to bed. She looked out at the forests and the hills beyond.

"I haven't heard from you, and it's beginning to scare me, Bonnie. You told me once that you might not be able to come to me anymore," she whispered. "Is it because you don't think I'll need you? I'll always need you. I want this child. It's a miracle. But I can't let you go. We've been together too long. It would be like losing you all over again."

Silence.

She touched her abdomen.

Hey, tell Bonnie we need her. I don't know if she had anything to do with making you come into our lives, but she might have. She's pretty special, and it wouldn't surprise me if she has influence. But we have to make sure that she sticks around for us, okay?

No answer there, either.

Of course not. What did she expect? The baby was trying to survive and become the child it was meant to be. It was Eve's job to handle everything else. She was being ridiculous, and she should go to bed and try to sleep.

She got as far as settling down in bed again. Then she was reaching for her phone and dialing.

Joe answered immediately. "What's wrong?"

"Nothing," she said. "Everything. I just wanted to hear your voice and know that you were all right. We're going to start off tomorrow trekking through some castle in the Highlands. I feel a million miles away from you right now."

"Me, too." He paused. "You're feeling okay?"

"Strong. Very strong. I could lift mountains."

"Exaggerating a bit?"

"A bit. But not that much. I remember I felt like this when I was pregnant with Bonnie. It was as if she was giving me her strength, too. The only problem was a few weeks when I couldn't keep anything down. So stop worrying. Everything's working out well with Manez?"

"Hell, yes. He's giving me more than I expected. Perhaps more than he expected. It may be a break for us."

"What are you talking about?"

"Just rumors right now. I'll let you know when I can confirm them." He paused. "I got a call from Les Carmody at the Forensics Department a couple hours ago. They wanted to assure me that they were making progress and should be able to tell me something fairly soon."

Not good. "I thought you said that it might be another day."

"I'm a cop." He grimaced. "They're trying their best to help me out. There's a good chance they're already suspecting the truth since they can't have recovered any trace of body parts yet. They just don't want to raise my hopes."

"And Salazar will probably know almost as soon as you do that there was no one in that car."

"I'd bet on it. And I'll be glad when you manage to lose yourself in those Highlands." He changed the subject. "How is Jane doing?"

"Better. Not as good as I'd like to see her, but she's healing. We can't ask for more than that right now."

"Does she know about the baby?"

"Not yet. I'm waiting. She's already trying to protect me. I don't want her worrying any more than she is already." She added teasingly, "And have her ask every time she talks to me if I'm surviving this pregnancy."

"Was that aimed at me?"

"Gently. Lovingly."

"I'll accept both with thanks. On that note, I'll let you go so that you can get some sleep. Don't overdo it tomorrow while you're trekking over that ruin, even if you think you can lift mountains."

"Joe."

He laughed and hung up.

She was smiling as she put her phone on the nightstand and turned over in bed. The news had not been all good, but merely talking to Joe made her feel a sense that they were on the move . . . and together.

Don't think that any minute Salazar and Franco might find out that they had been fooled.

They would still have to find out where she and Cara had gone. That would take time.

Lord, she hoped it would take enough time.

Joe hung up from talking to Eve and stared down at his phone. She had sounded good, but she would not have phoned if she hadn't needed to touch base with him. Eve's career as a forensic sculptor dominated her life, and she was used to working nonstop. She would never have chosen to uproot herself and go on this outlandish treasure hunt in the wilds of Scotland.

But he had chosen for her, and she was trying to adjust and make it work for them.

At possibly one of the most crucial points of her life.

He wanted to be *with* her, dammit.

Calm down. They were already involved and had involved Jane and Cara. It had to work.

But push it along, make it happen sooner.

He picked up his phone again and quickly dialed Manez.

"Don't you ever sleep?" Manez asked sourly when he picked up the phone. "You may be driven, but I need my rest after a day of dealing with this scum."

"You promised me an address."

"That was less than twelve hours ago. Nothing moves fast down here unless you want to end up hanging from a bridge without a head."

"Bullshit. You're just as driven as I am. I'd bet you dove into squeezing all available informants the minute you hung up from me."

"That doesn't mean I was able to tap into information that was accurate."

"Were you?"

"Maybe. I'm still exploring the —"

"Give me an address."

"I'd prefer to verify first."

"We may be running out of time. I need to get a handle on this."

"I don't want you jetting down here and causing a blowup before I'm ready."

"I need that address."

Manez was silent. "Very well, but you don't move without me."

"As long as you don't drag your feet."

Manez sighed. "You're a very difficult man, Quinn. The address is one forty-five El Camino Road."

Gaelkar Castle
Scotland
"Good God, MacDuff. It's magnificent."

186

Eve was gazing out the window of the Land Rover at the staggering beauty of the amethyst-slate mountains in the distance as they neared the castle. The dramatic towering starkness of the peaks, the barrenness that was the vast glens took her breath away. The sun was shining, and yet these Highlands still retained their moody, almost stormy, grandeur. "You didn't tell me."

"It's always best to be surprised." He smiled at her. "You think Cira chose well for her new kingdom?"

"You'd have to ask Jane. I think it probably suited her. There's a wildness here that I can see her appreciating."

"I refuse to ask Jane. She won't want to commit herself."

Eve looked back at Cara, who was sitting beside Jane. "Do you like it, Cara?"

She nodded, her eyes fixed dreamily on the mountains. "So much music . . . And did you see the eagles?"

"I'm afraid I didn't notice either of those things. I was just taking in the general impact." She turned back to MacDuff. "How long before we get to the castle?"

"It's just around the curve up ahead. It may disappoint you."

"It's ruins, for goodness sake. Low expectations."

But she still found herself eager to see that castle built so long ago at the dawn of this land.

"There it is." MacDuff pulled to the side of the road and got out of the Land Rover. He looked up the hill at the ruins of the castle while they waited for Caleb and Jock, who had opted to come in Caleb's car. "It's not very large, but it's in better shape than you would imagine for the lack of repair. That one wall of the battlements is as strong as when they built it. The dungeons are still entirely intact. Once the family left, they abandoned it. They were moving up in the world and concentrated all their energies on building their new home on the coast."

"MacDuff's Run, the castle where you grew up?" Eve asked, as she and Cara got out to stand beside him. "I'm certain that anyone would agree it's much more impressive than this one."

"I like it." Cara's gaze was fastened on the broken walls and tumbled stone of the castle. "It's . . . nice."

MacDuff chuckled. "You constantly amaze me. You criticize my humble hunting lodge, which granted is not in wonderful condition, but you're besotted with this ruin."

"I just think it feels like home," Cara said simply.

"Providing your home has a dungeon." He turned to Jane. "What do you think? Does it feel like home?"

"That's a leading question." She smiled at Cara. "But a castle can be a home as well as a fortress. When I was still trying to find out everything about Cira, I went on archaeological digs in Herculaneum. We had to be very careful not to destroy anything that would indicate how the people lived or died. We worked with spoons, carefully sifting."

"Is that what you're going to do here?" Cara asked eagerly.

Jane glanced at MacDuff. "It's how I'd prefer to do it. It's surprising what secrets can be revealed by using a spoon instead of a shovel. Since we have no idea where we're going with this, it might be a good idea to see if we can get a clue." She added, "But then, I'm not in charge."

"And you think I'm going to use a battering ram because I'm too impatient?"

"I know about impatience," Jane said. "I've been there. Ask Eve. It's your show, MacDuff."

He nodded. "And maybe we'll try a spoon . . . for a little while."

"Good." Jane turned to Cara. "Then would you like to grovel in the dirt with me? Warning. You'll have an aching back and bruised knees unless we can find someplace that sells knee pads."

"Could I do that?" Cara's face was lit with excitement. "I saw a show on *National Geo* that had one of those college digs. It looked like fun."

"Like I said, sore knees. But I found it worth it. There's no guarantee that we'll find anything, but there's always a chance." She looked at Eve. "You're invited, too."

"I didn't expect you'd leave me out. It will give me something to do. I'm not accustomed to sitting around twiddling my thumbs." Eve stood looking up at the hill. "Those people who built that castle didn't know the meaning of twiddling their thumbs. You can almost sense the energy and determination. I wonder how much was done by hand."

"It was Cira's home," Jane said. "Her first taste of real freedom and power after being born a slave. She would have gotten down on her knees and laid those tiles herself. She would have rigged a pulley like the Egyptians to drag those stones in place. She probably loved this castle."

"Then why would she have left it?" Eve asked.

"She didn't, it was her descendants who finally decided they needed to take the next step. She built this place as a kingdom, but I'm sure that she instilled that thirst for power in those who came after her. She grew up in Herculaneum realizing how weak a woman could be if she didn't have wealth and influence. She did the best she was able, became a famous actress, and gathered what wealth she could. Then, when the volcano erupted, she fled with every-thing she owned." Jane smiled. "And some things she didn't own. She probably hid out in the Highlands for a long time after she first arrived here until she thought she was safe. Then she decided it was time to start to build."

"Well, after her descendants decided to abandon this place, they apparently never looked back on what she'd built," MacDuff said dryly. "We have no record of any of her family returning here after they reached the coast, where they built MacDuff's Run."

"They might have looked back," Jane said. "They liked money; you say the family earned their title by raiding and robbing along the border. If they didn't take those coins with them, then I can see them going back to get them. Unless there was a reason not to do it."

"Can we find out?" Cara asked.

"Maybe," Jane said. "If they left us a clue

one way or the other."

"The spoon?" Cara grinned.

"The spoon," Jane said solemnly. She turned back to the Land Rover. "Let's start unloading our bags and supplies and get them up to the castle. I assume you didn't arrange for help here either, MacDuff?"

He nodded. "Jock and I will come back for the tents and camping supplies. Privacy appeared to be everything when Quinn called and asked me to take you. And it's a good rule to follow when you're going after a treasure trove, too."

"I can see that," Eve said. "But that hill looks like a climb." She was grabbing for her backpack. "Let's get to it."

"I'll do it." Cara was already helping Jane with her backpack. She was moving with alacrity, and her expression was eager. Eve was glad to see it. There was nothing better than purpose to make time pass quickly and give one a sense of worth.

"There's Caleb," Jane said as she watched his car come down the road toward them.

Eve was aware that Jane's easy casualness was abruptly gone. All she needed was to have Caleb show up on the scene, and she was charged, wary.

Jane looked at Eve and shrugged. "What can I say?"

"Nothing. I was just thinking that tutoring Cara in the art of the dig might be good for you, too." She started up the road, letting the barren beauty and austerity of the hills around her reach out and touch her, take her into the misty earth and blue sky. For this instant she could almost believe she belonged here.

Work.

Distraction.

It could be a solution for all of them.

Son of a bitch!

"It's not possible," Franco said through his teeth. "It's not true." He hung up, breathing hard as the fury tore through him. But it was true and he knew it. Jessup, that greedy bastard in Forensics, wouldn't lie to him. He knew what would happen to him if he did.

So what did he do now?

No choice.

He dialed Salazar. "We have a problem. Forensics found no body parts in the Toyota."

Silence. Then Salazar began to swear.

"You fool. How could you make a mistake like that?"

"I'm not a fool."

"You're worse, you stupid prick. You're

worse than Walsh ever was. Quinn played you. You lost the kid *and* Duncan."

He had no defense. He was humiliated. But he was going to kill Salazar for talking to him like that. "Not for long. I'll go after Quinn and find out where he sent them. I won't let him do this to me."

"He's already done it." Salazar's voice was harsh. "You've been keeping track of Quinn?"

"Of course, you wanted him dead."

"It's good that you didn't kill him yet. He's the only one who knows where the kid is. Is he at the Lake Cottage?"

"He left there to go to the precinct where he works. I followed him, but he didn't come out. He'll probably be back this evening."

"Probably? Find out for sure. I'll cut your heart out if you lose him, too." He hung up.

He meant it, Franco knew. This last mistake had made his position impossible. Salazar might cut his heart out anyway no matter what he did. He would try to make amends by butchering Quinn, but he had to prepare for the worst-case scenario. Salazar would more than likely send one of his primo killers to make sure that everyone knew he was a failure and what was done with a man who failed him.

Get ahead of the game. He was smart. He could find out where Quinn had sent Duncan and the girl for safety. Then he could either tell Salazar or go ahead and take care of them himself.

Then he would dispose of Quinn in the most brutal way possible, a true *rematar,* a bloodbath.

And then he would start planning how he would rid himself of Salazar without having to contend with the other members of the cartel. He was in a better position to do that than ever before.

He had an ace in the hole.

It would all come together. He just had to move fast. First, find Eve Duncan and Castino's brat.

"I need to talk to you," Salazar said. "Tonight at ten." He hung up.

He hadn't wanted to do this. This meeting was a risk when he didn't need any more risks.

He had no choice. Franco's failure had put him in a corner. He might need help, and he wasn't going to go through this alone.

It would be all right, they'd work it out.

All this hell would be worth it.

He got to his feet and moved out onto the

patio where his children were swimming in the pool. Beautiful children, he thought with satisfaction as he watched his son, Carlos, race across the pool. Three fine sons.

Castino had never been able to produce sons, just those two puny daughters, who had caused him such a headache during these last years.

But one child was dead and the other would soon be totally out of the picture, too. And then he would have his reward.

Yes, and the meeting tonight would be worth the risk.

Mexico City

One forty-five El Camino Road was an elegant creamy-tan stucco hacienda surrounded by trees behind a tall wrought-iron fence.

And the fence wasn't electrified, thank God, Joe realized, as he pulled himself up and over. He jumped to the ground, then darted behind the trees and made his way toward the house.

A soft glow issued from the windows at the rear of the house. Salazar?

There was no telling if Salazar would come to this house tonight, but, if what Manez said was true, there would never be a more likely time for him to show up. Tha was why Joe had jumped on a plane to fly down here when he'd been told the results from the Forensics Department.

He crouched behind a bank of large shrubs near the driveway, every sense alert.

Be patient, he told himself.

When you're playing a hunch, you have to be prepared for it not to pan out.

But that hunch was strong and burning bright. He needed a break, and this might be the one.

No one seemed to be moving around inside. There were no cars in the driveway.

But they could be parked in the back. The trees were so thick that any vehicles wouldn't be seen unless you were right on top of them.

So stake out the house.

And wait for lightning to strike.

Headlights from the sleek black Mercedes entering the gates, not surreptitiously as Joe would have thought, but boldly, recklessly.

The car was coming fast and was approaching the driveway in seconds.

A screech of brakes as the car stopped, and the driver's door flew open.

Come on, Joe thought, let me see you. Is 't true?

Then the driver jumped out of the car and

was striding toward the front door, every step emotion-charged and full of explosive anger.

Joe stiffened. Oh yes, it was true.

Moonlight fell on sleek dark hair.

And the beautiful face and winged brows that were so very like her daughter, Cara's.

Natalie Castino.

CHAPTER 7

Salazar flinched as the door slammed after Natalie came into the house.

"I see you're in fine temper," he said as he strolled out of the bedroom. "And you drove right up to the house instead of parking in the trees. Not smart, Natalie. The only way we've survived so far is to be careful. Do you want to get us killed?"

"I'd see that I wasn't the one killed." Natalie threw her handbag on the couch. "I'd just tell everyone that you lured me here to offer me information about the kidnapping of my little girls. A mother is always desperate and willing to take chances when it concerns a child. Of course, I'd have to shoot you so that it would make the story stick." Her eyes were glittering with anger as she strode toward him. "But I'm not desperate, I'm furious, because I think that you're going to tell me that you've made another mistake. Isn't that right?"

"Duncan and Cara weren't in the car. Franco doesn't know where they are."

"I knew it," she said through clenched teeth. "I could see it coming when you told me that Duncan had taken Cara to Atlanta. What are you doing about it? You're not relying on that stupid prick to find them?"

"I haven't taken him out of the action. I may be able to use him."

"What are you doing?" she asked again.

"I've tapped Jose Domingo, my distributor in Atlanta and told him to check out airline manifests on commercial airlines for the last two days. He's checking out train and bus, too. But I'd think that Quinn would want Duncan and the kid to go far and fast to get them to safety. So far, no records of them have surfaced. So Domingo is checking private and charter flights."

"How long before you'll know?"

"Only a few days. I have to be careful about pushing Domingo. His contacts are valuable to me. He doesn't want to make waves with ATLPD by any overt moves. After all, he could deal with any of the other cartels."

"Then go after Quinn," she said impatiently.

"We're getting there. He's been off the radar for the last several hours since we've heard about the forensic report. But Franco will locate him."

"Maybe he's gone to join Duncan and Cara."

"He went to the trouble of staging that elaborate red herring. He won't chance being followed and giving their hiding place away. He knows we're watching him. Franco will gather him up if he doesn't get another lead before that." He held up his hand as she opened her lips. "I know, an incompetent fool."

"You seem to hire no one else, first Walsh, now Franco. This entire thing has been bungled. You *promised* me. I trusted you." Her hands clenched into fists. "I gave you my daughters. You said that it would be over in a heartbeat, and no one would ever know."

"We've gone over this before. It didn't work out." He was sick to death of her attacking him. He just wished he was sick of her. He'd thought in the beginning that he'd grow tired of her and would be able to find a way to dispose of her and make his position more secure. It hadn't happened. He only had to see her, touch her, and he had to have her. Just thinking about her, and he got hard. He wanted her now. "And you wanted those girls dead as much as I did. I did you a favor."

"No, I told you I wanted them kidnapped. I didn't say you had to kill them."

"You knew that was the only safe way to handle it. You just closed your eyes. Why else were you so angry when I told you that Cara and that nurse got away?"

"Because at that point there was nothing else to do. I couldn't go back. I had to go on with it."

He slowly shook his head. "You wanted it." He moved closer to her. She smelled of vanilla and that exotic Russian perfume she'd worn since the day he'd met her. She'd told him her father sent it to her every year. Whether he screwed her or not, before he left her he always had to shower and get her scent off him before he went home to Manuela. His wife knew he had other women, but she couldn't know about Natalie, and that perfume was too distinctive. "And you wanted me. You still want me."

"Not now," she said impatiently.

"Now." He put his hand on her breast. "You're not sleeping with Castino. You need it. I can feel your nipples hardening." He rubbed at the sensitive tips through her silk shirt. "I'm doing everything you'd want me to do about the kid. It won't be long and you'll be safe." He unbuttoned her shirt.

"But I need encouragement . . ." His tongue touched her nipple. "Give it to me."

"I don't need you." She was starting to breathe hard. "There are other men."

"None that I wouldn't kill if I caught you with them." He bit down hard and felt the shudder that went through her. "Like I did when I heard you were screwing that chauffeur you hired to take you around to your fancy parties. Do you remember what I did to him?"

"Yes. It was . . . bloody."

"You liked it. You liked knowing that you'd caused it. That you had the power. It was difficult for me to do it in a way Castino wouldn't suspect had a connection with you." He pushed her away and took off her blouse and bra. "So I set him up to be caught in a Federales raid near the border. I protected you then, too, didn't I?"

"And yourself."

"It's the same thing."

She looked at him challengingly. "You only want me because I belong to Castino."

"Not only. You know better. It might have started out that way, but we're both caught now."

"Not me." She stared fiercely up at him. "I'll let you have me only as long as you amuse me. When I get bored, I'll walk away."

"I haven't bored you yet." His hands tightened on her breasts. "Get in bed."

She didn't move. "That's not why I came here."

"It's why I came here. Sometimes you're so concerned someone will find out about this place that I can't get you to come. But you came tonight, didn't you?"

"Let me go."

"Get in bed. Why not? We're here now. You're hot, you need it." He added thickly, "And I need you. I'll make you scream, Natalie."

She smiled. "Perhaps."

"Are you teasing me? That's very dangerous."

"I've heard nothing but what you want." She took off the rest of her clothes and stood there naked. "I want to hear what you want to give me." She took down her chignon and her hair flowed around her shoulders. "Oh, I'll scream for you." She came toward him. "And I'll make you scream. But I came here for a purpose, and you'll give me what I want."

"I told you that I was working on it. I have to be careful."

She rubbed against him like a cat. "Not good enough. I don't care about being careful any longer. I want a promise that you'll keep." She reached down, caressing him. "And you'll give it to me."

Her breasts brushing against him. The scent of her . . . "Shit."

"I need it to happen. You either give it to me, or I'll find someone who will."

"I'll kill you."

"No, you'll give me Duncan and Cara, and it won't be in a few days. You'll know where they are tomorrow. I don't care if it causes problems with your distributor in Atlanta. You'll do what you have to do." She went to the bed and lay down. "And before you leave here tonight, you're going to promise me that no matter what you have to do, I'll know where to find them."

"You?" He was over her, tearing off his clothes.

"Me. I can't leave it to you any longer." She gazed up at him as he came into her. "I have to make sure it's done." She whispered as she started to move, "Now promise me . . ."

3:15 A.M.

"Come back to bed," Salazar said thickly as he watched Natalie dress. "I'm not done with you."

"I'm done with you." She slipped on her shoes and went over to the mirror on the far wall. "You were right, I needed it. You were very entertaining." She ran her fingers through her hair. "We may have to arrange things so that we can do this more often. Would you like that?"

"I'd like to stay alive more," he said dryly. "Too dangerous."

"That's what I always say, but I'm beginning to think we should explore the possibilities. We need a change." She touched up her lipstick. "If you find me exciting enough?"

She knew damn well the effect she had on him. "Stop playing games and come back here."

"You don't have time. You have calls to make, don't you?" Her smile was brilliant as she turned back to him. "And I have arrangements to take care of, too. Changes . . . Salazar." She headed for the door. "I can hardly wait."

He watched the door close behind her and cursed low and vehemently. He was still horny as hell, and that wasn't his only frustration. He didn't like it that Natalie was being so demanding, but he knew it had been coming. He had barely been able to restrain her for the last few years.

He looked at his phone on the bedside table. Those calls Natalie had spoken about were against his better judgment. Not good business. It was clever to stay beneath the radar and not do anything to disturb either the Feds or the police department and make them pay too much attention to his operations. But if he didn't meet Natalie's deadline, she would be even more likely to become difficult.

What the hell, he thought recklessly. He was ready for a change, too. He was tired of being careful. How many years had it been since he had been like Franco and taken what he wanted and made everyone around him fear him? He wanted that heady feeling again.

He picked up the phone and dialed Franco.

"I need to know where Duncan and the kid are by tomorrow night. Do you have any possibilities?"

Franco hesitated. "Your man here in town said that he'd discounted all the commercial airlines and narrowed it down to four or five private airlines. Three Quinn has used in the past nine years. I thought I'd check those out. I'll be careful. Domingo said you wanted us to be discreet."

"I want to know tomorrow night. Screw being discreet." He hung up.

Joe watched Natalie Castino drive out of the gates and waited another fifteen minutes for Salazar to leave. He didn't come out of the house. The lights in the bedroom went off after another five minutes. He probably felt safe as long as Natalie wasn't with him.

You're not safe, you bastard.

He moved quickly toward the wrought-iron fence, and, a few minutes later, he was over the top and dropping to the grass.

A shadow in the bushes to his left!

He whirled and gave a roundhouse kick that hit the man in the throat, then moved in for the kill as he was falling.

"No!" Manez moved out of the bushes. "*Madre de Dios,* you've caused enough trouble, Quinn. I won't have you killing my men."

Joe stopped, breathing hard, trying to calm the rush of adrenaline. "Then you shouldn't have men who set themselves up to be taken out. I saw him the minute I hit the ground."

"Pedro is a very good man." Manez helped the man to his feet. "You're obviously just better. Go back to the car, Pedro. I'll take it from here."

Pedro gave Joe a glowering glance and turned and walked away.

"And you shouldn't expect me not to react if you don't tell me you're going to be on stakeout, Manez." Joe gazed after Pedro. "How much does he know about this house?"

"Why? Would you go after him and finish the job?" Manez said sourly. "He knows nothing. No one knows about this house but you and me and the prisoner who gave me the information. I just thought I might need backup."

"Against me?"

"Against Salazar. I'd be an even greater target than usual if he saw me here. Though I had an idea you might be popping in and causing trouble." He turned. "I need to get you off the street. I'll walk with you back to your car."

"I checked it out before I went to the house. Are you trying to protect me, Manez?"

"Only because I don't need you blowing the only lead I've had since —"

"I'm not blowing it," Joe interrupted. "I just had to verify so that I knew where I could go with it. I had to see what was happening."

"You should have left it up to me. I was going to bug the place and make sure that I had all I needed."

"This is Salazar and a woman he's been screwing for years. They both know the consequences. Do you think that he wouldn't take precautions? I had a listening device, and I should have been able to hear through the glass of the window and couldn't do it."

"So you found out nothing?"

"I found out that she went in angry and came out looking very sleek and satisfied. I don't know the dynamics, but they're definitely lovers." He stopped at his rental car. "And presumably have been lovers for a number of years according to your informant. The question is if she's his accomplice. I'd bet that she is."

"I'd . . . hesitate. A mother doesn't kill her children."

"We both know that's not true. It depends on what the stakes are and the personality of the mother." He paused. "It's the most unnatural crime imaginable, so the personality would have to be twisted beyond belief."

"Perhaps . . . she doesn't know?"

Joe looked at him.

Manez shrugged. "The idea offends me. What can I say?"

"You can say that you'll give me all the information possible on Natalie Castino. I suppose you got photos of her going through the gate?"

"I thought it might be useful."

"To stage an uproar between Salazar and Castino that would put the coalition in chaos? Not yet, Manez."

"I'll be the judge of that."

"No, not until Eve and Cara are safe." His lips tightened. "Salazar will have put precautions in place to make sure he's not connected to this place or Natalie Castino. That photo will mean nothing. Even if Castino makes a move on Salazar and takes him out, it won't be good for me. Then he won't be able to give the order to stop Franco and whoever else he's put on tracking Eve down. Let me take care of him myself."

Manez shook his head.

"You gave me a week."

"That was before Natalie Castino appeared on the scene. I can use her, Quinn."

"A week."

Manez shrugged. "Five days. Subject to change if I find it necessary."

"Done." Joe got in the car. "You won't find it necessary. I believe Salazar's attention is going to be focused away from anything to do with the cartels for the time being. He's going to be doing everything he can to find Eve and Cara."

"And what are you going to do?"

He pulled away from the curb. "Get back to Atlanta and make sure he comes up against a stone wall."

"I like this." Cara dug her spoon into the stony dirt of the courtyard and smiled at Eve. "I kind of thought Jane was joking about it, but she really gave me a spoon."

Eve chuckled. "I believe it's more of a way of teaching patience and care than necessity. I remember when she was digging at the site in Herculaneum, she was very impatient. She must have learned an important lesson."

"But MacDuff hasn't learned it." Cara's gaze went to the area where the Laird was working with Jock. "I didn't think I'd see an earl with his sleeves rolled up and sweating. And he has a shovel."

"It's his idea of a compromise. He let us have spoons and he's going for the big stuff. He believes that the chest might be in the dungeon area. It would take a long time for him to get down there with a spoon. We're only looking for possible clues, keys, boxes, scrolls, or anything else written by family members. They're looking for the chest itself." She put her spoon aside. "But I'll have to leave you to it by yourself for a

212

while. I have to go and take a look around the surrounding area and get my bearings."

Cara nodded. "It's a new place. Elena always used to look around the neighborhood when we moved to a different place. She said it made it safer for us."

Eve nodded as she got to her feet. She should have known Cara would not be alarmed. Her life had been one long flight for survival. "Stay close to Jane."

"You're going alone?"

"Jock was going to go with me, but he appears to be busy with MacDuff. I'll be fine."

"Yes, you will." Caleb was suddenly beside her. "But Jock thought that you'd be even better if you had someone to keep you company. He asked me to take his place." He grimaced. "A great compliment since he really doesn't trust anyone but MacDuff. I don't think he trusts me either, but he knows I can take care of you, and he knows where he can find me if he has to go after me."

Cara laughed. "But Jock wouldn't hurt you."

"Not if I could help it." He smiled at Cara. "You like him?"

She nodded. "He wouldn't hurt anyone."

Caleb looked at Eve. "I believe that's our cue to leave." He took her elbow to help her over the rocky terrain toward his car parked on the road. "I'll keep her safe, I promise, Cara."

Cara nodded and went back to her digging.

"Jock has her completely fooled," he said quietly. "She thinks he's some kind of Boy Scout. Are you going to tell her about him?"

"Not if I don't have to do it."

"Because she's a child?"

She shook her head. "She's not really a child. Because she's half-right, he wouldn't hurt anyone he didn't have to hurt. He is what she believes him to be. He didn't try to fool her, he was just being himself. I don't want her to think everyone she reaches out to is a threat."

"Well, I don't have that problem with Cara." He opened the car door for her. "If you've noticed, she regards me with the same wariness that everyone else does. I'm surprised that she permitted me to take her Eve away without her."

Eve glanced at him, her eyes twinkling. "But you were vouched for by Jock. That makes you totally acceptable."

He started the car. "Until she reaches the age of intimidation. Then I'd have my work cut out for me." He glanced at Jane sitting on a rock and going through a box o papers. "Wouldn't I, Eve?"

"Yes," she said bluntly. "But even Jane allowed me to go off with you without protest. She either trusts me to take care of myself, or you've made inroads on her trusting you."

"Which do you think?"

"I have no idea. I know you usually don't give a damn about anyone's trusting you. But Jane may be different." Her gaze narrowed on his face. "Is she different for you, Caleb?"

"She's a beautiful woman."

"Are you going to answer me?"

"So that you can rush to protect her?"

"I'll always do that."

"She's . . . different. I won't hurt her . . . if I can help it."

"That's not good enough."

He suddenly smiled recklessly. "It's all you'll get from me. It's more than I've ever given before. She fights me, and that makes me . . . angry."

"That's not what you were going to say." Her gaze was still reading him. "I think you were going to say it hurts. Were you?"

"Me?" He shook his head mockingly. "Why would you think I would succumb to that particular weakness? No one else believes that I would ever be that soft."

"I know you would never admit it. I don't know why I asked."

"Neither do I." He took out a folded paper from his pocket and handed it to her. "Jock gave me this map. He thought you might want to look it over. He told me to take you to the lake. It's the only area that has access from the north. From the south, anyone coming would be easily spotted."

She unfolded the map and checked it out. "By all means, let's go to the lake."

Gaelkar Loch was large, deep, crystal blue, and surrounded by craggy hills that fell steeply to its green banks. The north bank was bathed in thick gray mist that not only shadowed the lake itself but obscured a good fourth of the massive hills that hovered over it.

Eve felt suddenly small and overwhelmed as she stood on the edge of the steep slope nearest the road and looked out at the blue water and that ghostly mist. "What is it?" she murmured. "I've been to the Alps and I never felt . . ."

Caleb nodded. "It's principally that heavy fog. MacDuff tells me that it never goes away. Most unusual. It makes the place seem a bit menacing. It's easy to imagine that anything could happen in those mists.

There are all kinds of legends about it. The locals say that it could hide the beginning or the end of the world." He shrugged. "Some people feel it, some people don't. It does manage to capture the imagination. These Highlands have been battlegrounds and full of pain and savagery for centuries. I'm sure that Cira was a part of those battles."

"But you feel it? You weren't born here either, were you?"

"No, my family settled in Italy centuries ago." He grimaced. "Much to the dismay of the villagers who were there before them. It seems my ancestors were far more intimidating than I am, and the villagers didn't understand the gift that was passed down through the family."

"Imagine that," Eve murmured.

"But I do have a home a few hundred miles from here now. I like the wildness of the Highlands." He smiled. "I think I would have bonded with Cira."

"I believe you would, too." She looked back at the lake. "MacDuff believes Cira is Jane's ancestor."

He nodded. "But that means nothing to me. I want Jane exactly what she is, what she's made of herself." He inclined his head mockingly at Eve. "What you've made her."

His smile faded. "As usual, I have a number of purely selfish interests in coming here, but one of them is to help you, Eve. I won't let anything happen to you or Cara." Then the smile was back. "Jane would have my head, and that's not the part of my anatomy I'm interested in giving her."

Outrageous. Totally outrageous. But she still had trouble smothering a smile. "It depends on how you look at it. But I do thank you for any help. There are many reasons why I need everything to go smoothly while we're here."

"Smoothly. What a curious word to use in this case." He looked at her speculatively. "And you're usually very clear and concise."

"It's just a word, Caleb." She could have bitten her tongue. The word had come out of nowhere. Everything had to be smooth. She had to take every care so that the child would be able to survive these next weeks. But Caleb was sharp and intuitive, and he had caught that subtle inference. "Stop reading something into —" Her phone rang, and she breathed a sigh of relief. She took the cell out of her pocket and her relief was gone in an instant.

Joe.

"I've got to take this." She walked a few yards away from Caleb as she punched the access. "Is there a problem, Joe?"

"The forensic report came back yesterday. Salazar knows that you and Cara weren't in the car."

She drew a shaky breath. "We knew that was coming. Yesterday? Why didn't you call me when it first came in?"

"I was a little busy."

She stiffened. "I don't like the sound of that. Did Franco come after you?"

"He didn't get a chance. I made myself unavailable. Something else popped up, and I had to check it out."

"Joe."

"I'm going to tell you. That's why I'm calling. It may be a way we can manipulate the situation to keep Cara in the U.S. I was in Mexico City checking out a lead one of Manez's informants handed him." He paused. "For at least the past six years, Natalie Castino has been sleeping with Salazar. Probably longer than that, but that's the only time span Manez's informant knew for sure."

"What?" Eve was stunned. "There's got to be a mistake."

"I was at their little love nest in the hills outside Mexico City. I saw her. She was angry with Salazar. She'd probably just heard about the forensic report."

"Joe, that doesn't make sense. It had to be dangerous for her to conduct a liaison with Salazar. If her husband found out, she'd be killed."

"Maybe she thought it was worth it." He paused. "Or maybe she was caught in a trap and couldn't get out."

"You think that she helped him kidnap the girls," she whispered. It was almost too horrible to say the words. There was no child more helpless and vulnerable than when a parent was involved. They were automatically thought to be the protector, not the aggressor. "Why, Joe?"

"Manez is trying to find out. He's digging for more information about her." He added ruefully, "He didn't want to believe it. He's a tough guy, but he probably loves his own mom, and it's hard for him to make the connection."

"It's hard for anyone." She was having trouble herself. Though she had done a few reconstructions on children who she had later found out had been killed by their parents, it had almost always been an accidental blow. Or by the father to hide proof of molestation. She could remember only two murders committed by a child's mother, and the women had both been declared by the court to be insane. But then, maybe judges had the same problem as Manez about accepting that a mother could kill her own child. "I don't understand. It's not as if she had much to do with Jenny and Cara. You told me that nurses took care of the children, and she and Castino didn't see that much of them. I've seen photos of them while they were with their parents and . . . they were damn adorable." She had to steady her voice. "Why would she do it? Was it because she was so obsessed with her lover, Salazar, that she'd do anything he wanted?"

"It's a possibility, but I don't believe that's true. The woman I caught sight of outside that house last night was no weakling. She exuded power, lots of power. What she was doing with Salazar was what she wanted to do." He added, "And I'd bet that if she was involved in the children's kidnapping, she wanted that, too."

"Did Manez give you anything more to go on?"

"He came back with a bare-bones report by the time I got back here to Atlanta. I'll forward it to you. Not much. She married Castino when she was eighteen and had Jenny only a year later. In Russia, she was Daddy's little girl and lived the life of a princess. Sergai Kaskov is a Mafia boss, but he evidently adored her and gave her everything she wanted. But maybe she didn't want to be a princess, she preferred being a queen. When Castino came to Moscow and she heard how powerful his cartel was, he seemed to be what she needed. For the first few years, her life in Mexico was ideal, parties, a husband who was crazy about her, designer clothes, the power she'd never had in Russia."

"It changed?"

"Not on the surface. She had another child, Cara, a few years after Jenny. The word was that she hadn't wanted to have another child, but Castino was insisting. He wanted a boy."

"And he didn't get one that time either."

"No. So he wanted to try again. Natalie suddenly became ill and flew home to Moscow to visit her father. She came back eight months later, and she was in fine form and absolutely radiant. Manez said that everyone who saw Natalie and Castino together during that period remarked on how she managed to dazzle Castino again. He wasn't pleased about her long visit to her father and had taken a mistress. But within a few weeks, he'd sent her away, and Natalie was queen again. She kept him so busy, in bed and out, that he wasn't pushing about her getting pregnant immediately."

"If she was that busy with her husband, she wouldn't have had time to seduce or be seduced by Salazar."

"I don't know, it depends on what spurred them to get together. Manez didn't give me any more details about that period."

"What about the girls? Would she have had an opportunity to help with the kidnapping?"

"The afternoon before Jenny and Cara disappeared, Natalie had taken Jenny to perform at the garden party at a friend's house in the hills. Cara stayed home, taken care of by Elena. Natalie said she and Jenny returned to the house at about six, and she sent Jenny and Cara to bed about nine. No one discovered they were missing until the next morning."

"She sent them to bed at nine," Eve repeated. "Her nurse would have put their nightgowns on them, wouldn't she?"

"Presumably."

"But Jenny wasn't found in a nightgown when they took her out of that grave. She was wearing a white eyelet dress and a black-velvet ribbon in her hair." She moistened her lips. "As if she'd gone to a party."

"You're saying you think that the girls

were taken immediately after Jenny was brought back from that garden party?"

"It would give Salazar almost twelve hours more to whisk them out of Mexico before the search started." She felt sick. "Natalie gave him that time."

"But you still don't want to believe it." He said wearily, "Neither do I."

"I can't think why she would —"

"We'll find out eventually. We just have to accept that's almost certainly what happened." He was silent. "And be on guard against her."

"On guard?"

"Manez told me that she boarded a flight for Moscow this morning. It seems her father is ill and wants to see her. Convenient?"

"Perhaps she's panicking and going to him for protection."

"Or perhaps she'll surface somewhere other than Moscow. I just wanted to warn you that she may be a factor." He paused. "How are you? Everything okay with Cara?"

"She's digging in the dirt at the castle. She's smiling a lot and having a good time." She drew a shaky breath. "And how the hell do I tell her that her mother might have been responsible for killing her sister and Elena?"

"You don't tell her, not yet. Let it play itself out. You didn't answer me. How are you?"

"I'm digging in the dirt, too. And right now I'm with Caleb, gazing out at a lake that the Highlanders say might have been created to hide the beginning of the world or maybe the end of it."

"Caleb? If he showed it to you, then I'd bet on the end."

"Maybe. I can never tell about him. But Caleb's been more accommodating than usual." She changed the subject. "What are you doing?"

"Trying to keep Franco and Salazar from tracing you. I got behind when I flew down to Mexico. I'm on my way to Gainesville now to contact Jeff Brandel, the pilot who flew you to Scotland. I'm going to give him enough money to go out of the country for a while. He should have arrived back in Gainesville by now." He was silent for an instant. "Look, yes, the idea of Natalie Castino's killing her own child is horrible, but look at the good side that we found out about it. How likely is it that Immigration would send Cara back to a mother who's suspected of murdering her sister?"

"But how long would it take to prove that Natalie did that? It's hard to believe, people

225

push it away. She might persuade everyone that she's a victim."

"The glass half-empty?"

"I want hope for Cara, Joe. I just don't want to take chances. Not with her, not with you. I love you." She added unsteadily, "Take care of yourself." She hung up.

She gazed blindly out at the lake that had so intrigued her before. The beginning of the world, the end of the world. Mist and swirling waters and no one knew what was happening beneath that mist.

And no one knew what had happened to twist the heart of Natalie Castino, who should have loved and cared for her children and instead had tried to destroy them.

"Bad news?" Caleb was studying her expression. "Quinn?"

She nodded. "It looks as if Salazar will be on the move soon, if he's not now. I guess that's actually not bad news. We knew it was going to happen."

He shrugged. "You looked stunned."

"Joe just found out that Jenny and Cara's mother was probably involved in their kidnapping." She made a face. "I suppose stunned is the word, and sick, and bewildered. I can't understand it. A child's life is so precious. I can't see how any mother could do that."

"You're saying kidnapping, do you mean killing?" he asked bluntly.

"I'm having trouble saying the word when connected to Jenny and Cara." She deliberately said, "Killing. Because that was where it was going to end, and Natalie Castino must have realized that."

"I'm just being very clear." Caleb's lips turned up in a half smile. "No one minces words about me, and I generally return the favor." He tilted his head. "This is really disturbing you."

"You're damn right it does. I'm a mother. I instinctively want to protect any child." She added fiercely, "And I want to punish anyone who would try to hurt a child."

"Back to the primitive. I understand that concept though I generally operate from a different standpoint." Caleb looked out at the lake. "Have you seen enough? Would you like me to take you anywhere else?"

"No, we should probably go back to the castle." She started to turn away, and then realized he was studying her again. Why? Had she been too passionate about the idea of Natalie Castino's crime and betrayal? She couldn't have been anything else. Perhaps that wasn't why he was staring at her so curiously. He might not have even noticed how upset she'd been.

Though he probably had noticed and would analyze and bring it up at his leisure. Not that she couldn't just laugh it off. But she seldom laughed at whatever Caleb deduced about anything. He always came too close.

Face it now. She turned to look at him. "What? You're staring at me."

"I like looking at you. I like *you,* Eve." He took her arm and led her back toward the car. "I can see why you and Jane are so close. You're both painfully honest . . . most of the time. I find that infinitely refreshing." As they reached the car, his hands slipped down and he grasped her hands as he stood looking down at her. "Though it's usually not in the least complimentary to me. But even that's forgiven, I always know where I stand." He stared directly down into her eyes. "And here's where *you* stand. Don't worry, I'll make sure that you'll be safe. You have Jock and MacDuff, who are the soul of everything bold and noble, but every little while you need someone who's not at all noble. That's me." He was smiling as he opened the car door for her. "I have an incredible number of dirty tricks at my disposal. And I'm putting them all at your disposal."

She stared at him in surprise. "What

brought this on?"

He shrugged. "Occasionally something touches me, and I have to respond." He got in the driver's seat. "You seem to have hit it today." He started the car. "Don't tell Jane, she'll say I'm conning you."

"No she won't. She knows you better than you think."

He nodded. "But she'd still put up barriers and have me jump through hoops. She doesn't like the idea that I might do something that's not totally on the dark side. It confuses her."

"It confuses me, too." She paused. "What . . . touched you today, Caleb?"

His smile was mocking. "Now that would be a revelation. There's always a price for a revelation of my unique personality. You wouldn't want to pay it."

Would Jane want to pay it? Eve wondered.

"In time," he said as if he had read her thoughts. "If I prepared the way." He changed the subject. "Now tell me about Cara and that music that was luring me like a Lorelei the other evening. What do you intend to do about her when this is all over?"

Gainesville, Georgia
Still no answer.

Joe frowned as he hung up the cell.

It was the third attempt to reach Jeff Brandel he'd made since he'd gotten on the road today. Straight to voicemail on the first two calls, this time no connection at all.

He didn't like it.

Fifteen more minutes, and he'd be at the airport.

Nothing might be wrong.

But, dammit, he didn't like it.

CHAPTER 8

Gainesville Airport

"I need to see Brandel," Joe said as he strode into the small terminal that was more like an office. "Where is he?"

"In hangar Twelve E." A lanky young brunette woman in jeans and a plaid shirt looked up from the paperwork in front of her. "He's been there since this morning working on his plane. Should I call him for you?"

"I've been calling him." He left the terminal and strode out on the tarmac.

Hangar 12E.

And the metal door was pulled down.

It was a nice day, why the hell pull down the door?

Three minutes later he found out the answer.

Blood.

He stood there gazing at the man tied to the chair, who must be Jeff Brandel. It was impossible to tell because his face was cut and burned, and one eye was gouged out. His mouth was duct-taped shut.

"My God."

He moved closer and saw the drill beside the chair and the cuts on Brandel's body. The death wound was from the machete piercing his chest, and the blood was still flowing from it. He had gone through hideous torture, and had obviously tried to withstand it. He was a good guy and had probably not wanted to break and endanger Eve and Cara.

But there was no sign of the man who had done this so there was every chance that he had gotten the information he needed before he had killed Brandel.

He felt the anger rise as he looked again at the pilot. Anger and fear.

"Shit." He took out his phone and dialed Eve. "Brandel is dead. By the look of the body, he probably told them everything he knew."

"Dear God, no . . ." She was silent, trying to cope. "He had a wife. He told me he'd just gotten married two months ago. I . . . liked him."

"Yeah, so did I." He turned away from Brandel and walked to the open door. "But that's not important right now. Brandel talked. How much did he know? I only told him where he was to take you. Nothing else. Did you tell him anything?"

"No. He just said something about Cara and how he wanted kids and then about his wife."

"He couldn't hear anything you talked about with Cara?"

"No. The cockpit door was closed." She paused. "But he had to have seen Jane pick us up at the hangar. He was still sitting on the runway and hadn't pulled away yet."

Joe muttered a curse. "Even if he had no idea who she was, they'll be able to dig into our background and make a good guess fairly quickly."

"But that's all they'll know. MacDuff wouldn't have broadcast info about the hunt because he wouldn't want to have to deal with any other treasure hunters. Jane certainly wouldn't have talked about it. We arrived at the airport here in Scotland, then just vanished. It's not that bad."

"The hell it's not. They'll still be closer to you than I ever intended."

"But not closer than you thought might happen. I remember that remark you made about a Special Forces unit to protect us."

"*Might* happen. It wasn't supposed to happen." He looked back at Brandel. That wasn't supposed to happen either, a good man had suffered and died. "I'm going to call MacDuff and warn him what's going down. I wanted to tell you first."

"I can tell him. I'm almost back to the castle."

"Then go ahead and do it. I'll call him later. I need to phone the precinct and report Brandel's murder." He paused. "And break the news to his wife."

"I'm sorry. It's not going to be easy."

"None of it is easy," he said roughly. "And I don't want to stay here trying to heal wounds. I want to catch the next flight to you. I can't even do that because it's a sure thing I'm being followed. I can't risk leading anyone to you."

"Salazar and Franco," she reminded him. "I know you're feeling frustrated, but you might still be able to find them and take them down. Look how much you've already found out about Natalie Castino. We're safe for now, Joe."

"For now." He was gazing down at Brandel's bloody face. "I'll do what I can here. I don't know how long I'll be able to keep from saying to hell with it and just taking off. Watch everything that's going on around you. Take care." He hung up.

Only he should be the one taking care of

her, he thought in frustration. He shouldn't be thousands of miles away. He couldn't stand it.

He had to stand it.

He punched in the number for the precinct. "Joe Quinn. I need a forensic team and the medical examiner out here right away. I'll give you the address . . ."

"Nasty. Real nasty." Detective Pete Jalkown shook his head as he gazed at the covered gurney as it was wheeled out of the hangar. "You knew him?"

"Slightly. I hired him for a job."

"It wouldn't have anything to do with Eve?" Pete asked. "You know, the captain is very curious about that explosion. She was happy that Eve wasn't in that car but definitely curious."

"She'll have to stay that way," Joe said. "I'll talk to her as soon as I'm free to do it."

"If it were anyone but you, Quinn, you'd be in that interrogation room on general principle." His glance shifted back to the medical examiner's van. "And this isn't going to make it any better. Serial killers are a big headache when the captain has to deal with the press."

"Serial killer?"

"Possible," Pete said. "Three hours ago

we got a call from Travel-Rite Charter Service. They found one of their pilots, Zeke Dalkway, in the alley behind the terminal building. Worse condition than Brandel."

"Torture?"

"Four fingers missing and someone spent a long time on him before they killed him."

Because he hadn't been able to give them the information as Brandel had, Joe thought bitterly.

"The captain is going to jump on those cases with both feet," Pete said. "Much too visible and gory to ignore. It's like waving a red flag in front of a bull. Not smart."

Neither smart, nor discreet. Salazar had also jumped in with guns blazing. Nothing subtle about his attack mode. Patient for eight years of searching for Cara, but that patience had vanished overnight. He had gone for the jugular.

After he had spent the night with an angry Natalie Castino. Connection?

Blood and agony.

Two men ruthlessly tortured and dead because Joe had hired a pilot to help Eve and Cara escape. No more patience, no more careful planning to avoid confrontation. A complete change of modus operandi.

Yes, he could see a connection.

■ ■ ■ ■

"I've got it!" Franco said as soon as Salazar picked up the phone. "You wanted it by tonight, I'm hours ahead of you."

"Where are they?"

"Scotland. Brandel delivered them to Ardland Airport outside Edinburgh."

"And where did they go from there?"

"He didn't know. If he'd known, he would have told me."

"I'm sure he would," Salazar said. "But I need more than you've told me. You've given me a city and country. I need an address. I need *them*."

"I have the description of the woman who met them at the hangar. I think it might be Jane MacGuire. She's Duncan's adopted daughter and lives in London. That's pretty close."

"An address."

"I'm on it. I'm taking the next flight to Scotland. I'll find them."

"If I don't find them first. I'll see you in Scotland, Franco."

Silence. "You're going to Scotland? You don't have to bother. I'll take care of it."

"That hasn't been my experience so far. I'm allowing you the opportunity to convince me. Don't disappoint me." He added with a touch of cool menace, "In the meantime, I'll be on the spot and making sure that doesn't happen."

Music, Eve thought drowsily. Faint, far away . . . beautiful . . .

Cara.

Far away?

Her eyes flew open.

Cara wasn't in her bedroll a few yards away!

Easy. If she was playing her violin, then there was nothing seriously wrong.

She drew a deep breath. Her pulse was gradually steadying. Okay, find Cara.

She crawled out of the tent and knelt there, trying to locate the sound.

The stone wall near the top of the ruin.

Cara was sitting there, her violin tucked under her chin.

And the magic coming out of that instrument was breathtaking.

Eve should tell her to come back to the tent. Cara shouldn't be out there by herself. It was all very well for Eve to tell Joe that they had a window of safety, but she wanted to keep that window guarded and close to her. She'd have to go and disturb that magic and bring Cara back to the tent.

Or maybe not.

There was a familiar figure climbing up the stone blocks toward the top of the wall. Moonlight poured over his fair hair and slim, powerful body.

Jock.

She felt a surge of relief and sat back down outside the tent.

Jock would handle it.

Cara was safe with Jock.

There was someone there in the darkness, Cara realized vaguely. Someone was below her, climbing the stones. The presence was friendly, warm, and comforting.

Eve?

Instant guilt.

She probably shouldn't be doing this. She had thought if she got far enough away from the tent area that she wouldn't disturb anyone. Darn it, that must not be true if Eve had to get up and come after her.

She sighed and stopped playing. "I'm sorry. I didn't mean to bother anyone. I'll go back to —"

"As far as I know, you didn't bother anyone. I just thought you might want company." Jock Gavin climbed the last two stones and was standing there. He dropped down on the wall beside her. "Having

239

trouble sleeping?"

She stared at him in shock. She hadn't spoken to him since that night in the courtyard, but it wasn't as if she hadn't thought about him. He always seemed to be somewhere near, working with MacDuff, talking to Jane or Caleb. He was like the music, beautiful, warm, moving in and out, simple, complicated . . . stirring. Even when she wasn't looking at him, she was aware of where he was, what he was doing.

"Cara?"

He was gazing at her inquiringly. What had he asked?

Sleep.

"Usually, I sleep fine." She looked out at the hills. "But like I told you, there's music all around us here. Sometimes I wake up . . ."

"And have to go join the music?"

She nodded. "Crazy, huh?"

"Not at all. I envy you. How does it feel?"

"It . . . fills me. Whenever anything goes wrong, it makes me able to take it and go on."

"Everything?" he asked gently.

Elena. Jenny. Her index finger pressed hard on the violin string. "My sister and my friend were . . . killed. I didn't think anything would help. But the music was still there." She moistened her lips. "And some-how it became . . . part of them."

"That's a wonderful thing."

She nodded. "I was so angry. I wanted to reach out and hurt. I still do. I went to church and prayed, but it didn't help. But the music helps. Eve helps." She looked at him. "You help, Jock."

"Me?" His brows rose in surprise. "I'm happy to be of service, but I don't see how that ever came to be."

"You're beautiful," she said simply. "Like that Tchaikovsky I was just playing."

He threw back his head and laughed. "I wasn't expecting that."

"Why not? You know what you are. Lots of people must have told you." She made a face. "MacDuff even made fun of me be-cause he knew I was sort of dazzled. But it wasn't because you were like one of those princes in Disney movies, it was because of what you are inside. It kind of . . . shines."

"Really?" He was silent. "I'm flattered, but I'm not sure what you mean. And what you call my 'shine' could never come close to what I heard tonight."

"It does for me." But she didn't know how to put it in words. She didn't know why it had tumbled out. Yet it was strange that she didn't regret it or feel embarrassed. Not with him. "There are so many bad people in the world who kill and do terrible things. But you wouldn't do anything like that. Inside, you're clean and bright and warm. Just being around you makes me feel like that, too. Like Eve. Like the music."

He went still. "Cara. I'm not at all like Eve. The only similarity I have to your music is that I truly love it. I'm not what you think I am."

"Yes, you are." Her gaze went back to the violin she was holding. "Seth Caleb said something like that about you, but I don't believe it."

"Believe it," he said quietly. "Look at me, Cara."

Her gaze lifted to his face. It was hard, intense, and unsmiling. "I don't know what you're seeing, but it's not the man you want me to be. I've been every bit as terrible and violent as the people who have hurt you in the past. I try to tell myself that I had excuses, and I was a victim, too." His lips twisted. "But in the end we all have to accept responsibility for our own sins and try to come to terms and maybe change. There's nothing beautiful about me, Cara."

She gazed at him for a moment and shook her head. "You're wrong."

"You're not listening to me."

"Because I'd be afraid of you if you were bad. I had to learn that bad doesn't always look like bad. I did learn that, so now I have to rely on what I feel. I'm not afraid of you, Jock."

"Good. I would never do anything to hurt you. But you're too young to be able to judge the entire picture. I've done terrible things, Cara."

"But you wouldn't do them now."

He sighed. "How can I convince you? Yes, I would do them. It's difficult to stop once you've had that taste on your tongue. But I hope I would only do it to protect. But that's not a certainty, Cara."

But how she was feeling was a certainty. She was trying to frantically adjust that certainty to what he was telling her. "Protect. That's like the police or the FBI or the army or even those knights who lived here in this castle. They all did bad and bloody things, but it was for a good reason. Right?"

"Wrong. You're talking about heroes. I'm no hero. But if I could be anyone's hero, I'd want to be yours. I'd like to be your big brother, your knight, anything you want." He added gently, "I wish I could tell you that I'd qualify. I'd like the idea of you finding someone in this world to trust besides Eve and your music." He smiled. "Try

243

MacDuff. He has some heroic qualities."

She shook her head.

"Then you're on your own. Caleb would be insulted if I tried to tell you that he's a hero." He snapped his fingers. "But you have Joe Quinn. He should be more than sufficient."

"I'm not looking for a hero. Don't be silly. All I said was that I know you're a good man."

"Shining."

She smiled. "Now you're making fun of me."

He smiled back at her. "Because you took me by surprise, and I'm on the defensive." He dropped to the stones at her feet and linked his arms around his knees. "And I need soothing. Play me that Tchaikovsky that reminds you of me."

"I thought you were coming up to tell me to go back to my tent."

"Do you want to stop playing and go back down to reality?"

"No."

"Then play me that Tchaikovsky." He leaned his head back against the stones. "When you're ready, we'll go back."

She tucked her violin beneath her chin, then stopped. "You're not staying with me to protect me?"

"Why would I do that? That would be counter to everything I've been telling you. It would set me up to be a bloody hero." He airily waved his hand. "So let me be selfish and completely self-absorbed. Soothe me, Cara . . ."

She looked down at him and slowly lifted her bow. Not a hero? She still thought he was wrong about that. But she wouldn't argue with him anymore. He'd been so busy telling her all the things he couldn't be to her that he wanted to be. Big brother, knight, surely somewhere in that mix was . . . friend.

She started to play.

"You're awake," Cara whispered as she settled down in her bedroll an hour later. "Is that my fault, Eve? Did you hear me?"

"I heard you," Eve said. "You shouldn't have gone without telling me. It might not be safe. The only reason I let you go alone when we were at the hunting lodge was that I knew it was safe. I can't be sure of that here. I was going to come after you, but I saw Jock climbing the stones. I knew you'd be okay."

"It seemed safe," Cara said. "There wasn't anyone around. It was beautiful. This is a wonderful place. Do you know, sometimes I look out at the hills and mountains and I see something, a rock, a tree . . . and then an hour later it's gone. I know it's probably shadows, but it seems kind of . . . mystical. And when I'm up there on the wall, I can see forever."

"But would you be watching while you were playing? I've seen your face, and you're not aware of anything but the music."

"You're right." Cara stared into the darkness. "I guess I was stupid. I'm sorry to worry you. I won't do it again."

"Not without telling me. But you didn't worry me. I told you that I knew Jock was with you." She paused. "You couldn't sleep? Dreams?"

"No, I just needed to play. Sometimes everything gets all tight inside, and I have to let it out."

"And did you? You played for a long time."

"Yes, I was going to come back sooner, but Jock wanted the Tchaikovsky again." She smiled. "Or maybe he didn't. He knew I wasn't ready and wanted to give me the extra time. He . . . understood."

"I'm sure he did," Eve said quietly. "Jock is nothing if not empathetic. And I could tell he likes you very much."

"I like him, too."

"That's pretty obvious," Eve said dryly.

"You were very definite about what a great guy he is when Caleb was mildly critical."

"Because it's true. Or you wouldn't trust him."

Eve hesitated. "That doesn't mean he was always trustworthy, Cara. When he was just a little older than you, he fell into the hands of Thomas Reilly, a terrible man who was chemically and psychologically experimenting with mind control. Reilly was involved in all kinds of criminal and terrorist projects. Jock became his prime subject. While he was with Reilly, he did . . . things."

"I know that. He told me."

"He did?"

"Oh, not about that mind-control stuff, he just told me that he'd been very bad. He said that I shouldn't think that he was anything good." She was silent a moment. "But he *is* good. That wasn't his fault, and it was a long time ago. He's changed now, hasn't he?"

"Yes, it took a long time and Jane and MacDuff working with him, but he's changed."

"Jane helped him?"

Eve nodded. "She wouldn't stop until he was on his way back."

"That was good." She was silent again. "But he's not all the way back, or he wouldn't think he's so bad."

"Sometimes you can't return to what you were, you just have to go on," Eve said gently. "Jock is doing fine, Cara."

"He's wonderful," she said with sudden fierceness. "No one should have hurt him. No one should have made him think he was —" She broke off. "You're laughing at me."

"Yes, I was just thinking that you may have your first crush. You're getting toward that age."

"No, you have crushes on movie stars and rockers. Heather had them all the time. That's not like this."

"What is it like?"

She frowned. "I don't like the idea of the bad guys always winning. Elena . . . Jenny . . ." She paused, trying to work it out. "Jock. He still doesn't believe he's one of the good guys. He doesn't know about the shine."

"Shine?"

"Never mind. But he's still hurting, Eve."

"He'll work it out. It may take time." She added, "You can't do it for him, Cara."

She was silent.

What more could she say? Eve wondered. Cara had been surrounded by pain and loss since she was very young. Instead of growing callous, she had grown more sensitive to it. She had not been able to save the two people she loved most in the world, and now she couldn't bear to face Jock's being hurt. He had managed to reach out and touch her in a special way. Eve had known that when she had seen them together in the courtyard. "He won't appreciate your interfering in his life."

"I could try," Cara said stubbornly.

"Cara."

"Jane helped him before, but she's too busy now."

"Cara, he's a grown man, you're eleven years old. It should work the other way around. There's something wrong with this picture."

"That doesn't matter." She turned on her side and burrowed under the cover. "Jenny didn't think it was strange to tell me that I should take care of you."

"And one more doesn't make a difference?" Eve asked ruefully. "You're setting yourself up to take care of Jock Gavin?"

"Yes," she said drowsily as she rubbed her cheek on the pillow. "I'm going to take care of Jock . . ."

Edinburgh, Scotland
Salazar was walking toward the exit at the airport when he received a call from Franco.

"I'm in London," Franco said. "I've been scouting around Jane MacGuire's apartment and gallery, and she's definitely not here. She didn't leave any information with her agent about where she was going. Her landlord said he saw her leave in her car about the time that would coincide with an arrival at that airport in Scotland."

"Now you've told me about where she's not. Can you tell me where she is?"

"Not yet. But I think I've verified that she was the woman who picked up Duncan and the kid. I'm doing a complete background check on Jane MacGuire and her known contacts in London and Scotland now. I should have something for you soon."

"See that you do. My patience is gone. It's time we cleared this mess up." He hung up.

It wasn't only his patience that was gone. He hadn't heard from Natalie since he'd texted her the message about Duncan's arrival in Scotland. But he knew that he would soon.

That was fine with him. His adrenaline was pumping, and he felt more alive than he had in years. He was on the hunt. He could smell the blood.

He stepped outside the terminal and headed for the taxi line.

A sleek black Mercedes slid to the curb in front of him and a chauffeur jumped out and opened the passenger door. "Mr. Salazar."

Salazar stepped closer to the car and he was immediately enveloped in the familiar scent of vanilla and Russian perfume wafting from the backseat.

Natalie.

He hadn't expected to see her this soon.

It seemed she was smelling the blood, too.

He stepped forward and got into the car.

2:24 A.M.
Gaelkar Castle

Jane closed the ledger after she'd finished cataloging the afternoon's finds and leaned back in the chair. She should really go to bed. She had deliberately stayed up and worked in the research tent so that she'd be tired enough to sleep. She wasn't sure if it had done any good. She had trouble sleeping anyway, and the news that Eve had told them after she had talked to Joe was too disturbing. Working in this castle surrounded by the hills and winds and silences that whispered of the past had taken Jane away from the thought of the ugliness and violence of monsters who killed.

As they had killed Trevor.

As they might kill Eve and Cara.

"You're working late."

She looked over her shoulder to see Caleb standing in the doorway of the tent. He was dressed in black jeans and white shirt, with the sleeves rolled to the elbow. The night breeze was lifting his dark hair away from his face, which was, as usual, slightly mocking.

Darkness, flames, pure sensuality.

Her hand tightened on the ledger.

More disturbance that she didn't need.

"I'm done now." She forced herself to release the ledger and push it aside. "Or as done as I can be. What are you doing here? You startled me." Her lips twisted. "Which completely belies your claim that we can always sense each other."

He smiled. "I said I can sense you. You might possibly miss a tick occasionally with me. Though I don't see how considering how wary you are." He moved into the tent. "Why the burning of midnight oil? Are you getting close to something?"

"We've hardly scratched the surface. Though MacDuff has discovered a possible opening beneath the dungeons that might lead somewhere. Or not. It's all too vague to even guess." She got to her feet. "A wild-goose chase. If there's a treasure, I don't believe it's here."

"Why?"

"It's not the first time that the family has searched these ruins. The first expedition was in 1927, and there was another in 1969. Surely someone would have found a clue, something . . ."

"MacDuff's not stupid. Why is he here?"

She shrugged. "Because he's MacDuff and he thinks that he has a destiny. Hell, he was almost more involved with tracking down the Cira story than I was all those years ago. That's probably why he wanted me along. He's got this idea I'm part of his destiny, too. It's bullshit."

"No sudden psychic flashes from Cira?"

"I never had psychic flashes. Stop making fun of me, Caleb."

"I wouldn't think of it. But I've been watching you since we've been here. You're feeling something." He suddenly chuckled. "But then so am I. It's the Highlands, after all. In the courtyard, you told Cara that you could feel the music. Did you hear her playing tonight?"

"Yes, I went and stood outside the tent for a minute. I was worried. But then I saw Jock with her, and I knew it was okay."

"Because, in spite of Jock's wicked past, he has an honorable soul?" His tone was mocking. "Like Trevor."

"No, not like Trevor. Trevor didn't have an easy life, but he didn't go through the hell that Jock did." She met his eyes. "And Trevor did have an honorable soul. Even you could see that."

"Crystal clear. I even liked him except when he was getting in my way." He added deliberately, "But I don't have to worry about that now. I thought when Trevor died that he might pose an even greater threat than when he was alive. But I'm working my way through it." His gaze narrowed on her face. "And so are you. Every time we come together, I can see it happening."

She could feel her heart start to pound just looking at his face, that sensual mouth. No, she wouldn't let him do this to her. She forced herself to look away. "I'm going to my tent. I have to get up and start working in a few hours." She turned off the lanterns and started for the door. "You might not understand that, since you're not sweating and digging in the dirt like the rest of us."

"I understand, but I see no reason why I should join you in your misery. That's not why I came on this hunt. My job is to watch and listen and, if necessary, to act." He stepped aside to let her pass. "You'll find me much more valuable in that capacity."

"And is that why you dropped in on me at this hour tonight? Are you watching, listening?"

"All the time. And the hour didn't matter, I function better at night. But that's not why I came by when I saw the light streaming out of the tent. I've been debating all day if I should talk to you. Very unusual for me." He was strolling beside her toward her tent at the end of the row. "As you know, I seldom hesitate about anything. But this may be something sensitive that I should stay out of." He shrugged. "But since when am I sensitive? So I decided to go for it."

"I wouldn't expect anything else," she said dryly. They had reached her tent, and she stopped and turned to face him. Bright moonlight. She could see him almost as well as in the tent, and it was having just as powerful an effect on her.

Don't let him see it.

Get it over with and go into the tent.

"What is it, Caleb?" she asked impatiently. "It's been an upsetting day. I want to put a period to it."

"I know. You're upset about what Eve told you about Salazar closing in and finding out she's in Scotland."

"Dammit, of course I am. Aren't you?"

"Not as much as you. I knew it was going

to happen. It was only a matter of time. I'll just make adjustments."

"I'm not that philosophical. I love Eve."

"Do you think I don't know that? But that love can be complicated, that's why I hesitated."

She stiffened. "It's more dangerous than she told us?"

"Not as far as I know. But she might want to save you worry. You'll have to make up your mind about that."

"I'm going into this tent in ten seconds."

"That's enough time." He smiled down at her. "Eve was upset when Joe told her about Salazar and Natalie Castino. Very upset. Particularly when she told me that Natalie might have killed her own children."

"Of course, she was. Anyone would be upset."

"That's what Eve said, particularly anyone who'd had children, a mother who would never understand how anyone could do that to her own daughters. She was near tears, very passionate about it."

"What's your point, Caleb?"

"That Eve was so upset when she said those words that she reached down . . ." His hand moved to Jane's belly and put his hand on it. "Like this. Just for a second." His hand dropped away from her. "I'm sure that she didn't even realize she'd done it. Pure instinct."

Jane went rigid. "What are you saying?"

"It made me curious. It could have been nothing. Or it could have been something very important."

"It was nothing."

He shook his head. "As I said, I was curious. So when I took her back to the car I stood there and took both her hands while I talked to her. Like this." His hands grasped Jane's, his thumbs on her wrists. "Blood is powerful, it controls so many things. You can feel it pound through your body, can't you?"

"Yes." Her breathing was shallow. She felt his thumbs on her wrists, her pulse leaping more every second. Her skin hot, burning where he was holding her. "Let . . . me . . . go, Caleb."

"Soon. Only a demonstration. I made sure that Eve didn't feel any discomfort at all. But it's not really discomfort, is it, Jane?"

"Let me go."

"Reluctantly." He dropped her wrists. "I just wanted to remind you that I can do a few things with blood that other people can't." He grimaced. "Not entirely true. I wanted to touch you. I used it as an excuse."

She drew a deep, quivering breath. "What

a surprise." She moistened her lips. "And why did you reach out and hold Eve's hands?"

"I believe you've already guessed. The blood flow in all of us is very powerful, it can tell so much." He reached out again and ran his index finger across the vein of her left wrist. "But at certain times, it becomes even stronger and more definitive. It's incredible during that time."

Her pulse was leaping beneath that finger. Her mind was leaping even more frantically. "During what time?"

He lifted her wrist and pressed his lips to the pulse point. "Eve's pregnant, Jane."

"No!" She jerked her wrist away from him. "That's not true."

He sighed. "I was afraid that you'd be shocked."

"You can't be sure. You just touched her."

"I just touched you. Blood responds. In different ways, of course, depending on the demand. I was analyzing with Eve. If I'd had a little more time, I could have determined how far along she is, but that wasn't important. You can ask her."

"Yes, I can ask her," she repeated numbly. She shook her head to clear it. "If I decide I believe you. Which I'm not at all sure I do."

"Entirely your choice. I thought I'd give

you the option. You've taken Eve under your wing, I thought you should know you're responsible for more than you counted on."

"She would have told me."

"Would she?"

No, she might not, Jane thought. She and Eve were so much alike. Jane would not have wanted to lay an additional burden on her, and neither would Eve. "It might not be true. For God's sake, you're not a doctor."

Caleb was silent.

But he had saved Jane's life in that hospital only a few weeks ago when all the doctors had given up on her.

"How certain are you?"

"Very. Some of her blood is being directed to a different place. It's very interesting."

"Interesting?" She rubbed her temple. "Yes, I'd say that it's interesting. However, I'm not in any shape to examine or comment on it. I think . . . I'm scared, Caleb."

"You? Our brave, bold Jane? Nonsense."

"Screw you. This is Eve. It's important. I don't know what she's feeling. She's got to be . . . I don't know."

"Which is why I told you. I could have kept it to myself and let Eve play her own game as she wanted. But that would have cheated you." His lips tightened. "She wouldn't have meant to do it, but in the end, you would have been cheated. I won't allow that, even from Eve."

"It's not your call. You have nothing to do with this."

"But I appear to be very much involved, don't I? It comes from that habit of inserting myself whether I'm wanted or not." He reached up and stroked her cheek. "I find I can't do anything else with you. Now, go to bed and try to sleep. Though I've probably robbed you of that option."

"Almost certainly," she said unsteadily.

"I just want you to remember while you're tossing and turning that there's nothing to be afraid of. I told Eve that I'll be there, and I meant it." He made a face. "That sounds sickeningly noble. Forget I said it. Just remember that I hate to lose. I won't lose this either." He turned and strode away from her.

Leaving Jane staring after him with clenched hands and a chaotic collection of feelings. Trust Caleb to destroy any possibility of serenity this trip might hold.

She wasn't being fair. She wouldn't have wanted him to hold that information back. His presentation had been quintessential Caleb, a combination of sex and charged emotion, but he had given her what he thought she needed to hear. But it didn't alter the fact that he had thrown her a curve that had taken her breath away.

She went into her tent and dropped to her bedroll. She would get ready for bed later, now she had to sit and let that stunning news sink in. There were all kinds of ramifications of Eve's being with child. She wanted to solve them, help her, but how could she when she didn't even know how Eve felt about it?

Or how she felt about it.

This wasn't Eve taking in a lost child as she had with Cara. This was Eve with a baby that might dominate her life as her Bonnie had done.

That had the potential to hurt her as Bonnie's death had done.

No! She felt an instant rejection at the thought.

But she wanted above all for Eve to be happy.

She sighed and laid her head back on the pillow. She obviously would have to work her way through this bewilderment before she talked to Eve . . .

"Are you sure you want to do this, Cira?" Antonio moved to stand behind her. He put his hands gently on her shoulders, and whispered in her ear. "You don't have to say farewell to him here. We can go back to the castle and have the priest give the Gods' blessings and bury him near us."

"No." She looked down at the small casket she'd had the carpenters craft with such care. "I want it to be here by the lake. Marcus liked it here." She could feel the tears sting her eyes. "He told me someday he was going to go into that mist and bring me gifts of gold and jewels fit for a queen. I told him not to be foolish, that I had all the riches I could possibly want already." She looked over her shoulder at Antonio. "It's true, you know. This is a hard, wild land, but we've made it our own. I have everything I ever dreamed about in those days when I was a slave in Herculaneum. I have a husband I love who gave me five strong sons and two daughters who may be even stronger."

"You would think that." He kissed her temple. "You did not feel love for me when you were going through those birth pains."

"It just seemed unfair that a woman has to bear all that pain. But I can see why the Gods didn't trust having children to men. We do it so much better."

"Whatever you say, love."

She could feel his tears on her temple and knew he would not argue with her at this moment. He was feeling her pain at the loss of Marcus as well as his own. Marcus, eight years old, beautiful as the sun, who had been ravaged by the fever and fallen into darkness.

She couldn't stand here, looking down at that small casket any longer. It was time to say farewell and send her son to take his final journey.

She stepped away from Antonio and gazed into the mist. "We're lucky, you know. To have had him this long, to have him the only one of our children that the Gods wanted with them."

"It doesn't seem lucky to me."

"No. At first, I wanted to rage and beat my head on the stones. But then I started to think of Marcus, and I was still angry, but there's a kind of comfort in knowing that he'll be here where he wanted to be. I can ride down here and imagine him running out of the mist and telling me how he'd just been hiding and playing in the caves and had great adventures to tell me." The tears were running down her cheeks. "And now I believe we'd better go take him into that mist so that he can begin those adventures. Then we can go back to the castle and tell our other children that they must stop grieving and start living. Does that not sound like a good plan?"

"A fine plan," Antonio said thickly as he touched her damp cheek. "A magnificent plan, my own Cira . . ."

A dream, Jane thought drowsily as she came out of the heavy mists of sleep. Mists? Strange that she had seized on that word. A dream. Only a dream.

But she had not dreamed about Cira for years. Why now? Why tonight?

She was suddenly wide-awake. Her eyes flicked open and she stared into the darkness.

For God's sake, why was she even surprised that she'd had a Cira dream? She was at the castle Cira had built, MacDuff was constantly making comments about his belief that Jane was a descendant of Cira's. Pure power of suggestion. It didn't mean that Jane was back on that roller coaster of Cira dreams that had plagued her when she was seventeen.

And this dream had involved a child, a dead child, and that could have been triggered by her worry about Eve and her child. Or even her worry about Cara. She mustn't believe it had anything to do with Cira. She would not walk down that path again.

Now go back to sleep, she told herself. She could see the faintest hint of gray in the sky, and she didn't have long before she would have to get up and start to work.

Don't think of Cira and her Antonio.

Don't feel the pain that they'd felt when they'd carried their son into that mist.

It was all a dream.

And the tears that were running down her own cheeks had nothing to do with that little boy who had wanted to bring his mother gold and jewels fit for a queen . . .

CHAPTER 9

"I was right," Manez said when Joe answered. "Natalie Castino got off the plane in Moscow but immediately took a flight to Paris. From there she disappeared off the radar. I don't know where she went."

"Scotland," Joe said grimly. "I'd bet on it."

"Is that where you sent your Eve and Cara? You could have told me."

"You're in cartel heaven down there. You have too many leaks. Hell, we have too many leaks here, too. I actually counted on them when I was waiting for that report on the bomb." He paused. "I'm not going to tell you more than that they're in Scotland for that same reason. Salazar and Franco know that's where Eve and Cara have been taken. I hope that's all they know. They're probably scrambling like crazy to find out exactly where they are right now." He added, "But I don't know. I called a buddy at Scotland Yard to try to track them, but no luck yet. Who do you know over there?"

"I do have a few contacts."

"A few? You know every narcotics cop here and in Europe on a first-name basis. I met several of them when I went down to the cartel seminar you gave last year. All I need is one who is smart and has the informants who can find out what Salazar is doing and if he's getting close to finding out where Eve is."

"But then I'll owe him."

"And I'll owe you."

"That's right, it might be worth it," he said. "And what are you doing, Quinn?"

"Trying to keep myself from going over there and doing a major cleanup before Salazar even gets close to knowing where they are." He paused. "But I'm being watched."

"Salazar's men?"

"Yes, I spotted one of his men and ID'd him as Pauly Lomarto, who works for one of Salazar's local distributors. There's someone else, but I haven't been able to ID him yet. He's much better than Lomarto."

There was a silence. "He might not be working for Salazar."

Joe stiffened. There was something in Manez's tone. "What the hell do you mean?

What do you know?"

"I don't know anything. I only suspect. That's my job, right?" He paused. "But you should know that I've heard rumors that your Justice Department has been making inquiries in the past few days of several of our government departments about the kidnapping of the two Castino children."

"What?"

"In particular, the older child, Jenny. Inquiries about the possibility of a body being found on American soil and if we knew anything about it. Nothing on an official level yet, but it's heading in that direction. I found it curious that no inquiry was addressed to my attention. You were talking about leaks. There might possibly be a leak in the Sheriff's Department, it was suspected that the skeleton in that grave in California was really Jenny Castino."

"And you weren't going to tell me?"

"It's only rumors so far."

"And you thought I wouldn't be interested? You didn't, by any chance, leak it yourself?"

"That would have been self-destructive. Why would I do that when I might have used the information myself to manipulate you? But I don't want you putting down a state department investigator by mistake. It might be awkward for you. If the information was leaked about the skeleton, then it was probably also leaked regarding both yours and Eve Duncan's involvement in the removal of Cara Castino from Child Services."

He was right, Joe thought. "And they probably know by now about the explosion that was supposed to have killed Eve and Cara and my sending them out of the country. None of which was legal." He muttered a curse. "They're probably gathering evidence against me and just waiting to step in."

"Do you have any idea who leaked the information?"

"It could be Sheriff Nalchek, but I wouldn't think so. Maybe someone in his department." His hand tightened on the phone. "It doesn't matter, I have to concentrate on damage control. Who did your 'rumors' say was heading the investigation?"

"Agent Jason Toller. What are you going to do?"

"Move on Toller before he can move on me." He hung up. He drew a deep breath and sat there thinking. Direct attack or try to stave off Toller until he could better control the situation?

God, he wanted to go in now.

That was emotion and impatience. He knew what the right way was to handle it. He reached for his phone and called the FBI Headquarters at Quantico.

Thirty minutes later, he hung up and sat back in his chair to wait.

It was close to three hours later that there was a knock on the front door.

"Detective Quinn?" The man at the door was lanky, tall, with short, graying hair and a Southern drawl. "Agent Jason Toller. I understand that you wish to talk to me." His voice never lost the pleasant intonation as he continued, "But I should tell you that I do resent your pulling strings to bring me here. You could have called me and invited me."

"That would have taken time, and I don't know how much time I have at any given point." He gestured for Toller to come in. "I need to know where I stand with you. Are you going to cause me trouble, Agent Toller?"

"It's possible." He looked around the house. "Nice. Very nice." He looked at Eve's work area. "Is that where Ms. Duncan works? I've heard great things about her. I'm sure she's a fine woman. I was very upset when I thought you'd blown her up."

"Is that supposed to be a shock tactic?"

"No, I honestly thought you might have murdered her. I'm a suspicious man, and I usually believe the worst until I find out otherwise." He smiled. "It was at the beginning of my investigation and the facts were a little confused. I was very happy to discover that you probably weren't a murderer. Would you care to tell me where Eve Duncan and Cara Castino are now?"

"No."

His brows rose. "May I ask why not?"

"What would you do with Cara?"

"Child Services, and then we'd have to start negotiations with the Mexican government. Considering the identity of her father, the situation is very delicate."

"And she would probably be murdered before all the red tape had been cut."

Toller nodded. "It might happen. But it's not my job to make judgments. I'm only a lowly agent who is trying to do what's right and still keep my pension."

"Bullshit."

Toller shrugged. "I can understand why you might be upset. But you might be a little more tolerant. I could have caused you a good deal of trouble. In fact, I was planning on it until I did my research on you." He smiled faintly. "You're respected by your captain and the other detectives. You do favors, but you don't demand a return. It was the same when I investigated your years with the FBI and the SEALs. In fact, you were the golden boy at Quantico until you resigned and came to live here in Atlanta. You kept strong ties with them, even though you were dedicated to your job here." He grimaced. "But you did ask a return favor from the Director of the FBI today. I'm flattered. It must mean a lot to you."

"I can't have you getting in my way."

"But I will get in your way. It's inevitable." He tilted his head. "I believe you're an honest man and trying to do the right thing, but unfortunately the right thing isn't always the way the world works. So shall I tell you how this will play out?"

"I can hardly wait."

"Since you're clearly the key to our finding Cara Delaney, we'll continue surveillance. The moment we get a clue as to where to find her, we'll act immediately. At that point, we'll proceed as I've outlined. And no strings you can pull will stop us from doing it. Understand?"

"Absolutely."

"On the other hand, there will be no incarceration of the popular and influential Joe Quinn unless you do something that will cause me problems. At that point, I won't give a damn if you rot in jail." He turned to leave. "I'm glad that we had this chat. I was going to initiate a meeting anyway. I hope you're equally satisfied?"

"Not quite. I expected you to be more of a hard-ass toward me. Why weren't you?"

"You don't understand. My job is to investigate and, if possible, to smooth troubled waters. It's my particular specialty. This situation has the potential to cause the U.S. government headaches for the next ten years even if Cara Delaney isn't killed. She'll be an international incident that will attract all kinds of fringe groups until her case is settled."

"And I'm part of those troubled waters."

"You could be. You certainly *will* be if you do anything that will make me look inefficient to my superiors. We have to maintain control of the situation. Don't try to avoid surveillance, Detective."

Joe didn't answer.

Toller shrugged. "Have a nice day."

The next moment, he was gone.

Son of a bitch.

Joe's fists knotted at his sides. Toller had drawn the lines clearly, and it was going to be difficult as hell to work around him. He couldn't afford to be tossed in jail, and there was no way he could risk leading Toller to Eve and Cara. Now he had to deal not only with Salazar's men but Toller.

He called Manez. "I may be stuck here for a while, and it's going to drive me crazy. When I do get out of here, I'm going to have to move fast. I need you to get me that help to locate Salazar."

"You sound angry. A problem with Agent Toller?"

"He's going to try to block me. He's good, and he may be looking for a reason to throw me into jail. I'll have to be careful with him and not take him down. Which means I can't risk taking a chance on going to Eve yet unless I know Salazar's already found out where they are. Then I'll do what's necessary no matter what the consequences. But there won't be a risk to her if I go over and take care of business with Salazar. You can help me do that."

"There's a risk of an officer of the law breaking that law," Manez said quietly. "You're a hunter, and I recognize that you want to defend what is yours by going after the prey. But I can't condone your being an executioner, Quinn."

"Then don't condone it, but will you tap your man in Scotland to get me information? I need to know where Salazar is and what he's doing."

Manez was silent. "I'll ask Burbank at the Yard. He might be able to help." He hung up.

Joe knew he had pushed him too far. Manez was torn between an obsession to take the cartels down at any cost and his ingrained respect for the law. Hell, Joe had the same respect, but he was also driven by the primitive desire to protect the good against the scum of the world.

And that good in his eyes was embodied by Eve.

So try to hold back if he could, but get ready.

Salazar. Franco. Natalie Castino.

They were probably all in a position to strike.

Well, so would Joe be as soon as Manez gave him the information he needed.

Gaelkar Castle

"You're very quiet, Jane." Eve looked up from the dirt she was shifting and studied her as Jane gave her a bottle of water from the tray she was distributing. "And you have circles under your eyes. Did you have a bad night?"

"Not good," Jane said. "I was up late cataloging the day's finds, then Caleb dropped by, and he's never soothing." She opened the bottle and took a drink of water. "But we've come to expect that, haven't we?"

"Yes." Eve's eyes narrowed on Jane's face. "And that's all? Tell me that you didn't hear Cara playing."

"I heard her. She didn't keep me awake."

"It seems the whole camp heard her. The only one I haven't heard from yet is MacDuff." She made a face. "I promise you it won't happen again. I've had a talk with her. She'll be mortified that she might have disturbed you."

"Then don't tell her." Jane looked away from her. "It was beautiful, I was only worried that she was out there alone. But then I saw Jock, and I knew it was all right."

"That was my thought, too." Her gaze went to Cara, who was working on the other side of the ruins near Jock and MacDuff. "Though I'm not certain now. I think Cara has adopted Jock."

"What?"

"She thinks that he needs taking care of." Her eyes were twinkling. "And you're too busy."

Jane looked at Cara. "She's really extraordinary, isn't she? I don't know how Jock will take that."

"I don't either, but I don't intend to interfere. I'll leave it up to the two of them. It may be good for both of them." She took another drink of water. "This tastes good. It's cool here at night, but it heats up during the day. For the last half hour, I've been thinking wistfully about that lake Caleb took me to yesterday. All that cool mist."

Jane went still. "Lake? You didn't mention a lake when you came back yesterday."

"You can appreciate it wasn't my top priority," Eve said dryly. "Joe blew everything out of my mind when he told me about Natalie Castino and that Salazar might soon be breathing down our necks."

"It did the same thing to me," Jane said. "You could have told me you went to Timbuktu, and I would have accepted it." Her gaze slid away from Eve to the wall overlooking the hills. "Where is this lake?"

"Maybe ten miles north. Caleb showed it to me because he said the castle was vulnerable from that direction." She took another drink. "Beautiful place. But weird, lots of mist. Caleb and I agreed it looked like either the beginning or the end of the world."

"Interesting." She looked back at Eve. "I'd like to see it."

"Maybe after we finish for the day?"

"I'd like to go now."

Eve paused in raising the bottle to her lips to look at her. "Why?"

"You said it was the one place that was vulnerable, didn't you?" She smiled. "I should see it. I'll go tell MacDuff to keep an eye on Cara while we're gone. Why don't you go wash your hands and face and meet me at the Land Rover in five minutes?"

Eve frowned as she gazed after Jane as she crossed the courtyard. That smile had been forced, and Jane was definitely not herself. It was just as well she'd have the opportunity to get Jane alone to probe a bit.

But it appeared they were not to be alone. Caleb was sitting in the driver's seat of the Land Rover when she and Jane reached the road where it was parked.

"Good afternoon, ladies." He smiled at Jane. "You should have gone with us yesterday. It would have saved us this trip."

"I was busy." Jane shook her head. "And we don't need you, Caleb. Eve and I will do just fine on our own."

"I'm sure you would." He met Jane's eyes. "But I assure you I won't get in the way. Once we're there, I'll just sit in the car and keep an eye on you. I got a call from MacDuff the minute you left after telling him you were taking Eve back to the lake. He told me that since I was a total handicap on the dig, I might just as well make myself useful by acting as guard dog to make sure the two of you were safe." He shrugged. "I told him that it was a pleasant place, and I'd be accommodating this time. Get in."

Jane hesitated.

"Get in," he said softly. "I won't interfere."

"That would be a first." She got in the backseat. "Get in, Eve. I guess we'll be accommodating, too. I should have known that MacDuff would bring in the Marines."

"I appreciate the compliment," Caleb said as he started the car. "But I don't have the same philosophy. I'm of a more solitary nature."

"I hadn't noticed that," Eve murmured. "Who knows? You may be changing, Caleb. There seems to be something in the air."

"Here we are," Caleb said as he brought the Land Rover to a stop. "I'll stay here as I promised and commune with nature."

"There's a lot of nature to commune with," Eve said as she got out of the car and started down the steep slope toward the lake. "What do you think, Jane? The beginning or the end?" She looked over her shoulder when Jane didn't answer. "Jane?"

The same.

The mist.

The hills running down into the deep blue of the lake. The north shore that was completely obscured by the mist.

The mist.

I'll see him running out of the mist and telling me he'd only been playing in the caves . . .

"Jane!"

Eve. She sounded concerned, Jane thought vaguely. She had to answer her. She shook her head to clear it. She couldn't remember what Eve had asked her. Say something. Anything. "It's as beautiful as you said." She followed Eve down to the shore. "Do you know, when we were in the study with MacDuff looking at all those schematics, I didn't even pay any attention to any landscape features. Did MacDuff mention it? Was this lake on the map?"

"I don't remember." Eve's gaze was focused on Jane's face. "What does it matter?"

"It doesn't. I just wonder why I wasn't aware that it was here. I thought maybe MacDuff had mentioned it, and I'd just forgotten."

"You wouldn't have forgotten it."

"I might have. I might have been tired from the drive, and it just escaped me."

"It's no big thing. Why are you behaving like this?"

It was a big thing to Jane, but she was acting weird, and Eve had noticed.

Straighten out.

She smiled and looked back at the lake. "The beginning or the end? I guess it depends on what happens to you here. Or maybe it might not even happen here but it becomes a part of —" She stopped and turned toward the car. "I've seen enough. We can go back now."

"No, we can't," Eve said quietly. "Not yet. Something is wrong, and it has something to do with this place. What is it?"

"Why should it have anything to do with this lake? I've never seen it before."

"This conversation is so familiar. You said words like that a long time ago in the very same way," Eve said gently. "Do you think I'd ever forget? You were seventeen, and you were trying to convince yourself that those dreams of Cira were just made up of scraps you'd read on the Internet or stumbled on somewhere. But they didn't turn out that way, did they?"

"A temporary mental aberration."

"That came back, Jane?"

Eve wasn't going to give up. Jane still tried to distract her. "I just wanted to see the lake."

"Why?"

She gave a deep sigh, then surrendered. "Because I saw it last night, and Cira was there on that north bank."

She went still. "Another Cira dream?"

"Yes, I haven't had one for years. I didn't want this one."

"But it happened."

"Yes, I tried to tell myself it was MacDuff's pressuring me about Cira and the treasure. We were at the castle she built all those centuries ago. I told myself it was the power of all that suggestion going on in my head." Her eyes were stinging as she turned back to Eve. "I don't want dreams or knowing about someone else's life or how they're hurting. I've been hurting enough myself lately. I want to live in the real world and deal with real problems. It's the only way I can survive."

"You do yourself an injustice, you're very strong. You can take anything, do anything." Eve took a step closer. "I've never known why Cira was woven into your life during those years, but I know the experience didn't hurt you. I know that you only grew stronger and more compassionate. I was glad when the dreams stopped, but if they're back, then you'll accept them and make the best of it." She smiled. "And, if you like, share them with someone you love. I'll always be here for you."

"I know you will." She was filled with so much love that the words were unsteady. "You always have been." She took a step forward and slipped her arms around Eve and held her close. "I should be saying that to you. I don't say it enough."

"Because it's not necessary, we both know it's there." She hugged her once more, then pushed her away. "And we're both getting all weepy and emotional." She dropped down on the ground. "Sit down and talk it out. Like you did when you were a kid." She grinned. "Though you never acted like you were a kid." She waved at the mist-shrouded lake. "And this isn't the front porch, and that isn't our lake, but it will do. Right?"

"Right." Jane sat down beside her and linked her arms around her knees. "And you thought the lake was a little weird, but I don't believe it is. I think the mist is friendly. I think it must be full of love."

"Why?"

She hesitated. "Because my dream was about Cira and her lover, Antonio, and her son, Marcus." She stared out at the mist. "Cira loved her son so much, and he loved her. He must have been a very special little boy."

"Yes. But then Cira was special, too. She created a world to suit herself."

They were both silent, gazing at the mist for a long time.

Then Jane said quietly, "There's another reason why I was trying to tell myself that the dream was all power of suggestion."

"Why is that?"

"The dream was all about a child."

"It reminded you of Cara?"

Jane turned and looked her in the eye. "Not Cara."

Eve's eyes widened. She opened her lips to speak, then closed them again. She drew a deep breath. "Oh, shit."

Jane had to chuckle. "I suppose that's an affirmation?"

"How did you know? Joe?"

"Not Joe. Do you think he'd ever tell me anything as important as that if you didn't want him to?" She nodded at Caleb sitting in the car. "You let it slip to him."

"I did not," she said indignantly. "How?"

"He was curious. He held your hands. He said some of the blood was being directed to another place. He found it interesting."

"Nosy bastard." Then she had to laugh. "I didn't have a chance of keeping it to myself, did I?"

"If Caleb hadn't been around, you might

have. When he told me, I was stunned."

"So was I." She was silent. "You're not angry or hurt I didn't tell you?"

"No, I considered the source. The source is remarkably like me. You didn't want to burden me any more than you had to. I don't like it, but I understand. How far along are you?"

"Not even a month. I wouldn't have even known about it except Joe authorized a complete physical and tests when I was in the hospital with that concussion."

"And how do you feel about it?"

"I don't know. Scared, happy, bewildered . . . euphoric. Every time I think about having this child, it changes."

"But do you want it?" she persisted.

"Oh, yes," Eve said softly. "That's not even a question." Her smile was luminous. "I want to have this baby. I'm already beginning to feel . . . a presence. It's wonderful." The smile faded. "What's not wonderful is wondering if I'll be able to keep it safe. Or if I'll be so worried about trying to make sure nothing happens that I'll smother the poor kid."

"You'll muddle through," Jane said. "You did pretty well with me."

"You raised yourself, I was just there for support." She shook her head. "And I lost my Bonnie."

"Through no fault of your own." She reached over and touched Eve's hand. "And I'll be around to remind you of that the minute the baby makes an appearance." She gave a relieved sigh. "Though I'm glad we have a little time to prepare ourselves. I need it."

"I do, too. Another child after all these years . . ." She looked out at the lake. "Do you think this is a mistake, Jane?"

"Would you pay any attention to me if I said yes?"

"No. Well, I'd pay attention to you, but I'd seriously doubt your judgment." She looked back at her. "I know all the drawbacks. I'm not sixteen as I was when I had Bonnie. I'll have to be careful during the pregnancy. I have a career, and I'm set in my ways. You say I was a good mother, but I only remember my mistakes."

"What mistakes? I only remember the love," she said. "And, if there were mistakes, this isn't one of them. I think sometimes you were a little worried that I'd feel cheated because you loved Bonnie so much." She shook her head. "I understood. She was gone a long time before I came to you, but I could tell what she meant to you. She was the passion and tragedy of your life. I was your best friend. We were good together. But now you have a chance to bring someone else into your world." She added unsteadily, "It's going to be phenomenal, Eve. It will open doors. It will be different from me or Bonnie, but it will be like a new sunrise for you. And I'll fight like hell for that sunrise to come to you."

Eve was silent because she couldn't speak. "I can tell you're an artist. You're painting very beautiful pictures." She cleared her throat. "But that's down the road, and we just need to get through the next months so that it will be only clear sailing."

"I'll second that." Jane grinned and got to her feet. She reached down and offered a hand to Eve and pulled her to her feet. "And that means taking care of yourself while you're on the run from Salazar. Maybe you shouldn't be working on your knees in that courtyard."

"Don't start that," Eve said. "You sound like Joe. Exercise is good for me. I'm strong as a horse. Do *not* start pampering me."

"I'll try to remember," Jane said. "I'll do my best to forget you're pregnant and let you work yourself to the bone for the glory of MacDuff and Cira." She started up the hill. "I'll even refrain from telling MacDuff and Jock. I don't believe Caleb will discuss

287

it. He just thinks it's interesting."

"Good," Eve said. "All I'd need is all those protective males giving me the same treatment as Joe is doing."

"Yeah, you're too tough for that."

"I can but try."

"And come off very effectively in that area." She smiled. "Don't be too tough, Eve. I owe you too much. Let me pay back a little."

"I know. I know. You've already expressed your feelings on that score. I knew I didn't have a chance of convincing you." She waved at Caleb as he got out of the car to greet them. "Particularly not now. You invoked the mantra. Family, Jane. Family."

Gaelkar Castle

Jane waited until after they'd eaten supper and all started to scatter before she followed MacDuff to his tent.

She poked her head through the entrance. "May I come in?"

MacDuff's brows rose, and he gestured for her to enter. "By all means, step into my parlor. I've been trying to convince you for years that's where you belonged."

"You are not a spider, and I detest flies. I have no ambitions to be one. You could have at least personified me as a butterfly. They have artistic value." She stepped inside. "I wanted to ask you a question."

"In the privacy of my tent. I can hardly wait. Personal, I hope?"

"Only as far as it's the present love of your life." She gazed around the tent to the portable desk piled high with scrolled plans and loose papers. "Is there anything in that mess that has anything to do with the terrain of the countryside around the castle?"

His eyes narrowed. "Why do you ask?"

"Is there?"

"One. I didn't regard it as important since we're concentrating on the castle."

"May I see it?"

"Why? You and Eve left the dig this afternoon to go traipsing back to the lake where Caleb took her yesterday. She was exploring the area to gauge the threat it posed to her and Cara. Were you doing the same thing?"

"I want to keep Eve safe."

"That's noncommittal. I think there's more to it." He smiled. "But I'll accept it for the time being." He turned and went to the desk and searched through the scrolled maps and plans until he found one with a thin blue border. He spread it on the desk and adjusted the lantern so that the light fell upon it. "It's just a basic map of the area."

That's exactly what it was. But Jane would take what she could get. Her gaze went quickly over the trails and roads and hills and then up to the huge lake. It was strange gazing at those simple lines on paper when she remembered the dark blue water, the pale mist, the trees, the hills.

"You wanted to look at the lake again," MacDuff murmured, gazing at her face. "It appears to have a fascination for you."

"It is fascinating. I'd like to paint it sometime." She didn't take her gaze off the map. "I suppose you've seen it?"

"Of course. This isn't the first time I've been to this castle. Everything about the place is absolutely riveting for me. I know every legend, every myth. It's the place my clan originated, where we all began. I'm very passionate about it."

Is it the beginning of the world, or the end?

"You hide it very well."

"I'm a Scot." He smiled. "And I've learned not to let my emotions rule me. I'm the Laird, and many people look to me. It's a complicated world I live in, and I can't let my guard down." He paused. "But I've let my guard down with you, Jane. Because you're one of mine. You belong to Cira and to me."

"Bullshit."

He chuckled. "I knew that would cause you to bristle." He looked down at the map. "Is there anything you'd like to ask me? I may know a few things more than this map will tell you."

"Because, after all, you are the Laird," she said dryly.

"Exactly."

She pointed to a line that appeared to wind from the castle to the lake. "What is this?"

"It's a dirt trail that leads down to the lake. I'm told as far as anyone knows that it's been there since the castle was built. The road was only built by my orders about ten years ago. I thought it was time it was accessible."

"Why?" She tilted her head. "Don't tell me you're thinking of rebuilding this castle?"

"Anything is possible if I find that chest of coins." He grinned. "After all, it's mine."

"So would be the entire world if you had your way." She looked back at the map. "What about the lake itself. It's very . . . unusual."

"The mists?" He nodded. "For decades, we've had forestry and environmental experts from the universities wanting to come in and make their tests. They want to find out why those mists never disperse. Sunlight or storm, the mists remain. They have all their theories, but it's frustrating them to hell that they can't come here and get confirmation."

"And you won't let them do it?"

"I don't want to know." He gazed at her. "Do you?"

"It's none of my concern."

"Do you?" he repeated softly.

He would come running out of the mist and tell me he'd been playing in the caves.

"No." She asked before he could reply, "In the past, haven't any of your family gone on that north shore and explored beyond those mists?"

"No, it would take a full-scale expedition, those mists are very thick. You can't see more than a few feet in front of you. My grandfather tried and fell and broke his leg when the bank gave way. He almost drowned before he got back to the south bank."

"And no one else?"

"Ah, you are curious." His finger traced the north curve of the lake. "As a matter of fact, one of those very pushy professors from Oxford sent a few of his prize students up here to get answers in hopes that I wouldn't prosecute them. One of my caretakers, Ned Colin, saw the cars on the road and went after them."

She had seen his "caretakers," who were old Marine buddies, and she felt an instant of sympathy for those college kids. "He wasn't afraid of getting lost in the mists?"

"Colin only went a few feet and shouted for them to come out. He said they seemed relieved to come stumbling toward him. He confiscated all equipment, cameras, and notes, and sent the kids on their way."

She went still. "They took photos?"

"That caught your interest. It caught mine as well. But you'd be disappointed. They're only a white blur. The sketches weren't much better."

"Sketches?"

"I knew that would pique your interest. Yes, one of the students had a sketchbook. But, as I said, nothing much more revealing than the photos."

"And the notes?"

"They didn't have much time to take notes. Only maybe four, five hours. Nothing interesting."

She looked back down at the map. "Any mention of the topography? Rocks, caves, mud, sinkholes, cleared areas?"

"They couldn't see, they didn't have time to set up their lighting equipment." He added, "Of course, I'm not an expert at examining that kind of data. Would you like to look at them yourself?"

"Yes."

"That was instant and vehement. You clearly don't trust me to have noticed whatever you're looking for. Would you care to tell me what that is?"

"I don't know." She would not lie to him, but to tell the entire truth would immediately set off that very active mind. "I have no logical reason."

"And it has nothing to do with why I brought you here?"

"That's definitely not why I'm interested in those reports."

And now I believe it's time to take our son into that mist so that he can begin his great adventures.

A search for a dream, some small proof that it didn't really exist.

She met his eyes. "I don't want to discuss it, MacDuff. Do I have to do it to have you get those reports for me?"

"Oh, the temptation." He shook his head. "No, I'll have my assistant, MacTavish, dig out the originals and clarify them as much as possible and e-mail them to me. They'll be in your hands by tomorrow sometime."

"Thank you." She turned to leave.

"But you do know I'll be making guesses, and my imagination will run free?"

"I wouldn't expect anything else of you."

"By the way, what do you think of our progress here at the castle?"

She had half expected that question. "I don't see any progress, but something could happen at any moment. What do you think?"

"I think that it's worthwhile exploring the dungeon for a day or two more, then we'll reassess." He smiled at her. "I wouldn't want to waste the time you've so generously given me."

"It's good to be appreciated." She left the tent and drew a deep breath of the cool night air. She had found what information she could but she'd probably given up as much as she'd received. MacDuff was ultrasharp, and he'd been processing and analyzing every bit of what she'd said. He would weave scenarios, then come back to her and wouldn't stop until she told him what he wanted to know. And what he wanted to know was if the dreams of Cira had come back as he thought they might. It would only confirm to him how right he'd been to bulldoze her into coming on this hunt.

Okay, back off from that burst of annoyance. He'd also taken Eve and Cara under his wing at a danger to himself. You had to accept the bad with the good with MacDuff, and most of the time that good came out on top. He had his agendas, but he was loyal and you could count —"

"What were you doing in MacDuff's tent?"

She turned to see Caleb standing a few yards away. He was standing at ease, but there was a faint tension to the muscles of his shoulders and stomach. She could feel the edge of heat and darkness surrounding him. She instinctively stiffened defensively. "That's really none of your business."

He was silent, then the tension was suddenly gone, and he was smiling. "Of course it's not. Forget I asked. Or tell me, and then you'll know I'm not storing it away and letting it fester. Being the sexual creature I am, I immediately jumped to a conclusion that's probably totally wrong."

"Yes, but you shouldn't be lurking around like some peeping Tom anyway."

"I wasn't lurking, not that I'm not capable of lurking if it suits me. But I wanted to speak to you before you went to bed. It didn't make me happy to see you duck into MacDuff's tent. It was fortunate that you didn't spend more time than you did with him. That would have made me feel dangerously unhappy."

"Is that supposed to mean something to me? It's still none of your business."

"That's where we have a problem. It depends on the viewpoint. You see I have a small problem with MacDuff. Ordinarily, I think you have too many frictions to decide to go to bed with him, but he's one of the good guys. Not as good as Trevor was, but still in the same ballpark. And you have a tendency to lean that way."

She turned and walked toward her tent.

He caught up and strolled with her. "But all that indignation can't be directed toward my interference. Your time with MacDuff must have been squeaky clean."

"I believe this conversation is over."

"Almost." He stopped outside her tent. "I wanted to tell you that I was glad that you told Eve you knew about the child and that it came out all right."

"I didn't have any doubt. You see complications where they don't exist. We love each other. That makes all the difference."

"Does it? I'll have to bow to your superior knowledge." He paused. "I like to see the two of you together. It . . . warms me."

She gazed at him. The words had been almost . . . she didn't know what. But then she often didn't understand Caleb. "She told me that you said you would protect her.

Now, that warms *me,* Caleb."

He smiled. "You see, I can please you occasionally. I just never know when or where. But give me a chance, and I'll show you how."

That instant of rapport was gone, and she turned to go into her tent. "Good night, Caleb."

She heard him laugh as she entered the tent and turned on her lantern.

As usual, those few minutes had put Jane on edge and made her vibrantly, sensually, aware of Caleb. And this time she had thought she had sensed a vulnerability beneath the mockery.

Vulnerability? Not Caleb. There was no one tougher or more impervious to the forces around him. She had to keep thinking that way. If she softened, he would swoop down, and she might be lost.

Forget about Caleb. Think about Cira and that dream that had come out of the night after all these years. She had thought she had beaten it down and dismissed the idea that those dreams had any basis in reality. She had reluctantly accepted the idea of racial or ancestral memory being a vague possibility. But she had been grateful when those dreams had ceased, and she didn't want them to return. She wanted to deny them in any way she could.

But that lake of mists had definitely been the lake of her dream. The only way to disprove that it had nothing to do with Cira was to find out that the content was totally false.

No casket with the carnelian and copper inlays. No sign or clearing of a grave site where Marcus had been taken to start his final adventure. The small boy's body must have disintegrated to nothing in the centuries since he had died, but there might be pieces of that casket still intact.

Good Lord, she was playing a long shot. One she fervently wished to lose.

Because if the dreams were back, it might mean Cira was trying to tell her something.

And, with Eve pregnant and Cara in constant danger, the knowledge that the dream had been about a dead child gave Jane a feeling of chilling foreboding.

CHAPTER 10

Edinburgh, Scotland

"Aren't you done yet?" Salazar was standing in the doorway of the hotel bedroom, watching Natalie rub her vanilla body oil over her naked body. It was a lazy, sensual movement that was an act of pure seduction. "You've been in here an hour. Manuela never takes this long."

"Perhaps that's why you prefer me to your wife." She turned to face him and lifted her naked breasts and offered them to him. "I take time in everything I do. Haven't you noticed?"

"Yes," he said hoarsely, his gaze on her breasts. "Sometimes you drive me crazy. Why don't we just go back to bed and start over?"

"Because I have things to do." She pulled on her red-silk robe and came toward him. "And so do you. Before we leave Scotland, we're going to have this problem resolved."

She gave him a kiss as she passed him and went into the bedroom–sitting room. "And then we have to make other decisions." She sat down on the couch and reached for her phone. "But first, I have to call my father and prepare him."

"You think that Castino may call your father and check up to make sure that you flew to see him?"

"Perhaps, but that's not what I meant. I'll let you listen if you like." She started to dial. "Call room service and order breakfast, will you?"

Salazar shrugged and picked up the room phone. "That's not what I have an appetite for right now."

"Perhaps I'll concoct something wonderfully exotic for you after —" Her father had picked up, and she spoke into the phone, "Natalie, Daddy, I had to speak to you. Are you too busy to talk? I don't want to bother —"

"Hush," her father said impatiently. "When am I ever too busy to speak to you? What do you need?"

"Nothing. I just wanted to hear your voice, speak to you. I've been feeling so alone . . . without my girls." She cleared her voice. "It will be Cara's birthday in a few days. I don't even know if she's alive,

Daddy. Sometimes it gets to be too much."

"You should come home to me."

"It's my duty to stand by my husband. We've been through so much together. Jenny, Cara . . . You know he's been very good to me."

"And so he should be. You're the mother of his children and he should have kept them safe for you. I remember when you brought them to Moscow the summer before they were taken." His voice was hoarse. "It was like having you again when you were little and happy . . ."

"It was a great summer," she said unsteadily. "I never dreamed this could happen to my little girls. If I hadn't had you to talk to, I don't know what I'd have done." She paused. "I have to tell you something. I know you probably won't like it, but I'm desperate."

"Natalie."

"Just listen. I've had a telephone call from a man who says he has my daughters. He's promised to return them to me if I give him money."

Her father was cursing. "It's a scam, Natalie. After all this time? How much money?"

"Four million dollars."

"What does your husband say?"

"He says he won't pay it. He says it's a

scam, like you. But what if it isn't? What if I could have my girls back?" Her voice lowered. "Or what if they kill them because I don't pay?"

"Then I'll search them down and tear them apart."

"Too late . . ."

"I'll give you the money, Natalie."

"I know you will." Her voice was shaking. "But I can't ask that of you yet. I have to be sure they have my girls. I just wanted to tell you what was happening. I'll call you later after I hear from them again. Good-bye, Daddy." She hung up.

"Quite a performance," Salazar said. "Daddy's little girl. How long have you been playing him like this?"

"Don't be disrespectful of my father."

"How long?"

"We've understood each other from the time I was a teenager."

"And he's never caught you in a lie?"

"He never looked too deep. Everyone else lied to him. He needed to believe I wouldn't do it." She smiled. "So I made him happy, and he gave me what I wanted."

"What was all that business about ransom?"

"Preparation. What happens if you don't pay ransom? The kids end up dead. And

I'm not under suspicion."

"It would be tricky."

"I don't know if I'll do it. I just want to be prepared. I think I could work it out." She got up and wandered over to the table and took a piece of toast from the tray. "I've gotten this far, haven't I?"

"You've had me."

She nodded. "We've had each other." She sat down and lifted the dome off her plate. "Though you've been close to failing me, Salazar." She started to eat her eggs. "I did everything to make it easy for you, and you couldn't even follow through for me."

"It wasn't my fault. Walsh screwed up."

"We won't argue." She gave him a brilliant smile. "Just so it ends well."

He watched her eat with voracious yet delicate hunger. "You set it up to end well with your father."

"It's more complicated than that. He's very important in anything I plan. He has power, he has money. I just had to make sure he would believe me if the time came."

"Everyone believes you." He shook his head as he sat down opposite her. "They have from the beginning. No one thinks that a mother would have anything to do with the death of her children."

"Kidnapping. I have to keep correcting you."

"When you came to me and asked if I wanted to do something that would hurt Castino, you never mentioned kidnapping. You just said get rid of them. No specification."

"I assumed you'd know what I meant. But I left it up to you." She smiled serenely. "After all, I'm only a woman."

It wasn't the first time that he'd heard that from her. But she'd known that if she turned him loose on her children exactly what the result would be. "Manuela would never have thought about doing anything like that."

"Manuela was not married to Juan Castino. It was a completely different situation." She looked up at Salazar. "And she was a wimp who would never argue with you or hunt for a way to better herself."

"Is that what you did? Better yourself?"

"I defended myself." Her voice was suddenly fierce. "I'd had two girls, and Juan wanted sons. He blamed me. He'd started taking mistresses. It was only a matter of time before one of those whores gave him his damn boy. His current whore, Gracia, already had a son by another man."

"So?"

"He would have discarded me. He would have put that slut, Gracia, in my place. That would never happen. I liked being Castino's wife and having everyone bow down before me." She wrinkled her nose. "Even your dear Manuela. She came to my parties and applauded when my Jenny played the piano." Her lips tightened. "She told me about her boys. She even showed me photos. She was a little too pleased with herself." She poured coffee into her cup. "And that's when I decided we had to meet, Salazar."

"Why, Natalie? You've only told me you wanted to get rid of them, that they were in your way. But weren't you afraid that getting rid of the children would do exactly what you were trying to avoid? That Castino would leave you and go try to find some woman to give him a son?"

"Not if I handled it the right way. And I always handle my affairs in the right way." She leaned back and smiled at him. "I was never meant to be a mother. Can't you see that it would get in my way? But I tried, when that bastard, Juan, insisted. It wasn't my fault that he couldn't produce a son. He even tried to blame me. Did he think I was a breeding animal? I was ready to be done with him when he took that Gracia as his mistress."

"But you weren't ready to be done with being Queen of Mexico City," Salazar said softly.

"No, that would have been unfortunate." She took a sip of coffee. "And completely unfair to me after all I'd done. So I decided to go another way."

"Get rid of the children."

She nodded. "In such a way that I would be a tragic figure for the rest of my marriage to Juan." She smiled. "And everyone would think Juan was a monster if he even thought of divorcing me and going to another woman. Particularly my father. My father was the key to it all." She took another sip of coffee. "Did I mention that my father had a great fondness for Jenny and Cara? He didn't have Juan's foolish prejudice that a man must have sons. I saw to that. Did you know that I had a brother, Salazar?"

"No."

"Alex was a great disappointment to my father. He finally betrayed him on a drug deal and had to be disposed of. My father was very sad." She met Salazar's eyes. "But I comforted him. He learned once again how valuable a daughter could be."

"And you had nothing to do with his 'disappointment' in your brother?" Salazar asked sarcastically.

"Why, I don't know why you would think such a thing. My father certainly didn't." She leaned back in her chair. "He believes I'm close to perfect. He's correct in many ways. But Juan always knew that he'd better step lightly with me, or all his deals with the Russian Mafia could go right down the drain. He even pretended to be besotted with the girls to please my father." Her lips twisted. "But his obsession with having a son was growing all the time. I knew he'd take the risk of tossing me out soon."

"And what would your father have done then?"

"Cut off dealings with Juan, but my father is a practical man. He was making a good deal of money using Juan's connections in the U.S. He would have eventually resumed dealing, then tried to make it up to me in other ways." Her eyes were suddenly glittering in her taut face. "There would have been *no* other way that would have satisfied me. But I might have lost the power I had over both of them if I'd had to go to battle."

"So you used the children."

"Why shouldn't I? They were mine. I brought them into this world, and I had the right to do what I wished with them. I was the one who was important, they were nothing."

"And your father would have had a completely different viewpoint if Castino had broken up with you after the kids disappeared."

"Yes, I was a mother who'd had a tragic, life-changing experience. My father wouldn't have tolerated me being hurt more after that blow." She looked at him over the edge of her cup. "Would you like me to tell you how he would have retaliated? First, he would have broken off the deals, then he would have started undermining the cartel, then, after a discrete time had passed, Juan would have suddenly been terminated in a very painful manner. Juan is not stupid, he knew what would happen. So he became a very sympathetic husband, and I kept my position intact. It *will* remain intact, Salazar. I may have to shift strategies a bit, but I won't let your carelessness destroy me."

He was silent, gazing at her. "Why did you tell me all this?"

"You asked me."

"I've asked you before, and you've only put me off." He smiled grimly. "Which usually involved sex."

"Which you enjoyed enormously."

"Why did you tell me?" he repeated.

"We've reached a crossroads. You like to screw me, you regard me as an accomplice, but you don't have the respect for me that you must have."

"I respect you."

"Not enough. But after you think about what I've told you, it will get better. You'll think twice about acting without me."

"Not necessarily; all your future plans involve keeping Castino powerful. That's not going to happen. I'm bringing your husband down and his cartel with him."

"I said I might have to make adjustments." She shrugged. "If you succeed, and Juan is destroyed, I'll look at the situation and decide what's best for me to do." She put her cup down and leaned her arms on the table, smiling at him. "It may include you getting rid of your sweet Manuela."

He stiffened. "I like my life. I like my family. I'm not going to let what's between us interfere."

She chuckled. "Like all men, you want it all. We'll have to see how it all plays out. The only thing you can be sure about is that I will come out on top. With or without you." She got to her feet. "Now I have to go dress. Why don't you call Franco and see what he's found out about Jane MacGuire?" She headed for the bedroom. "Just a suggestion . . ." She closed the door behind her.

"Wake up, Natalie." Salazar came into the bedroom and started to dress. "I just heard from Franco."

"It's about time." It had annoyed her when Franco hadn't answered Salazar's call yesterday. She hated waiting for anything. "If I'd have had to stay in this hotel one more day . . ." She threw the coverlet aside and swung her feet to the carpet. "I told you that you should have put someone else on finding —" She stopped. Men were very touchy about I-told-you-so's, and she needed to know what was going on. "Anything happening?"

"Maybe. Franco was nosing around the gallery and talking to MacGuire's agent and other personnel. He found out that she was pretty much of a loner, but there were a few people she knew who occasionally dropped into the gallery." He looked down at the list on his phone. "A Seth Caleb, John MacDuff, he's an earl and Lord of MacDuff's Run, Michael Trevor. Scratch Trevor. He died recently. So we're left with Caleb and MacDuff who she might have

311

turned to for help."

"Does Franco have addresses?"

"I've got them. But Franco is already on his way to MacDuff's Run, where MacDuff lives most of the time. He tried to call him, but MacDuff wasn't picking up on the number the gallery gave Franco."

"Face-to-face is always better anyway from what you told me about Franco's success with that pilot," Natalie said. "Though he may have trouble using the same methods with an earl. Perhaps it would be better if we went to see him. I might have a better chance with him."

Salazar shook his head. "We'll go to Caleb's place. MacDuff might be a waste of time, and we have to hedge our bets." He got to his feet. "I told Franco to keep in touch. If he needs me, he'll let me know."

"Whatever you say." She got to her feet and headed for the bathroom. "I was only trying to help."

"And taking control of the action," Salazar added as he followed. "I'm not going to let that happen."

She smiled. "You sound defensive. I didn't mean to intimidate you." She opened the door. "Naturally, we'll work to do this together. Why else am I here with you?"

"I asked MacTavish to rush those notes and photos, and he said that he'd get right on it," MacDuff said the next morning as he paused to talk to Jane at the site where she was working next to Eve. "It may be awhile. He's trying to clarify the prints."

"Thank you." She sat back on her heels and looked up at him. "I suppose you're anxious to look through them again yourself? Do you think you'll find anything more at second glance?"

He shook his head. "Maybe. Perhaps I didn't know what I was looking for. What do you think?"

"You probably know as much as I do."

"Do I?" he murmured. "I'm not at all sure about that." He turned away. "I'd better get back to work. Though I'm not certain that we're getting anywhere. I'm having a few second thoughts."

Eve watched him walk away before turning to Jane. "What was that all about?"

"I asked him to have his assistant, MacTavish, send copies of notes and photos some college kids managed to get when they went exploring at that lake we went to yesterday."

"Why?"

"Just curious. It intrigued me." She looked

313

away. "You're the one who was telling me all about it before I asked to see it. It must have intrigued you, too."

Eve nodded. "But evidently not as much as it did you. I forgot it once Joe brought me back to the real world." She was silent. "But you were really fascinated when you were there yesterday." She added deliberately, "Almost as if you were in another world yourself."

Jane turned and looked directly at her. "Ask it."

"No, you tell me."

"The Cira dream," she said briefly. "It concerned the lake. As I told you, it might have been triggered by all kinds of influences to which we're being subjected here. I just wanted to get some proof that would discount any validity." She paused. "I didn't mean to be elusive. I just didn't want to worry you."

"I lived with those Cira dreams for years, we worked our way through them. Why should I worry about this one?"

Because there was a dead child that made me cry, Jane thought, and I didn't want you to take it as some kind of foreboding.

"I don't know," she said. "Maybe because pregnant ladies are supposed to be high-strung."

"High-strung? Me?"

"No, you're sturdy as a rock." She went back to work. "I'll let you see those photos after I pick them up if you like."

"If you wouldn't mind. Caleb said that area was vulnerable, and I'd like to know everything I can about it."

"I don't mind. I just don't know if those photos and sketches will help."

Eve shrugged. "They might." She was silent a moment, digging in the earth. Then she said, "Things aren't the . . . same with me. It bothers me. I should have paid more attention when you told me about the Cira dream yesterday, but then you blew me away when I realized you knew I was pregnant. It was all I could think about. Nothing seemed as important as the fact that you knew about my child."

"Perfectly natural, Eve," she said gently.

"Is it? Maybe I can't afford to be so absorbed. I have to be aware of everything around me." She looked out at the hills. "It's so beautiful out there, yet there's a . . . waiting, isn't there?"

"Waiting?"

"It seems as if this place has been here forever, but it's still waiting for something. You can almost feel it, can't you?"

"Maybe." Jane's gaze followed Eve's. Then

she moved her shoulders in a half shake. "Hey, I'm the one MacDuff is sure has a connection to this place. You're supposed to be practical and keep my feet planted firmly on the ground."

"Sorry." Eve was grinning. "Maybe it's just me that's waiting." She glanced down at her flat abdomen. "Waiting for the baby to change and grow. Waiting for Joe to come, so that we can be together." Her glance went across the courtyard, where Cara was sitting cross-legged on the stones, drinking a bottle of water and watching Jock shovel down at the dungeon level. "Waiting for her to be safe."

"Did Joe call you last night?"

Eve nodded. "He's very frustrated. I don't think he's going to last much longer." She made a face. "Which probably means an explosion. I guess I should be sensible and worry about it, but I'm feeling very primitive. I want Joe here with me." She sighed. "And I'm getting tired of digging with these damn spoons; I'm yearning for a shovel."

"So am I. I'm beginning to think it's a waste of time." Jane chuckled as she started back to work. "We'll have to do something about that soon. Jock and MacDuff may have to share."

Eve nodded. "Yes," she said absently. Her

gaze had returned to those green hills bathed in shadows and mists.

Waiting.

Waiting for something.

And it was almost here . . .

"You look hot and thirsty." MacDuff had stopped by the upper courtyard, where Jane was working. "I believe I'm feeling guilty about working you so hard."

"And pigs do fly," she said. "Where is this going, MacDuff?"

"Such a cynic." He smiled. "I just thought I'd ask if you wanted to come to my tent and take a break and have a bottle of water."

She looked at him.

"And maybe take a look at those e-mails that I just got in from MacTavish? I printed them out for you."

She sat back on her heels. "You're a devious man, MacDuff. You know I want to see them." She got to her feet and dusted the dirt from her hands. "He was quicker than I thought he'd be from what you told me. You must have stressed a certain importance."

"Of which I have no idea of the nature. But I'm always willing to try to please you, Jane."

"For a price."

"On occasion." He turned and started across the courtyard. "I assume you'll want to wash up a bit before you handle those papers. Ten minutes?"

"Would you mind if I bring Eve along to look at them?"

"I would actually. This is a private viewing." The next moment he'd moved out of hearing.

She shook her head as she brushed the hair away from her brow. Private viewing? That didn't bode well. And he had gone to the trouble of getting those copies at top speed, and it wasn't to please her. It didn't matter, they were here.

She entered MacDuff's tent five minutes later.

"Ah, just as eager as I thought you'd be." He handed her a bottle of water. "Take a deep breath and relax."

"I want to see the prints."

"And you will, but the timing is questionable. I think you're aware of that, Jane."

Yes, she had known it would come to this. She had only postponed the inevitability. "Blackmail, MacDuff?"

"Not at all. An exchange of information between two partners who are after the same prize." His voice hardened. "But I did you a service, and it's time for you to reciprocate. Why did you want these notes and photos, Jane? I want to know."

She didn't answer.

"You're not being fair, Jane."

No, she was protecting herself and the delicate balance that she'd always maintained about those damned dreams. But she wasn't going to get what she wanted unless she gave MacDuff what he wanted.

"Okay. I had a dream," she said flatly. "It was about Cira and the lake."

He went still. "Ah, I thought maybe it might be that." He grinned. "No, I hoped it might be that."

"Don't get your hopes up. It was a dream, and there were all kinds of reasons that might have caused me to have it."

"But my hopes are up," he said simply. "Don't dash them now. Tell me about it, Jane."

She looked at him for a moment, then briefly and concisely told him about the Cira dream. "I just wanted to —"

"I know what you wanted to do," he interrupted. "I thought it was something like that. I was going to give you the chance to tell me yourself. But it seems time's run out. Look at those photos and sketches, scan those notes. Let's see if we see anything that collates."

"You don't have to ask me twice." She looked at the photos. "They're blurry, nothing here."

"That was quick. You're looking for something."

"For something I don't think is there." She scanned the notes. "No mention here."

"What are you looking for, Jane?" he asked.

"Caves." She picked up the prints of the three sketches the students had made. "I thought I'd have a better chance with these sketches. It's what the artist saw, not a camera. I'm looking for some sign of caves on that north bank. There didn't seem to be any sign of them anywhere on the other banks of the lake. It would be reasonable that the north end wouldn't have them either."

"Except you said that Cira mentioned them repeatedly in your dream when she was talking about her son," he said. "He played in them, ran out of them to greet her."

"It wouldn't be reasonable." Jane was gazing at the first sketch, tossed it aside, looked at the second sketch. "See, I told you that there wouldn't be any —" She stopped, as her gaze was caught by something on the upper corner of the second sketch. "It could be anything. It's just a few scrawled lines, the artist was obviously in a hurry. It doesn't have to be . . ." She moistened her lips. "It's no proof."

MacDuff was looking down at the sketch. As Jane had said, it was only a few lines, shrubs, a boulder . . . that appeared to be blocking the front of an opening of some sort. "But it could be."

Jane glanced at the third sketch. "Nothing here." She tossed it on the desk. "No proof," she repeated.

"Stop struggling against it, Jane," MacDuff said gently. "Not proof, but definitely a reason to explore beyond those mists."

"You want to believe in that dream. It's what you've always wanted."

"I won't deny it. I'm a desperate man. Hunting for Cira's gold has always been an impossible dream on its own. I searched every practical avenue I can find and came up empty. Then I came across you, Jane MacGuire, and I knew that you could help me. I wanted a clue, a path, and I always knew you could give it to me."

She shook her head. "None of this helps you."

"Stubborn. Yet you clearly realized that those caves were important. I recognized the significance immediately."

"I . . . thought that Cira might have buried her son in one of them."

"And she very well might have done that." He met her eyes. "But she might also have buried that chest with the coins in one of them. Cira liked caves, remember? That chest was hidden in a cave in Herculaneum before she took it away with her when she escaped the volcano. She obviously thought they were safe."

"And she would have liked the idea of her son caring for it," Jane whispered. "It would have been a way of keeping him as part of the family."

"You *were* thinking about it," MacDuff said. "Fighting against accepting it but thinking about it."

He was right. It had been in her mind all along though she had tried to block it out. "So what are you going to do about it?"

"What do you think?" He smiled recklessly. "We're going to go down to the lake and see what Cira hid in those mists."

"Gently. Respectfully."

"Cira is my family. She's one of mine. Would I do anything else?"

"No." She smiled faintly. "But you've been searching for that treasure for a long time."

"She wants me to have it," he said. "Why

else would you have had that dream to help me along?" He shrugged. "And you know I was getting discouraged with searching here at the castle anyway."

"It's only been a few days."

"But you've been feeling that it's a waste of time, haven't you?"

"I didn't say that."

"No, you were very careful not to say it. Because you didn't want to lead me away from everything reasonable toward Cira and her son." He looked her directly in the eye. "But you wanted to go and see if she'd sent you a magnificent lifeline to save us all from having her legacy and everything she'd built tumble down around us."

"Saving *you*, MacDuff."

"I beg to differ. You're one of mine. Family is family."

Jane felt a ripple of shock. Family. How many times had that word come into play in the last days? She had used it, Eve had used it. Now MacDuff was throwing it at her.

And Cira had been involved in the most tragic of family duties in her dream.

"Strike a note?" MacDuff's gaze was fixed on her face. "You knew what this was about all along. It's not about the money, it's about saving what Cira created." He paused, then said, persuasively, "Let's go do that, Jane."

"It may be a red herring."

"Let's go see," he challenged softly. "I dare you."

She could feel a surge of the same recklessness she sensed in him. Why not? It was what she had wanted to do. Why else had she been so insistent about being proved wrong.

Because she had wanted desperately to be proved right.

"I don't take dares." She smiled at him. "But I have a boundless curiosity. When do we go?"

"*Yes.*" He threw back his head and laughed. "Now. A few hours. The sooner the better."

"A few hours? You're going to move camp?"

"That's what I said. Go back to your tent and pack up. I'll call Caleb and Jock and tell them to do the same." He turned toward the desk and rolled up the papers. "Then I'll call MacTavish and tell him to arrange to send special cameras and powerful floodlights that will let us pierce that thick mist."

"Those students didn't have those lights?"

"They were trespassers. They didn't know what they were getting into." He smiled.

"Neither do we. Isn't it exciting?"

She wanted to back off, to say no. But she did feel the excitement. She felt as she had when she was a very young girl, reaching out for adventure, wanting to see what was around the next curve in the road. She turned to leave. "Make sure MacTavish does his research and gets us the right equipment."

"I'll convey your concern." He was dialing his phone. "Go tell Eve and Cara to get moving. I want to have our tents set up at the lake by nightfall."

"By all means." She headed for the entrance. "We all have to do as the Laird decrees."

"As is right and proper." He chuckled. "I'm glad you understand that concept at last, Jane."

"I was joking." She looked back over her shoulder. "This is what I want, what I decree. Or I wouldn't be doing it." She smiled. "I'm just using you, MacDuff."

She heard him laughing as she left the tent. She was still feeling that charge of energy and adrenaline, but her smile was fading. She had started MacDuff on a new phase of his hunt for Cira's gold. She could have lied, she could have not said anything, but she had been infected with MacDuff's recklessness. How was she to explain the sudden move to Eve?

By telling her the truth. By telling her all the details of the dream. By telling her that Cira had emerged from the past, and she had to go with her one last time . . .

"Why didn't you tell me all this before?" Eve asked quietly. "You didn't give me any details. You just sort of brushed it off."

"I was fighting against believing that it had any significance. I'm still fighting."

"But not too hard." Her gaze was on Jane's face. "I'm seeing something in you that I haven't seen in a long time. So many things have happened to you . . . You've been hurt, and life hasn't been easy. You've lost a lover and discovered that you can still survive. I think one of the reasons you were fighting so hard to not let Cira back into your life was that was the time you met your Trevor. Another painful memory linked to Cira."

"None of the memories of Trevor were painful until the last one, when he was shot." Her lips were tight. "Cira was just a part of a grand adventure we played out together. He was like MacDuff and was after the treasure."

"And now the adventure is back." She

added shrewdly, "And you've discovered that you want to see it through. You want to do what Cira would want you to do."

She thought about it. "I guess that's true."

"But that still leaves the question, why didn't you tell me all the details of that dream before this?" She was silent, then said, "Never mind. I can figure it out. It's the child. You were afraid I'd read something into the fact that the dream was about a dead child. You mentioned a child, but not that the child was dead." She shook her head. "But that dream was also about hope and love and family. It was about life. And it may have been about how Cira intended to preserve the family fortunes far beyond what even she could imagine. You thought that I'd zero in on the little boy?"

"It occurred to me."

"Of course, it did. Because you're loving and protective, and there was something that could possibly hurt me."

"And it doesn't?"

"Look, if Cira is a fantasy, then the dream is a fantasy. If Cira is somehow reaching out and trying to tell you something, it wouldn't be to warn me that children sometimes die. I know that." She added fiercely, "And there's one way that Cira and I are very much alike. We take care of our own. I'm not going to let anything happen to my baby. I'll fight and I'll claw and I'll do anything I have to do. Cira would think it ridiculous that she would have to tell me that. No, any message she has is for you, not me, Jane."

"Well, I'm glad that's settled. I guess I was pretty foolish to worry about —"

"No." Eve took a step closer and gave her a warm hug. "Not foolish. Loving." She released her and stepped back. "And now I'd better go and tear Cara away from Jock and get her started on packing if you think MacDuff was serious about the camp being set up at the lake by nightfall?"

"He was serious." She gazed at Cara. "Are you going to tell her about the Cira dream?"

"If you don't mind." She smiled. "Cara and I had a discussion about dreams when we were flying over here. She's had some experiences with them. I think she regards your Cira dreams as a kind of wonderful fairy tale." She glanced at Jock. "And maybe Jock is part of a fairy tale, too. I've tried to gently disillusion her about both, but I don't have the heart to take all the fairy-tale ambience away. I'm not sure that she's ever believed in fairy tales unless they were full of beasts and monsters. Your Cira had a hard life, but she worked her way through to a happy ending." She motioned toward Jock. "And I don't know about the happy ending for him, but he's grown very strong, and he's actually quite wonderful. So yes, I don't mind letting Cara believe in those kinds of fairy tales."

"Neither do I," Jane said as she turned away and started for her tent. "Both Cira and Jock learned to defeat all the beasts and monsters. I'd say as role models they put Cinderella in the shade."

CHAPTER 11

"I'm at MacDuff's Run," Franco said when he called Salazar late that afternoon. "All I've found out so far is that the Laird is officially not in residence. It's not going to be easy to track him down. Hell, he may be there, and those guards are lying to me. Maybe Duncan and the kid are there, too. I'll have to find out what palms I have to grease to find out. I know that MacDuff has sentries guarding the perimeter of the castle. The people in the village seem to be a closemouthed bunch. The old woman I started to question looked at me as if I'd insulted her when I asked if she'd seen any visitors at the Run. She told me to go ask at the castle and walked away from me. All of these people seem to be protecting MacDuff."

"Then you'd better use your boyish charm and get answers," Salazar said. "Sometimes, bribes don't work."

"I know that," Franco said. "I'm just telling you that it may take a few days to get those answers here. MacDuff is protected. Have you found out anything about Seth Caleb? He could be easier."

"He's not easier," Salazar said sourly. "Caleb's house is closed up, and no one is trying to protect it or him. But everyone in town just fades away when I try to ask questions."

"That sounds like protection to me."

"Because you wouldn't recognize the difference between loyalty and fear. I've seen it. It would take longer to get past whatever they feel about Caleb. He doesn't need sentries to protect this place. I'll keep trying here, but work on finding everything you can from MacDuff."

"As soon as I can." Franco hung up.

"Aren't there any other leads we can follow?" Natalie asked impatiently.

"We're probing. These are the best we've got so far."

"What about Eve Duncan?" Natalie asked. "I've been thinking that she may be the key to the whole business. She's soft, and soft people can be manipulated. She was the one who took Cara into her home to keep her safe. Give me the chance, and I'll find a way to get what we want from her."

"In case you haven't noticed, we're searching for Duncan and Cara right now, dammit."

"Then go through Joe Quinn to get her. Press him harder. Make him hurt. If Duncan's soft about Cara, she'll be soft about Quinn."

"I'm handling Quinn. I'll do what I have to do. I don't need you to tell me." He looked at her. "Now, would you care to go to the pub and see if you can charm any of the locals into talking about Seth Caleb?"

"Why not?" She smiled. "I've got to do better than you have. I'm beginning to be interested in Seth Caleb. I want to see why everyone is so terrified of him. I might find him fascinating." She added slyly, "I don't believe anyone is that afraid of you, are they, Salazar? What a pity."

The sun was going down when Jane parked the Land Rover on the road above the lake. "Here we are." She jumped out of the car and started to unload. "What do you think about it, Cara?"

The red light of the setting sun was casting a glow over the mists and gave the scene a surreal, almost otherworldly air. Eve wasn't surprised when Cara instantly picked up on that aspect.

"Another planet," Cara said. "I saw a movie about this spaceship full of people who had to settle on another planet, and it looked something like this. Elena said that it was a little too convenient that the planet was that beautiful. She said it was pure Hollywood." She jumped out of the Land Rover and stood there looking down at the lake. "But this isn't Hollywood."

Eve got out of the car and came to stand beside her. "I told you it was a little strange. And I didn't see it at sunset."

"It's gorgeous." She took a step closer to the slope. "I love it, Eve. That mist . . ." She drew a deep breath. "Is that where we're going to be searching?"

"I don't know how much we'll be doing. It depends on how well we can light that area. I don't want either one of us blundering around in that heavy mist and falling into the lake."

"Or falling into a cave." Her gaze was fixed on the mist. "It's kind of weird, isn't it? Caves. I almost died in a cave not so long ago. I *would* have died if you and Joe hadn't saved me. Yet here we are again."

"It won't be a cave like that one. MacDuff thinks if the caves exist, they would probably be small, not huge caverns. But they may not exist. We don't know, Cara."

"But Jane thinks they do exist, doesn't she?"

"Maybe. Jane is a little confused, too."

"But she's excited, I can tell."

"Yes, she's excited," Eve said. "And no matter how this turns out, I'm glad to see it. She's more enthusiastic than I've seen her in a long time."

"And she's not afraid, is she?" Cara had not taken her eyes off the mist. "I think she's . . . welcoming it."

Eve stiffened, her gaze flying to Cara's face. "You think she should be afraid? You said you loved it. Are you afraid, Cara?"

"A little. I do love it. But it's kind of scary. In that other cave, where you saved me, I could see everything, the bad and the good. But I don't know what's in that mist."

"You don't have to know. You don't have to go near it. You can stay on the south side of the lake."

She shook her head. "I want to go." She smiled. "I'm like Jane, I want to see what's waiting for me there."

Eve nodded. "Okay, if you change your mind, just tell me." She made a face. "You're not the only one who had mixed feelings about that mist. Caleb was comparing it to the beginning or the end of the world. I much prefer your simplification." She turned back to the vehicle. "But, in the meantime, we're letting Jane unload our tents. We'd better stop looking and start working." She could see Caleb's car bringing him and Jock coming down the road, followed by MacDuff driving the equipment truck. "Or maybe we'll just let MacDuff and Jock take care of it. MacDuff's the one who was in such a big hurry to get us out here."

"I'll help them." Cara had already reached the Land Rover. "Jock would probably be the one to do most of the work. I'm not sure why, but he thinks he owes the Laird."

"He probably does, but I'm sure he wants to pay his own debts."

"I'll help him." Cara was pulling the tents and bedrolls out of the back of the Land Rover.

Eve noticed that the plural had become singular. She shook her head as she went to the other side of the vehicle to help Jane unload the Coleman lanterns. She was not sure if Cara was going to help Jock with the unpacking or if she had a more long-range goal in mind. At any rate, there was no battling that determination. "As Jock would say, it was just a wee joke, Cara. Of course, we'll do our share to help *them.*"

"I'll take that." Caleb took the bedroll Jane

was carrying and slung it by its strap on his back, then took the two lanterns. "You just had surgery a few weeks ago. You probably shouldn't be doing all this lifting and carrying yet."

"I'm fine, Caleb." She tried to take the two lanterns back, then gave it up. "And since when are you acting the pack mule? You didn't help set up at Gaelkar Castle."

"You weren't climbing up and down hills, and MacDuff was trying to make it as easy as possible on you so that you wouldn't get pissed off and leave the hunt." He reached in the Land Rover and took out her sketchbook and computer bag and handed it to her. "These aren't too heavy." He smiled. "So stop wasting time arguing. You'll notice that I waited until everyone else was halfway down to the lake before I stepped in to rescue you. Now no one will think you're shirking."

"I'll just come back up here and help with the rest of the equipment."

He shook his head. "You'll make yourself busy setting up tents and helping Eve and Cara. Because you will have done the impossible and convinced me that I should waste my valuable time and energy helping MacDuff and Jock do the rest of the setting up. Everyone will be amazed and applaud you." He started down the hill. "Come on. It's getting dark, and that will make it more difficult."

She hesitated, then started down the hill after him. "This is a total waste of your 'valuable energy.' I'm almost entirely well now."

"Almost. But when you were climbing this hill with Eve the other day, I noticed you were short of breath when you reached the top, your cheeks were flushed, and your pulse was pounding in your temple. You're not there yet, Jane."

She couldn't deny it. "You didn't mention it then."

"It wasn't the time. This is the time."

"It's my responsibility to take care of myself. I do a pretty good job of it. So go back to being concerned only about Seth Caleb."

"I'm having a good deal of trouble doing that. It's a matter of great alarm to me." He glanced down at MacDuff, Jock, Eve, and Cara, who had all reached the bank of the lake. The light was almost gone, but it appeared they were sorting the bedding and equipment. "I'm not like them, Jane. I don't want to be like them. Yet at times, you make me want to do what they would do. I felt like that with Trevor. Very dangerous."

"Then save yourself, I've no desire to change you. It's not my business."

"I'm not sure that I can save myself." He suddenly chuckled. "Unless I find a way to change you. Maybe that's what I've been trying to do all along. Care to walk on the dark side, Jane? I promise I'll make it entertaining."

"You couldn't do that for —" She glanced at him and suddenly lost track of what she'd been saying. He was framed against the mist, and darkness was all around him. But it wasn't the darkness that held her. Heat. Intensity.

His eyes were . . .

She couldn't breathe. She could feel her pulse racing.

"Don't do that," he said thickly. "*Now* it hits you? I've got my hands full of this damn equipment, and all those people down there might see anything I'd do to you. I wouldn't care, but in the end, you'd blame me." His eyes were suddenly glowing recklessly. "What the hell?" He dropped the lanterns on the ground and took a step closer. "So blame me already."

His thumbs were on the hollow of her throat, and he was tilting her head back. His mouth was on hers, his tongue playing wildly.

Her pulse was pounding crazily beneath the pressure of his thumbs. Crazy. Crazy. She had to move back.

But she was moving closer, her mouth opening wider, taking more of him.

"We can go back to the car," he whispered. "Or we can stop. But it has to happen now. Go? Stop?"

How could she say stop? It was too late. She *needed* him.

Needed him enough to act like a bitch in heat? This wasn't the way she behaved. This wasn't —

"You're stiffening," Caleb said between his teeth. "Second thoughts?" He pushed her back. "Then get away from me. Or I'll be damned if I let you go." He bent down and picked up the lanterns from the ground where he'd thrown them. "I'm not Trevor or Jock or MacDuff. I've wanted you for a long time, and this time, I almost had you." His voice was rough as he started back down the hill. "And you *wanted* it. You've wanted me as long as I've wanted you."

She was gazing at him, trying to get her breath, trying to think. "I didn't mean . . . I've never denied there's a certain chemistry between —"

"Certain chemistry? It's enough to blow us up if we ever come together. But you're

339

too wary to let that happen, aren't you? Well, it's going to happen. You almost lowered your guard enough tonight. Hell, but it came out of the blue. I wasn't expecting it."

"Neither was I," she said unsteadily. "One minute I was annoyed with you, then I —" She shrugged. "I must have gone a little crazy. It's not like me."

"Or is it? How do you know? Maybe it's exactly how you'll be with me. No analyzing, just feeling."

Feeling. Oh, yes, every cell of her mind and body had been feeling. She could still feel the throbbing of the pulse in her throat, his thumbs rubbing, pressing. Her breasts were still taut, aching.

Don't think about it.

It had been a moment that was completely wrong and shouldn't be repeated. "It's not how I want to be. And I'll fight not to be that way in the future." She moistened her lips. "This was my fault. I'd like to blame you, but I can't do it. I don't know why, but I must have been very vulnerable . . . and it happened. It won't happen again."

"The hell it won't." He looked back at her. "And you don't know why you suddenly wanted to screw me? Well, I do, Jane. I could see it, sense it. You're alive again. It's what

I've been waiting for, and I'm not going to let the opportunity escape me." He smiled mockingly. "Would you like to bet how long it will take us to end up in bed?"

"You're totally outrageous."

"It's my modus operandi." He looked down at the lake. "They're lighting the lanterns. It was dark enough so that they might not have seen what was going on up here. But you'd better compose yourself by the time we get down there. You're all loose and warm and passionate. I can hardly stand to look at you."

That's exactly how she felt, but the fact that he had put it into words annoyed her. "And what about you?"

"I'm going to disappear for a while. No hiding what I'm feeling."

No, and he was giving out sexual vibrations so strong that she was beginning to feel that same stirring just looking at him.

"It's okay." The anger was suddenly gone from his tone. "You'll work your way through it. Now you know how I feel about 90 percent of the time I'm with you. Being alive has its disadvantages."

"Staying away from you would also have advantages."

"But how can you do it? I've suddenly developed a fascination for this lake. I believe I'll have to offer my services to MacDuff at every turn." He waved at Eve as they neared the campground. "Don't you think that everyone will think I've turned over a new and noble leaf?"

"I think that I'm going to work like hell to get MacDuff what he wants and get out of here."

"I thought that would be your reaction." He wasn't looking at her but at the mist that floated ghostlike in the darkness of the far bank. "But it's a strange place, a strange time. I felt it the first time I saw it. I wasn't surprised that you had dreamed about it." He added softly, "Will you ever be able to get out, Jane?"

"Don't be ridiculous."

He chuckled. "Don't slap me down when I'm being mystical. Of course you'll get free because I'll be there to pull you out. I wouldn't let that mist take you any more than I would anyone or anything. I've devoted far too much effort to you. But I had you for a minute, didn't I?"

"No, you did not." It was the mist and the night and the thought of what lay beyond them that had shaken her for that long moment. "But you obviously need something to distract you." And she had to find a way to get rid of him until her defenses were back in place.

She quickened her pace and passed him as she reached the bank. She called, "Sorry to be so long. Caleb is inclined to dawdle. But he says he's willing to be taught, so maybe you and Jock can do the job, MacDuff. He's bored, and he volunteered to go bring the rest of the equipment down himself." She gave Caleb a glance over her shoulder. "He said it was the least he could do. Isn't that right, Caleb?"

"I did mention something like that." He was discarding the bedroll and lanterns, dropping them on the ground. "I'd almost forgotten." He smiled at MacDuff. "I'm at your disposal. Anything you want, and I'm there for you and the rest of the team." He didn't look at Jane, but the next words were aimed at her and held a hint of mockery. "It will be interesting for me to work shoulder to shoulder, so to speak."

When Eve woke the next morning, it was to see Cara sitting cross-legged beside her. She was fully dressed, with a steaming cup in her hand. "Hi." She smiled. "I went out to the campfire and got a cup of coffee for you." She carefully handed her the cup as Eve scooted up to a sitting position in her sleeping bag. "Jock is cooking bacon.

343

Doesn't it smell good?"

"Delicious." She sipped the coffee. "And so is this coffee. Thank you."

"You're welcome. If you want to wash up and brush your teeth, I'll go get you some bottled water."

"I believe I can do that for myself."

"But you shouldn't have to do it when I can do it for you. I should be taking care of you."

Eve gazed at her warily. "Has Jane been talking to you?"

Cara looked bewildered. "What?"

"Just a thought." She should have known that Jane wouldn't tell Cara about the baby. It would have just worried the child. "Don't tell me you dreamed about Jenny again."

"No. But I promised I'd take care of you, and I haven't been keeping my promise. I played the violin the other night when I shouldn't, and I've been spending too much time with Jock. I should have been doing stuff for you."

"No, you should not. You would have driven me crazy if you insisted on fetching and carrying for me. We discussed the playing and came to an agreement. And Jock would have sent you packing if you'd gotten into his way."

"I'm not sure he would," she said gravely.

"He . . . likes me. He wouldn't want to hurt me. So I have to watch out to make sure that I don't do anything that would be bad for him."

"So you're carrying the whole responsibility on your shoulders?" She shook her head. "For heaven's sake, Cara, be a kid for a change. Let yourself enjoy every minute you can. There's sure not many of those. Anything I do for you, I want to do. You don't owe me."

"Yes, I do." She suddenly smiled. "But I won't fetch and carry if you don't want me to do it. But was it all right that I brought you coffee?"

"Extremely all right." She took another sip of coffee and sighed blissfully. "As long as you let me do something for you in return."

"But that wouldn't be —" She stopped. "There is something that —" She stopped again.

"You want to play your violin? I never meant to keep you from doing that, Cara."

"I know." She moistened her lips. "It's not that, I was just thinking I'd like to — I couldn't sleep, so I opened the door and sat there for a while looking out at the lake." She added quickly, "I didn't go outside. I

just sat there. I was just wondering if I could
—"

"Cara."

"You said not to go beyond the mists on that north bank without you," she said in a rush. "I really would like to go there, Eve."

"I don't see why that wouldn't be possible. It's probably going to be fairly safe once MacDuff gets those lights he ordered."

Cara was shaking her head. "I want to go now. MacDuff and Jock were talking about the shipment of lights while Jock was cooking, and they should be here later in the day. Could we go before they get here?"

"You're that impatient?" Eve asked, puzzled.

She shook her head. "I started getting scared last night while I was looking at it. First, I was sitting there, and I felt . . . good. It was beautiful, like I said when I first saw it. And I thought whatever was behind that mist must be beautiful, too. But then I began to think of the forest, where Jenny died. That was beautiful, too, but it hid ugly things."

"That didn't change the beauty," Eve said gently. "Sometimes ugliness exists side by side with beauty. Jenny gave her life for you in that forest and that was beautiful, too."

"I know," she whispered. "But it still hurts

346

me to think of it. I remember how scared I was when she ran away from Elena and me. I began to get scared again last night when I was thinking of it. It sort of got mixed up in my head with the mist." She shook her head. "I can't be scared any longer, Eve. All my life I've been afraid, and I can't live like —" She reached out and touched Eve's hand. "I have to face it, Eve. I can't hide away from it. Will you help me?"

Help her? Eve felt a melting inside her as she gazed at this child who had lived a life of fear and death since she was a toddler. She wanted to take away that fear, shoulder the pain of those memories. But that wasn't what Cara was asking of her. She was asking her to show her how to handle the fear without flinching. And that would be a much harder task. "I'll help you. Of course I'll help you."

"Thank you." Cara suddenly launched herself at Eve and her arms closed tightly around her. "Thank you."

Eve froze in shock. Cara was not given to physical demonstrations, and Eve had told herself that it might be a long time before she was comfortable with any kind of affectionate gestures.

Don't question.

Accept.

She carefully put her coffee down and held Cara close. She was aware of the slightest stiffening but ignored it. Cara had made the first move. "You're welcome." She brushed a kiss on her temple. "I consider it a family obligation. But you'll have to let me know what I have to do. I'm a little confused about what you need from me."

Enough. Don't push it. Back away.

She let Cara go and picked up her coffee cup again. "So you need to go to the north bank? Why can't we wait for MacDuff's super-duper lights?"

"Because it would change what's there. It would be like wearing a bulletproof vest. I wouldn't be facing what I'm afraid of at all. Do you see what I mean?"

"I think I do. Though a bulletproof vest doesn't sound that bad to me." But she suddenly realized that Jane would understand what Cara was saying. "Without the mist it loses . . . integrity?"

Cara nodded eagerly. "I know MacDuff has to have those lights to find what he's looking for, but he'd be losing something, too." Her smile faded. "Right now there's a music to it. When you shine the lights, and the mist vanishes, will the music go, too?"

What could she tell her? Eve couldn't hear the music. "I don't know, Cara."

"I think it might. I want to face it all now." She paused. "With you, Eve. I don't want anyone else along."

Face the fear, face the beauty, with no protection, no raising of barriers. Wasn't that what Cira had done all those centuries ago when she had challenged a new land, a new life?

"Eve?" Cara was gazing at her.

Eve nodded. "Okay, no bulletproof vests," she said brusquely. "But it's not going to be easy pulling this off." She finished her coffee and got to her feet. "And we'd better get busy before MacTavish's truckload of lights and batteries comes rumbling down that road."

Cara eagerly jumped to her feet. "What are we going to do?"

"Finish getting dressed, cat breakfast, then go face MacDuff, Jock, and Caleb."

"I didn't see Caleb."

"Not surprising. He's not into hobnobbing. Jane?"

"She's still in her tent." Cara's eyes widened as she saw Eve reach into her suitcase and draw out her .38 revolver. "Why are you taking that? I was joking about the bulletproof vests. I meant —"

"I know what you meant." She tucked the gun into the pocket of her jacket but didn't put it on. "But if I can persuade MacDuff to let us go into that mist without them trailing after us, I want all the protection I can get. He told me that he has five of his Marine buddies in those hills near the north bank keeping an eye out for trespassers, but I don't want to have to count on them." She grinned at Cara. "And I may need it to shoot off a distress signal if we get lost in that mist. Though I hope not. It would be most humiliating."

Cara's gaze was still on the pocket into which the gun had disappeared. "I don't want to cause trouble. Am I being stupid, Eve?"

"No. There's no sign of anyone's knowing where we are, and MacDuff has given us adequate protection. The only danger is the mist, and, if we're careful, we can handle that." She grabbed her toothbrush and comb and headed for the portable canvas table against the tent wall. "But first I need to wash my face and brush my teeth. Go get us a plate of that bacon Jock is cooking and whatever else is available. Okay?"

"Okay." Cara's cheeks were flushed and her eyes shining with excitement. "Shall I tell them that —"

"No, leave it to me." She didn't want Cara to face the uproar alone. "After we have some hearty sustenance. We may need it. But first, I want you to go to Jane and tell her what we're doing. In a very real way, this is her lake, her territory. She has the right to know."

She shook her head ruefully after Cara ran out of the tent. It was true that there appeared to be no obvious danger, but that didn't mean that it was the safest thing on the planet to do. But Cara's problem was that she'd had to be careful, hide, always look behind her all her short life. How could Eve not understand and let her stop running if there didn't appear to be danger?

Appear was the key word, she thought dryly. She didn't know what was behind those mists.

With her luck, that north end of the lake was probably inhabited by a creature on the scale of the Loch Ness Monster.

When Eve and Cara left their tent fifteen minutes later, Jane was standing alone at the clearing, where only the embers of the campfire were still flickering.

"Let's go," she said quietly. "We don't have too much time. It took me quite a battle with MacDuff and Jock to get them to back off. They gave us ninety minutes; and then we can expect an invasion. Less if that truck with the power lights shows up while we're stumbling around out there." She gave flashlights to Eve and Cara and turned on her heel. "Come on, Cara. It's your show, you lead the way."

"Right." Cara started at a trot along the bank.

Eve fell into step with Jane as they hurried after her. "I didn't want to force you into coming with us. But you had a right to know."

"Yes, I did." She smiled faintly. "And you didn't force me to do anything. I don't know how I feel about this little foray into Marcus's kingdom, but I think there must be some reason Cara feels so strongly about it."

"It's not about Cira or Marcus or the treasure as far as she's concerned. It's about facing her devils."

"She's very young to have to confront them," Jane said. "And, who knows, maybe it's more about Cira and Marcus than she thinks. You told her the details about the dream?"

"Yes. I don't know, maybe she's somehow connecting Marcus's death with her sister's, Jenny's. She said something about Jenny's dying in a beautiful forest, too. She said she was too afraid that night, and she couldn't be afraid again." She glanced at Jane. "And you were close to her age when you had devils of your own to battle. So Cara isn't all that young."

"Young enough to be very fast. She's getting too far ahead of us to be safe." Jane's pace quickened. "She's entering the mist zone."

"Cara," Eve called. "Wait." She could barely see her in the mist, but at least Cara had halted and turned on her flashlight. Not that it was doing much good. Even though they were on the outer edge of the fogbank, the light was very weak.

But Cara's expression was glowing with eagerness as they reached her. "Isn't it awesome?" She held up her arm cloaked in mist. "I feel as if I could fly." She turned and started deeper into the mist. "Come on."

"Stay close," Eve said. "And don't drop your flashlight."

"I won't." Cara's voice was bright, excited in the smothering gray of the mist as she moved ahead. "I was wrong, Eve. There's nothing to be afraid of here. Oops." She laughed. "I almost slid into the lake. It's all muddy here on the bank. You warned me about that."

"Yes, I did. The bank probably never gets

enough sunlight to dry out. Be careful, the farther in we go, the denser the mist. These flashlights aren't doing much good. I can't see more than a foot in front of me."

"Neither can I," Cara said. "But that's okay; as long as I watch the bank, I'll be safe. Isn't it neat? It's like exploring our own private planet. I think there are some big rocks up ahead." She stopped. "I think we can go around them, then come back to the lake."

"How do you know there are rocks?"

"I hear the sound of the lake lapping against them, don't you? And the mist blows against them in a different way . . ."

"No, I can't say I hear that," Eve said. "I don't think those college students got much farther than this. This is a heavier mist than I've ever gone through. And I don't see how they sketched as much as they did. Jane?"

"No, I don't hear what she hears," Jane said softly. "But I'm not afraid either, Eve. It's . . . good here. I believe it's okay to go a little farther."

Eve hesitated, then started forward again.

There *were* boulders ahead, and they felt their way around them and were once more making their way around the lake.

Total grayness, no hint of light, the flashlights totally useless now.

"The hills come straight down to the lake up ahead," Cara said. "But I think the path around the lake widens there."

"How do you know?"

"It just seems like it should," Jane said simply. "Doesn't it, Cara?"

Cara looked back at her. "Yes."

"What's going on?" Eve asked.

"I have no idea," Jane said. "Tell us, Cara."

"It's the music. The music is so strong here. And it gets stronger up ahead." She looked at Jane. "And you hear it, too, don't you?"

"Not like you do. But I hear something. Words. Cira's words." She quoted softly, "I can ride down here from the castle and imagine him running out of the mist and telling me how he'd just been hiding and playing in the caves and had great adventures to tell me." She added, "That has a music all its own, doesn't it?"

Cara nodded slowly.

"And do you want to go farther and search out that other music right now? We could do it. Or do you think that you've been given what you were meant to have when you led us into this mist?"

Cara didn't answer for a moment. "I want to go on."

"Now?"

Cara was silent again. "No, not now. It's enough." She turned and headed back toward the boulders. "Let's go back to the camp."

"But not because you're afraid," Jane said. "That's all gone?"

"Yes." Cara's voice drifted back to them. "That's all gone . . ."

The truckload of power lamps and batteries that MacTavish had promised MacDuff didn't arrive until late in the afternoon. By the time they were unloaded and taken down to the encampment, it was almost dark.

Eve sat down in front of the fire beside Jock and watched MacDuff and Caleb checking over two huge power bulbs. "You're going out tonight?"

"Why not?" Jock lifted his cup of coffee to his lips. "We've got to experiment with the equipment. We might have to order something different. Though MacTavish seemed to think that it would be enough."

"What do you think?"

Jock shrugged. "I'm no expert. I have to yield to MacTavish."

"But MacTavish was never out in that mist, like you were, was he?"

He gazed at her face and smiled. "No, he

356

wasn't. How did you know I'd followed you?"

"Your boots. They were coated in mud when I caught sight of you right after we got back to camp. But you disappeared, and they were clean later."

"Very observant."

"Did you flip a coin to see who was going to follow us?"

"No, I was the logical choice. I didn't give anyone else an opportunity to argue." He took another drink of coffee. "It might have been blundered, and I never blunder."

"No, we had no idea you were anywhere near." She made a face. "Though I doubt if we would have known anyway. That mist is horrendous."

"Yes. It's . . . unusual. I was barely able to track you."

"I don't see how you could do it at all. We couldn't see anything."

"I've been trained to track in all situations and weather conditions." His lips twisted bitterly. "It was part of my schooling as a superassassin. That was why I was the logical choice. What's a little mist to someone like me?"

"You didn't have to follow us. We made it just fine."

"Correction. I did have to do it. I could

see how Cara felt bound to stretch her limits, but I had to be there to make sure that exercise didn't hurt her."

"It was all about Cara?"

"No, don't be foolish. You and Jane are important. I would have gone anyway. But Cara is . . . she's too young to know — She'll get in trouble if someone doesn't watch out for her."

"Jane and I managed to bring her back in one piece," Eve said dryly.

"No insult intended," Jock said. "You did fine."

"Thank you. But you'll still be there to keep us from screwing things up for her." She shrugged. "It's to be expected. She appears to feel the same about you." She got to her feet. "And I believe I'll go check on Cara now and see if she's okay. She was a little quiet after she came back from the north bank."

Jock looked down at his coffee. "I noticed."

"Yes, of course you did." She hesitated. "No matter what you think, that little trip into the mist was good for her. She learned . . . something."

"I'm not arguing." He got to his feet and threw the remainder of the coffee in his cup into the fire. "Learning is necessary. You just have to live through it." He started toward Caleb and MacDuff. "Now I have to go and see if MacTavish's equipment is going to work."

"You didn't answer me. Do you think it will?"

"No." He didn't look at her. "I've never seen a mist like that one. The light will bounce off that fog like a ball against a wall. We'll need something better. But MacDuff wants to give it a try."

Eve watched him join the other two men, then went into the tent to talk to Cara.

No questions.

No urging for confidences.

Just a silent affirmation that she was there if Cara wanted to talk.

She had no idea exactly what had gone on between Cara and Jane in that mist. She wasn't sure if Cara knew. So it was best for Eve to be silent and wait to be told.

"Hey. I just talked to Jock." She smiled as she stood looking at Cara, curled up in her bedroll. "They're going to try to see what those superlights are going to do tonight. Want to come out and sit by the fire and wait until they come back?"

Eve waited until the camp had quieted down and Cara was asleep that night before she called Joe. She was tired and bewildered and wanted to touch base. She wanted to hear his voice.

"Things are fairly crazy here," she said when he picked up. "Don't say anything. We're all safe. It's just that we took our first journey into woo-woo land and I have no idea where I'm fitting into this."

He chuckled. "Some would say that you should be an expert in that area. I take it you meant you went into the mist. Accomplish anything?"

"No, Cara heard music. Jane had a flashback to a Cira dream. I was merely stumbling along in that mist and trying to keep everyone from tumbling into the lake. The three of us had flashlights, but they were useless. That mist is crazy."

Silence. "Three? The three of you were alone out there?"

She knew that would be his reaction, but there was no way that she would have kept it from him. "Cara wanted it that way. It was kind of a rite of passage for her. Or something like that. It was fine."

"It's not fine."

"It was my decision. I thought it was worth it. I still think it was." She changed the subject. "And it turned out we weren't alone. Jock shadowed us all the while we were on that north bank. Amazing. How do you shadow anyone when you can't even see them?"

"Don't do it again," he said sharply.

It struck her the wrong way. "My decision," she repeated. "MacDuff had guards in the hills, and there was no report of Salazar or his crew anywhere in this part of the Highlands. I have to do what I think is right, Joe. I didn't call you to listen to you tell me what I should do."

"Then why did you call me?"

"I don't remember. Something about love and missing you. Maybe about talking about where we're going to send our kid to college? That seemed to be important at the time."

Silence. "That is important."

"Then can we skip the lectures and concentrate on that?"

"In a minute." He added roughly, "I have to know what's going on. It's driving me crazy not to know what's happening with you. I'm sitting over here and not able to —"

"I try to let you know what's happening. It's all fairly run-of-the-mill and pretty boring. Nothing to do with Salazar or Franco. We went for a walk in the mist. Then MacDuff, Caleb, and Jock went for a walk in the mist. They were experimenting with some high-powered lights, which turned out to be a complete failure. MacDuff is contacting some lab in London to explore using infrared technology. He thinks he can get some kind of apparatus up here by late tomorrow and —"

"Okay. Okay." Joe said. "I don't want to hear about that damn mist. I just want to know that you're not going into it alone. I don't like the idea of Jock's being able to creep behind you without your knowing it."

"I'll take it under consideration." She added, "But your nerves are pretty ragged, or you wouldn't have gone on the attack. What's happening with you, Joe?"

"Not a damn thing. Toller's man is being discreet but letting me know that he's ever-present. I saw Salazar's guy staking me out when I went to the precinct this morning." He added with leashed ferocity, "I feel like I'm in a box. I've got to get *out.*" He drew a harsh breath. "I'm in touch with Burbank, Manez's contact at Scotland Yard. He says that the word is that Salazar is on the hunt and gathering a team together from the local Mafia." He paused. "He's going to be ready once he finds out where you and Cara are. I can't wait for that to happen."

"You'll do what you think is best," she

said. "Just as I am, Joe." She tried to laugh. "But I really don't want to have to come back there and bail you out of jail. It would be really difficult keeping Cara under wraps if that happened."

"I just wanted to let you know. I'm trying to hold back. I won't do anything rash, but the situation is becoming . . . volatile." He suddenly changed the subject. "What about Harvard?"

"What?"

"You asked what school we should send the kid to. Harvard is good."

She was glad that he had chosen to switch gears. The conversation had gotten too heavy. "Too snooty."

"I went to Harvard."

"The defense rests. Your parents were snooty, and you just managed to escape the curse. If you'd grown up in the slums like me, you'd have a better perspective on education. But you still insisted on Jane's going to Harvard."

"Only because she wanted to go." He paused. "I believe we have a little time in which to make up our minds, don't you? What made you think of it anyway?"

"I don't know." She sighed. "Yes, I do. I was thinking of Cira's little boy and how he'd not had a chance to chase his dreams.

Thinking about the future is important even though sometimes that future never comes to be. I guess I'm feeling the need to plan for Cara, plan for our child. Maybe it's the nesting instinct."

"Cira's son . . ." Joe's voice was thoughtful. "A little boy . . . Do you know, I never even thought that we might be having a son. Somehow, I thought the child might be a girl."

"Why?"

"Didn't you? You lost your Bonnie. Maybe some kind of cosmic justice?"

"I haven't had time to think about the sex, cosmic justice, or anything else." But she was thinking about it now. "And I think that you're going down the wrong road. This isn't my child, it's our child. It will be what it will be."

"You don't want to know whether it's a boy or a girl?"

"No. Do you?"

"Maybe."

"Then maybe we'll find out. We'll talk about it. It's your child, Joe. Our child."

"Yeah." Silence. "But first we've got to make sure that our child is safe. So take care of yourself. No stumbling around in the fog and falling into the lake. It's not good for the kid."

"Point taken. I'll remember."

"I mean it, Eve. It's been too quiet. I've got a hunch that everything is going to explode."

"You included," she said dryly.

"Probably." He paused. "I want to be there to take care of you, take care of my child. I love you, Eve."

"Likewise." She cleared her throat. "I'll call you tomorrow, and I promise it won't be to tell you that I went strolling in the mist." She hung up.

Everything is going to explode.

She had felt a chill when he'd said that. It might be a hunch, but she believed in Joe's hunches. His instincts were infallible most of the time.

Everything is going to explode . . .

CHAPTER 12

Macduff's Run

The blood gushed onto Franco's wrists as his knife sliced across the guard's throat. More a sentry than a guard, Franco thought, as he wiped his hands on the man's shirt. He'd had a soldier mentality and endurance, too. He hadn't told Franco what he'd wanted to know until he'd cut off both his thumbs.

He pulled the guard's body into the bushes and carefully hid it. Then he started across the courtyard to the small side door facing the ocean. MacDuff's castle towered over the surf, and Franco had verified there were sentries on that side, too. But he could avoid them if he moved fast enough. And then all he had to do was get inside and find the target.

It was about time. It had taken too long, and Salazar was growing more impatient. None of MacDuff's people would talk, and it wasn't until he'd concentrated on the local village pub that he had hit pay dirt.

He'd spent a few hours schmoozing the employees, telling them he was a tourist who had been told about this castle and had come to see for himself. It had not been easy, but he'd finally found a young waitress who had told him enough to get him started.

It was true that MacDuff was not at the castle at present.

But his assistant, Rob MacTavish, was there and was an old and trusted employee.

He had known that he would have to make do with MacTavish. He only hoped he was as trusted by MacDuff as he'd been told. No problem getting to him. Franco had studied the positions of the sentries on that first day and could use one of them to get him to MacTavish.

It had all gone smoothly. Now Franco had the security alarm code from the sentry to get him into the castle.

And he knew where to find MacTavish.

Ten minutes later, he was moving quietly through the halls toward the study. Someday he'd have a place like this, he thought as he looked up at the high-arched ceilings. Only his castle would be new and lush, and there would a pool where all the women would be —

He reached the study, and paused outside the oak door. It was so thick and well made he couldn't see any light around the edges. But he could hear the sound of music. MacTavish evidently liked Madonna.

He braced himself. Move fast. Be prepared for anything.

Take him down.

He exploded through the door. He was across the room in seconds.

MacTavish jumped to his feet, his blue eyes wide and alarmed behind wire-rimmed spectacles. "What are you —" He whirled and was reaching into a top drawer in the desk.

Franco's machete sliced into his hand as he reached for the gun.

MacTavish screamed.

It was done. He *had* him.

Franco was behind him, freeing the knife from his hand and pressing it to MacTavish's stomach. "Don't move. Do exactly what I say." He pushed him back into the chair. "We're going to talk. I'm going to ask you questions, and you're going to answer."

"Who are you?"

He stuck the knife into his shoulder.

MacTavish screamed again.

"You aren't listening," Franco told him. "You don't ask the questions, old man. I ask the questions." He turned the knife in the wound. "Does that hurt?" MacTavish was groaning, biting his lip in agony. Franco felt the familiar surge of power and pleasure. "We've just started. Now let's have a talk about MacDuff and Jane MacGuire."

"I know where Jane MaGuire is," Franco said triumphantly when Salazar answered the phone five hours later. "I wasn't able to talk to MacDuff. He wasn't at the castle. But he had an assistant, Rob MacTavish, who had everything at his fingertips."

"And what is that?" Salazar put his phone on speaker, so that Natalie could hear. He pulled the rental car over to the curb. "What's everything, Franco?"

"MacGuire is with MacDuff and some friend, a Jock Gavin."

"What about Eve Duncan?"

"MacTavish didn't know anything about Duncan. I don't think MacDuff told him about her."

"Then he didn't have everything at his fingertips, did he?" Salazar asked sarcastically.

"He had enough. MacDuff has been planning a hunt for some kind of treasure for the last few weeks. Jane MacGuire was scheduled to go along. MacTavish ordered all the equipment for him and made arrangements with his property caretakers at all his properties."

"You're sure MacGuire didn't cancel at the last minute?"

"No, MacTavish e-mailed MacDuff some notes and photos that Jane MacGuire wanted to see just last night."

"What notes?"

"Something about a lake on the property where they're searching." He paused. "MacTavish said that he didn't think anyone would cancel out on a chance of getting a share of that treasure MacDuff was hunting. MacDuff has been gathering information and making plans for years, and he told MacTavish when he asked for the information that he thought he was very close, that this time he was going to find it."

"Eve Duncan," Salazar said impatiently, to bring him back to the subject at hand.

"I know. I'm sure she's with Jane MacGuire," he said hurriedly. "But you should listen to me. MacTavish thinks MacDuff is close to finding that treasure. It could be worth millions, maybe billions."

"Billions?" Salazar repeated. "Treasure hunt? It sounds like some kid's game."

"That's what I told MacTavish. He said that they're searching for a chest full of

ancient coins brought over from Herculaneum." He paused. "One of them was said
to be one of the pieces of silver Judas was
paid to betray Christ. It was supposed to
have been found by some professor a couple
years ago, but the Vatican refused to accept
it as authentic. That means it could still be
part of the treasure. That could be very big
money."

"Maybe," Salazar said. "But we can't deal
with that right now. We're going after Eve
Duncan and the kid."

"Don't be impatient," Natalie suddenly
spoke up. "Franco is right, we shouldn't
discount the possibility of raking in that
kind of money. You did very well, Franco."

Silence. "A woman?" Franco said warily.
"You have a woman there? Even if she's
your wife, you shouldn't involve her in —"

"I'm not his wife," Natalie said softly. "I'm
Natalie Castino. Do you know who I am?"

An instant of shocked silence. "Yes. I've
never met you, but I've seen you."

"I want you to know that I appreciate your
hard work. I look forward to meeting you. I
think with a little thought and planning, we
might be able to snatch that chest of coins
right from under MacDuff's nose."

"It will get in the way," Salazar said flatly.

"Not if we work it right." She smiled at

him. "You have power and a good deal of money in all your Grand Cayman accounts. But Franco and I have to think of the future, don't we, Franco?"

"It's . . . a lot of money."

"Of course, it is. And we should take a little time to see if MacDuff is as close as MacTavish said. You made sure that he wouldn't have lied to you?"

"He didn't lie."

She chuckled. "And you have a reputation for making it impossible for anyone to do that. Even my husband was impressed when he heard about you."

"Was he?"

"Absolutely. Now where is this hunt going on?"

"Gaelkar. It's in the Highlands."

"And that must be where we can find Duncan and Cara. Suppose you set out right away, and we'll meet together and talk."

"Salazar?" Franco asked.

"Come ahead," he said shortly. "I'll talk to you on the road." He hung up and glared at Natalie. "What the hell are you doing?"

"Exploring possibilities. There's a possibility that I won't be able to use you or my husband to give me what I need. You both have your own agendas. It would be very convenient to have a fortune of my own."

"A share of a fortune," he corrected sourly.

"It appears as if there might be plenty to share." She took out her computer and opened it. "You go ahead and GPS this Gaelkar. I'll see if I can Google any information about MacDuff and this chest of coins . . .

"Something's wrong, Jane," Eve murmured as she watched MacDuff stride toward them down the bank. His expression was more grim than she'd ever seen it. "And I don't think it has anything to do with that damn mist."

"Come to my tent," MacDuff said curtly as he stopped before them. "Both of you. Right now."

"Can you wait until we clean the mud off our shoes and wash our hands?" Eve asked. "We ran into a spot of —"

"No, right now." He turned on his heel. "I don't give a damn about that shit." The next instant, Eve and Jane were watching him stride down the bank. "I don't think you're going to give a damn either, Eve."

Eve felt a surge of fear and automatically looked toward Cara. As usual, she was with Jock and appeared perfectly okay. Whatever had happened hadn't touched her yet. "I don't like this."

She quickly followed Jane around the bank toward the tent area.

Not Cara.

Joe?

Possible. Danger was always possible where Joe was concerned.

Stop worrying. She'd know in a few minutes.

But, dear God, MacDuff had looked grim.

MacDuff still looked grim as they entered his tent. He had poured a shot of whiskey and was lifting the glass to his lips. He glanced at them. "Sorry to be rude. Would you like a drink? I felt the need of one."

"Why?" Jane asked as she came toward the desk. "What's happened, MacDuff?"

"I'm drinking to an old friend." He lifted his glass in a half toast. "Who was recently butchered by an acquaintance of yours, Eve."

Eve felt a ripple of shock. "What?"

"Rob MacTavish, my assistant." He took a drink of whiskey. "MacTavish has been with me for years and my father before me. He was a good man. He was planning on retiring soon. He was training his grandson to take over for him."

"What happened, MacDuff?" Jane repeated quietly.

"I received a call from Sean Donlachen, head of security at MacDuff's Run. He was abjectly apologetic." He took another drink. "Because he'd failed in his duty to me. Last night, the courtyard sentry was taken, tortured, and killed. But not before he'd given the alarm code to get into the castle. Early this morning, they found both the sentry and MacTavish. It appeared that MacTavish had received even harsher treatment than the sentry." His lips were tight. "Because he was a tough, loyal old man, and it must have taken a long time to break him."

"I'm so sorry, MacDuff," Jane said. "It was MacTavish you asked to send me those notes and sketches. Did that have anything to do with it?"

"No," Eve said unsteadily. She couldn't stop shivering. "I don't believe that what happened had anything to do with Cira's treasure. It sounds too much like what happened to those pilots in Atlanta. They were tracking you down to find Jane, Cara, and me, MacDuff. Isn't that what you're figuring?"

"That's what I'm thinking," MacDuff said. "I'm betting it was that Franco Quinn told me about. And they found a nice old man who knew where I was." He tossed back his whiskey. "And butchered him."

"Do you want Cara and me to leave?" Eve asked. "If we go, even if Salazar and Franco came, they might leave you alone if they see that we aren't here."

"You may have to leave. Since they know where you are, I won't risk you and the child. But not right away. I have to find a place for you that I consider safe." His lips twisted. "And by that time, they could be right on top of us." He turned back to Jane. "But they'll be coming from the north, over the hills to the lake. It would be the safest route for them. They wouldn't realize what they'd run into if they try to go through that mist." He paused. "I don't want anyone to go near that mist at the north end until I tell you it's safe."

"And when will that be?" Jane asked. "Because I don't think you're including yourself in that order, are you?"

"It occurred to me that it might be more efficient to get rid of the threat after I'm sure that Eve and Cara are safe." He poured himself another drink. "Picking Franco and Salazar off in that mist would be so much cleaner than having to keep those bastards from hunting Eve and Cara down. I'm sure MacTavish would approve."

"They might not even to try to go through

that mist," Eve said. "They might just go over the hills and hit us from the northwest."

"Maybe. But then they might decide that they should explore other lucrative goals while they're at it." His lips twisted. "And I won't let Cira's gold be taken by those sons of bitches who killed MacTavish."

"Is that a possibility?" Eve asked.

"The office was ransacked, and the file with the photos was taken. MacTavish must have told Franco everything concerning the hunt as well as where we are. Hell, he probably told him anything and everything to stop the pain. I even told MacTavish during that last call that I thought I was coming very close to finding Cira's gold. Yes, I'd say that it's a possibility Salazar might have an interest." He added through set teeth, "I almost hope they do. I'd like to repay a little in kind."

"I can see how you would," Eve said. "And I regret what happened to your friend MacTavish, but you can settle scores after I get Cara safe. Right now, I don't care about Cira's gold or preserving your estates or the fact that you want revenge." She turned to leave. "Now I'm going to call Joe and tell him that Salazar probably knows where we are and is moving fast." She looked over her shoulder. "And if you can find a safe house for Cara, do it. Or I'll do it myself."

She walked out of the tent.

She stood there for a moment, struggling against the anger and panic coursing through her. Two more deaths as Salazar and Franco moved nearer. Two strangers whom she had never seen had died for her and Cara. How many more would there be before this was over?

Get a grip. She drew a deep breath and straightened her shoulders. Cara. She had to find Cara. She headed back toward the bank.

She saw Cara immediately. She was still with Jock, and he was smiling down at her. Was it Eve's imagination, or was the closeness growing, the bonding between them becoming more firm? A bonding that would probably be broken when she snatched Cara away from Jock, and they went on the run. She felt a pang as she thought how many friendships had been lost when Cara had been forced to run in her short life.

It couldn't be helped. Her pace quickened as she hurried toward Cara. Get Cara to her tent, prepare her for what was to come.

Then make the call to Joe.

"Go ahead. I'll be there in a few minutes, Eve," Cara said, trying to smile. She had to be very calm, she told herself. She must not let Eve know how upset she was. She could tell that Eve was already upset herself, and she mustn't make it harder for her. "It won't take me long to get ready. Go call Joe."

"Cara . . ." She gazed at her, then at Jock. Then she nodded. "Don't be too long. MacDuff is going to be working on finding a safe place to take us. I don't know how much time we're going to have." She turned and headed back toward the tent area.

Cara's hands knotted into fists as she watched Eve leave. "She wants to give me a chance to say good-bye to you. Isn't that nice of her? Eve's always thinking about other people. Did I tell you that she saved my life once? She didn't even know —"

"Shut up," Jock said roughly. He was suddenly beside her, turning her to face him. "Stop pretending. I know what this is doing to you. How many times has it happened before? That's what Eve is thinking, too. It's hurting her to make you go on the run again." He took her shoulders in his hands and looked down into her eyes. "It's hurting me. So don't pretend. It makes me feel lonely."

"Does it? Why?"

"Because I like the way you play the violin." He smiled. "Because I like the way you smile at me. Because I've never had a sister, and you make me think it might be kind of nice to have one. Do I have to have any other reason?"

"No." She cleared her throat. "You . . . make me feel as if I'm not alone either. I don't want to leave you."

"Shh. We can get around that."

She shook her head. "You might need me. I think sometimes you have . . . pain. I should be here."

"I'll be fine."

He was smiling and so radiant that she wanted to reach up and touch his face. She repeated, "You might need me."

He was silent, gazing down at her. "I think I might always need you. But that doesn't mean we have to be together. Friends stay friends even when they're far apart."

She shook her head. "But then I won't know when you need me." But maybe he was trying to say that she was clinging too tight. "You're right." She tried to back away from him. "That's the way you're friends with Jane. It's just not my way. I'll work on being more like Jane." She moistened her lips. "I'd better go. Eve told me not to —"

"Hush," he said. "Jane is fine. Jane is great. But you don't have to be anyone but yourself. That's quite enough. Too much sometimes."

"Too much?"

"I'm not going to go into that," he said. "And do you really think that I'd let you get away from me? That's not going to happen."

"We're friends?" she whispered. "Really friends?"

"It couldn't be any more real," he said gravely. "And I'm not ever going to let you walk away unless that's what you want to do. I'll be closer to you than your Elena, closer than Eve. But you have a long way to go, and we can't be together all the time. I'll have to make do without you."

"You're not . . . joking?"

"Heaven forbid. Now, run along to Eve. I have to go see MacDuff. I knew MacTavish, too, and MacDuff may need someone to talk to about his old friend."

She nodded. "I tried to talk to Eve about Elena, but sometimes the words didn't come."

"And MacDuff may not say anything. In that case, we'll only have a drink. But he'll know I'm there, and that can be important, too." He yanked his thumb toward the tents. "Go. Let me see you safe in your tent before I leave."

"It's only a little way, Jock." She smiled at him as she turned to leave. "I couldn't be safer. I'm not worried."

"Neither am I. Not as long as I'm watching over you. You don't ever have to worry about anything happening to you while I'm keeping an eye on you." He smiled back at her. "You'll never have to look over your shoulder again. No one will ever hurt you. I'll always be there for you."

He was smiling, but Cara could sense that he could not have been more serious. "I don't want anyone to have to take care of me. Elena, Eve, Joe, Jane. Now you and MacDuff. Elena always told me I had to take care of myself, and she was right. It's my turn to take care of people now."

"We'll discuss it later." He nodded at the tents. "Go see what Joe's decided for you and Eve. Move."

Cara stood there, staring at him.

He frowned. "What's wrong?"

"I just wanted to look at you for a minute. Things . . . happen. I tried to remember what Elena looked like that last morning, and I couldn't do it."

"Cara." A mixture of expressions chased across his face. "Oh, shit. What can I say to that?" He leaned closer and cupped her face in his hands. "Hey, it's going to be fine. I promise nothing is going to happen to me or Eve or Jane or . . . should I go down the list?"

"You promise?"

He nodded. "You know it." He brushed his lips across the bridge of her nose. "Now will you go?"

"Sure." She smiled. "Of course, I will." She turned and flew across the bank toward the tents. She had spoken without thinking. The words had tumbled out. She knew that there was no way that he could guarantee that he or anyone in this camp would live even another day. Her sister, Jenny, had died. Elena had died. Both of them had been young and with their entire lives before them. Death came, but life should be held close to fight him off.

Maybe by making Jock give her that promise, he would think, remember, when death came too near him.

"Get out of there, Eve," Joe said harshly. "Now!"

"We're packing up. MacDuff is only waiting until he locates a safe house he'll be satisfied with."

"I'll call Burbank and see if he can find one. He's with Scotland Yard and should know the area. It's probably better if you go

383

back to the city anyway. You can get lost there."

"I could get lost here. You haven't seen those mists."

"Stay out of those mists. I told you I —"

"It was just a comment. I'll go where MacDuff tells me to go. Wherever I can keep Cara safe. I just wanted to call and tell you what had happened."

"I'll call MacDuff myself. And I'll get back to you as soon as I talk to Burbank."

"And then what?" she asked. "This is the explosion you thought would come. It's not all about me. What's your next move, Joe?"

"I think you know. I've made some advance plans. I have to get off this phone and get to work. I'll see you soon." He hung up.

She did know, Eve thought, as she hung up. Joe was in battle mode, and he'd be totally ruthless in execution. He had to extricate himself both from Salazar's tail and Toller's before he'd come to her, but he'd said soon, and he meant it.

Don't think of the danger and difficulties that he'd face. Just believe in him.

And concentrate on doing her part to keep Cara safe.

Joe's first call after hanging up from Eve was to Burbank at Scotland Yard. "I've just had word that Salazar is on the move, Burbank. See if you can find out what's happening?"

"I already know," Burbank said. "I've just had an informant tell me. Six men from Maitland's cartel in Liverpool, heading west on Salazar's orders. And not the usual run-of-the mill hired killers. The word is that Salazar requested specialists."

"What kind of specialists?"

"I don't know yet. I'm still checking."

Joe didn't like it. "I need to know, Burbank."

"I'll let you know when I do. I'd give you a destination, but Salazar hasn't told them anything but that he wanted them to rendezvous with him and Franco near Glasgow."

"Keep me informed." He paused. "I may send Eve and Cara to you if you can find a safe haven for them. Possible?"

"Possible. I'll ask around." He hung up.

Okay. Confirmation that Salazar was definitely heading toward the Highlands.

Now he had to get the hell out of here.

He made one more phone call.

Then he left the lake cottage and headed for the airport.

The airport was crowded, but Joe had only carry-on luggage, and he moved effortlessly through security. Then he took the train to the International concourse at Terminal E.

Lomoto, Salazar's man, was at the front of the car.

The tail Toller had assigned him was standing holding on to the iron bar by the sliding doors.

There was a dark amusement at seeing both of them caught on this train with him. If anything would have amused him right now.

He saw the boarding sign above the check-in counter the minute he got off the escalator that led from the train.

Geneva, Switzerland, with continuing service to Rome, Italy.

He checked in at the gate and went over to the window to watch the scurry of activity around the jet on the tarmac below.

His phone rang. Toller.

"Hello, Toller. I've been expecting you."

"What the hell are you doing, Quinn?"

"I thought I'd take a little trip to Switzerland. Does the agent you have following me ski? It would make it so much more pleasant for him."

"What are you up to? You know that there will be an agent waiting when you get off the plane in Geneva."

"And your agent here will make sure I

board this plane. I don't doubt that you're handling my departure with efficiency. By the way, what's his name?"

"Dixon."

"Dixon looks to be a clean-cut young man. Maybe a little too much government-issue. Crew cut, nice suit and tie. Just what I'd expect of you. Much more presentable than that scumbag, Lomoto, who Salazar assigned to me. He's wearing jeans and a red jacket, and I'll bet he's missing the gun he had to give up to get past security."

"What's happening, Quinn?"

"Probably what you thought would happen. But you'll notice I'm obeying your instructions and not even trying to avoid surveillance. I would have even made an attempt to become more compatible with your agent, Dixon, but I didn't want to make Salazar's hit man jealous. Lomoto is looking a bit uptight at the moment. He's obviously not sure whether to try to take me out here or wait for instructions from Salazar."

"You could neutralize the threat by coming in and having a talk with me about Cara Castino."

"Yes, I could do that." He glanced at the boarding desk. "I believe they're starting to call my flight. It was nice talking to you,

Toller." He hung up.

Time to rid himself of Lomoto.

He moved toward the restroom across the hall from the gates.

Lomoto followed only seconds later.

Good. The restroom was unoccupied except for someone in a stall at the far end.

Joe pressed back against the wall beside the entrance.

Waiting.

Not for long.

Joe saw a blur of jeans and red jacket.

He moved!

His arm encircled Lomoto's neck, and he jerked him into the urinal area. His leg swept out and brought him falling to the floor.

One savage and effective blow to the carotid artery.

Lomoto grunted and collapsed.

Joe caught him and dragged him into the nearest stall. He dumped him on the toilet, locked the door, and listened. The toilet flushed from the stall occupied down the long row. The sound of running water. No sound of anyone else's entering the restroom. Joe stepped on the toilet, and then pulled himself over the locked door and jumped to the floor. He had been lucky, any number of things could have gone wrong.

But they hadn't gone wrong, and he had rid himself of Lomoto. Now it was time to rid himself of Toller's man. But this removal would be infinitely more difficult and complex. He straightened his clothes and left the restroom.

Just in time.

Toller's agent had evidently decided not just to monitor but to investigate. He was walking toward the restroom.

Joe smiled and nodded. "Nice of you to be concerned about me. But I wouldn't miss this flight." Then he moved toward the boarding line.

Toller's agent, Dixon, hesitated, then turned back to watch Joe give his boarding pass to the agent.

Joe hadn't thought that he'd go into the restroom and investigate the sudden absence of Lomoto. Dixon didn't give a damn what happened to Salazar's man, he was only worried about keeping Joe in view.

Joe waved at him as he was given back his boarding pass and headed for the jetway door. Joe knew that he would probably stay there, watching, until the plane took off.

Joe moved slowly down the curving jetway. He'd deliberately waited until almost everyone had boarded before he started. He'd counted on the fact that there would be a last-minute scramble, with the flight attendants scurrying around, finding places for carry-on luggage and serving drinks. It would be the best time to make his move.

"You cut it close," Rick Stacy growled as Joe rounded the last turn in the jetway. Stacy's face was almost as green as his baggage handler's uniform, and he nervously moistened his lips. "We've got about five minutes before they shut the baggage doors."

"Then let's get moving." Joe took the green airline jacket that Stacy handed him and put it on. "That should be enough time." He pulled on the matching cap. "You set up the car for me?"

"Yes. Hertz." Stacy opened the jetway door that led down to the tarmac and baggage compartment access. "Just get into the truck and keep low. I'll have you back at the parking lot in ten minutes. When do I get the other half of my money?"

"When I'm sure that you didn't double-cross me. Not that you would, Stacy. I can tell you're a fine, upstanding man." He moved quickly to the truck, opened the passenger door, and jumped in. He glanced up at the windows at the gate. He was on the other side of the plane, and even if Toller's man was watching, he wouldn't be able to see him. But his bet was that Dixon was still watching the boarding gate to make sure Joe didn't come back.

He heard the cargo doors slam, then Stacy was in the truck beside him.

"Down!" Stacy muttered.

Joe slid down in the seat.

A few minutes later, the truck was cruising by the wire-enclosed airline lot that adjoined the regular passenger parking lot.

"Slow down," Joe said. "I'll jump out and hide behind those machines until you get back to baggage."

"My money," Stacy reminded him.

"I'll wire it into your bank account once I'm sure of you. This is just the first step for all of us, Stacy."

But a crucial first step, he thought. Once he got safely away from the Atlanta Airport, he'd drive to Birmingham and board a private jet to Edinburgh.

Seven hours at most and he'd be with Eve.

Hills of Gaelkar

"I want to talk to Eve Duncan, Salazar," Natalie said. "What can it hurt? Just give me ten minutes. She has no way of knowing that I'm involved in the kidnapping. To her, I'd just be a grieving mother as I am to everyone else. I might be able to set a trap for her and Cara. Much better than trying to blunder in and take them."

"Not everyone is fool enough to believe that you're what you pretend to be, Natalie," Salazar said.

"If they don't, they feel so guilty at being heartless that the effect is the same." She turned to Franco. "Don't you think it's a good idea?"

"Maybe," he said cautiously. "I don't know that she would —"

"Never mind." She waved her hand dismissingly. "You're so afraid of offending Salazar that you wouldn't admit I'm right. I forgive you." She stared down at the mist-shrouded lake hundreds of feet below them. "But then I believe we do need an example to show those people we're sincere. Perhaps one of those guards we skirted around when we were climbing up this perfectly exhausting mountain?" She smiled at Franco. "Could you do that for me, Franco?"

"If you want me to." He smiled. "An example . . . I think you're right."

"Franco," Salazar said warningly.

"With your permission . . . sir."

Franco was back in line, Salazar thought sourly, but he was clearly dazzled by Natalie and had been since the moment they had met. And Natalie wasn't above using Franco if it suited her purpose. Hell, she wasn't above using the devil himself. "An example might be beneficial. It might shake them up to realize how easily we can reach out and touch them. Go see what you can do."

"Eve Duncan," Natalie reminded Salazar softly. "Why not see what I can do, too?"

"Joe is on his way," Eve said to MacDuff as she hung up the phone. "He just boarded a flight in Birmingham. He wants me out of here and in a safe house by the time he gets here."

"And what do you want, Eve?"

"I want Cara safe." She gazed out at the lake. It wasn't only the lake that was misty today. The hills were draped, covered, in a suffocatingly heavy fog that was increasing every minute. "And, yes, I want to be safe, too. It's important right now." She looked back at him. "Have you found us a place?"

"Possibly. I'm exploring options. There's a flat in the Old Town section of Edinburgh that should be safe."

"Your men haven't seen anything of Salazar yet?"

"I would have told you." He added grimly, "Or you would have heard it. I guarantee that no one would get near you without our knowing it. Ned Colin is one of my best men, and I told him to call in at least eight or nine men to patrol those hills. There are four men just guarding the camp." He turned away. "I've got one more place to check out near London. We should be able to get you on the road within a couple hours." He frowned. "I hope. The weather forecast says this fog isn't going to lift for hours. If it really socks in, it will be impossible to travel. I'll try to get you moving right away."

And she wasn't helping anything by standing talking to him, Eve thought. She turned and strode back to her tent, where Cara was waiting.

"Joe's on his way," she told her. She glanced around the tent. "Everything seems to be packed up and ready. You've been very efficient."

"There wasn't much to pack. Not like when Elena and I had to move to a different city." She went to stand by the door and looked out at the heavy fog. "It looks . . . strange, doesn't it."

"We're just not used to the entire valley being foggy. Yes, it does look different."

"Could I go outside for a little while? I won't go far. I thought I'd go sit by the fire. I feel . . . closed in."

"Sure. MacDuff says the camp is guarded.

Want company?"

She shook her head. "I don't think so."

Because she was sad and maybe a little scared. Or maybe she wanted to go talk to Jock again. "I'll call you when MacDuff says we have to leave."

She watched Cara disappear into the fog. She wished MacDuff would make a decision so that they could get out of here. She was as on edge as Cara.

It would be better when Joe got here.

Everything would be better when Joe was here.

He had said six hours. It seemed a lifetime right —

Her cell phone rang.

No ID.

She hesitated. "Hello."

"Eve Duncan?" A woman's voice, rushed, broken. "Tell me they didn't lie to me again. You're the one who has my daughter?"

Eve stiffened. "This is Eve Duncan. Who are you?"

"Natalie Castino. You have my Cara?"

Shock jarred through Eve. "I don't know what you're talking about."

"Just tell me that she's safe. That those horrible men haven't hurt her." She was sobbing. "They told me that they killed my Jenny but that Cara is still alive. But that she won't be for very long if I don't do what they say. We've got to save her."

"What men are you talking about?" Eve asked cautiously.

"The people who kidnapped her. I think they have something to do with the leader of one of the rival cartels who hate my husband. But how could they do it? How could they hurt a child?"

The words and tone couldn't have sounded more genuine, Eve thought. If Joe hadn't told her about Natalie's meeting with Salazar, she might have even believed her. What was Natalie trying to do? Play it cautiously. "It's not a question of how, they obviously did kill Jenny. And you obviously have been told that there's a threat to Cara. Suppose you tell me what's happening?"

Natalie drew a shaky breath. "A few days ago, I received a telephone call and was told that my daughter Jenny had been killed and that Cara would also die unless I place four million dollars in an account in the Grand Cayman. My husband thought it was a scam and refused to pay, but my father agreed to transmit the funds if I could get them to prove they had Cara, and she could be safely extracted." Her voice broke. "He meant he thought they might kill her anyway. They sent me a school picture of her in some kind of choir robe . . . She looks like me. But she's so big now . . . My little girl is so big. My father said that photo didn't prove anything except that she'd still been alive sometime this year. He wanted a current photo and to set up a release." She drew a deep breath. "And then they told me that they didn't have her after all, that you'd stolen her away from them."

"If that's true, then you should have been relieved."

"Except they said that they would hunt her down and kill her. They said you'd taken her to Scotland, and they told me to come here and find a way to get them the money. Only they're angry now, and they want more. They said you'd found some kind of treasure or something, and they want that, too. Is that true?"

Eve was silent a moment. "It seems that they're well informed. What would they do if you refuse?"

"They told me it would only be days, maybe hours, before they either took Cara back or shot her. Please don't let them do that." She said in a rush, "My father looked you up, and he doesn't think you're part of this. You're some kind of sculptor or something, and you'd care if my daughter was hurt or killed. I hope he's right."

"Yes, I would care very much."

"Then help me, help us," she said. "I beg of you. You've been told my husband is a terrible man, and I suppose I have to say he can be terrible in many ways. I guess I'm a little bitter toward him because he doesn't seem to love our daughter as much as I do. But Cara shouldn't suffer because of his sins. I've already been forced to lose my Jenny."

So plausible. She was striking all the right notes. "We've been able to keep Cara safe so far. What makes you think we can't continue?"

"Because they hate my husband, and the only thing that would make them stop hunting for Cara is that money."

"And as soon as they had it, they'd kill her anyway."

"Do you think I'm not afraid of that? That's why I'm calling you. I want you to make a deal with Salazar. Tell him that you'll turn Cara over to my father if he gives him the money. Maybe give him that other treasure thing, too. My father will send a helicopter to pick her up with two of his most trusted men."

"And you?"

"Of course. I can't wait to see her. Did

you know in a few days it will be her birth-day?"

"No, I didn't."

"It's been so many years since I've been able to think of that day without tears. Has she ever spoken about me?"

"She doesn't remember much about you. All she remembers is her sister and her nurse, Elena."

"I guess I can't expect anything else. But I'm still bitter about the fact that Elena never brought her back to me."

"Bitter? She died saving Cara."

"And I'm grateful, but she should have known I'd have found a way to protect all of them." She paused. "But I have my chance now. I can save my Cara. If you'll help me. Will you do that?"

What to answer? Eve's mind was zooming, careening, as she tried to come up with the right thing to say. "I'm not certain if throwing my lot in with you is the right thing to do. One of the reasons that we took Cara away from the authorities in San Diego was that we didn't want to put her in a situation where she'd be sent back to Mexico to face danger from all sides. I'm still not sure that wouldn't happen. You say you love Cara, but you weren't able to prevent her kidnapping. How can you assure me that it wouldn't happen again?"

"Because my father would be involved. He loved his granddaughters. He wouldn't let anything happen to Cara now that he knows there is a danger."

Eve was silent. "Just what are you suggesting?"

"I contact Salazar and tell him that you've agreed to bring Cara to meet the helicopter my father will send with the ransom money. It will be your responsibility to get her to the helicopter safely, but once there, my father's men will take over. He'll whisk her away and you, too, if you wish. I understand that you've made yourself a target by interfering with Salazar."

"You could say that," she said dryly. "And we all fly away and live happily ever after?"

"Live is the key word," Natalie said quietly. "I've learned to value those words in the past eight years. Will I permit you to interfere with my relationship with my daughter once she's safe? I don't promise you that. What mother would give up her child because an outsider thinks she knows better than she does how to raise her? You'll have to do battle to get her back from me."

"I don't have to do battle, I still have Cara. The choice is mine."

"But you won't let her die, if you can help

400

it. I can tell that you care about her . . . just as I do." She rattled off a phone number. "You'll make the right choice. Call me when you do." She hung up.

Natalie Castino was a force to be reckoned with, Eve thought as she slowly hung up. She had gone through that conversation, pressing all the buttons, changing tone, altering character, as she went along.

If she was a killer, then she was an exceptionally clever one. If she was a grieving mother, fighting to keep her daughter alive, then she might have come up with a plan to do it. Yet Joe thought that she had helped Salazar to take the girls, and he was seldom wrong.

Still, they had no concrete proof of her involvement . . . except for the fact that Jenny had been buried in that white eyelet dress instead of her nightclothes. No sign that Natalie had been involved in MacTavish's death. All those tears, the sobs, the agony, might be real, but in the end, Eve would have to make her own decision.

And that decision would not only concern Cara and her but everyone in this camp.

She got to her feet and left the tent and was immediately assaulted by waves of fog. She could dimly see Cara's hazy figure sitting by the fire with Jock. What would she say if Eve told her that she'd just spoken to her mother?

She wasn't ready to find out. She turned and headed for Jane's tent.

"Did she believe you?" Salazar asked Natalie, as she hung up from talking to Eve Duncan. "I told you it was a waste of time. You should have stayed out of it."

"It wasn't a waste of time." Natalie smiled. "I was plausible. I gave her something to think about. If you do your part and frighten her enough, she might run right toward me."

"Toward us."

"That's what I meant, of course."

"Of course. You mentioned that treasure MacDuff's supposed to be hunting."

"I just wanted to get a feel for her take on that chest. She didn't laugh or ridicule the idea. MacTavish might have had it right." She glanced at Franco. "You were very clever to dig that out of him."

Franco nodded and smiled.

"A waste of time," Salazar repeated.

"We'll see. I certainly wouldn't want to do that. I don't want to spend any more time than necessary in these hills with those rather odorous men you've imported." She glanced around the camp, then at the man tied and gagged across the fire from them.

He was staring at her pleadingly. His face was bloody, and so was his throat. Franco had been playing with him after he'd captured him a few hours ago. She looked away from him and shrugged. "You gave me my chance. By all means, let me see what you can do, Salazar." She got to her feet. "In the meantime, I'll call my father and tell him how upset I am that I haven't heard any more about ransom for my Cara."

"You made two calls last night."

"How suspicious you are. One to my father, one to my husband. My father to reinforce the myth, my husband to tell him how much I missed him and that I couldn't wait to get home to him. One must always follow through with a lie and not let it just dangle in the wind." She tilted her head. "But you knew that, didn't you? You checked my phone after I went to sleep. One call to Moscow. One call to Mexico City. You just wanted to know why." She added softly, "You don't trust me, Salazar?"

"I'm not a fool. Our relationship is not based on trust."

She threw back her head and laughed. "True." She sauntered away from the fire. "It's based on getting my sweet daughter back to me. And perhaps acquiring a few other gifts along the way."

CHAPTER 13

"You don't actually think Natalie Castino is genuine?" Jane asked quietly.

"No, but I'm trying to be unbiased," Eve said. "We don't know enough about her. Most of it is hearsay, and who knows what a mother would do to find her child."

"You're in a very vulnerable state where that concept is concerned," Jane said. "You might not be thinking straight." She shook her head. "It could be a trap."

"That was my first thought." Eve grimaced. "I tend to trust Joe's judgment more than I do Natalie Castino's motherly love. But if it is a trap, can we turn it against them? I'm supposed to call her if I decide to help her whisk Cara away into the loving arms of her grandfather. There has to be some way we can use that."

"But we'd need help. You have to tell MacDuff, Eve."

She nodded. "I know that. I just wanted

to talk it out and get it straight in my head before I brought him into the picture. MacDuff can be overwhelming once he makes up his mind."

"Tell me about it," Jane said dryly. "But that doesn't alter the fact that he's the best game in town and certainly the one with the most cards he can play. Do you want me to talk to him?"

"No, I'll do it." Eve gave her a hug. "I have to check on whether he's located a safe house yet and whether we can travel in this fog. My guess is a big negative. And I'm getting more and more nervous about having Cara out in this wilderness." She moved toward the door. "I'll get back to you."

Jane followed her and watched until she disappeared into MacDuff's tent. She stood outside surrounded by the fog, which didn't appear to have abated at all. Then she turned to stare out at the lake.

The beginning or the end.

Today the lake appeared much more ominous than the day she had first seen it.

"You're very tense. It's not all that bad."

She turned to see Seth Caleb coming toward her and automatically stiffened. "I have a right to be tense. I have more at stake than you do, Caleb." She was suddenly aware of something different, charged, electric, about him. Not so different. She had seen him like this before when there was a threat, but it always disturbed her. "Or perhaps you haven't heard that Salazar is on the move. You haven't been around very much lately."

"I was merely being sensitive to your feelings." He was smiling recklessly as he came closer to her. "You were pedaling backward at top speed the last time I saw you, and I thought I'd allow you time to regroup. And I knew about Salazar at the same time you did. Perhaps a little earlier."

"Earlier?"

"I feel things sometimes. A sort of primal instinct. And we all know how primitive I can be."

"And how much you enjoy it."

"I can't help it," he said simply. "And I won't lie to you. If you expected me to stay close to the home fires and circle the wagon train, that wasn't going to happen. It's not how I operate. I took off for those hills and started hunting."

She went still. "And did you find anything?"

"Maybe. I didn't locate Salazar's camp. They're probably moving it every three or four hours. But there are only a couple ways they could cause us problems, and perhaps they won't think of them. And I have the lay of the land now. I know where I'd strike."

"I don't want them to strike at all. I want Eve and Cara out of here."

"So do I." His lips twisted. "They'll get in my way. Plus robbing the situation of any hint of fun. After all, I promised Eve I'd take care of her, and responsibility tends to be exceptionally boring."

"How unfortunate," Jane said. "No one asked you to take responsibility, Caleb. Eve is my responsibility." She turned to go back into her tent. "And when she leaves here, I'm going with her."

"Which means I'll have to tag along." He shrugged. "But I'll try to make it interesting as well as worthwhile. In the meantime, I'll go back to those hills and see if I can discover anything else of importance."

Jane suddenly whirled on him. "Why," she asked fiercely. "Do you just like to take risks? You've already found out what you wanted to know. Those bastards could be out there just waiting for a chance to —" She broke off. Why ask when she knew the answers? "Do what you wish. What do I care if you want to behave like a self-indulgent child?"

"But you do care," he said softly, his gaze on her face. "Why, Jane? You try so hard not to give a damn about me, but it just keeps coming back, doesn't it? Why do you suppose that happens?"

Her hands clenched into fists at her sides. "I'll get over it."

"Oh, no, I can't allow that to come to pass." He smiled. "I've worked too hard. Every time we come together, I get a step closer. I get to know you a little better."

"And I don't really know you at all, Caleb."

His smile faded. "True. I've been very careful about that, but I might have to relinquish a bit of who I am to make you feel safer."

"And would I feel safer?"

"I don't know. It would be a risk." The brilliance of his smile came back full force. "But then I like risks. You might learn to like them, too." He turned and started back toward the path to the hills. "But not when it concerns your Eve." He looked back over his shoulder at her, and she was again aware of that charged electricity, the suppressed excitement that was just below the surface. Dear God, she was beginning to feel that same reckless disturbance she saw in him, she realized. She wanted to follow him into that mist. She wanted to find the thrill of danger and adventure she could sense in him.

And he could see it. "Never Eve," he repeated. "Never anyone you care about and protect. No risks there, I promise."

And then he was gone.

But who was going to protect Caleb? Who had ever protected him?

Just another thing that she didn't know about Seth Caleb.

And why was it hurting her to realize that he could have been vulnerable and in pain, and she would not have been able to help him?

Forget Caleb.

Go back into the tent. Finish packing, then go find Eve.

And keep all risk away from her and Cara and the child.

2:40 P.M.
Southern Atlantic Charter Flight 1257
Somewhere over the Atlantic Ocean

Three more hours, Joe told himself as he checked his watch. He'd land in Edinburgh in another two hours and catch a helicopter to Gaelkar.

Three more hours.

It was too long. He felt caught, helpless, in this plane above the Atlantic. He couldn't get to her.

His phone rang, and he glanced at the ID. Manez.

"I trust that you're winging your way across the Atlantic even as we speak," Manez said when Joe answered. "You caused something of an uproar, you know. Toller was most upset that you slipped away from his agent. He didn't find out that you weren't on that plane until he managed to get a head count from the flight attendants right before the flight reached Geneva."

"And how did you know?"

"I've been keeping my eye on you . . . and on Toller. Things are becoming . . . interesting. I assume you're finding it necessary to go and rescue your Eve. Salazar is on the move?"

"He's found out where Eve and Cara are."

"A very determined man. But Toller is also determined. He wants no interference. If he finds out where you are, he'll have you arrested, Quinn."

"Do you think I don't know that?" He paused. "And are you going to tell him where I'm headed?"

"I really should, in deference to international cooperation."

"Are you going to do it?"

"I don't actually know where you're going, do I? Of course you mentioned Scotland, but you were careful not to pin down a location." He was silent a moment. "And I don't like the way Toller is handling this. As I told you, he's not involving me in his investigations into Jenny Castino's death. This is my city. No one knows more about the cartel bosses than I do, including Castino. My conclusion was that Toller wanted to remain in control and manipulate events to suit himself. That made me very curious, so I decided to dig very hard into Toller's sources to discover who had given the tip that Jenny was Castino's daughter."

"And you found out?"

"It wasn't Sheriff Nalchek or anyone in his office."

"I didn't believe it was Nalchek."

"But you weren't sure that it wasn't one of his men. A reasonable conclusion. I looked there first."

"And where else did you look?"

"In places that weren't at all reasonable. I found an agent in Toller's department who was a bit careless, and I have excellent hackers on my team. Would you like to know who tipped Toller?"

"Stop playing games, Manez."

"I don't play games. But Toller may think he's going to do so," he said grimly. "But the U.S. government can stay out of my business." He paused. "James Walsh tipped off Toller that the body in the grave was Jenny Castino's."

"What?" His hand tightened in shock on the phone. "No way. Walsh killed Jenny. He wouldn't have done that."

"Unless he was trying to protect his ass if he thought Salazar was getting impatient and might try to take him out. Maybe he was trying to make a deal." Manez added, "I've seen stranger things happen. It's dog eat dog in the cartels down here. And there have been a lot of rumbles on the street lately. Something is going to happen. I can smell it."

"Look, there's no way I can concentrate on Toller or his plans that might be upsetting you right now. I owe you, and I'll get around to it once Eve and Cara are safe. Later, Manez."

"I'm not asking for help. I can handle my own problems. I just thought you should know that not everything is what it seems." He paused. "And that you probably have only five or six more hours before Toller manages to track you down. He's working hard, and he's very clever. Not as clever as I am, but he doesn't know that. Or he wouldn't have made the mistake of trying

412

to ignore me. Good luck, Quinn." He hung up.

He might need good luck, Joe thought grimly. And he knew damn well that often nothing was as it seemed. But the information about Walsh had stunned him. But, as he'd told Manez, he couldn't think about anything right now but getting to Eve and finding a way to get rid of Salazar and Franco once and for all.

Three more hours.

4:45 P.M.
Loch Gaelkar

"We leave for Edinburgh in thirty minutes, Eve." MacDuff had suddenly appeared at the entrance of her tent, and his voice was curt. "Get ready."

Eve scrambled to her feet. "I thought we were waiting for the fog to lift. You said we couldn't even drive through this muck."

"We'll manage somehow. We can't wait any longer. I just got a report from Caleb, and it wasn't good. He saw signs of Salazar's force and activity in the hills. I don't like the idea of having you and Cara stranded out here when we don't know exactly where Salazar is located."

"We could find out." Caleb was suddenly standing beside them. "We know he's out

413

there in the hills, and he's not alone. He's moving fast, and I'd say he has at least nine or ten men with him. Hard to tell in this fog. You'd better warn your guards that they may be outmatched." He smiled. "Want to go hunting, MacDuff?"

"It appears you've already gone hunting," MacDuff said dryly. "And I'm not going to do anything until I get Eve and Cara safe. I checked with weather, and the fog is lighter in the valley beyond Gaelkar. It's about seven miles, and we can hike there, and I'll have a helicopter meet us. Where's Cara?"

"At the campfire with Jock. Where else? I'll go get her." Jane left the tent and hurried toward the campfire.

"We all go. I promised Eve," Caleb said quietly. "Though I'd prefer to take Salazar's goons down ourselves. Between Jock and me, I believe we'd have a good chance. And you're not too bad either, MacDuff."

"I'm flattered," MacDuff said dryly. "But I believe I'll call in Ned Colin and a few more of my men to accompany us until we get out of this fog. Not that I'd want to insult your —"

A shot shattered the words!

"What the hell!" MacDuff pushed Eve down to the ground and turned off the lantern.

Caleb was already out of the tent and zigzagging toward the campfire.

But Jock had already knocked Cara down and covered her with his body.

Another shot.

And a scream!

"Stay here." MacDuff was on his feet but crouching low as he ran out of the tent.

Eve rolled over and crawled toward the door. Let that scream not be Cara, she prayed. It had not sounded like a child, but it had been high-pitched.

Rat-a-tat-tat.

A rapid spate of bullets.

Another scream.

Not close. Somewhere in that gray mass of fog ahead.

She started to crawl across the ground toward the campfire. She caught up with MacDuff a moment later and rose to her feet.

"I told you to stay in the tent," MacDuff said, not looking at her. "You don't pay any more attention to orders than Jane." His gaze was raking the terrain. "Damn this fog." He took out his phone. "Don't worry, I'll call Colin and tell him to get down here."

Don't worry? "Do you see Cara or Jane?"

He was dialing rapidly. "Safe. Jock got them away from the fire and into those shrubs by the lake." He listened. "No answer. That's not good. I don't —"

"MacDuff?" The voice on the phone was so clear that Eve could hear it. "Alfredo Salazar. I'm afraid your man, Colin, is indisposed. Is Eve Duncan close by? I really need to talk to both of you."

MacDuff turned up the speaker. "I want to talk to Colin. What did you do to him?"

"I needed an example, and Franco ran across a prime candidate. He didn't want to cooperate, but we managed to convince him. Franco is very talented in that area. Are you listening, Eve Duncan? All of this is really for you and that annoying child."

"I'm listening."

"That's good. Then I can tell you that everything that happens from now on is on your head. Every scream, every death, is because you're here and causing me trouble. Do you hear that, MacDuff? All of this could end if you'd turn her and the kid over to us."

"Go to hell."

"Whatever you say," Salazar said. "And you Eve? You appear to be such a gentle person. Do you want to see MacDuff and your other friends die? And what about Jane MacGuire? You've managed to draw them all into something that wasn't your business in the first place."

"I'd be a fool to think that you'd let anyone live if I let Cara go to you," Eve said. "You'd never permit a witness to escape, Salazar."

"I might. If the price was high enough to make it worth my while. I understand that you and your friends might be able to pull something out of MacDuff's lake that would tempt me. Make me an offer."

"I'm not a fool."

"Oh well, first things first. Back to the example, MacDuff. We're taking your guard, Colin, to a place in the forest several hundred yards from your camp. He's still alive, but very frightened. Come and get him." He hung up.

Another shot.

An agonized groan from the depths of the fog.

"It's a trap," Eve said. "You won't be able to see them. They'll pick you off."

"I can't leave Colin out there," MacDuff said. "Salazar won't be able to see us either. I'll get Jock and Caleb to scout the area ahead, and I'll go in and get Colin. Go and stay with Cara and Jane. I'll call in the perimeter guards to protect you."

Before she could speak he was gone.

One more hour.

Joe strode across the tarmac toward the waiting helicopter. Providing he could get to Gaelkar in this pea soup of a fog, he thought bitterly. The weather forecast said that the fog wouldn't lift for that area for another eight to ten hours. Definitely not flying weather.

Screw it. He'd get there somehow. But first he'd check to see if MacDuff had managed to move Eve and Cara into a safe house here in Edinburgh.

His phone rang. Burbank. He'd asked Burbank to check on safe houses, too.

He accessed the call. "What's happening, Burbank?"

"Nothing," Burbank said. "Everything's at a standstill. We have a bit of a fog."

"So I've noticed. Why did you call?"

"You asked me to check on the specialities of the men Salazar hired from the Maitland Cartel. You seemed to think it important."

"It might be."

"Four of them are Afghani nationals and trained by the Taliban. Expert at explosives and setting *IEDs.*"

"Shit!"

"I take it you do think that it's important."

"I should have guessed. Franco has a fondness for bombs, and he'd gravitate in that direction." And in this fog, you wouldn't be able to see a booby trap even if it wasn't set by an expert. "Thanks, Burbank." He hung up and called Eve.

She didn't answer.

He tried again.

She answered on the third ring. "Joe? I can't talk now. Things are bad. Salazar has shown up, and he's hurt one of MacDuff's men. MacDuff has gone after —"

"IEDs," he interrupted. "Tell MacDuff to be careful of IEDs. Salazar has imported some experts."

"I'll go and tell —"

She'd hung up.

He tried to get her back.

No answer.

And it scared him to death. The last thing he'd wanted was to have Eve running around in that fog after what he'd just found out.

He had to get to her.

He ran for the helicopter.

Eve was dialing MacDuff even as she ran toward the direction she'd seen him take.

No answer.

She hadn't expected one.

He wouldn't take time out to answer a phone when he was trying to save the man Salazar had shot.

Jock.

She dialed his number.

He answered. "Not a good time, Eve."

"IEDs. Joe said to be careful of IEDs. Tell MacDuff."

Jock muttered a curse. "No sign of anything yet. Caleb and I have been scouting all around, and I see MacDuff up ahead. And Salazar didn't move Colin to this area until after we heard the shots. We may only have to worry about snipers."

"Is that all?" Eve asked shakily. "That's enough. But Joe said that Salazar brought in some Taliban specialists they could be using. It might be —"

"Taliban?" Jock's voice was sharp. "Shit. No IEDs. That's not what they're doing. I was sent to one of their training camps, and they'd go another route. Hang up. I've got to get through to MacDuff. *Hell. No time.* I'll go after him. He should be getting near to Colin." He didn't bother to hang up, and she could tell he was running. He shouted, "MacDuff! Stop! Now! MacDuff! Get away from —"

Kaboom.

The earth shook, throwing Eve to the ground.

The thick fog ahead was lit by flames.

An explosion, she realized dazedly. Jock was wrong. There had been an IED . . .

She lifted herself on her elbow.

Or maybe not, she realized in horror.

MacDuff!

She jumped to her feet and ran toward the fire.

She had only gone several yards when Caleb appeared beside her. "No." He grabbed her arm. "You don't want to go there."

"Salazar strapped explosives to Colin's body, didn't he?" she asked shakily. "*He* was the trap."

"Yes, that way they didn't have to stay close and risk being attacked by MacDuff's men. They just pressed a button when their infrared showed MacDuff was close to the body."

"Dear God." Eve felt sick. She tried to shake off Caleb's hand. "Let me go."

Caleb's grip tightened. "No way. We can't be sure that Salazar didn't stash a sniper in those trees just in case he might get lucky if one of the targets showed. Go back to the camp."

"The hell I will. I have to get to MacDuff."

"No, you don't."

Her gaze suddenly flew to Caleb's face. "What do you mean? Is he dead?"

"I don't know. The blast got him, but I don't know how bad. Jock was examining him when I got there. He told me to secure the area and make sure you were all protected."

"Maybe I can help him."

"Not now. I promised you, I promised Jane, I promised Jock. You stay alive. No one touches you. I don't want to hurt you, but I will. We go back to camp."

He meant it.

"Then hurt me," she said fiercely. "Because I won't leave MacDuff without —"

"You don't have to leave him." Jock was coming out of the fog carrying MacDuff's limp figure. MacDuff was a strong, tall man, but Jock seemed no more aware of his weight than if he were a child. "I'm bringing him back to camp."

"Is he —"

"Dead? No, but I don't know if I can keep him alive. I don't know what's wrong with him yet." His eyes were glittering with unshed tears. He seemed to be in shock, the agony twisting his features was stunning to see. "I probably shouldn't have moved him, but I couldn't leave him there."

"No, of course not," Eve said gently. "Get

him back to camp, and we'll take care of him."

"I will. They made a mistake hurting him. He's my friend, almost my brother. It was a bad mistake." He started toward the camp, then turned to look over his shoulder at Caleb. "There was someone in the trees when I got to MacDuff. He had a sniper rifle. After I was sure MacDuff wasn't dead, I decided I had time to take care of him. I broke him, but I didn't kill him. I thought that you might be able to get information out of him that might help."

"I'll do that."

"You don't have to hurry. I like the idea of his hurting." His tone was completely without expression. "If he doesn't talk, just leave him. He has to die anyway. They all have to die."

He disappeared into the fog.

Caleb gave a low whistle. "I believe Jock may be right. Salazar made a very bad mistake."

Eve called Joe the moment they got MacDuff back to his tent and settled.

"Thank God," he said when he heard her voice. "Are you safe?"

"I have no idea. Salazar is out there somewhere, and he's just blown up one of

MacDuff's men. MacDuff was hit by the blast, and we still don't know if he's going to live. But right now I guess we're as safe as we can be. Salazar is trying threats and intimidation rather than going into attack mode."

"That sounds like attack mode to me," Joe said grimly.

"Where are you?"

"On my way. But I won't be able to land anywhere near Gaelkar. You're still fogged in. Can you get out?"

"I don't want to leave MacDuff, and I have no idea —" A call waiting buzzed on her cell. She stiffened as she looked down at the ID. "I'd better take this call. It's Salazar." She put Joe on hold and accessed the call. "You failed, Salazar. I know you'll be disappointed. You didn't kill MacDuff."

"I'm not sure I believe you. He must have been very close, or Franco would never have pressed the button to blow up Colin. It was a pity you didn't see it, Duncan. His remains were scattered all over the clearing."

"You're a monster."

"He wasn't important. MacDuff *was* important. Aren't you tempted to give yourself and that kid up and save anyone else you care about from being blown up? You're trapped, you know. If you try to go through the hills, we'll be on the lookout and catch you. If you try to take that road to escape, you'll end up like Colin."

"You're bluffing."

"Am I?" He spoke to someone over his shoulder, then was back on the phone. "Look up at the road. On the count of three. One. Two." He paused, then said softly, "Three."

A shot.

And an explosion at the side of the road at the top of the hill!

"Trapped," Salazar repeated. "IEDs. Think about saving the people who tried to save you." He hung up.

She drew a deep breath as she gazed at the fire burning the grass at the side of the road. Then she went back to Joe's call. "I guess we got an answer. No, we can't get out. Salazar has planted IEDs on the road that leads out of Gaelkar."

Joe muttered a curse. "How much time do you have before Salazar makes a move?"

She tried to think. "I have Jock. I have Caleb. I still have MacDuff's men who are in the hills. But I don't want to bring all of them here to make them sitting ducks. I'd rather they stay in the hills and be a constant threat to Salazar. I think maybe the reason Salazar hasn't come after us yet is that he doesn't have enough men to make it completely safe."

"Then I have to clear that road fast," Joe said. "I'll take the helicopter as close as I can, then hike the rest of the way. I'll be there as soon as I can."

"Joe . . ."

"Can you think of any other way?"

"No." But she didn't want Joe to have to fight to disarm those IEDs when it was impossible to see anything more than a couple feet in front of him. She felt sick at the very thought. "Damn this fog."

"Don't be too eager to condemn it. It may turn out to be a good friend to us." His voice was suddenly rough with feeling. "You take care of yourself. I'll call you when I get close to the lake."

"How is he, Jock?" Jane whispered as she came into MacDuff's tent two hours later. "Has he regained consciousness yet?"

Jock shook his head. "Not yet. He has a broken left forearm and at least two broken ribs. I don't how much internal damage. Blasts can —" He stopped. "It can be bad. I might have hurt him myself by moving him."

"You couldn't do anything else. He was helpless. You had to get him to safety, or those bastards might have decided to strap explosives on him, too."

"That wouldn't have happened. I wouldn't have left him." He gently touched MacDuff's temple. "He never left me. No matter what I did, he fought for me. I remember when I was in that mental hospital because I kept trying to commit suicide, he found me and he took me home. He was there for me until I healed." He shook his head. "No, I never really healed, but he was there until I was strong enough to face what I'd done and live with it."

"It wasn't you who did it," Jane said. "You were a victim. You were just a boy, not even twenty years old, and those brainwashing chemicals they fed you made you helpless to think. You had no idea what you were doing. How many times do MacDuff and I have to tell you that?"

"I was a victim? That bastard, Reilly, proudly counted my kills at over twenty-two. All executed perfectly. I was an assassin par excellence. What about those victims?"

"MacDuff wouldn't like to hear you talk like that."

"And I don't, when he's around. I keep it inside so that he won't feel that he's failed me in any way." His lips twisted. "He hasn't failed me, Jane. You haven't failed me. But I have to work my way through this hell, and no one else can help me at this point." He looked back at MacDuff. "I love him, you know. There's nothing I wouldn't do for him. I'd die for him. Every bit of sanity and humanity I have left, I owe to him."

"No, that's not true. You were born with a soul, and, somehow, you were robbed and hurt. Even if MacDuff hadn't been there, I think that, somehow, you would have survived."

"We disagree." He smiled without mirth. "Right now, I'm leaning toward the thought that without MacDuff, my soul would have vanished in a puff of smoke. So I have to keep him alive, don't I?"

"Will you trust me to sit with him?" Jane asked. "I'll call you the minute he stirs."

He shook his head. "I trust you, Jane. But what if he doesn't stir? I have the foolish idea that if he starts to fade away from me, I might be able to bring him back."

"That's not such a foolish idea." She cleared her throat to rid it of tightness. She had felt like that when her Trevor had been dying. It had seemed impossible that he could leave her when she had wanted so badly for him to stay. "I'll be outside. Call me, if you need me, okay?"

"Okay." His gaze shifted back to MacDuff.

"Thank you, Jane."

She stood there, looking helplessly at him for an instant, then left the tent.

She didn't move for a moment, trying to rid herself of this feeling of discouragement and sadness. She had known MacDuff for years and Jock for almost as long. They were part of her past, part of her life, and she couldn't bear the thought of what was happening to them. There had to be something she could do.

"Is he still alive?"

She looked to her right and saw Cara sitting on the ground, leaning against the tent, her legs crossed, her face shimmering pale in the fog. "What are you doing here? I thought you were with Eve."

"She knows I'm here. She said it was okay. She wouldn't tell me, but I don't think she wanted to bother about me right now. She's worried about Joe." She paused. "Is the Laird still alive?"

"Yes."

"But Jock thinks he might die."

"How did you know that?"

"I saw his face when he carried him into the tent. It . . . hurt me."

"And you've been sitting out here ever since?"

"You were with Jock. He didn't need me."

"Well, evidently he didn't need me either." She wearily rubbed the back of her neck. "He told me to go about my business."

"Then is it all right if I go in and sit with him?"

"It's not the time, Cara. He won't want you either."

"May I try?"

Jane gazed at her. What could she say? The strain she saw on Cara's face was almost an echo of Jock's. "He might say things you won't want to hear. He's in pain."

"I know." Her lips were trembling. "And it's my fault."

Jane looked at her, shocked. "No!"

Cara nodded. "Salazar and Franco wouldn't have come here except for me. The Laird wouldn't have been hurt. Jock wouldn't have lost . . . It's my fault."

"Nonsense." She tried to make her voice firm. "It's Salazar and Franco who did all this. MacDuff and Jock had a choice. Eve had a choice. I had a choice. Sometimes you just have to fight the bad guys when you run across them. It's the way the world works. None of this was your fault, Cara."

She didn't speak for a moment. "May I go in to Jock?"

Jane wasn't sure she had gotten through to her, but she didn't want Cara sitting out here by herself. "I guess. I'll be in my tent or Eve's if you need me."

Cara nodded, and the next moment, she was on her feet and running into MacDuff's tent.

Jane shook her head and turned to go to find Eve, who was probably in just as much pain as the two people she had just left.

"What are you doing here?" Jock asked Cara, without looking away from MacDuff. "This is no place for you. You shouldn't be here, Cara."

"Yes, I should." She came closer to his camp chair and sat down on the floor at his feet. "I have to stay with you."

He shook his head. "Why? Do you want to see him die? That's what might happen. Go away."

"No. You need me."

"I don't need anyone." He looked away from MacDuff and down at her. "You're just a kid. Why should I need you?"

"I don't know. But you said some things . . . I think you do." She moistened her lips. "And I have to be here if you do."

"You were upset. I wanted to make you feel better."

"And you want to make me feel better now. You don't want me to be here if the

Laird dies." She paused. "But I remember what you said when you told me you had to go to the Laird after he heard that MacTavish had been killed. You knew he needed you. If only to keep him company, or be someone to drink with to say good-bye to an old friend." She tried to smile. "I can be company, Jock. If you want, I'll even drink to the Laird if he doesn't make it. But I'd rather pray that he does."

He looked at her for a long moment. "I'd rather you pray, too," he said gruffly. "Eve would have my head if I contributed to the delinquency of a minor."

"I can stay?"

"God, yes." He closed his eyes for an instant, then opened them and looked back at MacDuff. "Maybe I do need you." His hand touched her head at his knee for the briefest instant. "Stranger things have happened in my life. Just don't blame me if things don't go the way we'd like them."

"You're not the one to blame," she whispered. "I tried to tell Jane that but she wouldn't —" She stopped. She had gotten what she wanted, and he would probably argue as Jane had done. None of them understood. Jenny and Elena dead. Salazar hovering over them, ready to pounce. "I'll be quiet now. You won't want me to talk."

She leaned her head back against his chair. "Thank you for letting me be with you, Jock . . ."

CHAPTER 14

"Joe?" Eve leaped for her cell when it rang. She had been on pins and needles worrying about him for the past three hours. "Where are you?"

"I've reached a point on the road that's two miles east of the lake where I've just located and removed two IEDs. I'll have to take it very slowly from now on. It appears as if these two were planted very hurriedly and hopefully so will the others. They'll be a lot easier to disarm. But hurry breeds carelessness. I can't let my guard down." He paused. "Is either Jock or Caleb available? I haven't seen any sign yet of Salazar's men, but I could use another set of eyes and ears to watch my back."

"I'll check it out. I'll find someone."

"Tell them to stop on the slope and avoid the edge of the road and call me when they get close. I'll guide them to a safe access where I've already removed the IEDs."

"Right. Be careful, Joe." She hung up and drew a deep breath. Her heart was beating rapidly, and her palms were damp. She ran out of the tent to look up the long, steep slope that led to the road. She could see nothing, of course, but she knew that Joe was somewhere in that thick gray fog. The knowledge was filling her with hope and joy and a terrible fear.

Because he was alone and needed help.

She ran to Jane's tent. "Joe's here. He could use some help clearing the road. Where's Caleb?"

"He's scouting the perimeter with three of MacDuff's men." She reached for her phone. "I'll call him."

"Wait." She tried to think. MacDuff was down and perhaps dying. Jock's care might be the only barrier between MacDuff and death. Caleb was the only protection Cara and Jane had, and he might be forced to extend that protection to MacDuff. She couldn't let that protection be taken away from them. "Call Caleb. Tell him once he's finished to come back and stay on guard here until we get those IEDs cleared."

"We?" Jane repeated. She shook her head. "I don't like the sound of that, Eve."

"Neither do I. But we're stretched too thin. Joe needs help."

"Then let me go."

Eve shook her head. "Joe and I are a team. Sometimes he doesn't recognize that fact, but I'm not going to let him do that job alone. It's not as if I have to have a particular set of skills. I just have to do what Joe tells me to do. I watched him change the settings on that damn bomb Franco planted in our car, and I hated every minute of it. I won't let him push me out of the way now." She grabbed her flashlight and gun. "You'll keep Cara safe?"

"Of course, I will. But since she won't leave Jock, I may not have the opportunity for much interaction."

"Jock is more than enough protection. I'll be back as soon as I can, and we'll get the hell out of here." She gave Jane a quick hug and tore up the hill toward the road.

"Colin . . ."

The word was so weak that Cara barely heard it.

But she knew Jock had heard it because his entire body had stiffened, galvanized. He leaned toward MacDuff. "Don't talk. You've been —"

"Colin," MacDuff said, his voice stronger. "What happened to Colin?"

"Dead. The bastard strapped a bomb to him."

"Son of a bitch," MacDuff said. "Did you . . . get them?"

"Not yet. I've been busy."

"Just as well. I want to do it myself . . ."

"You might have to wait a bit. How do you feel?"

"Sore." He thought about it. "A bad headache. The blast?"

"Yes. You have a couple broken bones. I don't know about internal injuries. We need to get you to a doctor to check you out."

"I'll be fine." His glance fell on Cara. "What are you . . . doing here?"

"Praying." She smiled. "Jock said I shouldn't be allowed to drink with him. I'm glad you're back with us, sir."

"So am I. I guess that nonsense is supposed . . . to mean something. But I'm too tired to decode it at the moment." He closed his eyes. "Is everything okay, Jock? We can get out of here?"

"Everything is okay," Jock said. "We've got it under control. Quinn will be here any minute. We've just been waiting for you to come around so that we can start moving. But you can take a nap until we're ready."

"That sounds a little . . . condescending." His eyes were closing. "I'll have a word to say to you later . . ."

"You do that." Jock swallowed hard. "Later."

A moment later, Jock sat back in his chair as MacDuff's breathing steadied, then deepened.

"He's safe?" Cara whispered.

"I believe so. We'll have to see." He smiled down at her, that radiant smile that lit up his entire face. "He's complaining and trying to order me about. That's a good sign."

"Is it?" she asked eagerly. She was so happy to see that smile. "But he'll be angry when he wakes up and finds you've lied to him."

"Maybe when he wakes up, it won't be a lie." He reached down and helped her to her feet. "Now go and tell Jane that MacDuff has regained consciousness and everything that's happened. She'll want to know and come to check him out for herself."

Cara nodded. "I'll go right away." She flew toward the door. "I'll be right back."

"I know you will. You're very determined, Cara. And what a blessed quality that can be." He added gently, "Sometimes a mixed blessing, but in you it's pure gold."

Joe had said to call before she left the slope

to go on the road, Eve thought. Well, he hadn't actually been referring to her, but she was here, and he'd have to deal with it. With the fog still as thick as it was, the fact that she had come instead of Caleb should be the least of his worries. Not that he would look at it that way.

She dialed Joe's number. "I'm on the slope about one yard down and closest to the west approach to the road. Can you get me safely on the road?"

Silence. "Eve?" Then he was swearing. "Get the hell back down to that camp."

"Get me safely on the road," she repeated. "You needed someone to watch your back. I've been doing that job for years. Things are dicey down there at the camp. I'm the only one really available."

"Then I can do it alone. All I wanted was —"

"Someone to keep anyone from shooting you while you concentrated on disarming those IEDs. I can watch. I can shoot. And no one cares more than I do that you come out of this alive."

"Eve, for God's sake, you're going to have a baby. If you won't be careful of yourself, think of the child."

"Do you think that I'm not thinking of my baby? I haven't been thinking of anything else since I started up here." Her voice was shaking. "No, that's not true. I was also thinking about you. I was thinking that you have to live. My child needs a father, and it has to be you. Because you'll always be there, you'll always protect and keep our baby safe. Just as you're going to do in the next couple hours. You'll keep us all safe. Because that's what you do." She started to move up the slope. "I'm coming, Joe. Tell me where to go, where to step."

Silence. "Hang up the damn phone. You're so close I can hear you without it." He drew a harsh breath. "I think you're about ten feet to the left from me. I haven't had a chance to disarm that far on the road yet." He repeated. "Ten feet, Eve. Count those feet aloud to me so I can track your voice."

"One. Two. Three. Four." She was moving slowly, trying to be precise. How could she be exact when she could barely see where she was going? And how had Joe managed to disarm any of those explosives? He must have had to be painstakingly careful. No wonder he'd needed someone else to keep watch for Salazar's men when he'd had to concentrate on just keeping from being blown up. "Five. Six. Seven." She could smell the burned grass on the side of the road from the explosion Salazar had ignited to show her how helpless they all were. Screw you, Salazar. Joe wasn't helpless, and neither was she. They'd get through this. "Eight. Nine —"

"That's far enough." Joe was suddenly in front of her, grabbing her wrist and jerking her up on the road. "Keep still for a minute. Get your balance. This isn't time for a misstep." He held her close, burying his face in her hair. "Damn you, Eve," he said hoarsely. "You shouldn't have done —"

"Hush." She held him closer. She could feel his heart pounding against her, the scent of him, the warmth of him. "And you shouldn't swear at me when you're so scared I'm going to die. Think how you'd regret it if I did." Then she pushed him away. She had needed that moment. But they needed to get off this road more than she needed comfort. "Now let's get to it." She took a step back away from him. "You said no sign of Salazar's men up here yet?"

"No, but that doesn't mean he won't send a man up to check to make sure that someone isn't trying to destroy his booby traps. And that's why I can't just explode the IEDs. I had to have Burbank send one of his men to meet my helicopter with a military Stingray water-blade device so I could scramble the IEDs' firepower."

Eve nodded. "Whatever. I don't know what the hell you're talking about. But Salazar's more likely to think that he has us cowed down at the camp. He has to know that he injured MacDuff and that Caleb has been scouting the hill area. He doesn't know about you. He believes he has us all contained. His focus will probably be on attack and conquer." She looked down the road. "And does he have us contained? Do you have any idea how far these explosives are planted on the road?"

"I'd have to have a crystal ball to know that. All I can do is try to clear enough of the road to make it safe for us to get two vehicles up from your base camp and safely on the way out of the Gaelkar area. We'll need at least two since MacDuff is injured." His lips twisted. "And it's not going very quickly, Eve. It might take at least another couple hours."

"I can see how it might."

"Of course, we could wait for the fog to lift and just take the fight to Salazar. But I'd rather get you, Jane, and Cara out of here and somewhere safe. I'll be as fast as I can."

"As fast as it's safe," she corrected. "No hurry." She tried to smile. "Take your time. You have a great backup."

"Yes, I do." He turned away. "Keep behind

me and close. If I say jump, you don't question, you dive for the side of the road and roll down the slope. Promise me."

"I promise. What else?"

"Primarily, I need you to listen since you can't see a damn thing."

"How can you see the IEDs?"

"Very carefully." He took out a LED penlight. "I shaded the beam, and I'm focusing only on the ground and also blocking the light with my body. Hopefully, the fog is doing the rest."

"You said we might be grateful to this fog."

"At the moment. Up to now, it's been a royal pain in the ass."

He was crouching low, his gaze fixed intently on the ground, moving with extreme care. He was on task, fully focused on the job ahead.

Do your part, Eve told herself.

Keep close.

Listen, he had said.

Concentrate on everything around them so that Joe would not be forced to do it.

Listen . . .

"MacDuff's awake!" Cara burst into Jane's tent, her eyes shining with excitement. "Just now. He woke up and spoke to Jock. Well, me, too. But I think I just confused him,

443

but he knew me, and he —"

"Slow down." Jane jumped to her feet. "What are you trying to tell me." She hoped it was what she thought Cara was trying to say. "MacDuff is better?"

"That's what I said." Cara drew a deep breath. "He woke up, and he spoke to Jock. He asked about Colin, and when Jock told him that he was dead, he asked if Jock had taken care of Salazar. He said he was glad Jock hadn't had the time because he wanted to do it himself."

"That sounds like MacDuff," Jane said. "He *is* better."

"Jock thinks he's going to be okay." Cara's face was glowing. "But then he fell asleep again, and Jock told me to run and get you. He told me to tell you everything. He said he knew that you'd want to come and see for yourself."

"Yes, I do." She felt as if an enormous burden had been lifted. MacDuff was going to live. "I'll go right away."

"I'll go with you." Cara was heading for the door. Then she stopped. "No, I'll go to Eve's tent and tell her. She'll want to know."

Jane suddenly remembered that Cara wasn't aware that Eve had gone to help Joe. She wasn't about to worry her about another potential danger when she was so happy about MacDuff. "No, come back with me. Joe showed up while you were with Jock, and Eve's helping him find a way to get us out of here."

"Joe's here?" Cara smiled eagerly. "Everything's going right, isn't it, Jane?"

"It appears to be on the right path." She took Cara's arm. "Come on, let's get back to Jock."

They were out in the dark, and the fog closed in on them once more.

It was only when they were almost to MacDuff's tent that a thought occurred to Jane that caused a chill to go through her that had nothing to do with the fog.

She hesitated, almost stopped.

No. It didn't have to be true.

"Jane?"

Cara had caught the hesitation and was staring at her.

"Coming." Jane started forward again.

The next moment they were in MacDuff's tent.

"I brought her, Jock," Cara said. "You were right, she wants to see MacDuff for —" She stopped.

Jock was not in the tent.

MacDuff was sleeping peacefully on the cot, but Jock was nowhere in sight.

"Where's Jock?" Cara whispered.

It's what Jane wanted to know. But she didn't want to alarm Cara. "Maybe he needed to take a break. He's been cooped up in here since he brought MacDuff back. He'll probably be back in a minute."

"Jane." MacDuff's eyes were open. "All hell is breaking loose. You need to get Eve and the girl out of here."

"Shh." She went to him and took his hand. "We're working on it. Joe is here. That will be a big help. You just relax and let us handle it." She smiled. "This one time the Laird isn't going to give the orders."

"Then God help us." His eyes started to close again. "Maybe you should take over. After all, you're family. Cira might decide to give you a hand. It's not beyond the . . ." He was asleep again.

And Jane's hand tightened on his for a moment before she released it. God had already helped them, she thought gratefully. MacDuff was back with them. Like Jock, she was sure that he would be all right now.

Jock.

The chill returned as she turned away from MacDuff. "I think I'll go to Jock's tent and see what's keeping him, Cara. Will you stay with MacDuff while I'm —"

Cara was gone.

Panic.

"Shit!"

Jane ran out of the tent.

Fog. Darkness. Fear.

"Cara!"

Smother the panic. Maybe she'd gone to Jock's tent to look for him.

She ran down the row of tents.

Jock's tent was dark.

No Jock.

No Cara.

Jane's heart was beating hard, painfully.

But there was a note scrawled on a piece of paper pinned to the canvas beside the door.

It won't take long, Jane.

"Damn, damn, damn." She dialed Jock.

No answer.

She took a deep breath and phoned Caleb. "I need you to come back to the camp right away. Things are happening, and I need help."

"I'm already on my way," Caleb said. "Jock called me and told me that. I should be there soon."

"Jock called you? When?"

"About ten minutes ago. He said MacDuff was better but that you were going to need me."

"He must have called you right after he sent Cara to get me." Her hand tightened on the phone. "I was so damn happy about MacDuff that it didn't occur to me right away. Why would he have to send her to get me? Why not just phone me and tell me to come."

"He wanted to get rid of her." Caleb asked, "He's gone, Jane?"

"You're not surprised. Did he tell you?"

"No, but I knew it was bound to happen. Jock would have gone for Salazar after he found MacDuff if he hadn't had to try to save him. He cares about MacDuff. He wasn't going to let anyone who hurt him live. When he called to tell me that you'd need me, I thought that he judged it was time." He paused. "I wouldn't worry about him. From what I've heard about Jock, it's Salazar who should worry."

"I do worry about him. I know very well what Jock is capable of. Do you think I want him to start killing again?" Her voice was shaking. "And what about Cara? I suppose I shouldn't worry about her either?"

"Cara?"

"I turned away for a moment to talk to MacDuff, and she was gone. I'm sure she went after Jock. She's out there in the darkness and the fog looking for him. Hell, she wants to take *care* of him."

"We'll find her."

"Before Salazar finds her? Before Franco finds her?"

"I'll call Jock and tell him to locate her and bring her back."

"I tried. He's not answering. He obviously doesn't want anyone to interfere with what he's going to do. Which means Cara can't reach him either. She's alone out there."

"She won't be alone long. As soon as I assign some men to taking care of you and MacDuff, I'll start tracking her."

"I'm going with you. You assign men you can trust to care for MacDuff. I'm not going sit here and twiddle my thumbs while Cara is out there."

"I can travel faster without you."

"No, you can't. I'll do whatever I have to do. I promised Eve when she went to help Joe that I wouldn't let anything happen to Cara. I *promised* her. I'm not going to break that promise."

"Okay, calm down. We'll make it work. We already have a start."

"What start?"

"Jock took down a sniper on the scene where Colin was blown up. He told me he broke him but didn't kill him. He sent me to get information from him while he tended to MacDuff."

"You didn't tell me that."

"It wasn't pleasant, and what I did to get that information wasn't pleasant either. I didn't want to shock your delicate sensibilities."

"But you got the information? Will it help?"

"It will help." He hung up.

He was close, Jock thought as he moved silently through the forest. He could hear Salazar's men up ahead. No conversation, just breathing, and the sound of footsteps on the wet leaves. Salazar had probably told them to be quiet, so that the team Caleb had patrolling the perimeter wouldn't spot them.

But they were amateurs, Jock thought. Even Salazar and Franco would have been disposed of in a matter of moments if they'd been designated as prey by Reilly, the man who had trained Jock all those years ago.

He increased his pace. Get it over with. He didn't know how many men Salazar had stationed around their camp. He might have to get back and help Caleb take them out.

He stopped and listened. At least six men moving single file through the forest.

Single file. That would make it easier.

Remove them one by one until he got to the head of the column.

And hope it was Salazar.

No, not six men. One stride was lighter, shorter-spanned, the rhythm different. Boots, but not like the others.

A woman.

Natalie Castino?

It didn't matter. It wasn't as if he hadn't killed women before. And, according to what Quinn had told Eve, this woman might have tried to kill Cara.

So just block out the ingrained hesitance and concentrate on being the assassin that Reilly had created. It would be no problem. He could feel the past training slipping effortlessly into place.

No joy. There had never been joy. Just a steel-like intensity and determination that was focused on the prey.

No, there was something more that was involved. Because this was not the usual prey.

Revenge.

"Done."

Joe turned to face Eve. "We've cleared enough of the road for the cars. Let's get the hell out of here."

Eve breathed a sigh of relief. It hadn't taken as long as she'd thought it would for Joe to disarm those IEDs, but every minute that had passed had been excruciating. "I'll second the motion." She looked down at the lake, and she could see a faint watery outline in the darkness. "And it appears to be just in time. Some of the fog is dispersing. It was going to be easier for them to see what we were doing soon."

"But we'll be able to see his men if they try to plant any more explosives, too." He took her arm, led her across the road to the slope, then carefully helped her start down the slippery incline. "Now let's get down to the camp and get you all packed and out of here."

"We've already packed up most of it. It's MacDuff we have to worry about. Lord, I hope we have to worry about him." She took out her phone and dialed Jane. "When I left, I wasn't sure if he was going to make it. I know Jane knew what we're doing and wouldn't have called and disturbed me, but I have to check on —" She broke off as Jane picked up. "Jane, we're through up here. Joe got the job done. We're coming down."

"Thank God," Jane said. "At least, that's one thing that's positive."

Eve stiffened. "MacDuff?"

"No, he's doing better. Which freed up Jock to go hunting." She paused. "And for Cara to get it into her head to follow him."

"What?"

"I know. I'm as afraid as you are. Caleb and I are searching the forest for Cara now. We haven't found any sign of her yet. We've just got to hope that Cara finds Jock before anyone else finds her."

"Yes," Eve said numbly. "We've got to hope. Joe and I will start searching as soon as we get down. We'll split up the territory." She hung up and told Joe, "Cara's gone. She followed Jock when he went after Salazar."

Joe muttered a curse. "Why in hell would she —"

"We both know why she'd do it," Eve said. "She's had too many people die trying to keep her alive. She can't help but blame herself. She cares about Jock. She couldn't bear the idea of not going with him, helping him, if he was going to be in danger." She started at a half run down the slope, slipping and sliding, catching herself. "We've got to find her, Joe. There has to be some way . . ."

Jock twisted hard, and the man's neck snapped.

His knees buckled and Jock lowered him carefully to the ground.

Three down.

Four men to go.

And the woman.

She was clumsier than the men, and occasionally someone in the party would try to steady her, help her.

Everything was going smoothly.

He'd soon have them all.

His phone was vibrating again. He'd been ignoring it since he left the camp. It was a rule that you never answered a call when you were on a mission. Particularly this mission. Too many people he cared about would be trying to interfere.

He prepared to ignore it again. He moved down the path, making no sound, listening. There was a curve up ahead. He could detect the swish of bodies on the shrubs as they took the turn. If Jock cut left into the trees, he should be able to bring down the next prey before he made that turn.

He moved swiftly into the trees.

His phone vibrated again.

Ignore it, as he'd done since the hunt began. He should have turned it off. But he couldn't do it while MacDuff was lying in that tent injured.

It vibrated again.

He impatiently glanced down at the screen.

A text.

I CAN'T FIND YOU. I'M ON THE HILL NEAREST THE LAKE. WHY DON'T YOU ANSWER ME? YOU SHOULDN'T HAVE GONE. WHERE ARE YOU, JOCK?

Oh, my God.

Cara.

He was standing in the woods on the hill nearest the lake at this moment.

And he'd just killed three of Salazar's men on this hill.

Don't call her. Don't make a sound that would draw anyone's attention to her. His fingers flew over the keys.

PUT YOUR PHONE ON VIBRATE. DON'T MOVE. STAY WHERE YOU ARE.

I AM ON VIBRATE. IT WOULD BE PRETTY STUPID NOT TO BE. JUST AS YOU'RE STUPID TO HAVE TRIED TO FOOL ME. I TRUSTED YOU. NOW YOU COME BACK WITH ME. YOU'RE NOT GOING TO BE HURT. I WON'T LET THAT HAPPEN. IF YOU DON'T CARE WHAT I THINK, DO IT FOR MACDUFF. NEVER MIND, HE PROBABLY LIKES THE IDEA OF EVERYBODY'S KILLING EACH OTHER, TOO. IT'S NOT WORTH IT. DO YOU HEAR ME? IT'S NOT WORTH IT. NOW WHERE CAN I FIND YOU?

CARA, WHY ON EARTH DID YOU FOLLOW ME?

YOU WERE ALONE. I DIDN'T WANT YOU TO BE
ALONE.

Such a simple answer. An answer that had
led her to risk everything. Dear God, an
answer that he should have known would
be triggered when he'd left MacDuff's tent
tonight.

WHERE ARE YOU ON THE HILL? ARE THERE
ANY LANDMARKS? WHAT DO YOU SEE?

FOG. THOUGH IT'S NOT NEARLY AS BAD AS IT
WAS BEFORE. JUST TREES. LOTS OF TREES.

No help at all.

CARA, LISTEN TO ME. STOP LOOKING FOR
ME. FIND A PLACE WITH SOME COVER AND
HIDE. I'M NOT SURE HOW CLOSE SALAZAR IS
TO YOU.

WHERE ARE YOU?

CLOSE. STOP LOOKING FOR ME. TRUST ME.
I'LL COME TO YOU RIGHT AWAY. WAIT FOR
ME.

Silence.

I'LL WAIT FOR YOU.

Thank God. He had bought some time. But now he had to move fast and try to neutralize any threats to her. He could no longer hear Salazar and his men. They had passed out of his range while he was texting Cara. He dashed off a text to Caleb.

CARA. ON THE FIRST HILL NEXT TO THE LAKE.

He stuffed his phone in his pocket and took off through the woods in the direction he'd last tracked Salazar's men.

Find a place with cover and hide, Jock had said.

Cara had no idea where that would be, she thought desperately. As she had told Jock, there was no cover, no boulders. Just a few shrubs along the path. Well, then use what there was available. She scavenged around and found a few large branches on the ground, then dragged them deeper into the woods and tried to rig a barrier among the shrubs.

Hide.

She started to move behind her barrier.

She stopped.

A sound.

A footstep.

Jock?

Don't take a chance.

She had to take care of Jock.

Her fingers were flying over the keys.

STAY —

It was the only word she had time to type before the phone was knocked out of her hand.

Then an arm was around her neck, cutting off her breath.

"How nice to see you again, Cara." Ramon Franco's voice in her ear was the last thing she heard before a cloth was rammed over her mouth and nose. "I've been looking forward to this. You've been making me look very, very bad."

Chloroform.

Darkness.

STAY —

Jock gazed blindly down at the phone he'd just picked up from the ground where Cara had dropped it. Her phone and the single word that was tearing him apart.

A warning. Even at that moment when Cara knew she might be caught, lost, she was trying to save him. If she hadn't taken the time to type in that word, could she have saved herself?

He didn't know, he couldn't think. All he could do was look at that word.

She was the target. How long would they let her live? Maybe they'd killed her already. Maybe he'd find her body within yards of this barrier she'd built.

Agony. So deep, so sharp, that he couldn't bear it.

He had to bear it. Because there was a chance. He couldn't let that chance vanish.

STAY —

Block it. Look at the scene. Look at the footprints that usually told the story.

He knelt on the ground and examined the prints of the man who had taken Cara. Concentrate. Tell yourself she's alive. Don't give up and fall apart.

STAY —

"They've got her," Jock said jerkily as he handed Eve Cara's phone over an hour later, when Eve and Joe met with him in the woods. "I found this on the ground in the woods. She was trying to text me a warning, but she didn't get the chance."

When had Cara ever had a chance, Eve thought numbly as she gazed down at the one word on the screen. "You didn't find her body?"

"No. I don't think they've killed her yet. It was a single man who captured her. Not Salazar. This man was smaller, lighter. Probably Ramon Franco. And his footprints were heavier when he left the scene than when he came. He was carrying something heavy enough to be Cara." He handed her a white towel. "And this was tossed into the shrubs where I found the phone."

Joe took the towel and sniffed it. "Chloroform."

"Which means we have a chance to negotiate," Jock said. "They took her captive, but she's not dead." His lips thinned. "She's not going to be dead. Stall. I'll get her back."

"We'll get her back," Joe said quietly. "But we may not have much time. The intent was always to kill Cara and remove the evidence of who had taken her from Castino. Like Eve, I expected to find only her body if Salazar got his hands on her. Unless they wanted to dispose of it as they tried to do with Jenny's body."

"Of course, that's what they'd want to do." Eve shivered. "And they have a deep

460

lake and all of these hills to hide her." How could they be standing here talking about Cara's death? All she could think about was Cara's laugh, her wistful eyes, her absorbed, intent, expression when she was playing her violin.

And that's all she would think about, because she wouldn't accept that they could lose her.

Okay, then try to find a different outcome. There had to be some way. Her mind began racing frantically, weighing options, trying to recall her contacts with Salazar . . . and Natalie Castino.

Joe's gaze was fixed on her face. "Eve, she's alive. We have hope."

He probably thought she was in shock, she thought. He was only half-right. "They could have had another reason for not killing Cara right away. They want me, too. They believe I know too much. Maybe they want to find a way to get hold of us both."

"You mean use Cara as bait to trap you?" Jock asked.

"It's possible. And we might be able to turn it around to close the trap on them." Her lips tightened. "Or I'd be content just to get Cara out of their hands. No, I'd be ecstatic."

"No bait," Joe said flatly. "We'll try something else."

"We'll try whatever we think might work." Eve looked him in the eye. "Remember when we talked about a division of labor about keeping Cara safe? You stayed behind and worked behind the scenes to find out what was going on and put up a smoke screen. My job was to stay with Cara and keep her safe. You did your job. I didn't do mine. I didn't watch her close enough. Well, it's time I made that right."

"It was my fault," Jock said hoarsely. "I didn't think. I was just feeling, or I would have known what Cara would do."

"And it was Cara's fault for running after you because she was afraid that you'd be killed like her Jenny, like Elena," Eve said. "We can blame ourselves all night, and it's not going to bring her back. We have to stop it and get to work."

"You may be wrong," Joe said. "If we wait until Salazar puts out bait instead of going after him, Cara could be killed."

"No, we can't wait." She had a sudden thought. "But maybe we don't go to Salazar. Maybe we go around him."

"Around him?" Joe repeated. "What do you mean?"

"Natalie Castino. I told you about the fairy story she was handing me when she called me."

"She was trying to trap you."

"I don't doubt that for a minute. But she was wonderfully plausible, and I had to question my own instincts at the time. She's clever, and I'm sure she plays everyone around her as skillfully as Cara does her violin." She paused. "You got the impression that she was in control of everything she did. Was she in control of Salazar?"

"Possibly."

"Probably. She'd made the effort to keep him as a lover for all those years. But she wouldn't let him know that he was dispensable unless she was prepared to jettison him." She turned to Jock. "When you called us and told us to come here, you said that you'd been tracking Salazar's men. Was Natalie Castino with them?"

"There was a woman with them. I assumed that it was her. I never saw her."

"Then her story was definitely bogus. We have to work from there." She was thinking frantically, going over her conversation with Natalie sentence by sentence. "What are her priorities? She wants to be safe. She likes power and wants to maintain it. She doesn't want to be under her father's thumb or her husband's or Salazar's, but she's capable of using all of them. She wants to be queen

463

and will do anything to —" She stopped. "But a queen needs a crown and a treasury, doesn't she? That may be the bait we need to tempt her."

"Treasury," Joe repeated. "As in treasure?"

She nodded. "She mentioned the treasure while she was talking to me. She asked if we'd found it yet. And Salazar said something about the possibility of a deal later. There was definitely an interest from both of them in Cira's gold."

"Then maybe we should deal with Salazar if he wants it, too," Joe said.

"You have nothing with which to deal," Jock said. "We haven't found it yet, dammit."

"But we know where it might be," Eve said. "If I have to, I'll use that to strike a deal."

"Salazar is desperate," Joe said. "He's not going to risk Cara's being found and talking about his arranging for that kidnapping on the chance that there might be a big payoff. He'll take the safe road."

And the safe road was to kill Cara. Eve knew he was right, and she was desperate herself, or she wouldn't be considering taking the risk. "Then we deal with Natalie Castino. She's not desperate. I'm sure she wants Cara dead to protect herself, but if you could have heard her talking to me, you'd realize that she thinks she rules the world. Why not? She's convinced everyone that she had nothing to do with her daughter's disappearance for the past eight years. She has a superb self-confidence. She'll think she can deal and get the best of me and have it all. We just have to make sure that she's wrong."

"What can I do?" Jock asked. A muscle in his cheek jerked as he bared his teeth from tension. "I have to *do* something. I'm not thinking very well right now. Tell me how to help. Tell me how to get her back."

"Any way you look at it, we have to remove Salazar's men and try to leave him defenseless," Joe said. "From what you said, you were on your way to doing that before you found out about Cara. But we can't risk making him edgy until we're sure we have a way to get Cara. We'll just plan and set up, then execute when she's safe." He added, "You found Salazar once. Can you find him again?"

"I'll find him," he said grimly.

"Cara will probably be with them. You'll want to step in and take her," Joe said. "Don't do it. Don't take the chance."

Jock was silent.

"Don't do it, Jock," Eve said. "Just let us

know and keep watch over her."

He finally said, "I'll keep watch." He added, "And you won't have many men to take out by that time. But I don't promise anything." He turned to leave. "I'll let you know when I find them. It will be very soon."

Eve watched him walk away. She could almost feel his pain, which was making him as volatile as the IEDs Joe had disarmed tonight.

But nothing was going to disarm Jock but seeing Cara alive and free.

"I don't promise either," Joe said roughly. "I don't like any of this, and if I could see any other way, I'd take it. But I'm not going to let you sacrifice yourself to save Cara. That's not an option."

"Then let's hope that Natalie Castino can be persuaded that she can have it all." Eve turned to go back to the campsite. "I'm going to check with Jane about MacDuff, then I'm going to call Natalie. Time's running out."

He nodded curtly. "I'll get with Caleb, and we'll begin to throw together a plan." He strode away from her. "I meant what I said, Eve."

He always meant what he said, Eve thought wearily. But particularly when it came to her safety. She'd already stretched him to the limit tonight up on that road.

But sometimes there were no limits. Not when a child was concerned.

Jane.

She dialed her quickly. "Salazar has Cara. But she's alive. Franco, or whoever took her, used chloroform. We're moving to get her back."

"Oh, my God."

"We *will* get her back, Jane."

"How?"

"We have a few ideas. Where arc you?"

"Right now I'm back at camp with MacDuff. I started thinking while I was searching for Cara about how vulnerable MacDuff is right now with only a couple guards to watch over him. Salazar wanted him dead. Who's to say he won't try again? Cara has you and everyone else looking for her, and I couldn't let MacDuff be pushed aside." She added, "So I told Caleb to go on without me, and I came back. That's what he wanted anyway." She paused, then said with frustration, "Though I admit it's driving me crazy. I want to be out there with the rest of you."

"I know how you feel. But you're right, MacDuff was hurt because he was trying to help us. He deserves all the care we can give him. How is he?"

"I think he's better. I can't be sure. He goes in and out. But when he comes around, he's pure MacDuff." She added brusquely, "But we have to get him to a hospital. I was thinking of loading him into a vehicle and using that road that Joe cleared of explosives earlier to get him away from here. But it would be pretty bumpy, and I'd run the risk of running off the road."

"Very risky."

"The fog is lifting. It's worse in the valleys than anywhere else. I called an air ambulance, and they said they'd try to get to us as soon as possible, but they weren't sure when that would be." She added dryly, "Needless to say, I told them not to land on that road."

"And you're probably not going to have to worry about Salazar's men interfering with them if they land in the camp," Eve said. "I guarantee that they're going to be kept very busy in the next few hours. I have to go, Jane. Take care of MacDuff."

"That's why I'm here," she said. "You didn't tell me what ideas you have to get Cara back."

"There are a couple brewing."

"And you don't intend to tell me." She paused. "You think it would scare me or worry me. You're right, that's the name of the game right now. I'm feeling helpless. I want to be with you. But I can't, so all I can do is tell you to be careful and remember that I can't do without you. Now, go do whatever you have to do." She hung up.

Eve drew a deep breath, then did what she had to do. She dialed the number Natalie Castino had given her.

Would she even answer?

If she didn't, there was little hope that they could keep Cara alive.

One ring.

Two.

Three.

Then Natalie Castino picked up the call. "Eve Duncan? I can't tell you how glad I am that you called me back. I was so afraid that you wouldn't. You've decided to help me?"

Her tone held the same heartbreaking agony that it had the first time she'd called Eve. She was still playing the same role she'd assumed before. Poor victimized mother just trying to get her child returned to her. It seemed incredible that Natalie would still think that ploy would work.

But in order to get anywhere with the woman, Eve would have to jar her out of that role. "I was hoping that we might be able to help each other. But that can't happen unless you're honest with me, Natalie. There is no ransom, is there? It's all a hoax. You and Salazar were in together on the kidnapping of the girls."

Silence. "How can you say that? I wouldn't harm my own daughters."

"I don't expect you to confess. You're entirely too clever to incriminate yourself on the phone. I just want you to know that I'm aware of who and what you are. Though God knows I don't understand how you could do it. Jenny and Cara were extraordinary human beings and very lovable."

"Who would know that better than me, Eve?" Natalie said gently. "That's why I'm trying to save my Cara. If I'm not mistaken, I believe that you're trying to do the same thing. Why else did you call me?"

"Not to play your old game. I want to offer you a new one that would have advantages to both of us. Are you with Salazar now?"

"How did you guess? He forced me to come to meet him. He thought I might be useful in negotiating the ransom. I had no choice."

No agony. Her voice was smooth and almost without expression. She was not going to say anything incriminating but she was clearly willing to talk around the subject.

"Can he hear you now?"

"No, I demanded some privacy."

"He has Cara. I want her back."

Silence. "But I'd know if he had her, wouldn't I?"

"I believe you do know. She was chloroformed and taken to Salazar. He's going to kill her if you don't step in."

"I don't know what you're talking about."

"I'm talking about your daughter. I'm talking about death. I'm talking about your saving her."

"Everyone knows I'd do anything to save her." She paused. "Are you begging me, Eve? You don't have to beg me. Just tell me about this new game you wanted to offer me. The one you said might help all of us."

"Cira's treasure. It's a game centuries old, and that makes it all the more precious. MacTavish told Franco that some of those coins in the chest are priceless, but I'm sure an enterprising woman like you would be able to find a buyer. I've heard you like power, and money like that could put the world at your feet."

"And you're offering to give me this treasure?"

"I'm offering a trade."

471

"You've . . . found this chest?"

Make it sound totally convincing. "Yes."

"And you'll give it to me for Cara?"

"I will."

"Why? She's just a child. She can't be of any value to you."

For the first time, Eve realized exactly what she was dealing with in Natalie Castino. That question was asked with complete sincerity. Cara had no value for Natalie, and, therefore, she couldn't see any value in her for anyone else. Natalie was clearly a complete sociopath. And, therefore, it would be difficult for Eve to explain her affection for Natalie's daughter and make her believe it. "I've never cared anything about the treasure. But I don't want Salazar to get what he wants. He's caused me a good deal of trouble. Not to mention that he's tried to kill me."

"You're foolish not to want the treasure. But I can understand how you'd want to get back at Salazar."

Yes, Natalie could identify with anyone not giving her what she wanted. "So you'll deal with me?"

"How can I? I don't have Cara."

Eve smothered her exasperation. It was clear Natalie would never do anything to incriminate herself unless she knew she was perfectly safe. Eve could see how she had been able to deceive everyone about her innocence all these years.

"If you had Cara, would you deal? Hypothetically?"

"I do like money. It might be an answer for many troubles in my life. And, of course, I'd always want my dear child safe. But Salazar is a very dangerous man, and he might kill me if I got in his way. It's a very difficult situation."

"Give me an answer."

"And you might spread lies about my part in these negotiations for my daughter."

"You don't think you can handle my 'lies'?"

"Oh, I could handle them. It would just be a bother."

"Give me an answer."

Silence. "When would I get this treasure?"

"You get Salazar to release Cara, and I'll take you to where we hid it on the lake."

"That's not exactly . . . safe for me."

"That's the only way we can handle it. Your child is not that important to me. I might decide I want the treasure after all. Take it or leave it."

Another silence. "Naturally, I'll do everything possible to save my daughter. But you've got to keep Salazar from hurting me.

I'll call you and tell you when and where to come." She hung up.

It was done.

Eve drew a relieved breath as she hung up. It had been both harder and easier than she had anticipated. It was difficult trying to understand Natalie's thinking and make her believe that Eve was on the same page. It had been easier than she thought to make Natalie go for the deal itself. But Natalie was clever, and there might be all kinds of hidden agendas in her acceptance.

But the deal had been struck. Now all she had to do was tell Joe.

And to sit and wait for Natalie's call.

"She wanted a deal?" Salazar asked when Natalie hung up. "You look very pleased with yourself."

"I am very pleased with myself. They have the treasure and want to trade for Cara." She glanced at the girl slumped unconscious on the ground by a tree. "She may prove very valuable in more ways than the obvious." She smiled at him. "Unfortunately, you weren't included in the deal. Eve Duncan wants me to persuade you not to kill Cara, then set her free. Do you think I'm that persuasive, Salazar?"

"You made the deal?"

"It seemed the thing to do. We get Eve Duncan and the treasure. We already have Cara. A win-win situation." She glanced at Franco. "You've already come through for us by finding Cara. Do you think you can get Eve Duncan to tell us about the location of the treasure?"

"It won't be a problem. Women break easier than men."

"How very sexist. You just haven't been exposed to the right women, has he, Salazar?"

"When are you going to call her back?" Salazar asked. "I want this over. I've lost three men tonight. MacDuff's people must be better than we thought."

"I'll give it an hour. I want to make her sweat." She tilted her head. "Though she might not. I believe I'm beginning to have respect for Eve Duncan. How very strange. I don't remember ever respecting another woman before." She shrugged. "Oh, well, I'll still make her wait. I have to keep my word . . ."

CHAPTER 15

"I've located Salazar's camp," Jock said when he called Eve and Joe thirty minutes later. "Salazar's here, and so is Franco. Cara is still alive. They're keeping her knocked out. Every time she rouses, someone is there with that damn chloroform." He paused. "And that damn bitch just sits and watches them do it."

"How many men does Salazar have in that camp?" Joe asked.

"Including Franco, six." He paused. "Caleb and I could take them down."

"Not without a risk to Cara," Eve said. "You know that Jock."

Silence. "I know that. It's the only reason I'm calling you and not doing it."

"Because it's the right thing to do." She added, "But they're probably all going to be on the move soon. If you can unobtrusively eliminate a few of them on the trail, it would help."

"Oh, I can do that." He paused. "That woman in the camp, the one who's laughing and talking and letting them drug Cara. She's Cara's mother?"

"Yes, Natalie Castino."

"Can she be one of the ones I take down?"

"No, we need her."

"I don't need her. Cara doesn't need her." He added harshly, "Okay, okay. Maybe later." He hung up.

"He appears to be upset with our Natalie," Joe murmured. "Let's hope she survives to show up at our meeting."

"She will. Jock's not going to do anything to jeopardize Cara. This is very difficult for him."

"It's difficult for all of us," Joe said. "And I'm not blaming Jock for wanting to rid us of Natalie. I'm feeling the same way right now."

"She's keeping Cara alive. That's all that's important. Look, he'll take out a few of Salazar's men on the trail. You can set up an ambush once we find out where Natalie is arranging the meeting. We agreed that was the best way."

"But not the only way. That way involves you in the middle of the action."

"Joe."

"I'm being honest with you. If I see

another solution, I'm taking it." He turned and walked away from her.

"Six A.M. Three hours from now. The top of that craggy hillside that you can see from the lake. You show up alone and unarmed," Natalie Castino said when Eve picked up the phone an hour later. "I wasn't able to talk Salazar into releasing Cara, but I can guarantee we'll be there. I can guarantee that she'll be alive. After that, it's up to you. But I'll expect you to keep your part of our agreement regardless."

"You want Cira's gold."

"It will help. I'm a woman who has to make her way in a man's world," she said softly. "If I'd have been in control, I might never have lost my girls. I'm sure you can understand, Eve."

"Perfectly."

"I thought you would. We have some differences, but we're alike in many things."

God forbid, Eve thought. "You mean, we both want our own way."

"Exactly. I'll see you at six, Eve." She hung up.

"Alone and unarmed," Joe repeated. "She'd have to be crazy to expect you to go along with that."

"She doesn't expect me to go along with

it. You heard her. She said it was up to me." She smiled without mirth. "Or up to you, Joe. You have a little over three hours. Work it out."

He was already heading to the clearing where he could look up at the hill. There was still a light fog wreathing the slopes that plunged toward the lake, but the rising sun was shining weakly through the clouds to light the craggy, sparsely vegetated glade near the top. "It will be hard as hell to stage an ambush up there." He tilted his head thoughtfully. "Unless . . ." He was silent for a moment. "Why not? He's supplied us with everything we need . . ." He took out his phone. "I've got to call Jock back. I have something for him to do."

Joe was already thinking, planning, analyzing, Eve realized. She just hoped he'd come up with something that was relatively risk-free.

Risk-free? There was nothing that was going to be without risk in the next few hours.

She could only hope that they'd all survive.

Eve and Joe didn't start out for the meeting with Natalie and Salazar until over two hours later. It took them close to an hour's climb before they reached the final ap-

479

proach to the glade where they were to meet them.

"You know what to do." Joe's voice was sharp with tension. "Don't deviate, Eve. I may not be able to avert at the last minute."

"You make this sound like a SEAL raid," she said. "I have every intention of following your orders, Joe. But I can't guarantee I won't have to 'deviate.' "

"I know." He stopped. "I can't go any farther with you. Jock says Salazar has planted sentries in those trees up ahead. Jock and Caleb should be somewhere up there, too. But they're in place. I can't chance being spotted and endangering you. When you go into those woods, you have to appear totally alone." He looked at her, his hands clenching. "You don't have to do this, dammit."

"I know I don't. But I have to do what I can to save her." She said quietly, "I left Cara with Jane when I went up to the road to help you. I don't know if it would have made any difference if I'd been there with her when she got so upset when Jock left to go after Salazar. I might not ever know. But I chose you, Joe. This time I have to choose Cara."

"Change your mind. We can find another plan to —"

"Too late." She gave him a quick kiss and started down the trail. "That would be deviating." Don't look back. She didn't want to see him standing there, or she'd want to run back to him. Just concentrate on what lay ahead.

And hope that Natalie's greed was greater than her obsession for protecting herself.

Because if it wasn't, Eve would probably be shot by one of the sentries Salazar had planted as she entered those trees ahead.

Joe watched Eve until she disappeared into the trees before he started to move. He'd go to the edge of the forest and wait for the action to start.

He *hated* it. Even Jock and Caleb were closer to Eve and might be able to see if there was trouble. But there shouldn't be trouble, he told himself. He'd spent two hours up here making preparations before he'd gone down to the camp to bring Eve. He'd briefed Caleb and Jock against what he'd thought was every possible thing that could go wrong.

But it was always the things you didn't think could go wrong that invariably did.

It was the unexpected that could get you killed.

Could get Eve killed.

His phone was vibrating.

A text.

He went still. Jock? Caleb?

Relief. Manez from Mexico City. Not what Joe had been worried about. Surely not the unexpected blow that could put Eve in greater danger.

He read the text.

Shit!

"Hello, Eve." Natalie Castino smiled brilliantly at her as Eve walked out of the stand of trees into the glade. She was dressed in a cream-colored silk blouse, khaki designer trousers, and fine leather boots. She looked beautiful but totally out of place. "Salazar wasn't sure that you'd come, but I told him that you were a woman who knew what you wanted. Have you actually met Salazar?"

"Only by reputation. We've chatted." She stared coolly at Salazar, who stood there with an AK-47 held casually in his arm. "And he hired Walsh to kill Cara and me. I understand he still has a price on my head." She looked at Franco. "You'd know about that?"

"Search her," Salazar told Franco.

She stiffened as Franco came toward her. But she stood still and unresisting as his hands ran over her. When he stepped away from her, she glanced quickly around the clearing to get her bearings. The glade was surrounded by trees except for the cliff to the west that was rocky and contained several large boulders. Then her attention turned to Natalie Castino. Salazar. Franco. She had only seen photographs of them, but they were so familiar to her, she knew so much about them, that she felt as if she had known them for years. The only true strangers were two dark-skinned men dressed in boots, camouflage pants, and jackets, and carrying rifles. According to Jock, there were two more of Salazar's men acting as sentries in the forest. Eve couldn't be concerned about them. They were the responsibility of Caleb, Joe, and Jock. She had to focus on what was going to happen in this glade.

Cara. Where was Cara?

Cara was lying beside the trail, as if she'd been tossed there like some kind of garbage, Eve thought angrily. She looked smaller and more delicate than usual. Or maybe Eve was just more aware how fragile Cara's situation was at this moment. "Have you hurt her?" She strode over to Cara and fell to her knees beside her. "Cara." She gently brushed back Cara's dark hair away from her face. "Cara, it's Eve. Can you hear me?"

Cara didn't move.

"Cara."

"Eve?" Cara whispered. Her lids slowly opened. "So . . . sorry. Jock?"

"He's fine. So are you. Everything's going to be okay."

"No . . . Sorry . . ." Her eyes closed again.

"She's right, it's not going to be okay," Salazar said to Eve. "Not unless we get what we want. Maybe not then. You offered Natalie a deal. If it was true, there might be some reason to keep you alive for a while."

"She actually told you everything?"

"Are you surprised?"

"No, nothing she could do would surprise me." She glanced at Natalie. "But I thought there was a possibility that she might wish to surprise you."

"Why would I want to do that?" Natalie asked as she took a step closer to Salazar. "We're used to protecting each other, aren't we?"

"Yes." His gaze narrowed on Eve. "Why did you say that?"

"I was stating the obvious. She impresses me as a woman who doesn't like to be taken for granted." Don't challenge them. There were things to be done. She frowned as she gazed down at Cara. "She needs to be moved over on those rocks. The grass is too

484

wet here. All this dampness has to be bad for Cara."

"She's fine here," Salazar said flatly.

Eve tried not to show panic. Cara was lying too close to Salazar. And he wasn't going to let her be moved. Try Natalie, the wild card. She turned to her. "Cara needs to be moved."

"Does she?" Natalie gazed at her curiously. "I think you really do care about her. How very odd." She turned to Franco. "It won't hurt to do as she asks. Take the girl over to those rocks."

Franco glanced at Salazar. He didn't move.

"Franco," Natalie said. "Do it. You heard me."

He hesitated, then shrugged and strode over to where Eve was kneeling beside Cara.

"What do you think you're doing, Franco," Salazar said angrily. "Do as I say."

"I'm sorry, he won't be doing anything you tell him to do," Natalie said as she turned and strolled away from Salazar across the glade. "He belongs to me. He has for a long time."

Salazar muttered a curse as he watched Franco lift Cara and take her to the rocks. "What's happening here, Natalie?"

"It's over, Salazar. Our association has

become more trouble than it's worth. I've decided to terminate it." She turned and smiled at Eve. "Or I should say, I'm going to let Eve terminate it. I'm sure she's made all the necessary arrangements."

Salazar went still. "She has no weapon." He lifted his automatic rifle and pointed it at Eve. "Are you trying to get me to kill her?"

Eve was frozen as she stared into the barrel of the rifle. Natalie's move had stunned her. "I was wrong, Salazar. She did surprise me. But I have an idea she's trying to manipulate both of us. Are you going to let her do that?" She slowly got to her feet. "Now, I'm going to go over to Cara. This is between you and Natalie. All I want is to get the child out of here. Give me Cara, and I'll get you that treasure. I don't care who takes it as long as Cara and I come out of this alive." She was moving toward the rocks. "But I'd keep my gun pointed at Natalie or Franco if I were you. As you said, you know I'm no threat." Three more steps, and she'd be at the rocks. Jock had told her the rocks would be safe. She had to reach the rocks. "It sounded to me as if that might not be the case —" She'd almost reached the rocks where Franco was standing over Cara's body. "With your errand boy here.

Don't you think that you should —"

Now.

She dove on top of Cara! The next second she'd rolled off the rock, taking Cara with her. Two more rolls, and they were both behind the boulders.

She could hear Salazar cursing. "Get her! Get that bitch. I want her —"

A shot.

Jock's shot, aimed with deadly accuracy at the explosives Joe had taken from the IEDs on the road and planted a few hours earlier in the glade.

The glade exploded.

Screams. Smoke. Fire.

The rocks sheltering Eve and Cara were chipping, splintering. Eve held Cara closer, her arm over the child's head. She could hear Salazar screaming, moaning.

More explosions.

She couldn't hear Salazar anymore, but she heard Franco gasping, cursing, with pain. She lifted her head to see him beating at his pants to put out the flames. He looked up and met her eyes. She saw pure rage.

"I'm going to kill you." He started toward her.

Eve frantically looked around for something, anything, to defend herself. She reached for a rock.

"Get away from her, Franco." Natalie was suddenly beside them. Her face was streaked by smoke, and she had a tear in the sleeve of her silk shirt. "Now."

"I'm going to kill her."

"You'll do no such thing. She might be very valuable to me." She glanced at Cara. "She's alive, Eve?"

"Yes."

"Then she might stay that way if you co-operate." She pulled out a pearl-handled pistol and strode through the smoke, to where Salazar lay crumpled, bloody and torn apart by the explosion. "Dead. I knew he would be the first target. There had to be a reason why you wanted to get Cara as far away as possible from him. I thought it might be a sniper. I didn't expect you to blow everything up."

"Salazar conveniently supplied us with the explosives from the IEDs we disarmed on the road," Eve said. "Joe just grabbed them and came up here to give them back to him."

"It's a little messy, but I suppose it worked for you." She whirled and ran back toward them. "We have to move quickly, Franco. Grab the girl and let's get out of here. Eve's friends will probably be all over this place in minutes." She started running down the rocky slopes, away from the forest. "Coming, Eve?"

Eve had no choice.

Franco had lifted Cara in a fireman's lift over his shoulder and was running behind Natalie.

Eve couldn't let them out of her sight.

She ran after them.

This entire side of the hill was shale and loose stones.

Eve skidded, fell, got up, stumbled, and fell again. The smoke was drifting down, enveloping them as she ran. Her eyes were stinging, and she could just barely see Natalie ahead of her. She couldn't see Franco at all, and that frightened her. He had Cara, and he was a killer who was wounded and enraged. Her only hope was that he'd obey Natalie Castino. Which was a slim hope indeed. Since Natalie was proving to be more dangerous than Franco.

"Hurry," Natalie said over her shoulder. "We need to get out of here."

"Why? You're not going to get away. Joe will hunt you down, and he's got very lethal friends. Give it up and take your chances. You said that you weren't worried about anyone thinking you were guilty of having your girls kidnapped. You just called it a bother. Tell Franco to stop and put Cara down."

"Presently." Her brows lifted. "Do you really think that I'm just running blindly, that I have no plan? That's not the way I do things, Eve. We're almost there. Just around the next corner in the trail . . ."

Eve was already turning that next corner as she spoke.

She stopped short, her eyes widening as she gazed at the army-green helicopter tucked away and half-hidden by brush, rocks, and branches near the ledge of the slope. "What the hell?"

"I had to protect myself, didn't I?" Natalie waved at the pilot, and he started the engine. "Nikolai has been sitting in the valley below waiting for the weather to clear so that he could slip in here and wait for me. He managed to do it last night."

"Nikolai?"

"He's one of my father's men. My father put him at my disposal when I told him that I was trying to free my little girl. He was very worried about her. He'll be glad to know that Salazar didn't kill her, and I managed to take her away from him . . . and kill that terrible man in the process." She smiled. "My father believes in revenge. So do I. Salazar was enjoyable, but he didn't treat me with the respect I deserved." She called to Franco, "Put the girl in the helicopter. I have to get out of here."

Franco was opening the helicopter door and shoving Cara into the aircraft.

"He *does* belong to you," Eve murmured.

"Oh, yes. I've been planning this for a long time. When I saw how clumsily Walsh was handling the hunt for Cara, I decided to take matters into my own hands. I was tired of being Salazar's mistress and Castino's wife. I wanted something more." She smiled. "So I paid a visit to California. I found Franco, and I set him up to help me. He's ambitious, you know. All I had to do was convince him I'd be grateful, and he'd be rich if he went along with me. I had a long-term plan, but some of it had to be adjusted as I went along. But Franco didn't like Salazar, so that made it easier for me to keep him in line. He was very valuable when I was keeping so many balls in the air. When I decided that Salazar had to go down for taking the girls, Franco even pretended to be Walsh and alerted the U.S. Justice Department that the body in the grave was Jenny Castino."

"And was it your decision to let Franco go to that hospital and try to kill Cara?"

"It wouldn't have mattered in the long

run. Salazar had the right idea for the most part. I just had to work it into my plans."

So cold. Absolutely no feeling in her tone. "You're looking at me with horror. Not that I mind. There's a kind of respect connected with that emotion. I just thought you might understand." She shrugged. "But, as it turned out, I was glad that Salazar failed with Cara and you. When Franco told us about Cira's gold, I realized that you were holding the key to everything I'd ever wanted, everything I deserved."

"Dammit, I think I hear someone on the rocks on the hillside," Franco said. "Let's go."

"I'm going." She pulled out her gun. "It's time we left, Eve." She pointed it at her. "As I told Franco, I need you. You know where that treasure is located. It's going to be mine."

"What if I don't know? What if it was a bluff?"

"Not as good, but acceptable. Then I'd still need you. Franco said MacTavish was certain that you were going to find it. You'll find it for me."

"Natalie!" Franco's gaze was on the trail. "You don't have time for this."

"You're right." She motioned with her gun. "Why don't you stay and stop them

492

for me, Franco?"

"What?"

"No, on second thought, I've decided to rid myself of you now instead of later."

"You bitch." His eyes were blazing. "I've done *everything* for you."

"And now you can do the ultimate."

She shot him in the heart.

She watched him fall to the ground. "What a pity. But he really knew too much, Eve. He might have thought he could blackmail me later. My relationship with my father has to remain solid. He's all I have now."

"Now that you've gotten rid of Salazar?"

"No, I've burned all my bridges." She added softly, "If all went as scheduled, at five thirty a.m. GMT, my dear husband will have been gunned down outside the apartment he keeps for his current mistress. There will be abundant evidence that the kill was financed by Salazar because of his fear that my husband would learn that he'd kidnapped and killed Jenny and Cara."

Eve gazed at her in shock.

"I told you, I was tired of Juan Castino. I was tired of being forced to be Salazar's lover, so I could control him. It was time I got rid of both of them and became my own woman. So I had Franco contact his sources in Mexico City and arrange it."

"I suppose that would be the obvious solution in your eyes."

"There were others, but I was impatient. I want to start a new life."

"With Cira's gold."

"Yes. The minute I heard about it, I knew it was meant for me." She opened the helicopter door. "Get in the helicopter, Eve."

"She's not going anywhere." Joe was standing by the trail with a gun pointed at Natalie. "Back away from the helicopter and put down your weapon."

Natalie stiffened. "You must be Joe Quinn? I've heard about you. Could we come to an agreement?"

"No way in hell."

"I didn't think so, but I could probably persuade you if I had the time."

"Put down that weapon."

"You're afraid for Eve?" She turned the gun on Eve. "Yes, I can see that you are."

"Put it down, Natalie," Eve said.

"That wouldn't be intelligent. He's not going to press the trigger because he knows that even if it was a great shot, I still could kill you." She backed toward the helicopter door. "But it appears that I'd be wise to cut my losses and avoid this confrontation. It's not as if I still won't win in the end."

"Get away from that helicopter," Joe said.

Natalie shook her head. "I'm getting on board, and Nikolai is taking off." She looked Eve in the eye. "I have Cara. We can still come to a deal. It will be a little complicated for me, but I can keep Cara alive until you give me what I want."

"Let her go, Natalie."

Natalie got in the helicopter. "Or I can do what I always do and look out for myself. It will be up to you. Now I'm going to point the gun away from you and on Cara. Will Quinn take the chance of killing her?" The helicopter was lifting. "I don't think so. Most men are so soft about children . . . It's always amazed me." She was suddenly looking out the window at Eve, and her eyes were cold. "I don't like to lose, Eve. I did very well, but this was only a partial victory for me. I want it all. I think I need to do something to impress you with that."

She was lifting her gun.

Aiming it.

Aiming it at Joe!

"No!"

Eve was running toward him.

Tackling him, bringing him down.

She could feel the bullet as it passed her cheek.

And as it struck Joe.

Then she could feel the blood.

"Eve."

Her arms tightened around him.

"Eve, it's okay."

How could it be okay? She had felt the bullet as it struck Joe. She could feel his blood on her arm . . .

He was pushing her away and sitting up. "It's only a flesh wound. My side . . ." He looked down at his left side. "I think you did more damage tackling me than she did with that bullet. She must be a lousy shot."

"You're wrong. I think she must be a very good shot." Eve was shaking with both fear and intense relief. "I watched her shoot Franco. She knew what she was doing. She probably was doing exactly what she told me she was going to do. Showing me that she had no intention of losing." She reached out and touched the blood on his shirt. "I guess we're both lucky that she didn't want to drive the point home." She turned and looked out at the horizon. The helicopter was still in view, but it was almost out of sight.

"She *will* lose, Joe. We can't let her win." She shook her head to clear it. She couldn't think of Natalie right now. She had to take care of Joe. She began to unbutton his shirt. "You're right, it's only a flesh wound. Hardly more than a scratch." She tore up his shirt and began to dab the wound. "She told me that she'd arranged for Castino to be assassinated. She said it was supposed to be done this morning."

"She was telling the truth. I got a text from Manez right after you left me. Castino is dead."

She nodded jerkily. "I didn't doubt her. She's capable of anything." She moistened her lips. "And she makes it work, Joe. She thinks she can get away with any atrocity, and she finds a way to do it."

"But we know her now. What we know, we can beat."

"She has Cara, Joe. We don't know what she'll do with —"

"That bitch got away?" Jock was striding down the rocky path. "I saw the helicopter from the top of the hill. She got away?"

"Yes." Eve gestured to Joe. "After taking a shot at Joe. It's not bad, thank God."

"Good," Jock said absently as he strode to the edge of the cliff and looked out at the horizon. "Cara? I didn't see Cara. Is she still alive?"

"Yes. She's with Natalie Castino." She'd finished bandaging Joe, and she rose to her feet and went to stand beside Jock. "But Natalie still wants Cira's gold. That means we can still save Cara."

"I thought we'd done that. Hell, we blew up Salazar and his men, and I thought she'd be safe." His voice was low but vibrating with agony. "I told her once I'd keep her safe, that she'd never have to look over her shoulder again. I didn't do enough. I should have done more."

"We didn't know that Natalie had an escape plan. You did all you could."

"If I'd done all I could, Cara would be here with us now. I'm going after her. I'll get her back."

"We think Natalie Castino is going to Moscow to be with her father."

"I don't care if she's going to hell. It's where I'll send her anyway." He turned and strode back up the trail.

"He's hurting." She went back to Joe. "But we can't let him move too fast. If Natalie gets spooked, she might decide that Cara's not worthwhile to her."

"We don't know what's fast or slow right now." Joe was getting slowly to his feet, and Eve moved closer to help him. "It's a whole new ball game, and Natalie is writing the rules." He began walking toward the trail. "But right now I'm just happy that she seems to believe she needs you. It will be good not to have you designated as a target."

Not at the moment, Eve thought. But Natalie had no compunctions about using people, then killing them. Salazar, Castino, Franco. It would be just as well not to bring that up to Joe right now.

And right now, Natalie also needed Cara. After she got what she wanted from holding her daughter hostage, would she hesitate about killing her?

Not for a minute.

Joe's arm slid around her waist. "It's going to be okay," he said quietly. His hand gently moved to her abdomen. "The three of us have gone through a hell of a lot in the past weeks. We can get through the rest."

She nodded and stepped closer to him. She needed to feel his warmth and strength. "I know that." She did know it, but she was tired and scared and wanted nothing more than to go home with Joe and Cara and this new, ever-changing life in her body.

But there was no Cara yet.

But there would be. There would be.

She had to believe it . . .

Jane watched the EMTs load MacDuff's stretcher into the air ambulance before turning to Jock. "The doctor examined

MacDuff before they moved him from his tent. He believes that there won't be any serious consequences from his injury."

"I didn't think there would be once he regained consciousness. MacDuff is tough." Jock started toward the ambulance. "I'm going to the hospital with him just to make sure."

"But you're not going to stay there long."

"No." He looked back at her. His silver-gray eyes were ice cold and without expression. "Not long at all, Jane." He climbed into the helicopter and shut the door.

She was still feeling the chill as she watched the air ambulance take off. Chill and despair and helplessness. "I wasn't sure that he'd be going with him," Caleb said as he came toward her. "Jock isn't quite himself right now."

Jane shook her head. "I knew he'd want to be with him until he was positive of his condition. He loves MacDuff."

"But he's burning inside." Caleb smiled faintly. "I know a lot about that."

"I imagine you do." Jane glanced one last time at the helicopter before she turned away. "I expected Joe to be down here getting some first aid. When Eve called me, she said that he'd been wounded."

"Just a scratch. He's still up in the hills

dealing with damage control because of several bodies that have to be dealt with. Not to mention, MacDuff's men. They were pretty upset about Colin's murder, then MacDuff's injury. And they didn't like it that they were left out of that blowup that took out Salazar." He shrugged. "I don't blame them. I would have felt the same if I'd missed all the fun."

"I won't even address that remark," she said. "Eve wouldn't tell me what was happening, but I guarantee I wouldn't have thought it was 'fun.' "

"You just did address it. In the way that was predictably your own." His smile faded. "And if anything had happened to Eve, I wouldn't be saying that. I don't believe I would have had the nerve to send her in to face Natalie Castino and Salazar. I know Quinn didn't want her to do it. It was her choice. She wanted to be sure that Cara would be protected."

"She still wants her to be protected."

"We all do." He lightly tapped his chest. "Even my callous, barbaric self." He turned away. "And now I've got to get back to Quinn and offer my help. I'm actually becoming accustomed to being a team player. No, that's not true, but it sounds good, and I thought you'd like to hear it."

He met her eyes. "I just wanted to check to see how you were doing. I know it was harder for you to stay out of the action than it was for Colin's men."

"Yes, it was, but it was the right thing to do."

"Boring." He smiled. "I promise I'll never make you do the right thing, Jane." Before she could answer, he had turned away. "But I brought Eve down from the hills with me, and she might need someone to talk to about right and wrong. She's much more on your wavelength than I am." His voice drifted back to her. "She's down by the lake . . ."

Jane stood watching him for a moment. Why was it always so difficult to look away from Caleb? He seemed to gather all the light and darkness around him until it became a part of him. She forced herself to look away and down at the lake.

But Eve wasn't at the lake as Caleb had said. She was standing beside her tent, and she was looking down at Cara's violin, which she was holding.

Not good.

"Eve." Jane walked quickly toward her. "The air ambulance just took MacDuff and Jock to the hospital. Everything seems to be —"

"Easy." Eve looked up and met Jane's eyes. "I'm not going to fall apart. I've just been scared and having trouble remembering that Natalie Castino isn't infallible. She's just a smart woman who is evil beyond belief." She glanced back at the violin. "But Cara is smart, too. Smart and good and gifted. She's already survived more than anyone would think she could. She can survive this, too." She bent down and carefully put the violin back in its case. "All she needs is help from the people who love her. She's going to get that, Jane." She moved down the slope toward the lake. "And it's going to be enough to save her."

"Yes." Jane moved down to stand beside Eve on the bank. The fog was gone, but the heavy mist that always wreathed the north bank was still there. So much violence and killing had echoed through these hills in the last days, but that eternal mist was still beckoning, calling, as it had for centuries. "We'll make it enough."

But, Cira, we could use a little help from you if you can see your way clear. This is about a child, too. Your Marcus would have liked her. You would have liked her. Don't let us lose her as you did Marcus. Please, don't let Eve lose her.

Eve was gazing out at the mist, too. "It

503

seems . . . different today." She tried to smile. "What do you think? The beginning or the end?"

Jane moved a step closer and took her hand. "The beginning," she said. "Definitely, the beginning."

ABOUT THE AUTHOR

Iris Johansen is *The New York Times* best-selling author of *Shadow Play, Your Next Breath, The Perfect Witness, Live to See Tomorrow, Silencing Eve, Hunting Eve, Taking Eve, Sleep No More, What Doesn't Kill You, Bonnie, Quinn, Eve, Chasing the Night, Eight Days to Live, Blood Game, Deadlock, Dark Summer, Pandora's Daughter, Quicksand, Killer Dreams, On the Run, Countdown,* and more. And with her son, Roy Johansen, she has coauthored *The Naked Eye, Sight Unseen, Close Your Eyes, Shadow Zone, Storm Cycle,* and *Silent Thunder.*